Books by V. S. Pritchett

The Sailor, Sense of Humour, and Other Stories
   (1956)
The Spanish Temper
   (1954)

THESE ARE BORZOI BOOKS, PUBLISHED
IN NEW YORK BY ALFRED · A · KNOPF

*The Sailor, Sense of Humour,
and Other Stories*

The Sailor,
Sense of Humour,
and Other Stories

by V. S. PRITCHETT

NEW YORK

Alfred · A · Knopf

1 9 5 6

The following stories originally appeared in The New Yorker: *"Passing the Ball," "The Landlord," "The Ladder."*

L.C. *catalog card number: 56–5775*

© *V. S. Pritchett, 1956*

THIS IS A BORZOI BOOK
PUBLISHED BY ALFRED A. KNOPF, INC.

FIRST EDITION

Preface

For one, like myself, who has laboriously scattered his time in the writing of novels, literary criticism, and books of travel, the practice of the short story has been the delightful and compensating art and the only kind of writing that has given me great pleasure. It has always elated me. The famous difficulties—and they are very real—have always stimulated. For, in the end, the story-writer always knows that, however good or bad the thing is, he will see it instantaneously and whole. In this he has the luck of the lyrical poet, the sculptor, or the painter of water-colours; and behind him he has Edgar Allan Poe's belief in the value of those works of art that can be seen at a glance. In a nervous and restless age which is overwhelmed by enormous experience, we have inevitably formed the habit of seeing it crystallized rather than at insupportable length, in fragments rather than as solid mass, obliquely rather than full face; and, because of this, the brief, quickly moving, epigrammatic, allusive habit of the short story usually seems to me a more natural form for our story-telling than the novel. I do not say that the short-story writer has notably risen to the occasion, but I do think he has equipped himself for it. He has contrived a glancing mode that lies between lyrical poetry, plain reporting, and aphorism, a mode in which the

v

echoes and shadows within a tale are as important as the tale itself.

The present volume is a selection from the large number of stories I have written in the last twenty-five years, and these are a small part of the innumerable stories I have written a page or two of and have never finished. I regret the waste, but I believe in the habit of writing and console myself with the theory that these ruinous fragments have played their part in shoring up the occasional success; or with the excuse that I have been too idle to stereotype some manner of writing which automatically turned every note into a tale. I have never found that accumulated experience in writing helps very much; on the contrary, one of the disgusts of the writer's life is that he finds himself having to learn from the beginning again every time he puts pen to paper. One of the things, indeed, that I recall, as I reread these tales, is the amount of muddle and indecision from which they have emerged. How strange that *this* is the version of "Sense of Humour" that I decided on, or that "The Sailor"—written so many times in the third person—appeared at last in the first. How many disguises the narrating "I" is made to assume; how unfailingly, when the first person singular has been myself as I think I am, the story has congested before his tedious and ignorant obstruction, and has not succeeded until he was deleted from it. The number of times one has altered the plot totally when the story was three parts done.

Every short story is a drama, but every writer of short stories has his own idea of what is dramatic. A story moves towards a disclosure and that may be an event, a complete revelation of character, the close of a mood, the changing of an emotion, the clinching of an idea, the statement of a situation now completed. It is difficult for a writer to define his own interest, but I think that I find the drama in human personality, in character rather than in events. There, in the absurdities or the pathos of the private imbroglio, has been

my story. The drama has lain in the portrait, in the unconscious self-revelation of people, in the sight of them
floundering amid their own words, and performing strange
strokes as they swim about, with no visible shore, in their
own lives. They are heads sticking out of the water of their
own dreams. It strikes me that the story lies in their double
lives, in the fact that they are themselves story-telling animals, living and yet living by telling a story about this living
at the same time. They dwell—and this to me is the moving
and dramatic thing about people—in a solitude which they
alone can populate. If this is a pretentious description, I am
willing to withdraw it and to say simply that for me the
drama, the event, the plot, is the person; and the more
fantastic, the more certain to be true.

V. S. Pritchett

ACKNOWLEDGMENTS

SOME OF THE STORIES included in this collection appeared in *The Atlantic, Harper's Magazine, Harper's Bazaar,* and *The New Yorker,* to the editors of which acknowledgment is made for permission to reprint. Others of the stories appeared in *You Make Your Own Life,* published in England in 1938 by Chatto and Windus, and in *It May Never Happen,* published in New York by Reynal and Hitchcock in 1947.

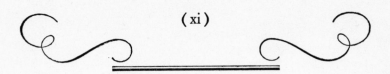

CONTENTS

CONTENTS

The Sailor, Sense of Humour,
and Other Stories

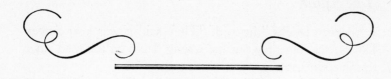

The Sailor

He was lifting his knees high and putting his hand up when I first saw him, as if, crossing the road through that stinging rain, he were breaking through the bead curtain of a Pernambuco bar. I knew he was going to stop me. This part of the Euston Road is a beat of the men who want a cup of tea or their fare to a job in Luton or some outlying town.

"Beg pardon, chum," he said in an anxious hot-potato voice. "Is that Whitechapel?"

He pointed to the traffic clogged in the rain farther down where the electric signs were printing off the advertisements and daubing them on the wet road. Coatless, with a smudged trilby hat on the back of his head so that a curl of boot-polish black hair glistered with raindrops over his forehead, he stood there squeezing the water in his boots and looking at me, from his bilious eyes, like a man drowning and screaming for help in two feet of water and wondering why the crowd is laughing.

"That's St. Pancras," I said.

"Oh, Gawd," he said, putting his hand to his jaw like a man with toothache. "I'm all messed up." And he moved on at once, gaping at the lights ahead.

"Here, wait," I said. "Which part of Whitechapel do you want? Where have you come from?"

The Sailor

"Surrey Docks," he said. "They said it was near Surrey Docks, see, but they put me wrong. I bin on the road since ten this morning."

"Acton," he read a bus sign aloud, recalling the bottom of the day's misery. "I bin there," and, fascinated, watched the bus out of sight.

The man's worried mouth dropped open. He was sodden. His clothes were black with damp. The smell of it came off him. The rain stained from the shoulders of his suit past the armpits over the ribs to the waist. It spread from dark blobs over his knees to his thighs. He was a greasy-looking man, once fat, and the fat had gone down unevenly like a deflating bladder. He was calming as I spoke to him.

A sailor, of course, and lost. Hopelessly, blindly lost. I calculated that he must have wandered twenty miles that day exhausting a genius for misdirection.

"Here," I said. "You're soaked. Come and have a drink." There was a public-house nearby. He looked away at once.

"I never touch it," he said. "It's temptation."

I think it was that word which convinced me the sailor was my kind of man. I am, on the whole, glad to say that I am a puritan and the word "temptation" went home, painfully, pleasurably, excitingly and intimately familiar. A most stimulating and austerely gregarious word, it indicates either the irresistible hypocrite or the fellow struggler with sin. I couldn't let him go after that.

Presently we were in a café drinking acrid Indian tea.

"Off a ship?" I said.

He looked at me as if I were a magician who could read his soul.

"Thank Gawd I stopped you," he said. "I kep' stopping people all day and they messed me up, but you been straight."

He gave me his papers, his discharge paper, his pension form, official letters, as he said this, like a child handing himself over. Albert Edward Thompson, they said, cook, born

4

'96, invalided out of the service two years before. So he was
not just off a ship.

"They're clean," he said suspiciously when I asked him
about this. "I got ulcers, riddled with ulcers for fourteen
years."

He had no job and that worried him, because it was the
winter. He had ganged on the road, worked in a circus, had
been a waiter in an Italian restaurant. But what worried him
much more was getting to Whitechapel. He made it sound to
me as though for two years he had been threshing about the
country, dished by one job and another, in a less and less
successful attempt to get there.

"What job are you going to do?" I said.

"I don't know," he said.

"It's a bad time," I said.

"I fall on my feet," he said, "like I done with you."

We sat opposite to each other at the table. He stared at the
people in the café with his appalled eyeballs. He was scared
of them and they looked scared too. He looked as though he
was going to give a yell and spring at them; in fact, he was
likelier to have gone down on his knees to them and to have
started sobbing. They couldn't know this. And then he and I
looked at each other and the look discovered that we were
the only two decent, trustworthy men in a seedy and grabbing world. Within the next two hours I had given him a job.
I was chum no longer, but "sir." "Chum" was anarchy and
the name of any twisty bleeder you knocked up against, but
"sir," for Thompson (out of the naval nursery), was hierarchy, order, pay-day, and peace.

I was living alone in the country in those days. I had no one
to look after me. I gave Albert Thompson some money; I
took him to Whitechapel and wrote down the directions for
his journey to my house.

The bungalow where I lived was small and stood just
under the brow of a hill. The country was high and stony

there. The roads broke up into lanes, the lanes sank into woods, and cottages were few. The oak woods were naked and as green as canker. They stood like old men, and below them were sweet plantations of larch where the clockwork pheasants went off like toys in the rainy afternoons. At night you heard a farm dog bark like a pistol and the oceanic sound of the trees and sometimes, over an hour and half's walk away, the whistle of a train. But that was all. The few people looked as though they had grown out of the land, sticks and stones in cloth; they were old people chiefly. In the one or two bigger houses they were childless. It was derelict country; frost with its teeth fast in the ground, the wind running finer than sand through a changeless sky or the solitary dribble of water in the butts and the rain legging it over the grass—that was all one heard or saw there.

"Gawd!" said Thompson when he got there. "I thought I'd never strike the place." Pale, coatless again in the wet, his hat tipped back from a face puddingy and martyred, he came up the hill with the dancing step of a man treading on nails. He had been lost again. He had travelled by the wrong train, even by the wrong line, he had assumed that, as in towns, it was safest to follow the crowd. But country crowds soon scatter. He had been following people—it sounded to me—to half the cottages for miles around.

"Then I come to the Common," he said. "I didn't like the look of that. I kept round it."

At last some girl had shown him the way.

I calmed him down. We got to my house and I took him to his room. He sat down on the bed and told me the story again. He took off his boots and socks and looked at his blistered feet, murmuring to them as if they were a pair of orphans. There was a woman in the train with a kid, he said, and to amuse the kid he had taken out his jack-knife. The woman called the guard.

After we had eaten and I had settled in, I went for a walk

6

that afternoon. The pleasure of life in the country for me is in its monotony. One understands how much of living is habit, a long war to which people, plants, and animals have settled down. In the country one expects nothing of people; they are themselves, not bringers of gifts. In towns one asks too little or too much of them.

The drizzle had stopped when I went out, the afternoon was warmer and inert, and the dull stench of cattle hung over the grass. On my way down the hill I passed the bungalow that was my nearest neighbour. I could see the roof as pink as a slice of salt ham, from the top of my garden. The bungalow was ten years old. A chicken man had built it. Now the woodwork was splitting and shrinking, the garden was rank, two or three larches, which the rabbits had been at, showed above the dead grass, and there was a rosebush. The bush had one frozen and worm-eaten flower which would stick there half the winter. The history of the bungalow was written in the tin bath by the side door. The bath was full of gin, beer, and whisky bottles, discarded after the weekend parties of many tenants. People took the place forever and then, after a month or two, it changed hands. A business man, sentimental about the country, an invalid social worker, a couple with a motor bicycle, an inseparable pair of school-teachers with big legs and jumping jumpers; and now there was a woman I hardly saw, a colonel's daughter, but the place was said to belong to a man in the Northampton boot trade.

A gramophone was playing when I walked by. Whenever I passed, the colonel's daughter was either playing the gramophone or digging in the garden. She was a small girl in her late twenties, with a big knowledgeable-looking head under tobacco-brown curls, and the garden fork was nearly as big as herself. Her gardening never lasted long. It consisted usually in digging up a piece of the matted lawn in order to bury tins; but she went at it intensely, drawing back the fork until her hair fell over her face and the sweat stood on her brow. She

7

always had a cigarette in her mouth, and every now and then the carnation skin of her face, with its warm, dark-blue eyes, would be distorted and turned crimson by violent bronchial coughing. When this stopped she would straighten up, the delicacy came back to her skin, and she would say: "Oh, Christ. Oh, bloody hell," and you noticed at the end of every speech the fine right eyebrow would rise a little, and the lid of the eye below it would quiver. This wink, the limpid wink of the colonel's daughter, you noticed at once. You wondered what it meant and planned to find out. It was as startling and enticing as a fish rising, and you discovered when you went after it that the colonel's daughter was the hardest-drinking and most blasphemous piece of apparent childish innocence you had ever seen. Old men in pubs gripped their sticks, went scarlet, and said someone ought to take her drawers down and give her a tanning. I got a sort of fame from being a neighbour of the colonel's daughter. "Who's that piece we saw down the road?" people asked.

"Her father's in the Army."

"Not," two or three of them said, for this kind of wit spreads like measles, "the Salvation Army." They said I was a dirty dog. But I hardly knew the colonel's daughter. Across a field she would wave, utter her obscenity, perform her wink, and edge off on her slight legs. Her legs were not very good. But if we met face to face on the road she became embarrassed and nervous; this was one of her dodges. "Still alone?" she said.

"Yes. And you?"

"Yes. What do you do about sex?"

"I haven't got any."

"Oh, God, I wish I'd met you before."

When I had friends she would come to the house. She daren't come there when I was alone, she said. Every night, she said, she locked and bolted up at six. Then the wink—if it was a wink. The men laughed. She did not want to be

8

raped, she said. Their wives froze and some curled up as
if they had got the blight and put their hands hard on their
husbands' arms. But the few times she came to the house
when I was alone, the colonel's daughter stood by the door,
the full length of the room away, with a guilty look on
her face.

When I came back from my walk the gramophone had
stopped. The colonel's daughter was standing at the door of
her bungalow with her sleeves rolled up, a pail of water beside her, and a scrubbing-brush in her hand.

"Hullo," she said awkwardly.

"Hullo," I said.

"I see you've got the Navy down here. I didn't know you
were that way."

"I thought you would have guessed that straight away," I
said.

"I found him on the Common crying this morning. You've
broken his heart." Suddenly she was taken by a fit of coughing.

"Well," she said, "every day brings forth something."

When I got to the gate of my bungalow I saw that at any
rate if Thompson could do nothing else he could bring forth
smoke. It was travelling in thick brown funnel puffs from the
short chimney of the kitchen. The smoke came out with such
dense streaming energy that the house looked like a destroyer
racing full steam ahead into the wave of hills. I went down
the path to the kitchen and looked inside. There was Thompson, not only with his sleeves rolled up but his trousers also,
and he was shovelling coal into the kitchener with the garden
spade, the face of the fire was roaring yellow, the water was
throbbing and sighing in the boiler, the pipes were singing
through the house.

"Bunkering," Thompson said.

I went into the sitting-room. I thought I had come into
the wrong house. The paint had been scrubbed, the floors

9

polished like decks, the reflections of the firelight danced in them, the windows gleamed, and the room was glittering with polished metal. Doorknobs, keyholes, fire-irons, window-catches, were polished; metal that I had no idea existed flashed with life.

"What time is supper piped—er, ordered," said Thompson, appearing in his stocking feet. His big round eyes started out of their dyspeptic shadows and became enthusiastic when I told him the hour.

A change came over my life after this. Before Thompson everything had been disorganized and wearying. He drove my papers and clothes back to their proper places. He brought the zest and routine of the Royal Navy into my life. He kept to his stocking feet out of tenderness for those orphans, a kind of repentance for what he had done to them; he was collarless and he served food with a splash as if he allowed for the house to give a pitch or a roll that didn't come off. His thumbs left their marks on the plates. But he was punctual. He lived for "orders." "All ready, sir," he said, planking down the dish and looking up at the clock at the same moment. Burned, perhaps, spilling over the side, invisible beneath Bisto—but on time!

The secret of happiness is to find a congenial monotony. My own housekeeping had suffered from the imagination. Thompson put an end to this tiring chase of the ideal. "What's orders for lunch, sir?"

"Do you a nice fried chop and chips?" he said. That was settled. He went away, but soon he came back.

"What pudding's ordered, sir?" That stumped both of us, or it stumped me. Thompson watched me to time his own suggestion.

"Do you a nice spotted dick?" So it was. We had this on the second day and the third, we changed on the fourth, but on the fifth we came back to it. Then Thompson's mind gave a leap.

"Do you grilled chop, chips, spotted dick *and custard?*" he said. That became almost our fixed menu. There were bouts of blanc-mange, but spotted dick came back.

Thompson had been sinking towards semi-starvation, I to the insidious Oblomovism of the country. Now we were reformed and happy.

"I always fall on my feet," he said, "like I done with you." It was his refrain.

The winter dripped like a tap, the fog hardly left our hill. Winter in England has the colourless, steaming look of a fried-fish-shop window. But we were stoking huge fires, we bunkered, the garden spade went through coal by the hundredweight. We began to talk a more tangy dialect. Things were not put away; they were "stowed." String appeared in strange knots to make things "fast," plants were "lashed" in the dying garden, washing was "hoist" on the lines, floors were "swabbed." The kitchen became the "galley." The postman came "alongside," all meals were "piped," and at bedtime we "piped down." At night, hearing the wind bump in the chimneys and slop like ocean surf in the woods, looking out at the leather darkness, I had the sensation that we were creeping down the Mersey in a fog or lumping about in the Atlantic swell off Ushant.

I was happy. But was Thompson happy? He seemed to be. In the mornings we were both working, but in the afternoons there was little more to do. He sat on a low chair with his knees close to the bars of the range or on the edge of his bed, darning his clothes. (He lived in a peculiar muddle of his own and he was dirty in his own quarters.) In the evenings he did the same and sometimes we talked. He told me about his life. There was nothing in it at all. It was buried under a mumble of obscurity. His memories were mainly of people who hadn't "behaved right," a dejecting moral wilderness with Thompson mooching about in it, disappointed with human nature. He didn't stay to talk with me much. He preferred the kitchen, where, the oil-lamp smoking, the range smoking, and himself smoking, he sat chewing it all over, gazing into the fire.

"You can go out, you know," I said, "whenever you want. Do what you like."

"I'm O.K.," he said.

"See some of the people," I said. Thompson said he'd just as lief stand by.

Everyone knows his own business best. But I was interested one night when I heard the sound of voices in the kitchen. Someone had come in. The voices went on on other nights. Who was it? The milker from the farm probably or the cowman who cleaned out cesspits by lantern light at night and talked with nostalgia about burying bodies during the war. "If there hadn't been a war," this man used to say, "I wouldn't have seen nothing. It was an education."

I listened. Slow in question, slow in answer, the monotonous voices came. The woodcutter, the postman? I went into the kitchen to see who the profound and interminable crony was.

There was no one. There was only Thompson in the kitchen. Sitting close to the fire with all windows closed, a shallow, stupefied, oil-haired head in his own fug, Thompson was spelling out a story from a *Wild West Magazine*. It was old and dirty and his coal-blackened finger was moving from word to word.

So far Thompson had refused to go out of the house except as far as the coal-shed, but I was determined after this discovery that he should go out. I waited until pay-day.

"Here's your money," I said. "Take the afternoon off." Thompson stepped back from the money.

"You keep it," he said, in a panic. "You keep it for me."

"You may need it," I said. "For a glass of beer or cigarettes or something."

"If I have it I'll lose it," he said. "They'll pinch it."

"Who?" I said.

"People," Thompson said. I could not persuade him.

"All right, I'll keep it for you," I said.

"Yes," he said eagerly. "If I want a bob I'll ask you. Money's temptation," he said.

"Well, anyway," I said, "take the afternoon off. It's the first sunny afternoon we've had. I'll tell you where to go. Turn to the right in the lane . . ."

"I don't like them lanes," said Thompson, looking suspiciously out of the window. "I'll stay by you."

"Well, take a couple of hours," I said. "We all need fresh air."

He looked at me as if I had suggested he should poison himself; indeed as if I were going to do the poisoning.

"What if I do an hour?" he began to bargain.

"No, the afternoon," I said.

"Do you half an hour?" he pleaded.

"All right, I don't want to force you," I said. "This is a free country. Go for an hour."

It was like an auction.

"Tell you what," he said, looking shifty. "I'll do you twenty minutes." He thought he had tricked me, but I went back into the kitchen and drove him to it. I had given him an overcoat and shoes, and it was this appeal to his vanity that got him. Out he went for his twenty minutes. He was going straight down the lane to where it met the main road and then straight back; it would take a smart walker about twelve minutes on a winter's day.

When an hour passed, I was pleased with myself. But when four hours had gone by and darkness came, I began to wonder. I went out to the gate. The land and the night had become one thing. I had just gone in again when I heard loud voices and saw the swing of a lamp. There came Thompson with a labourer. The labourer, a little bandy man known as Fleas, stood like a bent bush with a sodden sack on his shoulders, snuffling in the darkness, and he grinned at me with the malevolence of the land.

"He got astray," he said, handing Thompson over.

"Gawd," exclaimed Thompson, exhausted. His face was the familiar pale suety agony. He was full of explanations. He was sweating like a scared horse and nearly hysterical. He'd been on the wrong course. He didn't know where to steer. One thing looked like another. Roads and lanes, woods and fields, mixed themselves together.

"Woods I seen," he said in horror. "And that Common! It played me up proper."

"But you weren't anywhere near the Common," I said.

"Then what was it?" he said.

That night he sat by the fire with his head in his hands.

"I got a mood," he said.

The next morning cigarette smoke blew past my window and I heard coughing. The colonel's daughter was at the kitchen door talking to Thompson. "Cheero," I heard her say and then she came to my door and pushed it open. She stood there gravely and her eye winked. She was wearing a yellow jersey and looked as neat as a bird.

"You're a swine," she said.

"What have I done?"

"Raping women on the Common," she said. "Deserting your old friends, aren't you?"

"It's been too wet on the Common," I said.

"Not for me," she said. "I'm always hopeful. I came across last night. There was the minister's wife screaming in the middle of it. I sat on her head and calmed her down, and she said a man had been chasing her. 'Stop screaming,' I said. 'You flatter yourself, dear.' It was getting dark and I carried her shopping-bag and umbrella for her and took her to her house. I often go and see her in the evenings. I've got to do something, haven't I? I can't stick alone in that bungalow all

14

day and all night. We sit and talk about her son in China. When you're old you'll be lonely too."

"What happened on the Common?"

"I think I'm drunk," said the colonel's daughter, "but I believe I've been drunk since breakfast. Well, where was I? I'm losing my memory too. Well, we hadn't gone five minutes before I heard someone panting like a dog behind us and jumping over bushes. Old Mrs. Stour started screaming again. 'Stand still,' I said, and I looked and then a man came out of a tree about ten yards away. 'What the hell do you want?' I said. A noise came back like a sheep. 'Ma'am, ma'am, ma'am, ma'am,' it said."

"So that's where Thompson was," I said.

"I thought it was you," the colonel's daughter said. " 'There's a woman set about me with a stick on the Common,' he said. 'I didn't touch her, I was only following her,' he said. 'I reckoned if I followed her I'd get home.'

"When they got to the wood, Thompson wouldn't go into it and she had to take his hand; that was a mistake. He took his hand away and moved off. So she grabbed his coat. He struggled after this, she chased him into the thicket and told him not to be a fool but he got away and disappeared, running on to the Common.

"You're a damn swine," the colonel's daughter said to me. "How would you like to be put down in the middle of the sea?"

She walked away. I watched her go up the path and lean on the gate opposite to stroke the nose of a horse. She climbed into the field and the horses, like hairy yokels, went off. I heard her calling them, but they did not come.

When she was out of sight, the door opened behind me and Thompson came in.

"Beg pardon, sir," he said. "That young lady, sir. She's been round my kitchen door."

15

"Yes," I said.

He gaped at me and then burst out: "I didn't touch her, straight I didn't. I didn't lay a finger on her."

"She didn't say you did. She was trying to help you."

He calmed down. "Yes, sir," he said.

When he came back into the room to lay the table I could see he was trying to catch my eye.

"Sir," he said at last, standing at attention. "Beg pardon, sir, the young lady . . ."

His mouth was opening and shutting, trying to shape a sentence.

"The young lady—she'd had a couple, sir," he said in a rush.

"Oh," I said, "don't worry about that. She often has."

"It's ruination, sir," said Thompson evangelically.

She did not come to the house again for many days, but when she came I heard him lock both kitchen doors.

Orders at the one extreme, temptation at the other, were the good and evil of Thompson's life. I no longer suggested that he go out. I invented errands and ordered him to go. I wanted, in that unfortunate way one has, to do good to Thompson. I wanted him to be free and happy. At first he saw that I was not used to giving orders and he tried to dodge. His ulcers were bad, he said. Once or twice he went about barefoot, saying the sole was off one of his boots. But when he saw I meant what I said, he went. I used to watch him go, tilted forward on his toes in his half-running walk, like someone throwing himself blindly upon the mercy of the world. When he came back he was excited. He had the look of someone stupefied by incomprehensible success. It is the feeling a landsman has when he steps off a boat after a voyage. You feel giddy, canny, surprised at your survival after crossing that bridge of deep, loose water. You boast. So did Thompson —morally.

"There was a couple of tramps on the road," Thompson

said. "I steered clear. I never talked to them," he said. "Someone asked me who I was working for." He described the man. "I never told him," he said shrewdly. "I just said 'A gentleman.' Meaning you," he said.

There was a man in an allotment who had asked him for a light and wanted to know his business.

"I told him I didn't smoke," said Thompson. "You see my meaning—you don't know what it's leading up to. There warn't no harm, but that's how temptation starts."

What was temptation? Almost everything was temptation to Thompson. Pubs, cinemas, allotments, chicken-runs, tobacconists—in these, everywhere, the tempter might be. Temptation, like Othello's jealousy, was the air itself.

"I expect you'd like to go to church," I said. He seemed that kind.

"I got nothing *against* religion," Thompson said. "But best keep clear. They see you in church and the next thing they're after you."

"Who?" I asked.

"People," he said. "It's not like a ship."

I was like him, he said, I kept myself to myself. I kept out of temptation's way. He was glad I was like that, he said.

It was a shock to me that while I observed Thompson, Thompson observed me. At the same time one prides oneself, the moment one's character is defined by someone else, on defeating the definition. I kept myself to myself? I avoided temptation? That was all Thompson knew! There was the colonel's daughter. I might not see her very often; she might be loud, likable, dreary or alarming by turns, but she was Temptation itself. How did he know I wasn't tempted? Thompson's remark made me thrill. I began to see rather more of the colonel's daughter.

And so I discovered how misleading he had been about his habits and how, where temptation was concerned, he made a difference between profession and practice. So strong was

The Sailor

Thompson's feeling about temptation that he was drawn at once to every tempter he saw. He stopped them on the road and was soon talking about it. The postman was told. The shopkeepers heard all his business and mine. He hurried after tramps, he detained cyclists, he sat down on the banks with road-makers and ditchers, telling them the dangers of drink, the caution to be kept before strangers. And after he had done this he always ended by telling them he kept himself to himself, avoided drink, ignored women, and, patting his breast pocket, said that was where he kept his money and his papers. He behaved to them exactly as he had behaved with me two months before in the Euston Road. The colonel's daughter told me. She picked up all the news in that district.

"He's a decent, friendly soul," muttered the colonel's daughter thickly. "You're a prig. Keep your hair on. You can't help it. I expect you're decent, too, but you're like all my bloody so-called friends."

"Oh," I said hopefully, "are prigs your special line?"

I found out, too, why Thompson was always late when he came home from his errands. I had always accepted that he was lost. And so he was in a way, but he was lost through wandering about with people, following them to their doorsteps, drifting to their allotments, back yards, and all the time telling them, as he clung to their company, about the dangers of human intercourse. "I never speak to nobody"—it was untrue, but it was not a lie. It was simply a delusion.

"He lives in two worlds at once," I said to the colonel's daughter one morning. I had sent Thompson to the town to buy the usual chops, and I was sitting in her bungalow. This was the first time I had ever been in it. The walls were of varnished matchboarding like the inside of a gospel hall, and the room was heated by a kerosene stove which smelled like armpits. There were two rexine-covered chairs, a rug, and a table in the room. She was sorting out gramophone records as

I talked and the records she did not like she dropped to the floor and broke. She was listening very little to what I said but walked to the gramophone, put on a record, stopped it after a few turns, and then, switching it off, threw the record away.

"Oh, you know a hell of a lot, don't you?" she said. "I don't say you're not an interesting man, but you don't get on with it, do you?"

"How old are you? Twenty-five?" I said.

Her sulking, ironical expression went. She was astonished.

"Good God!" she exclaimed with a smile of sincerity. "Don't be a damn fool." Then she frowned. "Or are you being professionally clever?

"Here," she said. "I was damn pretty when I was twenty-five. I'm thirty-nine. I've still got a good figure."

"I would have put you at twenty-seven at the most," I said truthfully.

She walked towards me. I was sitting on the armchair and she stood very close. She had never been as close to me before. I had thought her eyes were dark blue, but now I saw they were green and grey, with a moist lascivious haze in them and yet dead and clock-like, like a cat's on a sunless day. And the skin, which had seemed fresh to me, I saw in its truth for the first time. It was clouded and flushed, clouded with that thickened pimpled ruddiness which the skin of heavy drinkers has and which in middle age becomes bloated and mottled. I felt: "This is why she has always stood the length of the room away before."

She saw what was in my mind and she sat down on the chair opposite me. The eye winked.

"Keep control of yourself," she said. "I came down here for a rest and now you've started coming round."

"Only in the mornings," I said.

She laughed. She went to a bookshelf and took down a bottle of whisky and poured out half a tumblerful.

The Sailor

"This is what you've done coming in here, early bird," she said. "Exciting me on an empty stomach. I haven't touched it for ten days. I had a letter this morning. From my old man."

"Your father?"

I had always tried to imagine the colonel. She gave a shout of cheerful laughter and it ended in coughing till tears came to her eyes.

"That's rich. God, that's rich. Keen observer of women! No, from my husband, darling. He's not my husband, damn him, of course, but when you've lived with someone for ten years and he pays the rent and keeps you, he is your husband, isn't he? Or ought to be. Ten years is a long time and his family thought he ought to be married. He thought so too. So he picked up a rich American girl and pushed me down here to take it easy in the country. I'm on the dole like your sailor boy. Well, I said, if he felt that way, he'd better have his head. In six months he'll tire of the new bitch. So I left him alone. I didn't want to spoil his fun. Well, now, he writes me, he wants to bring his fiancée down because she's heard so much about me and adores the country. . . ."

I was going to say something indignant.

"He's nice too," she said casually. "He sells gas heaters. You'd like him all the same. But blast that bloody woman," she said, raising her cool voice. "She's turned him into a snob. I'm just his whore now.

"Don't look so embarrassed," she said. "I'm not going to cry.

"For ten years," she said, "I read books, I learned French, educated myself, learned to say 'How d'you do?' instead of 'Pleased to meet you,' and look down my nose at everything in his sort of way. And I let him go about saying my father was in the Army too, but they were such bloody fools they thought he must be a colonel. They'd never heard of sergeant majors having children. Even my old man, bless his heart," she smiled affectionately, "thought or let himself think as they did. I was a damn silly little snob."

"I don't know him," I said. "But he doesn't sound much good to me."

"That's where you're wrong," she said sharply. "Just weak, poor kid, that's all. You don't know what it is to be ashamed your mother's a housemaid. I got over it—but he didn't, that's all."

She paused and the wink gave its signal.

"This is more embarrassing than I thought," she said.

"I am very sorry," I said. "Actually I am in favour of snobbery, it is a sign of character. It's a bad thing to have, but it's a bad thing not to have had. You can't help having the diseases of your time."

"There you go," she said.

The suffering of others is incredible. When it is obscure it seems like a lie; when it is garish and raw, it is like boasting. It is a challenge to oneself. I got up from my chair and went towards her. I was going to kiss her.

"You are the sentimental type," she said.

So I didn't kiss her.

Then we heard someone passing the bungalow and she went to the window. Thompson was going by. The lock of black hair was curling over his sweating forehead and he gave a hesitant staggering look at the bungalow. There was a lump of fear on his face.

"He'd better not know where you've been," she said. She moved her lips to be kissed, but I walked out.

I was glad of the steady sense of the fresh grey air when I got outside. I was angry and depressed. I stood at the window of my house. Thompson came in and was very talkative. He'd been lost, of course. He'd seen people. He'd seen fields. He'd heard trees. He'd seen roads. I hardly listened. I was used to the jerky wobbling voice. I caught the words "legion" and "temptation," and thought he was quoting from the Bible. Presently I realized he was talking about the British Legion. The postman had asked him to go to a meeting of the British Legion that night. How simple other people's problems are! Yet "No" Thompson was saying. He was not going to the British Legion. It was temptation.

I ought to have made love to her and kissed her I was thinking. She was right, I was a prig.

"You go," I said to Thompson, "if you want to. You'd enjoy it."

But how disgusting, obvious, stupid, to have made love to her then, I thought.

"Do as you like," I said.

"I'm best alongside you," said Thompson.

"You can't always be by me," I said. "In a month, perhaps less, as you know, I'll be leaving here and you'll have to go."

"Yes," he said. "You tol' me. You been straight. I'll be straight with you. I won't go to the Legion."

We ate our meal and I read.

"In every branch of our spiritual and material civilization we seem to have reached a turning-point," I read. "This spirit shows itself not only in the actual state of public affairs. . . ."

"Well," I thought, "I can ask her over tonight. I needn't be a fool twice." I went out for an hour. When I returned, Thompson was fighting Temptation hard. If he went to the Legion how would he get back? No, best not. He took the Legion on in its strength. ("She is a type," I thought.) At four he was still at it. At five he asked me for his money. ("Well, we are all types," I was thinking.) Very shortly he brought the money back and asked me to keep his pension papers. At half past six I realized this meant that Thompson was losing and the Legion and all its devils winning. (What is a prig, anyway?) He was looking out at the night. Yet, just when I thought he had lost, he had won. There was the familiar sound of the Wild West monologue in the kitchen. It was half past eight. The Legion was defeated.

I was disappointed in Thompson. Really, not to have had more guts than that! Restlessly I looked out of the window. There was a full moon spinning on the tail of a dying wind. Under the moonlight the fields were like wide-awake faces, the woods like womanish heads of hair upon them. I put on my hat and coat and went out. I was astonished by the circle of stars. They were as distinct as figures on a clock. I took out my watch and compared the small time in my hand with the wide time above. Then I walked on. There was a sour smell at the end of the wood, where, no doubt, a dead rabbit or pigeon was rotting.

I came out of the wood on to the metalled road. Suddenly my heart began to beat quickly as I hurried down the road, but it was a long way round now. I cut across fields. There was a cottage and a family were listening to a dance-band on the wireless. A man was going the rounds of his chickens. There was a wheelbarrow and there were spades and steel bars where a water mill was being built.

Then I crossed the last fields and saw the bungalow. My heart throbbed heavily and I felt all my blood slow down and my limbs grow heavy. It was only when I got to the road that I saw there were no lights in the bungalow. The colonel's daughter, the sergeant's daughter, had gone to bed early like a child. While I stood I heard men's voices singing across the fields. It must have gone ten o'clock and people were coming out of the public-house. In all the villages of England, at this hour, loud-voiced groups were breaking up and dispersing into the lanes.

I got to my house and lit a candle. The fire was low. I was exhausted and happy to be in my house among my own things, as if I had got into my own skin again. There was no light in the kitchen. Thompson had gone to bed. I grinned at the thought of the struggles of poor Thompson. I picked up a book and read. I could hear still the sound of that shouting and singing. The beer was sour and flat in this part of the country, but it made people sing.

The singing voices came nearer. I put down the book. An argument was going on in the lane. I listened. The argument was nearing the cottage. The words got louder. They were going on at my gate. I heard the gate go and the argument was on my path. Suddenly—there could be no doubt—people were coming to the door. I stood up, I could recognize no voice. Loud singing, stumbling feet, then bang! The door broke open and crashed against the wall. Tottering, drunk, with their arms round each other, Thompson and the colonel's daughter nearly fell into the room.

Thompson stared at me with terror.

"Stand up, sailor," said the colonel's daughter, clinging to him.

"He was lonely," she said unsteadily to me. "We've been playing gramophone records. Sing," she said.

Thompson was still staring.

"Don't look at him. Sing," she said. Then she gave a low laugh and they fell, bolt upright on the sofa like prim, dishevelled dolls.

A look of wild love of all the world came into Thompson's eyes and he smiled as I had never seen him smile before. He suddenly opened his twitching mouth and bawled:

> *"You've robbed every tailor,*
> *And you've skinned every sailor,*
> *But you won't go walking Paradise Street no more."*

"Go on. That's not all," the colonel's daughter cried and sang: "Go on—something—something, deep and rugged shore."

She put her arms round his neck and kissed him. He gaped at her with panic and looked at her skirt. It was undone.

He pointed at her leg in consternation. The sight sobered

24

him. He pulled away his arms and rushed out of the room. He did not come back. She looked at me and giggled. Her eyes were warm and shining. She picked leaves off her skirt.

"Where's he gone? Where's he gone?" she kept asking.

"He's gone to bed," I said.

She started a fit of coughing. It strained her throat. Her eyes were dilated like an animal's caught in a trap, and she held her hand to her chest.

"I wish," she cried hysterically, pointing at me in the middle of her coughing, "I wish you could see your bloody face."

She got up and called out: "Thompson! Thompson!" And when he did not answer she sang out: "Down by the deep and rugged shore—ore-ore-ore."

"What's the idea?" I said.

"I want Thompson," she said. "He's the only man up here."

Then she began to cry. She marched out to his room, but it was locked. She was wandering through the other rooms calling him and then she went out, away up the path. She went calling him all the way down to her bungalow.

In the morning Thompson appeared as usual. He brought the breakfast. He came in for "orders." Grilled chop, did I think? And what about spotted dick? He seemed no worse. He behaved as though nothing had happened. There was no guilty look in his eyes and no apprehension. He made no apology. Lunch passed, teatime, and the day. I finished my work and went into the kitchen.

"Tell me," I said, "about last night."

Thompson was peeling potatoes. He used to do this into a bucket on the floor, as if he were peeling for a whole crew. He put down the clasp-knife and stood up. He looked worried.

"That was a terrible thing," Thompson said, as if it was something he had read about in the papers. "Terrible, sir. A young lady like that, sir. To come over here for me, an educated lady like that. Someone oughter teach her a lesson. Coming over and saying she wanted to play some music. I was took clean off my guard. It wasn't right," said Thompson. "Whichever way you look at it, it wasn't right. I told her she'd messed me up."

"I'm not blaming you. I want to know."

"And she waited till you was out," Thompson said. "That's not straight. She may class herself as an educated young lady, but do you know what I reckon she is? I reckon she's a jane."

I went down to the bungalow. I was beginning to laugh now. She was in the garden digging. Her sleeves were rolled up and she was sweating over the fork. The beds were thick with leaves and dead plants. I stood there watching her. She looked at me nervously for a moment. "I'm making the garden tidy," she said. "For Monday. When the bitch comes down."

She was shy and awkward. I walked on and, looking back, saw her go into the house. It was the last I ever saw of her. When I came back, the fork she had been using was stuck in the flower bed where she had left it. She went to London that night and did not return.

"Thank Gawd," Thompson said.

There was a change in Thompson after this and there was a change in me. Perhaps the change came because the dirty February days were going, the air softer and the year moving. I was leaving soon. Thompson mentioned temptation no more. Now he went out every day. The postman was his friend. They used to go to the pub. He asked for his money. In the public-house the labourers sat around muttering in a language Thompson didn't understand. He stood them drinks. At his first pint he would start singing. They encouraged him. He stood them more drinks. The postman ordered them for him and then tapped him on the pocket book. They emptied his pockets every night. They despised him and even brought complaints to me about him after they had emptied his pockets.

Thompson came back across the Common alone, wild, enthusiastic, and moaning with suspicion by turns. The next day he would have a mood. All the countryside for ten miles around knew the sailor. He became famous.

Our last week came. He quietened down.

"What are you going to do?" I asked.

"I'll stay by you."

"You can't," I said. "I'll be going abroad."

"You needn't pay me," he said. "I'll stay by you." It was hard to make him understand he could not stay with me. He was depressed.

"Get me out of here safe," he pleaded at last. "Come with me to the station." He could not go on his own because all the people he knew would be after him. He had told them he was going. He had told them I was saving his pension and his last fortnight's pay. They would come creeping out of cottage doors and ditches for him. So I packed his things and got a taxi to call for us. How slowly we had lived and moved in these fields and lanes! Now we broke through it all with a rush as the car dropped down the hill and the air blew in at the window. As we passed the bungalow with the sun on its empty windows, I saw the fork standing in the neglected bed. Then we swept on. Thompson sat back in the car so that no one should see him, but I leaned forward to see everything for the last time and forget it.

We got to the town. As the taxi slowed down in the streets, people looked out of shops, doors; a potman nodded from the pub.

"Whatcha, Jack," the voices called.

The police, the fishmonger, boys going to school, dozens of

people waved to him. I might have been riding with royalty. At the station a large woman sweeping down the steps of the bank straightened up and gave a shout.

"Hi, Jacko!" she called, bending double, went into shrieks of laughter and called across to a friend at a first-floor window. It was a triumph. But Thompson ignored them all. He sat back out of sight.

"Thank Gawd I've got you," he said. "They skin you of everything."

We sat in the train. It was a two-hour journey.

"Once I strike Whitechapel," he said in the voice of one naming Singapore, "I'll be O.K." He said this several times, averting his face from the passing horror of the green fields.

"Don't you worry," he said. "Don't fret yourself for me. Don't you worry." His optimism increased as mine dwindled as we got nearer London. By the time we reached London he was almost shouting. "I'll fall on my feet, don't you worry. I'll send you my address."

We stood on the curb and I watched him walk off into the yellow rain and the clogged, grunting, and mewing traffic. He stepped right into it without looking. Taxis braked to avoid him. He was going to walk to Whitechapel. He reckoned it was safer.

The Œdipus Complex

Good morning, Mr. P.," said Mr. Pollfax, rinsing and drying his hands after the last patient. "How's Mr. P.?" I was always Mr. P. until I sat in the chair and he switched the lamp on and had my mouth open. Then I got a peerage.

"That's fine, my lord," said Mr. Pollfax, having a look inside.

Dogged, with its slight suggestion of doggish, was the word for Mr. Pollfax. He was a short man, jaunty, hair going thin, with jaunty buttocks and a sway to his walk. He had two lines, from habitual grinning, cut deep from the nostrils, and scores of lesser lines like the fine hair of a bird's nest round his egg-blue eyes. There was something innocent, heroic, and determined about Mr. Pollfax, something of the English Tommy in tin hat and full pack going up the line. He suggested in a quiet way—war.

He was the best dentist I ever had. He got you into the chair, turned on the light, tapped around a bit with a thing like a spoon and then, dropping his white-coated arm to his side, told you a story. Several more stories followed in his flat Somerset voice when he had your mouth jacked up. And then removing the towel and with a final "Rinse that lot out," he finished with the strangest story of all and let you go. A month or so later the bill came in. Mr. Pollfax presents his compliments and across the bottom of it, in his hand: "Be good." I have never known a dentist like Mr. Pollfax.

"Open, my lord," said Mr. Pollfax. "Let's see what sort of life his lordship has been leading. Still smoking that filthy pipe, I see. I shall have to do some cleaning up."

He tapped around and then dropped his arm. A look of anxiety came on his face. "Did I tell you that one about the girl who went to the Punch and Judy show? No? Nor the one about the engine-driver who was put on sentry duty in Syria? You're sure? When did I see you last? What was the last one I told you? That sounds like last April? Lord, you *have* been letting things go. Well," said Mr. Pollfax, tipping back my head and squirting something on to a tooth, "we'll have a go at that root at the back. It's not doing you any good. It was like this. There was a girl sitting on the beach at Barmouth with her young man watching a Punch and Judy show . . ." (Closer and closer came Mr. Pollfax's head, lower and lower went his voice.)

He took an instrument and began chipping his way through the tooth and the tale.

"Not bad, eh?" he said, stepping back with a sudden shout of laughter.

"Ah," I mouthed.

"All right, my lord," said Mr. Pollfax, withdrawing the instrument and relapsing into his dead professional manner. "Spit that lot out."

He began again.

There was just that root, Mr. Pollfax was saying. It was no good there. There was nothing else wrong; he'd have it out in a couple of shakes.

"Though, my lord," he said, "you did grow it about as far back in your throat as you could, didn't you, trying to make it as difficult as you could for Mr. Pollfax? What we'll do first of all is to give it a dose of something."

He swivelled the dish of instruments towards me and gave a tilt to the lamp. I remembered that lamp because once the bulb had exploded, sending glass all over the room. It was fortunate, Mr. Pollfax said at the time, that it had blown the other way and none of it had hit me, for someone might have brought a case for damages against someone—which reminded him of the story of the honeymoon couple who went to a small hotel in Aberdeen. . . .

"Now," said Mr. Pollfax, dipping things in little pots and coming to me with an injection needle; "open wide, keep dead still. I was reading Freud the other day. There's a man. Œdipus complex? Ever read about that? Don't move, don't breathe, you'll feel a prick, but for God's sake don't jump. I don't want it to break in your gum. I've never had one break yet, touch wood, but they're thin, and if it broke off you'd be in a nursing home three weeks and Mr. Pollfax would be down your throat looking for it. The trouble about these little bits of wire is they move a bit farther into the system every time you swallow.

"There now," said Mr. Pollfax. "Feel anything? Feel it prick?" he said. "Fine."

He went to a cupboard and picked out the instrument of extraction and then stood, working it up and down like a gardener's secateurs in his hand. He studied my face. He was a clean-shaven man and looked like a priest in his white coat.

"Some of the stories you hear!" exclaimed Mr. Pollfax. "And some of the songs. I mean where I come from. 'The Lot that Lily Lost in the Lottery'—know that one? Is your skin beginning to tingle, do you feel it on the tip of your tongue yet? That's fine, my lord. I'll sing it to you."

Mr. Pollfax began to sing. He'd give it another minute, he said, when he'd done with Lily; he'd just give me the chorus of "The Night Uncle's Waistcoat Caught Fire."

"Tra la la," sang Mr. Pollfax.

"I bet," said Mr. Pollfax sadistically, "one side of his

lordship's face has gone dead and his tongue feels like a pin cushion."

"Blah," I said.

"I think," he said, "we'll begin."

So Mr. Pollfax moved round to the side of me, got a grip on my shoulders, and began to press on the instrument in my mouth. Pressing and drawing firmly, he worked upon the root. Then he paused and increased the pressure. He seemed to be hanging from a crowbar fixed to my jaw. Nothing happened. He withdrew.

"The Great Flood begins," said Mr. Pollfax putting a tube in my mouth and taking another weapon from the tray.

The operation began again. Mr. Pollfax now seemed to hang and swing on the crowbar. It was not successful.

"Dug himself in, has he?" muttered Mr. Pollfax. He had a look at his instruments. "You can spit, my lord," he said.

Mr. Pollfax now seized me with great determination, hung, swung, pressed, and tugged with increased energy.

"It's no good you thinking you're going to stay in," said Mr. Pollfax in midair, muttering to the root. But the instrument slipped and a piece of tooth broke off as he spoke.

"So that's the game, is it?" said Mr. Pollfax withdrawing. "Good rinse, my lord, while Mr. Pollfax considers the position."

He was breathing hard.

Oh well, he said, there were more ways than one of killing a cat. He'd get the drill on it. There were two Jews standing outside Buckingham Palace when a policeman came by, he said, coming at me with the drill, which made a whistling noise like a fishing line as he drew it through. The tube gurgled in my mouth. I was looking, as I always did, at Mr. Pollfax's, at the cowls busily twirling on the chimneys opposite. Wind or no wind these cowls always seemed to be twirling round. Two metal cowls on two yellow chimneys. I always remember them.

"Spit, my lord," said Mr. Pollfax, changing to a coarser drill. "Sorry old man, if it slipped, but Mr. Pollfax is not to be beaten."

The drill whirred again, skidding and whining; the cowls twirled on the chimneys, Mr. Pollfax's knuckles were on my nose. What he was trying to do, he said, was to get a purchase.

Mr. Pollfax's movements got quicker. He hung up the drill, he tapped impatiently on the tray, looking for something. He came at me with something like a buttonhook. He got it in. He levered like a signal man changing points.

"I'm just digging," he said. Another piece of tooth broke off.

Mr. Pollfax started when he heard it go and drew back. "Mr. Pollfax in a dilemma," he said.

Well, he'd try the other side. Down came the drill again. There were beads of sweat on his brow. His breath was shorter.

"You see," exclaimed Mr. Pollfax suddenly and loudly, looking angrily up at his clock, "I'm fighting against time. Keep that head this way, hold the mouth. That's right. Sorry, my lord, I've got to bash you about, but time's against me."

"Why, damn this root," said Mr. Pollfax, hanging up again. "It's wearing out my drill. We'll have to saw. Mr. Pollfax *is* up against it."

His face was red now, he was gasping, and his eyes were glittering. A troubled and emotional look came over Mr. Pollfax's face.

"I've been up against it in my time," exclaimed Mr. Pollfax forcefully between his teeth. "You heard me mention the Œdipus complex to you?"

"Blah," I managed.

"I started well by ruining my father. I took every penny he had. That's a good start, isn't it?" he said, speaking very rapidly. "Then I got married. Perfectly happy marriage, but

33

I went and bust it up. I went off with a French girl, and her husband shot at us out in the car one day. I was with that girl eighteen months and she broke her back in a railway accident and I sat with her six months watching her die. Six ruddy months. I've been through it. Then my mother died and my father was going to marry again, a girl young enough to be his daughter. I went up and took that girl off him, ran off to Hungary with her, married her, and we've got seven children. Perfect happiness at last. I've been through the mill," said Mr. Pollfax, relaxing his chin and shining a torch down my mouth, "but I've come out in the end.

"A good rinse, my noble lord," said Mr. Pollfax.

"The oldest's fourteen," he said, getting the saw. "Clever girl. Very clever with her hands."

He seized me again. Did I feel anything? Well, thank God for that, said Mr. Pollfax. Here we'd been forty minutes with this damned root.

"And I bet you're thinking why didn't Lord Pollfax let sleeping dogs lie, like the telephone operator said. Did I tell you that one about the telephone operator? That gum of yours is going to be sore."

He was standing legs apart, chin trembling, eyes blinkng, hacking with the buttonhook, like a wrestler putting on a headlock.

"Mr. Pollfax with his back against the wall," he said, between his teeth.

"Mr. Pollfax making a last-minute stand," he hissed.

"On the burning deck!" he gasped.

"Whence," he added, "all but he had fled."

"Spit," he said. "And now let's have another look." He wiped his brow. "Don't say anything. Keep dead still. For God's sake don't let it hear you. My lords, ladies and gentlemen, pray silence for Mr. Pollfax. It's coming, it isn't. No, it isn't. It is. It is. There," he cried, holding a fragment in his fingers.

34

He stood gravely to attention.

"And his chief beside,
Smiling the boy fell dead,"

said Mr. Pollfax. "A good and final spit, my lord and prince."

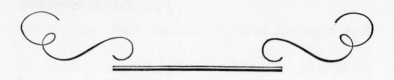

The Saint

When I was seventeen years old I lost my religious faith. It had been unsteady for some time and then, very suddenly, it went as the result of an incident in a punt on the river outside the town where we lived. My uncle, with whom I was obliged to stay for long periods of my life, had started a small furniture-making business in the town. He was always in difficulties about money, but he was convinced that in some way God would help him. And this happened. An investor arrived who belonged to a sect called the Church of the Last Purification, of Toronto, Canada. Could we imagine, this man asked, a good and omnipotent God allowing His children to be short of money? We had to admit we could not imagine this. The man paid some capital into my uncle's business and we were converted. Our family were the first Purifiers—as they were called—in the town. Soon a congregation of fifty or more were meeting every Sunday in a room at the Corn Exchange.

At once we found ourselves isolated and hated people. Everyone made jokes about us. We had to stand together because we were sometimes dragged into the courts. What the unconverted could not forgive in us was first that we believed in successful prayer and, secondly, that our revelation came from Toronto. The success of our prayers had a simple foundation. We regarded it as "Error"—our name for

Evil—to believe the evidence of our senses, and if we had influenza or consumption, or had lost our money or were unemployed, we denied the reality of these things, saying that since God could not have made them they therefore did not exist. It was exhilarating to look at our congregation and to know that what the vulgar would call miracles were performed among us, almost as a matter of routine, every day. Not very big miracles, perhaps; but up in London and out in Toronto, we knew that deafness and blindness, cancer and insanity, the great scourges, were constantly vanishing before the prayers of the more advanced Purifiers.

"What!" said my schoolmaster, an Irishman with eyes like broken glass and a sniff of irritability in the bristles of his nose. "What! Do you have the impudence to tell me that if you fell off the top floor of this building and smashed your head in, you would say you hadn't fallen and were not injured?"

I was a small boy and very afraid of everybody, but not when it was a question of my religion. I was used to the kind of conundrum the Irishman had set. It was useless to argue, though our religion had already developed an interesting casuistry.

"I *would* say so," I replied with coldness and some vanity. "And my head would not be smashed."

"You would not say so," answered the Irishman. "You would not say so." His eyes sparkled with pure pleasure. "You'd be dead."

The boys laughed, but they looked at me with admiration.

Then, I do not know how or why, I began to see a difficulty. Without warning and as if I had gone into my bedroom at night and had found a gross ape seated in my bed and thereafter following me about with his grunts and his fleas and a look, relentless and ancient, scored on his brown face, I was faced with the problem that prowls at the centre of all religious faith. I was faced by the difficulty of the origin of evil. Evil was an illusion, we were taught. But even illusions have an origin. The Purifiers denied this.

I consulted my uncle. Trade was bad at the time and this made his faith abrupt. He frowned as I spoke.

"When did you brush your coat last?" he said. "You're getting slovenly about your appearance. If you spent more time studying books"—that is to say, the Purification literature—"and less with your hands in your pockets and playing about with boats on the river, you wouldn't be letting Error in."

All dogmas have their jargon; my uncle as a business man loved the trade terms of the Purification. "Don't let Error in," was a favourite one. The whole point about the Purification, he said, was that it was scientific and therefore exact; in consequence it was sheer weakness to admit discussion. Indeed, betrayal. He unpinched his pince-nez, stirred his tea, and indicated I must submit or change the subject. Preferably the latter. I saw, to my alarm, that my arguments had defeated my uncle. Faith and doubt pulled like strings round my throat.

"You don't mean to say you don't believe that what our Lord said was true?" my aunt asked nervously, following me out of the room. "Your uncle does, dear."

I could not answer. I went out of the house and down the main street to the river, where the punts were stuck like insects in the summery flash of the reach. Life was a dream, I thought; no, a nightmare, for the ape was beside me.

I was still in this state, half sulking and half exalted, when Mr. Hubert Timberlake came to the town. He was one of the important people from the headquarters of our Church and he had come to give an address on the Purification at the Corn Exchange. Posters announcing this were everywhere. Mr. Timberlake was to spend Sunday afternoon with us. It was unbelievable that a man so eminent would actually sit in our dining-room, use our knives and forks, and eat our food.

Every imperfection in our home and our characters would jump out at him. The Truth had been revealed to man with scientific accuracy—an accuracy we could all test by experiment—and the future course of human development on earth was laid down, finally. And here in Mr. Timberlake was a man who had not merely performed many miracles—even, it was said with proper reserve, having twice raised the dead—but had actually been to Toronto, our headquarters, where this great and revolutionary revelation had first been given.

"This is my nephew," my uncle said, introducing me. "He lives with us. He thinks he thinks, Mr. Timberlake, but I tell him he only thinks he does. Ha, ha." My uncle was a humorous man when he was with the great. "He's always on the river," my uncle continued. "I tell him he's got water on the brain. I've been telling Mr. Timberlake about you, my boy."

A hand as soft as the best-quality chamois leather took mine. I saw a wide upright man in a double-breasted navy-blue suit. He had a pink square head with very small ears and one of those torpid, enamelled smiles which were said by our enemies to be too common in our sect.

"Why, isn't that just fine?" said Mr. Timberlake, who, owing to his contacts with Toronto, spoke with an American accent. "What say we tell your uncle it's funny he thinks he's funny."

The eyes of Mr. Timberlake were direct and colourless. He had the look of a retired merchant captain who had become decontaminated from the sea and had reformed and made money. His defence of me had made me his at once. My doubts vanished. Whatever Mr. Timberlake believed must be true, and as I listened to him at lunch, I thought there could be no finer life than his.

"I expect Mr. Timberlake's tired after his address," said my aunt.

"Tired?" exclaimed my uncle, brilliant with indignation. "How can Mr. Timberlake be tired? Don't let Error in!"

For in our faith the merely inconvenient was just as illusory as a great catastrophe would have been, if you wished to be strict, and Mr. Timberlake's presence made us very strict.

I noticed then that, after their broad smiles, Mr. Timberlake's lips had the habit of setting into a long depressed sarcastic curve.

"I guess," he drawled, "I guess the Al-mighty must have been tired sometimes, for it says He re-laxed on the seventh day. Say, do you know what I'd like to do this afternoon?" he said turning to me. "While your uncle and aunt are sleeping off this meal let's you and me go on the river and get water on the brain. I'll show you how to punt."

Mr. Timberlake, I saw to my disappointment, was out to show he understood the young. I saw he was planning a "quiet talk" with me about my problems.

"There are too many people on the river on Sundays," said my uncle uneasily.

"Oh, I like a crowd," said Mr. Timberlake, giving my uncle a tough look. "This is the day of rest, you know." He had had my uncle gobbling up every bit of gossip from the sacred city of Toronto all the morning.

My uncle and aunt were incredulous that a man like Mr. Timberlake should go out among the blazers and gramophones of the river on a Sunday afternoon. In any other member of our Church they would have thought this sinful.

"Waal, what say?" said Mr. Timberlake. I could only murmur.

"That's fixed," said Mr. Timberlake. And on came the smile as simple, vivid, and unanswerable as the smile on an advertisement. "Isn't that just fine!"

Mr. Timberlake went upstairs to wash his hands. My uncle was deeply offended and shocked, but he could say nothing. He unpinched his glasses.

"A very wonderful man," he said. "So human," he apologized.

"My boy," my uncle said, "this is going to be an experience for you. Hubert Timberlake was making a thousand a year in the insurance business ten years ago. Then he heard of the Purification. He threw everything up, just like that. He gave up his job and took up the work. It was a struggle, he told me so himself this morning. 'Many's the time,' he said to me this morning, 'when I wondered where my next meal was coming from.' But the way was shown. He came down from Worcester to London and in two years he was making fifteen hundred a year out of his practice."

To heal the sick by prayer according to the tenets of the Church of the Last Purification was Mr. Timberlake's profession.

My uncle lowered his eyes. With his glasses off, the lids were small and uneasy. He lowered his voice too.

"I have told him about your little trouble," my uncle said quietly with emotion. I was burned with shame. My uncle looked up and stuck out his chin confidently.

"He just smiled," my uncle said. "That's all."

Then we waited for Mr. Timberlake to come down.

I put on white flannels and soon I was walking down to the river with Mr. Timberlake. I felt that I was going with him under false pretences; for he would begin explaining to me the origin of evil and I would have to pretend politely that he was converting me when already, at the first sight of him, I had believed. A stone bridge, whose two arches were like an owlish pair of eyes gazing up the reach, was close to the landing-stage. I thought what a pity it was the flannelled men and the sunburned girls there did not know I was getting a ticket for *the* Mr. Timberlake who had been speaking in the town that very morning. I looked round for him and when I saw him I was a little startled. He was standing at the edge of the water looking at it with an expression of empty incomprehension. Among the white crowds his air of brisk efficiency had dulled. He looked middle-aged, out of place, and insignificant. But the smile switched on when he saw me. "Ready?" he called. "Fine!"

I had the feeling that inside him there must be a gramophone record going round and round, stopping at that word.

He stepped into the punt and took charge.

"Now I just want you to paddle us over to the far bank," he said, "and then I'll show you how to punt."

Everything Mr. Timberlake said still seemed unreal to me. The fact that he was sitting in a punt, of all commonplace material things, was incredible. That he should propose to pole us up the river was terrifying. Suppose he fell into the river? At once I checked the thought. A leader of our Church under the direct guidance of God could not possibly fall into a river.

The stream is wide and deep in this reach, but on the southern bank there is a manageable depth and a hard bottom. Over the clay banks the willows hang, making their basket-work print of sun and shadow on the water, while under the gliding boats lie cloudy, chloride caverns. The hoop-like branches of the trees bend down until their tips touch the water like fingers making musical sounds. Ahead in mid-stream, on a day sunny as this one was, there is a path of strong light which is hard to look at unless you half close your eyes, and down this path on the crowded Sundays go the launches with their parasols and their pennants; and also the row-boats with their beetle-leg oars, which seem to dig the sunlight out of the water as they rise. Upstream one goes, on and on between the gardens and then between fields kept for grazing. On the afternoon when Mr. Timberlake and I went out to settle the question of the origin of evil, the meadows were packed densely with buttercups.

"Now," said Mr. Timberlake decisively when I had paddled to the other side. "Now I'll take her."

He got over the seat into the well at the stern.

"I'll just get you clear of the trees," I said.

"Give me the pole," said Mr. Timberlake standing up on the little platform and making a squeak with his boots as he did so. "Thank you, sir. I haven't done this for eighteen years, but I can tell you, brother, in those days I was considered some poler."

He looked around and let the pole slide down through his hands. Then he gave the first difficult push. The punt rocked pleasantly and we moved forward. I sat facing him, paddle in hand, to check any inward drift of the punt.

"How's that, you guys?" said Mr. Timberlake looking round at our eddies and drawing in the pole. The delightful water sished down it.

"Fine," I said. Deferentially I had caught the word.

He went on to his second and his third strokes, taking too much water on his sleeve, perhaps, and uncertain in his steering, which I corrected, but he was doing well.

"It comes back to me," he said. "How am I doing?"

"Just keep her out from the trees," I said.

"The trees?" he said.

"The willows," I said.

"I'll do it now," he said. "How's that? Not quite enough? Well, how's this?"

"Another one," I said. "The current runs strong this side."

"What? More trees?" he said. He was getting hot.

"We can shoot out past them," I said. "I'll ease us over with the paddle."

Mr. Timberlake did not like this suggestion.

"No, don't do that. I can manage it," he said. I did not want to offend one of the leaders of our Church, so I put the paddle down; but I felt I ought to have taken him farther along away from the irritation of the trees.

"Of course," I said, "we could go under them. It might be nice."

"I think," said Mr. Timberlake, "that would be a very good idea."

He lunged hard on the pole and took us towards the next archway of willow branches.

"We may have to duck a bit, that's all," I said.

"Oh, I can push the branches up," said Mr. Timberlake.

"It is better to duck," I said.

We were gliding now quickly towards the arch; in fact, I was already under it.

"I think I should duck," I said. "Just bend down for this one."

"What makes the trees lean over the water like this?" asked Mr. Timberlake. "Weeping willows—I'll give you a thought there. How Error likes to make us dwell on sorrow. Why not call them *laughing* willows?" discoursed Mr. Timberlake as the branch passed over my head.

"Duck," I said.

"Where? I don't see them," said Mr. Timberlake turning round.

"No, your head," I said. "The branch," I called.

"Oh, the branch. This one?" said Mr. Timberlake finding a branch just against his chest and he put out a hand to lift it. It is not easy to lift a willow branch and Mr. Timberlake was surprised. He stepped back as it gently and firmly leaned against him. He leaned back and pushed from his feet. And he pushed too far. The boat went on, I saw Mr. Timberlake's boots leave the stern as he took an unthoughtful step backwards. He made a last-minute grasp at a stronger and higher branch, and then there he hung a yard above the water, round as a blue damson that is ripe and ready, waiting only for a touch to make it fall. Too late with the paddle and shot ahead by the force of his thrust, I could not save him.

For a full minute I did not believe what I saw; indeed, our religion taught us never to believe what we saw. Unbelieving I could not move. I gaped. The impossible had happened. Only a miracle, I found myself saying, could save him.

44

What was most striking was the silence of Mr. Timberlake as he hung from the tree. I was lost between gazing at him and trying to get the punt out of the small branches of the tree. By the time I had got the punt out, there were several yards of water between us, and the soles of his boots were very near the water as the branch bent under his weight. Boats were passing at the time but no one seemed to notice us. I was glad about this. This was a private agony. A double chin had appeared on the face of Mr. Timberlake and his head was squeezed between his shoulders and his hanging arms. I saw him blink and look up at the sky. His eyelids were pale like a chicken's. He was tidy and dignified as he hung there, the hat was not displaced, and the top button of his coat was done up. He had a blue silk handkerchief in his breast pocket. So unperturbed and genteel he seemed that as the tips of his shoes came nearer and nearer to the water, I becamed alarmed. He could perform what are called miracles. He would be thinking at this moment that only in an erroneous and illusory sense was he hanging from the branch of the tree over six feet of water. He was probably praying one of the closely reasoned prayers of our faith, which were more like conversations with Euclid than appeals to God. The calm of his face suggested this. Was he, I asked myself, within sight of the main road, the town Recreation Ground and the landing-stage crowded with people, was he about to re-enact a well-known miracle? I hoped that he was not. I prayed that he was not. I prayed with all my will that Mr. Timberlake would not walk upon the water. It was my prayer and not his that was answered.

I saw the shoes dip, the water rise above his ankles and up his socks. He tried to move his grip now to a yet higher branch—he did not succeed—and in making this effort his coat and waistcoat rose and parted from his trousers. One seam of shirt with its pant-loops and brace-tabs broke like a

crack across the middle of Mr. Timberlake. It was like a
fatal flaw in a statue, an earthquake crack that made the
monumental mortal. The last Greeks must have felt as I felt
then, when they saw a crack across the middle of some statue
of Apollo. It was at this moment I realized that the final
revelation about man and society on earth had come to nobody and that Mr. Timberlake knew nothing at all about the
origin of evil.

All this takes long to describe, but it happened in a few
seconds as I paddled towards him. I was too late to get his
feet on the boat and the only thing to do was to let him sink
until his hands were nearer the level of the punt and then to
get him to change hand-holds. Then I would paddle him
ashore. I did this. Amputated by the water, first a torso, then
a bust, then a mere head and shoulders, Mr. Timberlake, I
noticed, looked sad and lonely as he sank. He was a declining
dogma. As the water lapped his collar—for he hesitated to let
go of the branch to hold the punt—I saw a small triangle of
deprecation and pathos between his nose and the corners of
his mouth. The head resting on the platter of water had the
sneer of calamity on it, such as one sees in the pictures of a
beheaded saint.

"Hold on to the punt, Mr. Timberlake," I said urgently.
"Hold on to the punt."

He did so.

"Push from behind," he directed in a dry businesslike
voice. They were his first words. I obeyed him. Carefully I
paddled him towards the bank. He turned and, with a splash,
climbed ashore. There he stood, raising his arms and looking
at the water running down his swollen suit and making a
puddle at his feet.

"Say," said Mr. Timberlake coldly, "we let some Error in
that time."

How much he must have hated our family.

"I am sorry, Mr. Timberlake," I said. "I am most awfully

sorry. I should have paddled. It was my fault. I'll get you home at once. Let me wring out your coat and waistcoat. You'll catch your death—"

I stopped. I had nearly blasphemed. I had nearly suggested that Mr. Timberlake had fallen into the water and that to a man of his age this might be dangerous.

Mr. Timberlake corrected me. His voice was impersonal, addressing the laws of human existence rather than myself.

"If God made water it would be ridiculous to suggest He made it capable of harming His creatures. Wouldn't it?"

"Yes," I murmured hypocritically.

"O.K.," said Mr. Timberlake. "Let's go."

"I'll soon get you across," I said.

"No," he said. "I mean let's go on. We're not going to let a little thing like this spoil a beautiful afternoon. Where were we going? You spoke of a pretty landing-place farther on. Let's go there."

"But I must take you home. You can't sit there soaked to the skin. It will spoil your clothes."

"Now, now," said Mr. Timberlake. "Do as I say. Go on."

There was nothing to be done with him. I held the punt into the bank and he stepped in. He sat like a bursting and sodden bolster in front of me while I paddled. We had lost the pole of course.

For a long time I could hardly look at Mr. Timberlake. He was taking the line that nothing had happened and this put me at a disadvantage. I knew something considerable had happened. That glaze, which so many of the members of our sect had on their faces and persons, their minds and manners, had been washed off. There was no gleam for me from Mr. Timberlake.

"What's the house over there?" he asked. He was making conversation. I had steered into the middle of the river to get him into the strong sun. I saw steam rise from him.

I took courage and studied him. He was a man, I realized,

in poor physical condition, unexercised and sedentary. Now the gleam had left him, one saw the veined empurpled skin of the stoutish man with a poor heart. I remember he had said at lunch:

"A young woman I know said: 'Isn't it wonderful? I can walk thirty miles in a day without being in the least tired.' I said: 'I don't see that bodily indulgence is anything a member of the Church of the Last Purification should boast about.'"

Yes, there was something flaccid, passive, and slack about Mr. Timberlake. Bunched in swollen clothes, he refused to take them off. It occurred to me, as he looked with boredom at the water, the passing boats, and the country, that he had not been in the country before. That it was something he had agreed to do but wanted to get over quickly. He was totally uninterested. By his questions—what is that church? Are there any fish in this river? Is that a wireless or a gramophone?—I understood that Mr. Timberlake was formally acknowledging a world he did not live in. It was too interesting, too eventful a world. His spirit, inert and preoccupied, was elsewhere in an eventless and immaterial habitation. He was a dull man, duller than any man I had ever known; but his dullness was a sort of earthly deposit left by a being whose diluted mind was far away in the effervescence of metaphysical matters. There was a slightly pettish look on his face as (to himself, of course) he declared he was not wet and he would not have a heart attack or catch pneumonia.

Mr. Timberlake spoke little. Sometimes he squeezed water out of his sleeve. He shivered a little. He watched his steam. I had planned, when we set out, to go up as far as the lock, but now the thought of another two miles of this responsibility was too much. I pretended I wanted to go only as far as the bend we were approaching, where one of the richest buttercup meadows was. I mentioned this to him. He turned and looked with boredom at the field. Slowly we came to the bank.

We tied up the punt and we landed.

"Fine," said Mr. Timberlake. He stood at the edge of the meadow just as he had stood at the landing-stage—lost, stupefied, uncomprehending.

"Nice to stretch our legs," I said. I led the way into the deep flowers. So dense were the buttercups there was hardly any green. Presently I sat down. Mr. Timberlake looked at me and sat down also. Then I turned to him with a last try at persuasion. Respectability, I was sure, was his trouble.

"No one will see us," I said. "This is out of sight of the river. Take off your coat and trousers and wring them out."

Mr. Timberlake replied firmly: "I am satisfied to remain as I am."

"What is this flower?" he asked, to change the subject.

"Buttercup," I said.

"Of course," he replied.

I could do nothing with him. I lay down full length in the sun; and, observing this and thinking to please me, Mr. Timberlake did the same. He must have supposed that this was what I had come out in the boat to do. It was only human. He had come out with me, I saw, to show me that he was only human.

But as we lay there I saw the steam still rising. I had had enough.

"A bit hot," I said, getting up.

He got up at once.

"Do you want to sit in the shade?" he asked politely.

"No," I said. "Would you like to?"

"No," he said. "I was thinking of you."

"Let's go back," I said. We both stood up and I let him pass in front of me. When I looked at him again, I stopped dead. Mr. Timberlake was no longer a man in a navy-blue suit. He was blue no longer. He was transfigured. He was yellow. He was covered with buttercup pollen, a fine yellow paste of it made by the damp, from head to foot.

"Your suit," I said.

He looked at it. He raised his thin eyebrows a little, but he did not smile or make any comment.

The man is a saint, I thought. As saintly as any of those gold-leaf figures in the churches of Sicily. Golden he sat in the punt; golden he sat for the next hour as I paddled him down the river. Golden and bored. Golden as we landed at the town and as we walked up the street back to my uncle's house. There he refused to change his clothes or to sit by a fire. He kept an eye on the time for his train back to London. By no word did he acknowledge the disasters or the beauties of the world. If they were printed upon him, they were printed upon a husk.

Sixteen years have passed since I dropped Mr. Timberlake in the river and since the sight of his pant-loops destroyed my faith. I have not seen him since, but today I heard that he was dead. He was fifty-seven. His mother, a very old lady with whom he had lived all his life, went into his bedroom when he was getting ready for church and found him lying on the floor in his shirt-sleeves. A stiff collar with the tie half inserted was in one hand. Five minutes before, she told the doctor, she had been speaking to him.

The doctor, who looked at the heavy body lying on the single bed, saw a middle-aged man, wide rather than stout and with an extraordinarily box-like thick-jawed face. He had got fat, my uncle told me, in later years. The heavy liver-coloured cheeks were like the chaps of a hound. Heart disease, it was plain, was the cause of the death of Mr. Timberlake. In death the face was lax, even coarse and degenerate. It was a miracle, the doctor said, that he had lived as long. Any time during the last twenty years the smallest shock might have killed him.

I thought of our afternoon on the river. I thought of him hanging from the tree. I thought of him indifferent and golden in the meadow. I understood why he had made for himself a protective, sedentary blandness, an automatic smile, a collection of phrases. He kept them on like the coat after his ducking. And I understood why—though I had feared it all the time we were on the river—I understood why he did not talk to me about the origin of evil. He was honest. The ape was with us. The ape that merely followed me was already inside Mr. Timberlake eating out his heart.

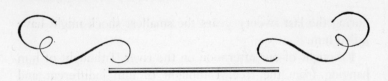

Many Are Disappointed

Heads down to the wind from the hidden sea, the four men were cycling up a deserted road in the country. Bert, who was the youngest, dreamed:

"You get to the pub, and there's a girl at the pub, a dark girl with bare arms and bare legs in a white frock, the daughter of the house, or an orphan—maybe it's better she should be an orphan—and you say something to her, or, better still, you don't say anything to her—she just comes and puts her arms round you, and you can feel her skin through her frock and she brings you some beer and the other chaps aren't there and the people don't say anything except laugh and go away, because it's all natural and she doesn't have a baby. Same at the next place, same anywhere, different place, different girl, or same girl—same girl always turning up, always waiting. Dunno how she got there. Just slips along without you knowing it and waiting like all those songs . . ."

And there the pub was. It stood on the crown of the long hill, straight ahead of them, a small red-brick house with out-buildings and a single chimney trailing out smoke against the strong white light which seemed to be thrown up by great reflectors from the hidden sea.

"There's our beer, Mr. Blake," shouted Sid on his pink

racing tires, who was the first to see it, the first to see everything. The four men glanced up.

Yes, there's our beer, they said. Our ruddy beer. They had been thinking about it for miles. A pub at the cross-roads, a pub where the old Roman road crossed this road that went on to the land's end, a funny place for a pub, but a pub all right, the only pub for ten miles at Harry's ruddy Roman road, marked on the map which stuck out of the backside pocket of Harry's breeches. Yes, that was the pub, and Ted, the oldest and the married one, slacked on the long hill and said all he hoped was that the Romans had left a drop in the bottom of the barrel for posterity.

When they had left in the morning there had been little wind. The skylarks were over the fields, and the sun itself was like one of their steel wheels flashing in the sky. Sid was the first, but Harry with the stubborn red neck and the close dull fair curls was the leader. In the week he sat in the office making the plan. He had this mania for Roman roads. "Ask our Mr. Newton," they said, "the man with the big head and the brain." They had passed through the cream-walled villages and out again to pick up once more the singing of the larks; and then cloud had covered the sun like a grey hand, west of Handleyford the country had emptied, and it was astonishing to hear a bird. Reeds were in the small meadows. Hedges crawled uncut and there had been no villages, only long tablelands of common and bald wiry grass for sheep and the isolated farm with no ivy on the brick.

Well, they were there at last. They piled their bicycles against the wall of the house. They were shy before these country places. They waited for Ted. He was walking the last thirty yards. They looked at the four windows with their lace curtains and the varnished door. There was a chicken in the road and no sound but the whimper of the telegraph wire on the hill. In an open barn was a cart tipped down, its shaft white with the winter's mud, and last year's swallow nests,

now empty, were under the eaves. Then Ted came and when
he had piled his bicycle, they read the black sign over the
door. "Tavern," it said. A funny old-fashioned word, Ted
said, that you didn't often see.

"Well," Sid said, "a couple of pints all round?"

They looked to Harry. He always opened doors, but this
door was so emphatically closed that he took off his fur
gauntlet first and knocked before he opened it. The four men
were surprised to see a woman standing behind the door,
waiting there as if she had been listening to them. She was a
frail, drab woman, not much past thirty, in a white blouse
that drooped low over her chest.

"Good morning," said Sid. "This the bar?"

"The bar?" said the woman timidly. She spoke in a flat
wondering voice and not in the singsong of this part of the
country.

"Yes, the bar," Ted said. "It says 'Tavern,' " he said,
nodding up at the notice.

"Oh yes," she said, hesitating. "Come in. Come in here."

She showed them not into the bar but into a sitting-room.
There was a bowl of tomatoes in the window and a notice
said "Teas."

The four men were tall and large beside her in the little
room and she gazed up at them as if she feared they would
burst its walls. And yet she was pleased. She was trying to
smile.

"This is on me," Sid said. "Mild and bitter four times."

"O.K., Mr. Blake," Ted said. "Bring me my beer."

"But let's get into the bar," said Bert.

Seeing an armchair, Ted sank into it and now the woman
was reassured. She succeeded in smiling but she did not go
out of the room. Sid looked at her, and her smile was vacant
and faint like the smile fading on an old photograph. Her hair
was short, an impure yellow and the pale skin of her face and
her neck and her breast seemed to be moist as if she had just

54

got out of bed. The high strong light of this place drank all colour from her.

"There isn't a bar," she said. "This isn't a public-house. They call it the Tavern, but it isn't a tavern by rights."

Very anxiously she raised her hands to her blouse.

"What!" they exclaimed. "Not a pub! Here, Harry, it's marked on your map." They were dumbfounded and angry.

"What you mean, don't sell beer," they said.

Their voices were very loud.

"Yes," said Harry. "Here it is. See? Inn."

He put the map before her face accusingly.

"You don't sell beer?" said Bert. He looked at the pale-blue-veined chest of the woman.

"No," she said. She hesitated. "Many are disappointed," she said, and she spoke like a child reciting a piece without knowing its meaning. He lowered his eyes.

"You bet they ruddy well are," said Ted from the chair.

"Where is the pub?" said Sid.

She put out her hand and a little girl came into the room and clung close to her mother. Now she felt happier.

"My little girl," she said.

She was a tiny, frail child with yellow hair and pale-blue eyes like her mother's. The four men smiled and spoke more quietly because of the resemblance between the woman and her child.

"Which way did you come?" she asked, and her hand moving over the child's hair got courage from the child. "Handleyford?" she said. "That's it. It's ten miles. The Queen's Arms, Handleyford, the way you came. That's the nearest pub."

"My God!" said Bert. "What a country!"

"The Queen's Arms," said Ted stupefied.

He remembered it. They were passing through Handleyford. He was the oldest, a flat wide man in loose clothes, loose in the chin too, with watery rings under his eyes and a small golden sun of baldness at the back of his head. "Queen's Arms," he had called. "Here, what's the ruddy game?" But the others had grinned back at him. When you drop back to number four on the hills it comes back to you: they're single, nothing to worry about, you're married and you're forty. What's the hurry? Ease up, take what you can get. "Queen's Arms"—he remembered looking back. The best things are in the past.

"Well, that's that!" said Sid.

"Queen's Arms, Harry," Ted said.

And Bert looked at the woman. "Let's go on," he said fiercely. She was not the woman he had expected. Then he blushed and turned away from the woman.

She was afraid they were going and in a placating voice she said: "I do teas."

Sid was sitting on the arm of a chair, and the child was gazing at a gold ring he wore on his little finger. He saw the child was gazing and he smiled.

"What's wrong with tea?" Sid said.

"Ask the man with the brain," said Ted. "Ask the man with the map."

Harry said: "If you can't have beer, you'd better take what you can get, Mr. Richards."

"Tea," nodded Sid to the woman. "Make it strong."

The woman looked at Sid as if he had performed a miracle. "I'll get you tea," she said eagerly. "I always do teas for people." She spoke with delight as if a bell had suddenly tinkled inside her. Her eyes shone. She would get them tea, she said, and bread and butter, but no eggs, because the man had not been that morning, and no ham. It was too early, she said, for ham. "But there are tomatoes," she said. And then, like a child: "I put them in the window so as people can see."

"O.K.," Sid said. "Four teas."

She did not move at once but still, like a shy child, stood watching them, waiting for them to be settled and fearful that they would not stay. But at last she put out her hand to the child and hurried out to the kitchen.

"Well, Mr. Blake," said Ted, "there's a ruddy sell."

"Have a gasper, Mr. Richards," said Sid.

"Try my lighter," said Ted.

He clicked the lighter, but no flame came.

"Wrong number," said Ted. "Dial O and try again." A steak, said Sid, had been his idea. A couple of pints just to ease the passage and then some real drinking, Ted said. But Bert was drumming on a biscuit tin and was looking inside. There was nothing in it. "Many," said Bert, "are disappointed."

They looked at the room. There were two new treacle-coloured armchairs. There was a sofa with a pattern of black ferns on it. The new plush was damp and sticky to the hands from the air of the hidden sea. There was a gun-metal fender and there was crinkled, green paper in the fireplace. A cupboard with a glass door was empty except for the lowest shelf. On that was a thick book called *The Marvels of Science*.

The room was cold. They thought in the winter it must be damn cold. They thought of the ten drizzling miles to Handleyford.

They listened to the cold clatter of the plates in the kitchen and the sound of the woman's excited voice and the child's. There was the bare linoleum on the floor and the chill glass of the window. Outside was the road with blown sand at the edges and, beyond a wall, there were rows of cabbages, then a bit of field and the expressionless sky. There was no sound on the road. They—it occurred to them—had been the only sound on that road for hours.

The woman came in with a cup and then with a plate. The child brought a plate and the woman came in with another cup. She looked in a dazed way at the men, amazed that they were still there. It seemed to Ted, who was married, that she didn't know how to lay a table. "And now I've forgotten the sugar," she laughed. Every time she came into the room she glanced at Bert timidly and yet pityingly, because he was the youngest and had been the most angry. He lowered his eyes and avoided her look. But to Ted she said: "That's right, you make yourselves comfortable," and at Sid she smiled because he had been the kindest. At Harry she did not look at all.

She was very startled then when he stood at the door and said: "Where's this Roman road?"

She was in the kitchen. She told him the road by the white gate and showed him from the doorway of the house.

"There he goes," said Sid at the window. "He's looking over the gate."

They waited. The milk was put on the table. The woman came in at last with the bread and butter and the tea.

"He'll miss his tea next," Ted said.

"Well," Ted said, when Harry came back. "See any Romans?"

"It's just grass," Harry said. "Nothing on it." He stared in his baffled, bull-necked way.

"No beer and no Romans," Ted said.

The woman, who was standing there, smiled. In a faltering voice, wishing to make them happy, she said:

"We don't often get no Romans here."

"Oh God!" Bert laughed very loudly and Ted shook with laughter too. Harry stared.

"Don't take any notice of them, missus," Sid said. And then to them: "She means gypsies."

"That come with brooms," she said, bewildered by their laughter, wondering what she had done.

When she had gone and had closed the door, Bert and Ted touched their heads with their fingers and said she was dippy, but Sid told them to speak quietly.

Noisily they had drawn up their chairs and were eating and drinking. Ted cut up tomatoes, salted them, and put them on his bread. They were good for the blood, he told them, and

Harry said they reckoned at home his granddad got the cancer he died of from eating tomatoes day after day. Bert, with his mouth full, said he'd read somewhere that tea was the most dangerous drink on earth. Then the child came in with a paper and said her mother had sent it. Sid looked at the door when it closed again.

"Funny thing," he said. "I think I've seen that woman before."

That, they said, was Sid's trouble. He'd seen too many girls before.

He was a lanky man with a high forehead and a Hitler moustache and his lips lay over his mouth as if they were kissing the air or whispering to it. He was a dark, harsh-looking, cocksure man, but with a gentle voice and it was hard to see his eyes under his strong glasses. His lashes were long and his lids often half-lowered, which gave him an air of seriousness and shyness. But he stuck his thumbs in his waist-coat and stuck out his legs to show his loud check stockings and he had that ring on his finger. "Move that up a couple and he'd be spliced," they said. "Not me," he said, "look at Ted." A man with no ideals, Bert thought, a man whose life was hidden behind the syrup-thick lens of his glasses. Flash Sid. See the typists draw themselves up, tilt back their heads, and get their hands ready to keep him off. Not a man with ideals. See them watch his arms and his hands, see them start tapping hard on the typewriter keys and pretending to be busy when he leaned over to tell them a story. And then, when he was gone, see them peep through the Enquiry window to watch where he went, quarrel about him, and dawdle in the street when the office closed, hoping to see him.

"Well," said Harry when they had cleared the table and got out the map.

Sid said: "You gen'lemen settle it. I'll go and fix her up."

Sid's off, they said. First on the road, always leading, getting the first of the air, licking the cream off everything.

He found her in the kitchen and he had to lower his head because of the ceiling. She was sitting drably at the table, which was covered with unwashed plates and the remains of a meal. There were unwashed clothes on the backs of the chairs and there was a man's waistcoat. The child was reading a comic paper at the table and singing in a high small voice.

A delicate stalk of neck, he thought, and eyes like the pale wild scabious you see in the ditches.

Four shillings, she said, would that be too much?

She put her hand nervously to her breast.

"That's all right," Sid said, and put the money in her hand. It was coarsened by work. "We cleared up everything," he said.

"Don't get many people, I expect," he said.

"Not this time of year."

"A bit lonely," he said.

"Some think it is," she said.

"How long have you been here?" he said.

"Only three years. It seems," she said with her continual wonder, "longer."

"I thought it wasn't long," Sid said. "I thought I seen you somewhere. You weren't in—in Horsham, were you?"

"I come from Ashford," she said.

"Ashford," he said. "I knew you weren't from these parts."

She brightened and she was fascinated because he took off his glasses and she saw the deep serious shadows of his eyes and the pale drooping of the naked lids. The eyes looked tired and as if they had seen many things and she was tired too.

"I bin ill," she said. Her story came irresistibly to her lips. "The doctor told us to come here. My husband gave up his job and everything. Things are different here. The money's not so good—" Her voice quickened. "But I try to make it up with the teas."

She paused, trying to read from his face if she should say any more. She seemed to be standing on the edge of another country. The pale-blue eyes seemed to be the pale sky of a far-away place where she had been living.

"I nearly died," she said. She was a little amazed by this fact.

"You're O.K. now," Sid said.

"I'm better," she said. "But it seems I get lonely now I'm better."

"You want your health, but you want a bit of company," Sid said.

"My husband says: 'You got your health, what you want company for?'"

She put this to Sid in case her husband was not right, but she picked up her husband's waistcoat from the chair and looked over its buttons because she felt, timorously, she had been disloyal to her husband.

"A woman wants company," said Sid.

He looked shy now to her, like Bert, the young one; but she was most astonished that someone should agree with her and not her husband.

Then she flushed and put out her hand to the little girl, who came to her mother's side, pressing against her. The woman felt safer and raised her eyes and looked more boldly at him.

"You and your friends going far?"

He told her. She nodded, counting the miles as if she were coming along with them. And then Sid felt a hand touch his.

It was the child's hand touching the ring on his finger.

"Ha!" laughed Sid. "You saw that before." He was quick. The child was delighted with his quickness. The woman put the waistcoat down at once. He took off the ring and put it in the palm of his hand and bent down so that his head nearly brushed the woman's arm. "That's lucky," he said. "Here," he said. He slipped the ring on the child's little finger. "See," he said. "Keeps me out of mischief. Keep a ring on your little finger and you'll be lucky."

61

Many Are Disappointed

The child looked at him without belief.

"Here y'are," he said, taking back the ring. "Your mother wants it," he said, winking at the woman. "She's got hers on the wrong finger. Little one luck, big one trouble."

She laughed and she blushed and her eyes shone. He moved to the door and her pale lips pouted a little. Then, taking the child by the hand she hurried over to him as if both of them would cling to him. Excitedly, avidly, they followed him to the other room.

"Come on, Mr. Blake," said Ted. The three others rose to their feet.

The child clung to her mother's hand and danced up and down. She was in the midst of them. They zipped up their jackets, stubbed their cigarettes, folded up the map. Harry put on his gauntlets. He stared at the child and then slowly took off his glove and pulled out a sixpence. "No," murmured Ted, the married man, but the child was too quick.

They went out of the room and stood in the road. They stretched themselves in the open air. The sun was shining now on the fields. The woman came to the door to see them. They took their bicycles from the wall, looked up and down the road, and then swung on. To the sea, the coast road, and then perhaps a girl, some girl. But the others were shouting.

"Good-bye," they called. "Good-bye."

And Bert, the last, remembered then to wave good-bye too, and glanced up at the misleading notice. When they were all together, heads down to the wind, they turned again. "Good God," they said. The woman and the child had come out into the middle of the road hand in hand and their arms were still raised and their hands were fluttering under the strong light of that high place. It was a long time before they went back into the house.

And now for a pub, a real pub, the three men called to Harry. Sid was ahead on his slim pink tires getting the first of the new wind, with the ring shining on his finger.

Passing the Ball

Two years ago, when I had finished at the hospital and I was waiting for a grant to come through, I put in a month as a locum for a country doctor.

When I first went to see him the doctor switched on his desk lamp, turned it to shine full in my face, and said in a rough voice, as if he were finishing a mouthful of hay:

"How old are you?" he said. "If I may ask? Married? Do you hunt? I mean where were you at school?"

He began pulling out the drawers of his desk one by one and, shutting them recklessly with a number of bangs, rang for his dispenser and said something to her about a horse. After this he leaned forward and fell to tapping the side of his tin wastepaper basket with a riding-crop in slow, trotting time. His look was uninterested.

"Yes, yes, yes," he said lazily from the saddle. "We don't want a lot of your newfangled ideas here. This isn't the usual kind of practice. The man I have here has got to be a gentleman. You can hand out your penicillin and your M. & B. You can put the whole parish in an iron lung, fill them with American drugs—I know that's the modern idea—but it's my experience of forty years of doctoring that a gentleman's worth the lot. Have a drink? Do you know the Fobhams?"

I could see up the doctor's meaty nose and underneath his chin when he raised it to utter this name in the voice of one who had suddenly put on court dress. By nature Dr. Ray was a man of disguises, and a new one with every sentence. Two whiskies stabilized him. A heavy, guilty blush came down from the middle of his head, enlarged his ears, and went below his collar. His hands became confidential; one of them was put on my shoulder; his voice lowered and, if shrewdness was in one blue eye as sharp as a pellet, the other became watery with anxiety.

"What it boils down to, old man, is this," he said, sneering at himself. "Half the village at the surgery door thinking they're going to die because they've cut their fingers, and threatening to write to the Ministry of Health because you won't issue free crutches and corsets. The usual thing. The day's work, eh? All in it. Forget it. The important thing is this."

"Yes?" I said.

"I'm telling you." He sharpened. "The only people who count here are fifteen families: the private patients. That's where the living is. I've been here most of my life and I've made quite a nice thing out of it. I don't want it spoiled. They're the people to watch. I get a call from them—I go at once. I don't want anyone coming in here and ruining it with a lot of newfangled stuff."

"Frankly," he added, "I can't afford it."

The doctor stepped back, opened his mouth wide and felt his face in several places.

"I think you're the right sort of chap," he said. "Have another drink? There are only three illnesses in this place—bridge, horses, and marriage—you're not married? Glad to hear it. And there's only one medicine: tact. In any case," he said, "it's August. Everyone's away."

In that month the woods in the small estates seemed to lie under glass. The cottages fluffed like hens in the sun; the large houses had a sedate and waxen gleam. The air seemed to hang, brocaded, from the enormous trees. I drove on my

64

rounds from one tropical garden to the next. Men like cock pheasants drove out of Georgian houses in their shooting brakes; their women's voices went off like the alarm call of game. In the rivers, large, clever trout, living like *rentiers* on their capital, put themselves at the disposal of the highly taxed fishermen on the banks of the beautiful river. There was the warm bread smell of the harvest in the fields and of tweed, roses, and tobacco in the bars. In their houses, most of them built in the eighteenth century, the fifteen families were hidden. There Mrs. Gluck ordered more honeysuckle so that next year it would climb into *every* bedroom; there the Admiral did his jigsaw puzzle and the young Hookhams came down from the week's climb towards the Cabinet in London; two miles off, Lord Fobham, wearing plimsolls, let off a wing of his house at a tremendous rent and spent his evenings stiffening himself with gin in the company of Mr. Calverley, a cultivated alcoholic who often—I was to discover—lost his clothes and had slept, against the will of their owners, in most of the houses round about. Mrs. Luke sat moustached and quietly chewing on her fortune in a house famous for its monkey puzzles. At Upley was the financier Hicks, who had shot the head off the stone pelican on the gate of his drive; in the mill house near the water meadows was Mrs. Scarborough ("Pansy") Flynn, three times divorced, nesting like a moorhen and listening for the voices of men. And then there were the Bassilleros, who brought into the country an odour of Claridges; indeed, his violet complexion gave "Jock" Bassillero's face the surprised appearance of one cut out of a hotel carpet and seen in fluorescent light.

I have conveyed an impression of tropical luxury in my account of this August, but in fact it was the coldest August for many years. We had influenza in the village. The tropical quality came from the fifteen families; at a certain stage, portions of civilization reach a Tahitian condition and are hot enough to be moved to a climate less mild than the English one; indeed, there was a good deal of talk among the fifteen families of emigrating to Jamaica. I found this tropical tendency almost at once. A few days after I had taken over from the doctor, there was a party at the Hickses'.

I heard there had been a party when Mr. Calverley was brought into the surgery. He had a cut on top of his head and was supported by a few friends. Mrs. Bassillero was among them.

"What have you been up to?" I said as I dressed the wound.

Mr. Calverley was wearing no collar and no jacket and smelled strongly of ivy. He had curling black hair and looked gentle, savage, and appealing.

"The gutter fell on him," said one of the women. "Is it deep? Is it all right? Poor Tommy. He was climbing after Pansy Flynn."

The sympathy annoyed Calverley. He knocked the dressing out of my hand, jumped up, and drove his friends back to the door.

"I'll kill you all," he said.

Hicks, the financier, a man who illustrated the Theory of Conspicuous Waste, by the habit of dropping the first letter of many of his words, said: " 'hut up, Tommy. 'it down. 'ook at Ray, he's making 'ight of it."

"That's not Ray," someone said. "Ray's on holiday."

" 'ood 'od," said Hicks. " 'an't have quacks here."

I had got Calverley back in the chair.

" 'ight poison us. State 'octor? No?"

Calverley looked up at me with a quiet, intimate, head-hunting smile.

"I'll kill you," he said to me in a soft and cultivated voice.

Mrs. Bassillero started talking loudly to someone on the other side of the surgery about the sexual life of a couple called Pip and Dottie.

I found Calverley's tie on my carpet the next morning.

In the next two or three days I heard odds and ends about the Hickses' party. Calverley had got half-way up the ivy at the side of the house. Hicks had put his foot through his drawing-room window. One or two cars were having their wings straightened at the garage and Lady Fobham, to whom I was called, had been in the lily pond.

And then there was a telephone call from the Bassilleros. I was out on my rounds and the message followed me from house to house. It was half past twelve before I got to the Bassilleros'. Mr. Bassillero (the message said) had had "one of his attacks."

The Bassilleros lived in a house built in 1740. I noticed, as I went in, paintings of several famous dead horses, a great many medals. With its white and its gold, the house was a pretty example of the architecture of the period. A Spanish servant let me into a wide hall where a large naval battle was going on in a gilt frame on the wall opposite the door. It was a picture filled with impudent little waves, clouds, and sails, like Mrs. Bassillero's blue-grey curls. She came to me wearing a smart, sand-coloured version of the county's tweed uniform. She walked with the artificial jerk of the hips taught to débutantes in her time. One eyelid was lowered in a little, trained, quarter-wink. She was five feet high, broad-chinned, thin-limbed, and narrow like a boy.

"I had a message at the surgery . . ." I began. Mrs. Bassillero had a pretty voice and the seductive, abrupt, bad manners of her generation which set it off.

"I rang for Ray."

"He's on holiday," I said.

"That's a body blow," she said. "We always have Ray." She stood there, her violet eyes picking me over, preparing to haggle with me, do a deal, or ask me what I bet her that she could not get Ray back at once from the other end of the earth if she wished to.

"You're using Ray's car," she accused me. "He said he'd

lend it me." Mrs. Bassillero put her head on one side to see if
this "try on" would succeed.

"It belongs to the practice," I said.

Mrs. Bassillero gave the faintest jerk to her head and one
eyebrow moved, as if she were shaking off a very close
bullet.

"Hard luck on me," she said.

"I am sorry about Mr. Bassillero," I said. "May I see
him? What is the trouble?"

Mrs. Bassillero considered me and hummed. Then again
came that jerk of the head, shaking off the bad news: the
bad news was myself.

"I rang up to ask Ray to luncheon," she said. "I forgot
he's away." And then, doing a deal again: "Will you stay?"

"I was told Mr. Bassillero had had an attack," I said.

"He has," she said. "He's lost his voice again."

"He can't speak," she said. Her direct eyes now were
made to mist with skilful appeal.

"I had better look at his throat," I said.

Mrs. Bassillero suddenly laughed like a man.

"If you really want to," she said. "You don't understand.
What a bore Ray isn't here! When I say he can't speak, I
mean he *won't* speak. We're not on speaking terms. We had
a row after the party at Hickses'. You must stay to luncheon.
There's no one to pass the ball. Everyone's away. We always
get Ray when my husband's voice goes. You'll stay? Now I
will take you to my husband."

She trod out of the room slowly like a cat and I followed
her to the door of her husband's study.

"Look at his throat, doctor," she said loudly as she opened
the door.

Mr. Bassillero was a short person, too. He was considering his fishing rods and did not look up at once when I came
into the room.

"Damn glad you're here, doctor," he said. "Trouble."

"I'm sorry to hear that," I said.

Then Mr. Bassillero looked up and said: "Who are you?"

Tact, I remembered, was the thing. I did not say Mrs. Bassillero had sent for me. Mr. Bassillero had that kind of dark handsomeness which is fixed like a pain to one aspect of a luxurious head. He was only about forty-five, but he seemed to have receded into the loud pattern of his clothes. He was wearing a plum-coloured tweed suit with green lines squared on it, a design that made him nearly invisible in any well-furnished room. His violet cheeks had been embossed on him twenty-five years ago. Mr. Bassillero, I was to find out, had undergone a severe cure for drinking. His cure had left him stupefied. His main occupation during the day, I soon gathered, was to consider whether he would change his clothes. He was a man who knew he was dressed for something—but for what escaped his mind.

"I think I shall go in and change," was one of his frequent sentences. Or "I shall put on my other boots and go down to the village."

Mr. Bassillero was looking at my worn grey suit.

"Mrs. Bassillero has very kindly asked me to luncheon," I said.

"We usually have Ray," said Bassillero. "Always passes the ball. Understands women. Can cap anything. She," Mr. Bassillero pointed a neutral finger at the door, "better warn you—has lost her voice. Can't speak."

"It is damp weather for August," I said.

"Yes, put on a Burberry this morning," Mr. Bassillero agreed. "Cold enough for a coat. Difficult speaking to someone who doesn't answer, difficult to keep it up. We've got Spanish servants—never stop."

Mr. Bassillero had talked a lot, but now his supply of words went. We stared at a silver dog on his desk. We were saved by one of the Spaniards calling us to luncheon.

We went into a room so high and large that the Bassilleros

69

were like a pair of mere anemones at the bottom of a tank. I, on the contrary, had the sensation of growing uncomfortably tall; one of my difficulties during the meal was a dread that I would shoot up and hit the ceiling.

"If you will ask my husband he will, I am sure, give you something to drink," Mrs. Bassillero said as we sat down.

"I wonder if I could get you to trouble *her* to pass us down the bread. Spanish servants always forget something," said Mr. Bassillero.

I had become wired in as a telephone for Mr. and Mrs. Bassillero. I found myself bobbing in my chair from right to left, collecting one set of remarks, passing them on, and then collecting and disposing again. I found myself very soon telling Mr. Bassillero that his wife was going to London on the evening train, I found myself telling her that Mr. Bassillero was going to Scotland. Mr. Bassillero told me he had found "some damn Spanish thing" in his cutlets; Mrs. Bassillero asked *if* I had just bought a new motor mower, *would* I allow it to be left out in the rain, considering the price of things now. I sat trying to make myself shorter. We had arrived, I thought, at last at a safe topic: the weather. As I have said, it was a cold August. The Bassilleros had put on their heating. Mr. Bassillero eased now that we had returned to his favourite, indeed his only, subject.

"Thought of changing my shirt this morning," he said. "Putting on a warmer one. Not a single warm shirt in my drawer."

If the Bassilleros could not speak they could, of course, hear.

"I imagine, doctor, when you can't find a shirt where you are lodging, you go to the linen room or you go to Mrs. Thing?" said Mrs. Bassillero.

Mr. Bassillero asked me if I did not agree that in a properly run house, as my lodgings probably were, there was a place for everything and you did not have to turn the house upside down to get it. Not only that, he said, my Mrs. Thing probably spoke English.

Mr. Bassillero spoke mainly to the salt at his end of the table; Mrs. Bassillero looked at a large picture of a horse called Bendigo, which had won the Jubilee Stakes in the eighties.

Mrs. Bassillero said: "I'm sure you, doctor, speak foreign languages well."

A group of Cupids above my head seemed to be beckoning me up. I fought my way down to the subject of the weather.

"It is clouding over again," I said.

The attempt did not help us.

"In any case," said Mrs. Bassillero, "I'm sure you never change into warm shirts at this time of the year. You wear a light summer overcoat."

"I haven't got one," I said.

"What?" said Mr. Bassillero.

I repeated the sentence to his end of the table.

"Good God," he said.

"Did you lose it?" said Mrs. Bassillero with sharp interest.

"Some fellow pinch it?" asked Mr. Bassillero.

For a moment they were almost united. They even looked at each other for a second, then their glances skidded away.

"No, I just haven't got one," I said.

Mr. Bassillero sank back, like an invalid, into his handsomeness. He looked at me with total unbelief.

"I thought you were going to say," he said bitterly, "some fellow took it. Tom Calverley took mine at the Hickses' on Saturday. I took his. Only thing to do."

"Men are too extraordinary, doctor," said Mrs. Bassillero. "You are no taller than my husband, but I'm sure you wouldn't be such a fool as to come home in Tommy Calverley's overcoat. He's six foot three. I mean right down to your boots. Polar. I mean, surely you'd pick one your own size. Even after a party."

"Calverley took mine. I took his. Fair's fair," said Bassillero, speaking to me.

"On a cold night," I said.

"Two in the morning," said Bassillero.

"I see you are not on my side, doctor," said Mrs. Bassillero giving the shake to her grey curls.

"After a party I might come away in mink," I said. I risked a lie: "I once did," I said. I looked hopefully at both of them to see if we were happier now.

Mrs. Bassillero had a gay but humourless manner; a joke about mink was unacceptable.

"What an *odd* thing to do," she said coldly.

I had offended Mr. Bassillero too; he looked at me with distaste. In mixing up men's and women's clothes, I had been sartorially disagreeable. He rang off, so to say, and spoke to himself.

Mrs. Bassillero said to me in her short, crushing style: "I hope you returned the coat."

"Of course," I said.

"Because I do think if one wilfully takes someone else's coat one ought to return it, don't you? Or not? I don't know about men. I mean, there's Tommy Calverley's ridiculous coat hanging up in the cloakroom still. I expect you saw it?"

I don't like being snubbed. "I thought of selling it," I said.

Mr. Bassillero looked up. His colour had become a darker violet.

"Sold it!" exclaimed Mr. Bassillero.

"No," I calmed him. "I was speaking to Mrs. Bassillero about a coat I took."

"Oh," said Mr. Bassillero, "if Tom Calverley's sold my coat . . ."

Mr. Bassillero was unable to go on with this idea. He

looked at me suspiciously: it appeared to him I was trying to get him away from the ground on which he was making his stand.

"Took my coat and hadn't the grace to bring it back," he said to me.

Mr. Bassillero became magnetic.

"Daren't," he said. "Daren't bring it back."

There was a long silence at the table. At either end of it the Bassilleros had receded into the events of the Hickses' party. Mr. Bassillero was the first to speak, and his voice seemed to come from three days away.

"Wouldn't pay him either," he said.

He glanced at the window and the sky, looked at his jacket wondering if he would change again.

"Knows what he left in his pocket," he said.

Mrs. Bassillero's head made a small dodge. She got up.

"Shall we have coffee next door?" she said. She walked ahead and opened the door. Bassillero held me back.

"You a married man, doctor?" he said.

"No," I said.

"Neither is Ray," he said.

Mr. Bassillero looked lost, as if by some misfortune he was the only married man in the world.

"Are you coming?" called Mrs. Bassillero.

"Engaged?" said Bassillero, recovering hope.

"No," I said.

Mr. Bassillero thought this over.

"It makes no odds," said Mr. Bassillero. "A fellow takes your coat, eh? You take his? All right. You find your wife's gloves in his pocket. Now what do you do? Where are you, I mean to say—what? You've got a scientific brain—explain it. Eh? See what I mean?"

I passed into the drawing-room, where Mrs. Bassillero's thin legs looked like scissors, and one cutting and racketing knee appeared from under her skirt as she sat pouring the coffee.

"Do sit down, you look so unsteady," said Mrs. Bassillero as I took my coffee. She poured out a cup for her husband and turned her back to him when he took it.

"I *do* think," she said in a gush, turning to me. "I *do* think it's too extraordinary about men. I mean the way they have become humble in the last two hundred years. I mean they used to dress up to please women and to be admired by them; hours doing their hair and their faces. Now it's the other way on. I do think it's sweet of you to give it all up. So self-effacing. I mean you all dress alike, and take each other's clothes."

She paused. Not only her face, but the hard-headed knee seemed to be advancing at me. The dealer's voice in her suddenly came out.

"After a couple of martinis, when you've got one eye on the man who is making a pass at you and the other ripping around for somewhere to put your gloves, one has no idea which coat is which. You stick them anywhere. They all look alike. One might be married to anybody."

When she said this, Mrs. Bassillero's pleasant violet eye gave its trained quarter-wink.

"That, at any rate, is the story you've got to sell for me to Mr. Bassillero," she appeared to be signalling.

I saw that this was the crisis; this was where Ray, having "passed the ball" for half an hour, would now rise to the occasion and administer his medicine. What would he do? Would he distract Mr. Bassillero with some anecdote about a tailor, a horse, or a fish; or entangle Mrs. Bassillero in some social crossword puzzle about the first Fobham marriage? To show how unsuited my mind was to the situation—I tried, as they say, to get at the facts and to reconstruct the incident. I got back to the scene in my surgery on the night of the Hickses' party. Who was there? What were they wearing? I

74

went over the people one by one and then I saw Calverley sitting in my chair.

"Good heavens," I said. "I've just remembered something. You know when Calverley came to my surgery that night, he wasn't wearing an overcoat. Actually, he hadn't even got a jacket on."

I didn't know what Mrs. Bassillero's relations with Mr. Calverley were; but Mrs. Bassillero's startled eyes suddenly stared into a scene that neither Mr. Bassillero nor I knew about; she was too taken aback to wink.

"I see," she said. "You mean he hadn't taken my husband's coat at all?"

"Or," I said, making it worse, "he'd probably left it somewhere."

She looked at me scientifically in a way that suggested that I was the kind of man who couldn't keep his mouth shut even if it were stitched. Then she gave the small flick of her head and, turning to her husband, she spoke to him directly for the first time.

"That is why he hasn't brought it back," she said. "It's at Pansy Flynn's. . . ."

Into that name Mrs. Bassillero might have been pouring machine-gun fire.

"Not the first time your coat has been there, my dear," she followed up. "It probably walked there by itself, it knows the way."

The astonishment in Mr. Bassillero's face was chiefly that of a man who finds himself, through no fault of his own, suddenly on speaking terms with his wife again. He could not believe it. Then he slowly saw the innuendo. He appeared to be about to shoot back at his wife—indeed, his arms moved nervously; I suppose he felt he was not dressed in the right clothes for uttering a domestic sarcasm, for all he did was suddenly to pull down his two waistcoat ends with a force that made his collar stand out.

75

Passing the Ball

And then I had the only sensible idea that occurred to me during the luncheon party.

"I'm passing there"—I did not say where—"on my way to the surgery. I will pick up your coat for you, Mr. Bassillero. In fact, if you like to give me Mr. Calverley's, I will make the exchange. I'll drop yours in for you this evening."

I looked from one Bassillero to the other and I saw that, having done my worst, I was beginning to triumph. I saw the embarrassment of two people who are about to lose the object of a very satisfying quarrel. Reluctantly Mr. Bassillero saw his grievance go; suspiciously Mrs. Bassillero considered the peace. Presently they fell into an argument about who was going to London and who to Scotland and when. It ended where so many of the discussions of the Bassilleros' must have done on the central situation of their marriage; that Mr. Bassillero couldn't go to Scotland—indeed, anywhere else—until he could freely decide which coat to wear, and that Mrs. Bassillero never made up her mind until she saw what he was doing first.

It is pleasant to do good to people. As I put Calverley's coat in the car and drove off from the Bassilleros', I felt that Dr. Ray would congratulate me. I had been a telephone for the Bassilleros, I had been the catalyst, I had administered "the only medicine." Calverley's coat, like Calverley disembodied, sagged beside me on the seat. Long, a dim, grey herringbone cloth, it was not in fresh condition. The collar was greasy, there were the spots of Calverley's personal life on it; it was worn at the pockets and the second button hung loose. It had been left in so many places; it had been returned by so many hands; it had hung on so many alien hooks. It probably smelled of whisky. As it lounged there in its creases, I could imagine Calverley's head sticking out of the collar, the face with the gentle eyes, the violent mouth, and the head-hunting smile. An ordinary stretch of herringbone tweed, with its tradition of decorum, can never before have conveyed such sensations of rampage and free will, though now it lay sly, slothful—conceivably, I fancied, in remorse.

I drove for a couple of miles through the long settled greenery of this part of the country. It was the time of the year when the chestnut leaves are dark and drying. I had no intention of stirring up a mare's nest at Mrs. Flynn's, but went to Calverley's house. He lived in a small white lodge, a pretty, even arty place with a peacock cut out of the yew hedge. I got out, picked up the coat, and knocked at the door and listened to the bees humming under the windows as I waited. A cottage woman who said she came in to clean and cook for Mr. Calverley opened to me.

"I have brought back Mr. Calverley's coat," I said. "I believe he and Mr. Bassillero took the wrong ones the other day."

The cottage woman took the coat in the guarded way of one who had been taking in the discarded clothes of Mr. Calverley from all kinds of undesirable people for many years.

"Where is the jacket?" she said. "He had a jacket."

"I don't think they swapped jackets," I said. "Perhaps I could take Mr. Bassillero's coat back, if you know where it is."

The cottage woman became a defender of private property.

"Mr. Calverley's gone to London," she said.

She had stepped back to hang the coat up in the little hall of the house and I followed her in.

"He didn't say anything to me about a coat," the woman said.

"Isn't it hanging up there?" I said.

"There's nothing there," she said pointing to the mackintoshes and jackets hanging on the pegs. There was, I saw at once, a short grey herringbone coat hanging among them.

"I think I *see* Mr. Bassillero's coat behind the mackintosh," I said, advancing eagerly.

The woman backed towards the peg, made herself swell, and barred the way.

"Oh no," she said, "that is Mr. Calverley's coat."

"Oh—I mean the one behind the mackintosh. . . ."

The cottage woman folded her hands on her apron and stuck her elbows out.

"That's his best one," she said. "He only got it three days ago."

"Three days—but that's extraordinary. Are you quite sure?"

"I look after all Mr. Calverley's things. I'm mending it. It's the one," she said, playing her trump card with dignity, "that had the accident."

The woman's cheeks puffed with offence.

"You can see for yourself," she said, stepping scornfully out of the way.

I went to the peg and got the coat off the peg. As I did so, a peculiar thing happened. It divided into two pieces. It had been ripped almost in two from tail to collar. Half of one pocket was hanging off. The woman's face swelled with a purple blush.

"Mr. Calverley had a few friends in and it got torn," she said.

"No buttons either," I said.

The woman did not like my grin.

"Mr. Calverley," she said, "often buys new things and gets dissatisfied. He is very particular about his clothes. He said it was too short on him."

Naturally, Bassillero was the name on the tape.

At the end of the month Dr. Ray came back. My last interview was in some respects like the first. He had a new disguise; he was sunburned. He put his hands in the pockets of his navy-blue jacket, tightening it at the waist; on his head

78

was an imaginary yachting cap; and he swung from side to side in his swivel chair. After hunting, he said, yachting was the finest training for any profession. It taught you not to cross the line before the gun goes off.

"Which is what you did," he said; "you weren't very bright when you let Calverley have his coat back before you got Bassillero's."

"But how could I take that back?" I said. "It was ripped to pieces."

"Did you ever notice Calverley's hands?" said the doctor. "Ever see him on a horse? Or pick up a head waiter by the collar?"

Dr. Ray buzzed for his dispenser, and when the girl came in he asked her to find out whether Mr. Bassillero was still in Scotland. Then, as it were, swinging the tiller over and coming round into the wind, Dr. Ray looked me in the face.

"I think you've made the right decision. Keep out of general practice. Now did you have any other trouble? The Fobhams—all quiet there? No heavy weather? Very odd—perhaps they're away too."

Things as They Are

Two middle-class women were talking at half past eleven in the morning in the empty bar of a suburban public-house in a decaying district. It was a thundery and smoky morning in the summer and the traffic fumes did not rise from the street.

"Please, Frederick," said Mrs. Forster, a *rentier* who spoke in a small, scented Edwardian voice. "Two more large gins. What were you saying, Margaret?"

"The heat last night, Jill. I tossed and I turned. I couldn't sleep—and when I can't sleep I scratch," said Margaret in her wronged voice. She was a barmaid and this was her day off.

Mrs. Forster drank and nodded.

"I think," said Margaret, "I mean I don't mean anything rude, but I had a flea."

Mrs. Forster put her grey head a little on one side and nodded again graciously under a flowered hat, like royalty.

"A flea, dear?" she said fondly.

Margaret's square mouth buckled after her next drink and her eyes seemed to be clambering frantically, like a pair of blatant prisoners behind her heavy glasses. Envy, wrong, accusation, were her life. Her black hair looked as though it had once belonged to an employer.

"I mean," she began to shout against her will, and Frederick, the elderly barman, moved away from her. "I mean I wouldn't have mentioned it if you hadn't mentioned it."

Mrs. Forster raised her beautiful arms doubtfully and touched her grey hair at the back and she smiled again.

"I mean when you mentioned when you had one yesterday you said," said Margaret.

"Oh," said Mrs. Forster, too polite to differ.

"Yes, dear, don't you remember, we were in here—I mean Frederick! Were we in here yesterday morning, Frederick, Mrs. Forster and me . . ."

Frederick stood upright, handsome, old, and stupid.

"He's deaf, the fool, that's why he left the stage," Margaret said, glaring at him, knowing that he heard. "Jill, yesterday? Try and remember. You came in for a Guinness. I was having a small port, I mean, or were you on gin?"

"Oh, gin," said Mrs. Forster in her shocked, soft, distinguished way, recognizing a word.

"That was it, then," said Margaret, shaking an iron chin up and down four times. "It might have hopped."

"Hopped," nodded Mrs. Forster pleasantly.

"I mean, fleas hop, I don't mean anything vulgar." Margaret spread her hard, long bare arms and knocked her glass. "Distances," she said. "From one place to another place. A flea travels. From here, at this end of the bar, I don't say to the end, but along or across, I mean it could."

"Yes," said Mrs. Forster with agreeable interest.

"Or from a person. I mean, a flea might jump on you—or on me, it might jump from someone else, and then off that person, it depends if they are with someone. It might come off a bus or a tram." Margaret's long arms described these movements and then she brought them back to her lap. "It was a large one," she said. "A brute."

"Oh, large?" said Mrs. Forster sympathetically.

"Not large—I mean it must have been large, I could tell by the bites, I know a small flea, I mean we all do—don't mind my mentioning it—I had big bites all up my leg," said Margaret stretching out a long, strong leg. Seeing no bites there, she pulled her tight serge skirt up with annoyance over her knee and up her thigh until, halted by the sight of her suspender, she looked angrily at Frederick and furtively at Mrs. Forster and pulled her skirt down and held it down.

"Big as pennies, horrible pink lumps, red, Jill," argued Margaret. "I couldn't sleep. Scratching doesn't make it any better. It wasn't a London flea, that I know, Jill. I know a London flea, I mean you know a London flea, an ordinary one, small beastly things, I hate them, but this must have been some great black foreign brute. Indian! Frederick! You've seen one of those things?"

Frederick went with a small business of finger-flicking to the curtains at the back of the bar, peeped through as if for his cue. All bars were empty.

"Never," he said contemptuously when he came back, and turning his back on the ladies, hummed at the shelves of bottles.

"It's easy," Margaret began to shout once more, swallowing her gin, shouting at her legs, which kept slipping off the rail of the stool and enraged her by jerking her body, "I mean, for them to travel. They get on ships. I mean those ships have been in the tropics, I don't say India necessarily, it might be in Egypt or Jamaica, a flea could hop off a native onto some sailor in the docks."

"You mean, dear, it came up from the docks by bus," said Mrs. Forster. "You caught it on a bus?"

"No, Jill," said Margaret. "I mean some sailor brought it up."

"Sailor," murmured Mrs. Forster going pale.

"Ted," said Margaret, accusing. "From Calcutta. Ted could have brought it off his ship."

Mrs. Forster's head became fixed and still. She gazed mistily at Margaret and swayed. She finished her drink and steadied herself by looking into the bottom of the glass and waited for two more drops to come. Then she raised her small chin and trembled. She held a cigarette at the end of her thumb and her finger as if it were a stick of crayon and she were writing a message in blue smoke on the air. Her eyes closed sleepily, her lips sucked, pouted, and two tears rolled down her cheeks. She opened her large handbag and from the mess of letters, bills, money, keys, purses, and powder inside she took a small handkerchief and dabbed her eyes.

"Ah!" said Margaret, trying to get her arm to Mrs. Forster, but failing to reach her because her foot slipped on the rail again, so that she kicked herself. "Ah, Jill! I only mentioned it, I didn't mean anything, I mean when you said you had one, I said to myself: 'That's it, it's an Indian. Ted's brought it out of the ship's hold.' I didn't mean to bring up Ted, Jill. There's nothing funny about it, sailors do."

Mrs. Forster's cheeks and neck fattened amorously as she mewed and quietly cried and held her handkerchief tight.

"Here," said Margaret mastering her. "Chin—chin, Jill, drink up, it will do you good. Don't cry. Here, you've finished it. Frederick, two more," she said, sliding towards Mrs. Forster and resting one breast on the bar.

Mrs. Forster straightened herself with dignity and stopped crying.

"He broke my heart," said Mrs. Forster panting. "I always found one in the bed after his leave was over."

"He couldn't help it," said Margaret.

"Oh no," said Mrs. Forster.

"It's the life sailors live," said Margaret. "And don't you forget, are you listening, Jill? Listen to me. Look at me and listen. You're among friends, Jill. He's gone, Jill, like you might say, out of your life."

"Yes," said Mrs. Forster nodding again, repeating a lesson. "Out of my life."

"And good riddance, too, Jill."

83

"Riddance," murmured Mrs. Forster.

"Jill," shouted Margaret. "You've got a warm heart, that's what it is, as warm as Venus. I could never marry again after what I've been through, not whatever you paid me, not however much money it was you gave me, but you're not like me, your heart is too warm. You're too trusting."

"Trusting," Mrs. Forster repeated softly, squeezing her eyelids.

"I tell you what it was," Margaret said. "You were in love, Jill," said Margaret, greedy in the mouth. "Can you hear me?"

"Yes, dear."

"That's what I said. It was love. You loved him and you married him."

Margaret pulled herself up the bar and sat upright, looking with surprise at the breast that had rested there. She looked at her glass, she looked at Mrs. Forster's; she picked up the glass and put it down. "It was a beautiful dream, Jill, you had your beautiful dream and I say this from the bottom of my heart, I hope you will have a beautiful memory."

"Two months," sighed Mrs. Forster and her eyes opened amorously in a grey glister and then sleepily half-closed.

"But now, Jill, it's over. You've woke up, woken up. I mean, you're seeing things as they are."

The silence seemed to the two ladies to stand in a lump between them. Margaret looked into her empty glass again. Frederick lit a cigarette he had made, and his powdered face split up into twitches as he took the first draw and then put the cigarette economically on the counter. He went through his repertory of small coughs and then, raising his statesman-like head, he listened to the traffic passing and hummed.

Mrs. Forster let her expensive fur slip back from her fine shoulders and looked at the rings on her small hands.

"I loved him, Margaret," she said. "I really did love him."

84

"We know you loved him. I mean, it was love," said Margaret. "It's nothing to do with the age you are. Life's never over. It was love. You're a terrible woman, Jill."

"Oh, Margaret," said Mrs. Forster with a discreet glee, "I know I am."

"He was your fourth," said Margaret.

"Don't, Margaret," giggled Mrs. Forster.

"No, no, I'm not criticizing. I never criticize. Live and let live. It wasn't a fancy, Jill, you loved him with all your heart."

Jill raised her chin in a ladylike way.

"But I won't be hit," she whispered. "At my age I allow no one to strike me. I am fifty-seven, Margaret, I'm not a girl."

"That's what we all said," said Margaret. "You were headstrong."

"Oh, Margaret!" said Mrs. Forster delighted.

"Oh yes, yes, you wouldn't listen, not you. You wouldn't listen to me. I brought him up to the Chequers, or was it the Westmoreland?—no, it was the George—and I thought to myself I know your type, young man—you see, Jill, I've had experience—out for what he could get—well, honest, didn't I tell you?"

"His face was very brown."

"Brown! Would you believe me? No, you wouldn't. I can see him. He came up here the night of the dance. He took his coat off. Well, we all sweat."

"But," sighed Mrs. Forster, "he had white arms."

"Couldn't keep his hands to himself. Put it away, pack it up, I said. He didn't care. He was after Mrs. Klebs and she went potty on him till Mrs. Sinclair came and then that Mr. Baum interfered. That sort lives for trouble. All of them mad on him—I bet Frederick could tell a tale, but he won't. Trust Frederick," she said with a look of hate at the barman, "upstairs in the billiard room, I shan't forget it. Torpedoed twice, he said. I mean Ted said: he torpedoed one or two. What happened to him that night?"

"Someone made him comfortable, I am sure," said Mrs. Forster always anxious about lonely strangers.

"And you were quite rude with me, Jill, I don't mean rude, you couldn't be rude, it isn't in you, but we almost came to words. . . ."

"What did you say, Margaret?" said Mrs. Forster from a dream.

"I said at your age, fifty-seven, I said you can't marry a boy of twenty-six."

Mrs. Forster sighed.

"Frederick. Freddy, dear. Two more," said Mrs. Forster.

Margaret took her glass, and while she was finishing it Frederick held his hand out for it, insultingly rubbing his fingers.

"Hah!" said Margaret blowing out her breath as the gin burned her. "You bowled over him, I mean you bowled him over, a boy of twenty-six. Sailors are scamps."

"Not," said Mrs. Forster reaching to trim the back of her hair again and tipping her flowered hat forward on her forehead and austerely letting it remain like that. "Not," she said getting stuck at the word.

"Not what?" said Margaret. "Not a scamp? I say he was. I said at the time, I still say it, a rotten little scamp."

"Not," said Mrs. Forster.

"A scamp," said Margaret.

"Not. Not with a belt," said Mrs. Forster. "I will not be hit with a belt.

"My husband," began Margaret.

"I will not, Margaret," said Mrs. Forster. "Never. Never. Never with a belt.

"Not hit, struck," Mrs. Forster said, defying Margaret.

"It was a plot, you could see it a mile off, it would make

you laugh, a lousy rotten plot," Margaret let fly, swallowing her drink. "He was after your house and your money. If he wasn't, what did he want to get his mother in for, a big three-storey house like yours, in a fine residential position? Just what he'd like, a little rat like that. . . ."

Mrs. Forster began a long laugh to herself.

"My grandfather," she giggled.

"What?" said Margaret.

"Owns the house. Not owns. Owned, I say, the house," said Mrs. Forster tapping the bar.

"Frederick," said Mrs. Forster. "Did my grandfather own the house?"

"Uh?" said Frederick, giving his cuff links a shake. "Which house?"

"My house over there," said Mrs. Forster pointing to the door.

"I know he owned the house, dear," Margaret said. "Frederick knows."

"Let me ask Frederick," said Mrs. Forster. "Frederick, you knew my grandfather."

"Uh?" said Frederick, leaning to listen.

"He's as deaf as a wall," Margaret said.

Frederick walked away to the curtain at the back of the bar and peeped through it. Nervously he came back, glancing at his handsome face in the mirror; he chose an expression of stupidity and disdain, but he spoke with a quiet rage.

"I remember this street," he raged, "when you could hardly get across it for the carriages and the footmen and the maids in their lace caps and aprons. You never saw a lady in a place like this."

He turned his back on them and walked again secretively to the curtain, peeped again, and came back stiffly on feet skewed sideways by the gravity of the gout and put the tips of his old, well-manicured fingers on the bar for them to admire.

87

"Now," he said, giving a socially shocked glance over the windows that were still half-boarded after the bombing, "all tenements, flats, rooms, walls falling down, balconies dropping off, bombed out, and rotting," he said. He sneered at Margaret. "Not the same people. Slums. Riff-raff now. Mrs. Forster's father was the last of the old school."

"My grandfather," said Mrs. Forster.

"He was a gentleman," said Frederick.

Frederick walked to the curtains.

"Horrible," he muttered loudly, timing his exit.

There was a silence until he came back. The two women looked at the enormous empty public-house, with its high cracked and dirty ceilings, its dusty walls unpainted for twenty years. Its top floor had been on fire. Its windows had gone, three or four times.

Frederick mopped up scornfully between the glasses of gin on the counter.

"That's what I mean," said Margaret, her tongue swelling up, her mouth side-slipping. "If you'd given the key to his mother, where would you have been? They'd have shut you out of your own house and what's the good of the police? All the scum have come to the top since the war. You were too innocent and we saved you. Jill, well, I mean if we hadn't all got together, the whole crowd, where were you? He was going to get into the house and then one night when you'd been over at the George or the Chequers or over here and you'd had one or two . . ."

Jill looked proudly and fondly at her glass, crinkled her childish eyes.

"Oh," said Jill in a little naughty-faced protest.

"I mean, I don't mean plastered," said Margaret, bewildered by the sound of her own voice and moving out her hand to bring it back.

"Not stinking, Jill, excuse me. I mean we sometimes have two or three. Don't we?" Margaret appealed to the barman.

"Uh?" said Frederick coldly. "Where was this?"

"Oh, don't be stupid," said Margaret turning round suddenly and knocking her glass over, which Frederick picked up and took away. "What was I saying, Jill?"

A beautiful still smile, like a butterfly opening on an old flower, came onto Mrs. Forster's face.

"Margaret," she confided, "I don't know."

"I know," said Margaret, waving her heavy bare arm. "You'd have been signing papers. He'd have stripped you. He might have murdered you like that case last Sunday in the papers. A well-to-do woman like you. The common little rat. Bringing his fleas."

"He—was—not—common," said Mrs. Forster, sitting upright suddenly, and her hat fell over her nose, giving her an appearance of dashing distinction.

"He was off a ship," said Margaret.

"He was an officer."

"He *said* he was an officer," said Margaret, struggling with her corsets.

Mrs. Forster got down from her stool and held with one hand to the bar. She laughed quietly.

"He—" she began.

"What?" said Margaret.

"I shan't tell you," said Mrs. Forster. "Come here."

Margaret leaned towards her.

"No, come here, stand here," said Mrs. Forster.

Margaret stood up, also holding to the bar, and Mrs. Forster put her hands to Margaret's neck and pulled her head down and began to laugh in Margaret's ear. She was whispering.

"What?" shouted Margaret. "I can't hear. What is it?"

Mrs. Forster laughed with a roar in Margaret's ear.

"He—he—was a man, Margaret," she whispered. She pushed her away.

"You know what I mean, Margaret," she said in a stern

clear voice. "You do, don't you? Come here again, I'll tell you."

"I heard you."

"No, come here again, closer. I'll tell you. Where are you?"

Mrs. Forster whispered again and then drew back.

"A man," she said boldly.

"And you're a woman, Jill."

"A man!" said Mrs. Forster. "Everything, Margaret. You know—everything. But not with a belt. I won't be struck." Mrs. Forster reached for her glass.

"*Vive la France!*" she said holding up her glass, drank and banged it down. "Well, I threw him out."

A lament broke from Margaret. She had suddenly remembered one of *her* husbands. She had had two.

"He went off to his work and I was waiting for him at six. He didn't come back. I'd no money in the house, that was seventeen years ago, and Joyce was two, and he never even wrote. I went through his pockets and gave his coats a shake, wedding rings poured out of them. What do you get for it? Your own daughter won't speak to you, ashamed to bring her friends to the house. 'You're always drunk,' she says. To her own mother. Drunk!" said Margaret. "I might have one or perhaps two. What does a girl like that know!"

With a soft, quick crumpling, a soft thump and a long sigh, Mrs. Forster went to the floor and full-length lay there with a beautiful smile on her face, and a fierce noise of pleasure came from her white face. Her hat rolled off, her bag fell down, open, and spilling with a loud noise.

"Eh," said Frederick coming round from behind the counter.

"Passed out again. Get her up, get her up quick," said Margaret. "Her bag, her money."

"Lift her on the side," she said. "I will take her legs."

They carried Mrs. Forster to the broken leather settee

and laid her down there. "Here's her bag," Margaret wrangled. "It's all there."

"And the one in your hand," said Frederick, looking at the pound note in Margaret's hand.

And then the crowd came in: Mrs. Klebs, Mrs. Sinclair, Mr. Baum, the one they called Pudding, who had fallen down the area at Christmas, and a lot more.

"What's this?" they said. "Not again? Frederick, what's this?"

"They came in here," Frederick said in a temper. "Ladies, talking about love."

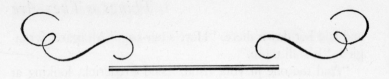

It May Never Happen

I shall not forget the fingers that fastened me into the stiff collar. Or how I was clamped down under the bowler hat, which spread my rather large ears outwards, and how, my nose full of the shop smell of new suit, I went off for the first time to earn my living.

"You are beginning life," they said.

"You have your foot on the first rung of the ladder," they said.

"Excelsior," my new Uncle Belton said.

I was going to work in the office of one of my uncles, a new uncle, the second husband of my mother's sister, who had just married into the family. His name was Belton, a man of forty-four with a tight, bumptious little business in the upholstery trade, a business that sounded so full of possibilities that it would blow up and burst, out of sheer merit. The push of Mr. Belton, the designing of Mr. Phillimore, his partner, made it irresistible. The name of the firm was Belton & Phillimore.

On my first day I met Mr. Belton outside our railway station. I watched a horse eating and I read all the hoardings while I waited. Mr. Belton was half an hour late. He was one of those cheerful, self-centred men whose tempers shorten when they are in the wrong. They put themselves right by sailing out into general reflections.

"Punctuality, Vincent, is everything," said Mr. Belton, bitterly. "How long have you been here?"

"Half an hour."

"*Why* have you been here half an hour?"

Mr. Belton was looked upon as a sharpshooter, a raider, in our family. He had been around his new relations trying to raise capital for his business, he had carried off my mother's sister, in marriage, he was carrying me off to his office. He was a small, round, dominant, and smartly dressed man, who usually wore brown. His black hair was parted in the middle, and when he arrived anywhere he arrived with aplomb, bouncing down as hard as a new football on asphalt and very nearly on one's toes.

A new business, a new marriage, a new outlook on life— my brand-new uncle looked as though he had come straight out of a shop window. He had been hardly more than quarter of an hour in our house before we thought our paint looked shabby and the rooms small. The very curtains seemed to shrink like the poor as he talked largely of exports, imports, agencies, overheads, discounts, rebates, cut prices, and debentures. And when he had done with these, he was getting at what we paid for meat, where we got our coal and how much at a time, telling us, too, where to buy carpets and clothes, gas-fires, art pottery, and electric irons. He even gave us the name of a new furniture polish. It sounded like one of the books of the Old Testament. He walked about the house touching things, fingering picture-frames, turning chairs round, looking under tables, tapping his toes thoughtfully on the linoleum. Then he sat down and, lifting his foot restfully to his knee and exposing the striking pattern of his socks, he seemed to be working out how much we would get if we sold up house and home. The message "Sell up and begin again" flashed on and off in the smiles of his shining new face like Morse.

"I can get all these things," he said, "in the trade."

When he and I sat in the train that morning, I thought Mr. Belton looked larger.

"I don't want you to think I'm lecturing you, boy," he said, "but there are many boys who would give their right hand to walk straight into this business as you are doing."

"Yes, Uncle," I said.

"A little thing—you must call me 'sir.' "

"Yes, Uncle," I said, "sir."

"And you must call Mr. Phillimore 'sir.' "

I had forgotten all about Mr. Belton's partner.

"But for Mr. Phillimore you would not have this chance," Mr. Belton said, detecting at once that I had forgotten. "It's a very remarkable thing, it's really wonderful, some people would think more than wonderful, that Mr. Phillimore agreed to it. He's a very busy man. A man with a great deal on his mind. There are people in the trade who would be glad to pay for the privilege of consulting Mr. Phillimore. His word is law in the firm and I want you to be most respectful to him. Don't forget to say 'Good morning, sir,' to him when you see him, and if he should offer to shake hands you must, of course, shake hands with him. I think he may offer to shake hands, but he may not. If he rings his bell or asks you to do anything, you must do it at once. Be quick and mind your manners. If he is going out of the room, open the door for him. Mr. Phillimore notices everything."

Naturally, Mr. Belton had seemed all-powerful to me, and it awed me to hear that behind this god was yet another god to whom even he deferred.

It distressed me that there were other people in the compartment who might hear this conversation. The day was damp and a low smoke from the train blew along the window as though we were travelling through cloud into another universe.

My face must have looked strained and pale. I had eaten very little for breakfast and my head ached where the bowler hat pressed a red mark on my forehead. My uncle relaxed a little. At the next station two girls got out and we were alone in the compartment.

"I shall always remember the first time I stayed with Mr. Phillimore and his mother." So far my uncle had been hectoring and glum; but now a luminous gravity of expression came on his big, experienced face and covered it like the skin on a balloon. He looked curiously light, as if he had been inflated with hydrogen and would rise from the seat of the empty railway carriage and blow away out of the window. He had what is called a common accent, none too certain about aitches and double negatives, but his voice was musical and now became rarefied when he spoke of his partner.

"In Mr. Phillimore's 'ouse—ahem, house, the gentlemen give up their chairs to the ladies when they come into the room. And when the ladies leave the room you have to let them walk in front of you," my uncle said. He stared at this picture in his memory with wonder. He seemed to hang in the higher air, and then gradually he subsided and became himself again, a shade coarser than he had been before. His brown eyes looked unsteadily, a thick smile began nervously by his nose and slowly spread over his face, and a twist of deprecation came to the corners of his lips.

"You see, Mr. Phillimore is a gentleman. It may seem peculiar to you and me," he said.

"But people are peculiar," he said. And the smile slowly deepened as it will on the face of a baby until he began to look fondly and sentimentally at me.

"I'll give you a little tip, boy," he said, putting his hand on my knee, a touch that sent an uncomfortable thrill through my body and flushed me with all the shyness of my age. "Do you mind if I give you a little piece of advice, something helpful?"

"No, Uncle," I murmured. "Sir."

"You needn't call me sir now," he said kindly. "If Mr.

95

Phillimore should ring for you," he said, "just remember the infant Samuel. You remember how when our Lord called Samuel the boy said: 'Speak, Lord, Thy servant heareth.' Well, just pause and say that, just quietly to yourself, before you go and see what Mr. Phillimore wants. Don't hang around, of course. Sharp's the word. But say it."

My throat pinched, my tongue went dry. I should have said that Mr. Belton was a religious man. His expression became dreamy.

"I think there'd be no harm in your saying it if I ring, too," he said. Even he looked surprised after making this suggestion.

The office and workshops of Belton & Phillimore, makers of Butifix furniture and especially of the Butifix armchair and sofa, were at No. 7, in a row of old stained houses standing behind railings. The street was flogged by trams and dray horses. Dust flew into one's eyes from the vans. The doorstep of No. 7 was the only whitened one in the street.

"Step over it," Mr. Belton said. I nearly fell over it. From Mr. Belton's manner, from his militant walk, I had imagined I was going to work in a large factory, where hundreds of workers were frizzling under acres of glass roof. But Belton & Phillimore occupied only the ground floor of this old house, whose window-sills slanted and gave a leer of depression to its aspect. A number of small businesses—a tailor or two, a lampshade-manufacturer, and agents for pulleys, gloves, and shop fittings—worked in single rooms above. A smell of glue hung like a dead animal about the doorway and there were packing-cases stored in the hall. A notice that was never taken down all the time I was there said: "Young Improvers Wanted. Apply Schenk." Someone had written: "April 26 Holborn Baths," in pencil underneath. On my uncle's floor there was first a small room, made by new glass partitions, where a typist sat. She was a large-boned, round-shouldered girl of seventeen with fine yellow hair, who worked in a green overcoat. Her office smelled of gas, paint, and tea. Next door was the room occupied by Mr. Belton and Mr. Phillimore and beyond, down the passage, was the large workroom under a top light where one could hear the sound of a turning machine, the swish of a plane, and the noise of hammering. Patterns of cloth, samples of hair, kapok, and down were on the large desk where the two partners sat in their office, and there I waited alone listening to the typewriter—an old-fashioned one—clumping up and down like the police. My uncle had changed into a white dust-coat and marched out to find Mr. Phillimore. Before he went he leaned down and smelled a bowl of flowers on the table. "Colour," he smiled patriotically, "we're colourful people."

"Speak, Lord . . ." I gabbled, but I was too afraid to get to the end of the sentence. I had had many daydreams about Mr. Phillimore. He was a myth in our family. No one had ever seen him; but it was agreed that he had been the making of my uncle. Indeed, people said he had been my uncle's salvation. I foresaw a tall, clean, sarcastic man with a deep stiff collar, as clean as a doctor. Or perhaps one of those bullying, morally overweighted figures from the north of England whose minds pass like soft steam-rollers over you, suffocating rather than flattening you with the eiderdown gospel of work and righteousness. The door opened. I was startled by a high-pitched, eager feminine giggle; a small man stumbled towards me.

"Er—er—hullo, 'llo, my dear," the voice said. I saw a white dust-coat. I saw a pair of agonized yellow-blue eyes popping with an expression of helplessness out of a badly pimpled face. Really, Mr. Phillimore looked raw and bleeding. Then I saw his untidy wheat-coloured hair, with a pink scalp showing through it; and after that, loose lips drawn back, rabbit fashion, from a set of protruding teeth, each tooth shooting out in a different direction. It was a mouth that looked ravenous and could not close; and saliva, therefore, fizzed out of it when he was excited. He was young, no more than thirty-five, and my first sight of Mr. Phillimore suggested the frantic, yelping disorganized expression of a copulating dog.

Before he got to me Mr. Phillimore caught the pocket of his white dust-coat on the door-handle, dropped a ruler from his pocket, and trod on a pencil.

"Oh dear, oh dear!" cried Mr. Phillimore, going down on his knees with a sigh of inexpressible fatigue.

"Pick it up," said my uncle to me bitterly, giving me a push.

"Oh no, *no*, my dear!" said Mr. Phillimore from the floor. "My fault, Mr. B. I'm most frightfully sorry. How are you? At last, after all these months! Are you quite recovered from your illness?" He was on his feet now, a weak damp hand clung will-lessly to mine, and he gazed eagerly into my eyes.

"I haven't been ill, sir," I said.

"You don't look well," he said doubtfully. Then his spirit rose again: "The moment I heard of you I *longed* for you to come. We've been waiting for you for months. We're simply *killed* with work, my dear, you've no idea."

Mr. Phillimore sat down at the partners' desk and looked at me reproachfully. He looked congenitally exhausted.

"Ah, Vernon," he said.

"Vincent, sir," I murmured.

"Vincent," he said. "You and I have not the energy, the decision, of the remarkable Mr. B. He is a remarkable man, Vernon, he has been my salvation. Vincent, I mean, I'm *so* sorry."

My uncle, who had sat down at his desk and was tapping a sheet of figures with a pencil, glanced up at this remark and smiled mechanically. My confusion was natural. I had always gathered Mr. Phillimore was the saviour; now I heard the

98

roles reversed. I blinked. The two men were saving each other.

"With two more machines, Phillimore," my uncle said, ignoring the worship of his partner and acting a part, "we could treble these figures." And he brought his soft fist down like a sponge on the desk, not heavily, but strongly enough to make Phillimore strain to attention.

Though I had been only a few minutes in the office I felt already (when I heard those words) the swirl of urgency and importance in the affairs of Belton & Phillimore. I stared at Mr. Phillimore until he must have thought I was trying to get instructions from him by hypnosis. To my disappointment a look of despair and appeal came into Mr. Phillimore's face. The telephone bell rang and, with a shudder, Mr. Phillimore took up the telephone, saying before he answered it:

"P'please, Mr. B., don't expand the business any more for a moment." Then, mastering his stammer, dropping his voice into his throat, Mr. Phillimore concentrated on answering the telephone efficiently. Copying and practising Uncle Belton's gesture, Phillimore weakly hammered the air with *his* fists as he talked, glancing at my uncle nervously as he did so. When he had finished his telephone conversation and had told my uncle about it, Mr. Phillimore looked at me and said:

"It is true. I'm not exaggerating." He nodded towards my uncle, who was still tapping his pencil on the figures. "He saved my life." Then he smiled and said to my uncle: "Do you like the flowers I brought for us?"

"I'd sooner you brought me an order, Phillimore," said my uncle.

Nothing happens in an office. One day is like another. When I look back upon that year the only thing I see is a love-affair—the love-affair of Mr. Belton and Mr. Phillimore. They sat in their office like husband and wife in a sitting-room. It was not really a love-affair, but a salvation

affair. Mr. Belton had the rippling mind of the natural sales-
man, and strengthening it was a powerful evangelical notion
that he must save people from their own undoing. He did not
sell: he saved. He saved people, when he was travelling in
towels or electric irons or cretonne, for example, from the
sadness of not having these things. When he was in the
stocking business, he rescued people from the misery of not
having so many hundreds of dozens of stockings. The world
needed to be saved from its parsimony, its uncreative caution.
Mr. Belton pumped salvation into the world, rescued men
from the Slough of Despond. Giant Despair—I have heard
him say to customers—is man's greatest enemy. And when
he came to have businesses or agencies of his own after he
had married my mother's sister, and his relations put money
into these enterprises, he was rescuing *them*. He was rescuing
their savings from the ignominy of two and one-half per
cent or whatever it was, in some prim nibbling bank.

"Oh, ye of little faith," he said, cocking his dark eyebrow.
And if things went wrong the eyebrow would straighten.

"It was an experience," he would rebuke his critics. "I
had to buy *mine*."

It was my new Uncle Belton's gift of salvation that had
captured Mr. Phillimore.

Now that I had seen Mr. Phillimore, Uncle Belton modi-
fied the Phillimore myth and said to me when I went home
with him in the tobacco smoke of the train:

"Mr. Phillimore is peculiar. We all have our peculiarities.
He is really an artist. He does our designs. When I met
Mr. Phillimore three years ago he had a tiny chair-making,
arts and craft shop in Somerset. He was living under his
mother's thumb. Imagine a man of thirty-five who can't go
out in the evening without his mother's permission. Terrible."

Uncle Belton scowled.

"The poor devil was drinking himself to death," he said.

"He shut himself in his room and drank whisky out of a hot-water bottle."

Uncle Belton's face went pale as lichen.

"It might have led to women—anything," he said. Then he blinked. He had evidently been struck by the thought that he ought not to have said this to me about his partner. His voice became bland and expansive.

"There he was—and independent, mind you, he had money —going downhill as fast as I have ever seen a man go—a gentleman, paralyzed, hypnotized, you might call it. I told him straight what was the matter with him. I saw it at once —he had to get away from that mother. I told her: 'You're a mother. You don't know nothing about your son.'"

His voice now became merry. "It's marvellous, reely," he said. "Marvellous the way things work out. I just went down there to look around."

Uncle Belton saw those two provincial people with their neat lifeless little business. He saw in them a temporary gold-mine. But there was more in my uncle's passion than acquisitiveness. He had a horror of drink; he had a greater horror of spiritual disasters. He stepped back from the cat-astrophic crashes of the inner life. His remedy lay in that part of the Protestant tradition which deals with the conflicts of the inner life by annihilating the inner life altogether. When Uncle Belton and Mr. Phillimore left Somerset to start the firm of Belton & Phillimore, their departure was like an elopement.

"It has been an experience for me, knowing your uncle," said Mr. Phillimore to me again and again. He had borrowed the word "experience" from Mr. Belton. His voice rose into the treble. "What drive, Vernon, Vincent—which is it? Vincent! What drive!"

My day's work at the office was monotonous, like family life. For if my new Uncle Belton and Mr. Phillimore were husband and wife, I was the only child who strays listlessly from room to room trying to find something to do. I stuck on stamps, I copied letters. I put clean water in the flower-bowl, which Mr. Phillimore kept filled. They were a love-offering. I took messages. I went across the road to buy buns for the typist, or my uncle would send me out to collect a shirt from a shop or to buy a bottle of hair-cream at his barber's. My uncle had thick glossy hair as still as glass on his head. We lived in all the intensity of domestic life. Uncle was always willing to stop his work and address a manly midweek sermon to Mr. Phillimore. Mr. Phillimore was always willing to stop what he was doing and talk to me. He would follow me ravenously about, open-mouthed as if he would graze on my hair. We had been brought up on the myth of the unapproachability of Mr. Phillimore; the myth had a germ of truth: it was he who, continuously, made the approaches.

"Ah, youth, youth, golden-headed youth," he would say as he passed me in the workshop. I had thick black hair not unlike my uncle's and I was trying to make it look glossy. Through the window in the partition Miss Croft, the typist, kept her little eyes on all of us. One of my anxieties was to make Miss Croft smile, but she was in her wooden teens, and her lips set firmly when I stood in the room with her. She looked at me with the swollen face of an elder sister. It was a long time before I saw that she was piqued because once *she* had been the only child in this family and now I had supplanted her. A woman's life is swayed by her feelings, but Miss Croft was not yet a woman: she was learning about her feelings, how to use them, like a young girl who is learning to play scales on the piano, and she was still awkward with them.

Mr. Phillimore would often stand at the door of her room talking to me, and as he did so, his look would pop anxiously, intimately, apologetically in Miss Croft's direction. Mr. Phillimore's eyes seemed to say: "In my life I need all the help I can get from *everyone*. Don't be jealous and hurt!" One could see what had happened. Miss Croft silently reproached him.

"You are wasting Mr. Phillimore's time. That poor man is run off his feet," she said abruptly to me.

"*He* started talking to *me*," I said.

Miss Croft sat back from her typewriter.

"He is the brains of this firm," Miss Croft said. "I have been here from the beginning. I've seen it all. That man," she was developing her simple possessive instinct as if she were doing arm exercises, "tells me everything." She always called him "that man."

Yes, and now Mr. Phillimore had started telling me everything.

Miss Croft gave her head a short upward jerk. She put a lump in her chin by running her tongue round her lower gum and began typing again with her big red fingers. I loved watching the quickness of her fingers. There were two or three other things about her that were pretty; her little starry violet eyes and her small waist; the curve of her legs was becoming lovely. And she had a lisping childlike voice. But she was changing; what was pretty one week became plain the next. She was like a creature in a chrysalis.

"One thing," she said complacently, "that man won't be here long. I can see things."

When she saw how astonished and impressed I was by this remark, Miss Croft was very satisfied.

"Why do you say that?" I asked.

There were things, she said primly to me, that were confidential.

My Uncle Belton was a man who was unaware of the little situations that were simmering all day long around him. He lived juicily, like an orange, within the containing rind of his objects in life. He was out two or three times a week seeing customers and walking in his dream of making the business larger and getting larger premises. When he wasn't tapping his pencil on columns of figures or abusing someone on the telephone, he was gazing vehemently at the plans of new premises he had seen. One afternoon he came back in a hearty mood and sent me to tell Mr. Phillimore he had brought *him* a present.

"A present," cried Mr. Phillimore, who was working on the frame of a sofa. Up he jumped. "How exciting," he said.

We had a foreman with bloodshot eyes, who always winked at me when I came with a message for Mr. Phillimore. He winked now.

"You've got a present for me!" cried Mr. Phillimore, almost running to Uncle Belton's office. "What a thrill."

My uncle did not give Mr. Phillimore the parcel. He wanted some of the surprise for himself. He wanted a part of everything for himself; it was not greed but part of his gregarious generosity. He would have eaten your lunch for you so that you and he could feel more genially at one. We watched Uncle undo the parcel. It contained a small framed picture. He stood it on the desk and turned it to face Mr. Phillimore.

"Just made for you, Phillimore," he said. The picture was simply a text done in poker work. The words were: "Don't Worry—It May Never Happen."

"Don't worry—it may never happen," Phillimore read with delight and he rubbed his hands together.

"Don't Worry—it may never happen," ruminated my uncle in his deep, golden, optimistic voice.

"Wonderful," cried Phillimore. "Oh, good." Like a boy clapping a catch at cricket. Then he looked serious. He shook his head. "Very true. Very true," he said thoughtfully. "I'll tell you what—we'll hang it on the wall."

"That's an idea," said Uncle.

"Over the mantelpiece? Or over the desk, do you think?" said Mr. Phillimore.

He danced about, holding the picture now in this place and now in the other. Uncle helped him. They were like a newly married couple hanging up a picture.

"Over the mantelpiece, where you can see it," said Mr. Belton.

"Here, do you think?"

"No—a little higher. There! No, a bit to the left." Yes, it was a marriage. Mr. Phillimore and Mr. Belton sat down exhausted, gazing at the picture now hanging on the wall. Phillimore read it aloud again.

"True," he said. "Very true. Yes," he sighed, shaking his head. "It's just made for me. Why worry? There's no need to. One's desires, one's wishes, one's hopes—they won't come off. Nothing changes."

"Here," cried my uncle. "It doesn't say that. It says don't be held back by your fears, the thing you're afraid of just won't occur. You're not afraid of what you want coming true, are you? That would be ridiculous."

"My dear Vincent," said Mr. Phillimore, getting my name right for once, "that only shows how different Mr. B. is from the rest of us."

"Good godfathers," said my uncle. "Phillimore, you're morbid."

"Yes, yes, I know," said Mr. Phillimore with a primness and secretiveness I had never noticed before. "But one preserves one's integrity."

And Phillimore lifted his nose and one could hear a hissing intake of air like a gas escape. It was a little terrifying. Uncle scowled playfully, but he was put out. For a few seconds the two men considered each other, and my uncle, being by far the shorter and stouter, had the advantage of weight. Many men who were taller than my new Uncle Belton were intimidated by his vehement shortness. He seemed to be shooting upwards at one like a howitzer.

After his expeditions to the warm and buzzing platters of

the world, Belton was often irritable; when he came back, he was obliged to return to earth, where he found an order had been delayed, or some timber had a flaw in it, or they were short of cloth because Phillimore had advised Belton to go easy on the buying. And now after the difference over the meaning of the picture, Belton went irritably off to the workroom.

"I hope," said Mr. Phillimore, "dear Mr. B. won't upset the hands. I shall feel it is my fault." And then turning to me, begging for support, he said: "Yet how frightful, how terrifying it would be, Vincent, if what one wished came true. How futile life would be if one's fears were not realized. Don't you think?" He watched me.

"I should die!" he cried and his hands hung limply from the wrist like wet leaves.

This kind of conversation was beyond me. And he often spoke like this in front of the workers, who winked at me all the time. On the other hand, I could not be sure that Mr. Phillimore wasn't mocking me. And then I suppose in our family—my own and my uncle's—we were stamped with a reserve about our personal lives. We had no private lives. We simply had secret lives, like secret drinkers. We were the natural opponents of private life. We regarded ourselves as units of will or energy directed upon our various purposes. Mr. Belton saw himself (for he was religious) as a new kind of fusion of science and religion, a successful sperm, fertilizing the Christian endeavour. Contact with a man like Phillimore who appeared to put feebleness, illness, fright, incapacity, and failure in life first, was bewildering. Phillimore's eagerness to cut a bad figure was like an indecent physical exposure. He was the sperm which fails.

So when Mr. Phillimore cried out "I should die," I saw something new in his expression, something watchful, crystalline, and with the madman's order, in his eye. For a second or two I had the impression that Mr. Phillimore was *not* a fool; that he was cunning and obstinate, and long-sighted. The impression dissolved and indeed I forgot about it or he made me forget it by a sudden change of his mood. He was as limp as a willow. What I would call his good-bye air appeared. I mean that after some gust of confidence, some anxious tail-wagging spaniel-like prance of intimacy, Mr. Phillimore would draw back and fade. He would gradually back to the door and stand there getting dimmer. It was like being in a train which is moving out and Mr. Phillimore stood on the platform stammering about how lucky you were to be going away, while he was left behind. The weak hands seemed to wave. It was his vanity to be left behind.

"Ah well, Vernon," he said (I was beginning to think he got my name wrong out of malice), "where shall we all be in ten years' time? You—I see you—rich, successful, in the arms of some superb mistress—Miss Croft, shall we say, but in a tiger skin. And I—alas, in my solitary room. . . ."

He had gone.

Every firm has its Devil—that is to say, its chief competitor. And this Devil is always a firm of the same size or perhaps a little more important. Belton & Phillimore were not afraid of their big competitors: the huge furniture-manufacturers and upholsterers who devoured the trade like ranging wolves. Belton & Phillimore admired these great firms. They were afraid of the little ones and especially of one little one.

If my uncle wanted to give Mr. Phillimore a fright he would say: "Salter's on the move again. He's cut his prices." Or, holding up a letter: "Look at this. Salter's giving six months' credit."

My uncle would look bitter and belligerent. One was warring against Sin. Salter, my uncle conveyed, was a cheat, a fraud, a sinister figure who was plotting against their lives. Salter copied our designs and cheapened them. He stole our customers. He would try and get hold of our workers. Like a highwayman, he preyed on our labour. He wanted to strangle us. My uncle was not eloquent about this; he was as curt, as stubborn as a soldier. Salter might have been outside on the street sniping at him.

"We can't fight *that*," my uncle would say, meaning, of course, the opposite.

"That defeats us," Phillimore eagerly agreed. He put down his ruler and his pencil, leaned back in his chair, and made a noise in his throat like the death-rattle—a noise natural to him. He also had an irritating habit of whistling through the gap in his front teeth, a whistle of surrender. It was he, at these times, who appeared to be "saving" my uncle; one saw the emergence of Phillimore's hatred of success, the trembling of compassion in his nature. An expression of one lying blissfully in hospital came on Phillimore's face. He would have done anything for Belton at that moment, and if Belton had observed the character of his partner—which, of course, he had not; he did not believe in anyone's character but his own—he would have chosen this moment to say to Mr. Phillimore:

"Go down to your mother, tell her we are on the edge of bankruptcy, get her to give us this extra capital we need. Tell her it is a terrible risk, that we may very likely lose it. Tell her it's desperate. Tell her we may not last another month. Go out and get drunk, it's the only thing to do."

The prospect of ruin would have been irresistible to Mr. Phillimore. He would have done in this mood what in a more confident one he would have resisted. Alas, Belton was no reader of the heart. He turned and attacked Phillimore.

"Defeat us," he said, setting his chin. "I don't understand the meaning of the word, Phillimore. There is no defeat. What's Salter? A draper"—Uncle's lowest word of contempt—"a draper, Phillimore. Give me the price list. Get me Dobson's on the phone. Miss Croft, come and take these letters. Boy, take this note up to the bank. . . ."

The crisis of sacrifice, loss, abandonment was passed. Like a wife who sees her husband recover and so free himself from helpless reliance on her, Phillimore saw his compassion scattered. Phillimore would have liked to rock my uncle like a baby—and indeed Belton often looked like one. But optimism had won. And when my uncle did raise the question of getting more capital, Mr. Phillimore became evasive. The "goodbye" look came back. He admired my uncle's resilience, but the admiration itself exhausted him and left him—how shall I say it? I can remember only his appearance, the open mouth, the choking open mouth under the dropping teeth—it left him in a condition of—nausea. And one heard the sound, the sinister air rushing up his nostrils, like a preparation for suicide.

About this time I used to go out to lunch with Mr. Phillimore, and one day I saw this Devil who haunted our firm and planned our destruction. Phillimore and I were in a teashop.

"Oh dear," said Phillimore, "there's that poor wretch, Salter." My heart jumped. The devilries of Salter had so impressed me that I was ready to run out of the place.

"Has he seen us?" I said, trying to look undisturbed. I ought not to have been surprised by the self-possession of Phillimore: Salter meant disaster.

"That man might have ruined us," said Phillimore sadly. "But for your wonderful uncle, Vernon, we should be in Queer Street, up the spout, right in the middle of the purée."

Phillimore sighed and shook his head. He gazed in Salter's direction with affection. He gazed, I now suspect, with nostalgia. And I, gazing there too, saw a stringy and dejected man, bald but not sufficiently so, with pince-nez like a dismal pair of birds on either side of his nose, and a grey moustache, damp with tea. The teashop was under a railway arch and we could hear the trains rumbling over our heads like rollers. They seemed to flatten and crush the figure of Mr. Salter in his old raincoat. I suppose he knew us, for he looked at us miserably and I have never seen a figure that conveyed more resignation to injustice, more passive disquiet. To judge by the look he gave us, this hypocrite Salter was muttering aloud that we were cheating and ruining him. We were copying *his* designs, undercutting *his* prices, stealing *his* customers. He got up and went to pay his bill listlessly just as I was putting a spoonful of Queen's pudding into my mouth. I was relieved when he gave an accusing nod to Phillimore as he passed our table. He did not speak. We saw him stand on the step of the restaurant for a moment, looking at the traffic; and when he at last chose to cross the road and walked northward, I tried to work out which of our customers he was going to steal. But Phillimore said:

"Salter has an ulcerated stomach through living on tinned food on a hospital ship in the war. He was in the Middle East."

Phillimore said this in a subdued enthusiastic voice. The illness, the cheatings, the plots of Salter excited Phillimore's imagination. To my uncle he talked about nothing else for days.

The year passed and another year began. I found myself growing. I spent more time in the workroom now, working with my hands. I would check the timber or the cloth or help with the packing or sort certain kinds of hair and down. I was not penned in the little glass room with Miss Croft. I was free to walk about. I liked the workroom because it had a glass roof and through that one sometimes saw the white clouds smoking in the sky and I would think of the country you would be able to see if you could lie on top of one of those clouds. I liked to think that fields and woods existed, but that I too existed and was working. I wished I was in love and the wish itself was delightful, for there was no pain nor melancholy in it, no emptiness and defeat. I was in love already. I had fallen in love with myself, a lover as close as my own skin.

One morning in May the firm was delivering some chairs in the West End, and I was sent in a hired van with them, riding high up with the driver, to see that the chairs were delivered without damage, to an important special customer. I did not go straight back to the office. I left the van. Up till then I had never been in a restaurant north of the Thames, but now I decided to try a place in some narrow alley of the city. One after the other I rejected. The thoughtless traveller wanders in circles. I was delighted to wander and, in fact, wandered so long that I found myself near the office and in the teashop under the arches. There I saw a most remarkable person. No, not Salter. I saw Miss Croft.

A Miss Croft I had never seen in my life before because I had never seen her outside the office. As surprised as I was, she blushed like a country rose, she smiled, she beckoned to me. Her awkwardness had gone, mine went too. Our eyes, our tongues were excited. I sat down at her table.

"Don't have the fish. It's awful," she said. "Dry."

"I won't have the poached egg, either," I said.

These two sentences seemed brilliant to us. A beautiful waitress, much more beautiful than Miss Croft, came up and looked at us sulkily. And the sneer on the waitress's face made us feel we were even more brilliant. We were escaped prisoners.

The new thing about Miss Croft was that she had put her hair up. Before it had hung, tied in a schoolgirlish black bow, on her shoulders. Now her head was lighter, like a flower that had long been sheathed by its leaves; and her body was lighter too. She parted her lips when she spoke instead of mumbling; the sisterly, sermonizing line had gone from her brows and she looked arch when she caught me looking at the two small hills in her white blouse and even leaned forward to tempt and confuse me more. For my part, I made one or two brilliant remarks about the people in the restaurant, remarks which made her say: "Oh, you are!"

"I'm coming to sit on your side of the table," I said, very encouraged, for I had the insane idea of putting my arm round her waist; but a waitress dropped a tray and I think Miss Croft did not hear me, for she began to talk very quickly about the only subject that really interested us: our daily bread, the air we breathed, the latest instalment of the inner story of Belton & Phillimore.

"Where did you take those chairs this morning?" she asked me. I parried this. I was not sure whether I was supposed to say.

"To Naseley, wasn't it?" she said.

"Yes."

"Mr. Phillimore has gone to Somerset," she said, "to get money. Dadda says there's something going on." I ought to have said that when she wanted to give authority to anything she said, she always quoted her father. She called him Dadda.

"Dadda says: 'You wait—there's another man.' " She said this in the voice a woman uses when she says "There is another woman."

"I don't believe it," I said, not because I did not believe it, but because I did not like the idea of Miss Croft having a father.

"Mr. Belton and Mr. Naseley are on the 'phone to each other every day. When he says he's going out to a customer, he's going to see this Naseley. He knows I know. I can read faces."

She said this not in the moralizing, maternal way she had had a year before, but with a new feminine recklessness. She was tasting the new feminine delight in saying anything that came into her head; and as she said this she leaned forward, touching the back of her hair and looking over the faces of the people in the restaurant, so that she could give me another chance of looking at her throat and her neck and have the pleasure of catching me do so.

"I can," she said, catching me. I coloured. And then she went on to soothe the wound:

"Why are you so vain?" she said. Then quickly changed to: "I said to Mr. Phillimore, when he left to catch the train, 'I can read faces, Mr. Phillimore.' He looked at me. You should have seen the look he gave. Really I'm sorry for that man. He said to me: 'Can you.' Just that, nothing more," she said, her small eyes brightening. She closed her handbag and said firmly:

"Dadda says Naseley and Belton will buy him out if he doesn't get that money from his mother." And she got up to go.

Two days later Phillimore returned from Somerset. It was clear, after he came out of my uncle's office, that there was a change in him. He had always been anxious to chatter with me, but for a while he said nothing to me. He nodded, stared, paused: there was that hissing intake of breath and then he said nothing. I became familiar.

"Coming out to lunch?" I called to him, forgetting to call him "sir." He looked at me coldly.

"No, Vincent," he said, "go to your beautiful waitress alone."

And the next day "Not today, Vernon," he said, "but beware of the auburn glory at the dyers' and cleaners'."

And his Adam's apple came up offensively over the top of his collar.

He said these things before Miss Croft, who laughed at me. "Vincent is so susceptible," she said. She looked with yearning at Mr. Phillimore. Always Mr. Phillimore had made the advances to everyone; now when Miss Croft seemed to be lifting herself on a dish towards him, he was taken aback. He hesitated, open-mouthed. He looked around him, like a man surrounded by plots and enemies and worked his way back to the door.

And now Miss Croft talked of nothing but Mr. Phillimore.

It May Never Happen

She would not leave till he left in the evening. She followed him to the end of the street. She watched his moods. She set her own by them. If he came into the room and went out without speaking, she refused to speak to me or to answer my uncle. If he spoke, she would flirt with me, saying:

"He's so *serious*, Mr. Phillimore. What shall we do with him?"

"Ah, youth!" began Mr. Phillimore. Then he changed his mind and said in a savage way: "I'd know what I'd do with him if I were you, Miss Croft. Look into his eyes."

"Oh, don't, you'll make him shy."

"Innocent!" said Mr. Phillimore. "Innocent eyes! How can you allow him to be innocent?"

Miss Croft blushed and turned indignantly away; but the indignation was for me. Both Phillimore and I gazed at her waist as she turned her back to us.

"Go away, both of you," said Miss Croft stamping her foot. We both, to her annoyance, looked with astonishment at her foot and went away.

"The Croft," said Phillimore, bitterly to me. "Do you fancy the embraces of the Croft?" In his most withering way: "All the indiscriminate vitality of a girl's secondary school going to waste," he said. "One almost has a duty— No, Vernon. With your energy, Vernon—"

It struck me that Mr. Phillimore was a man to avoid. He felt himself betrayed and looked as though, now, blindly, he would betray us all. One morning he arrived at the office a little late. His hat was on the back of his head and he had a spectacle-case in his hand. It had a spring in the lid which made it go "pop" when he closed it.

"Pop," said Mr. Phillimore, snapping the spectacle-case at me.

"Pop," he said again, pointing it at Miss Croft. And then he put it to his forehead and said: "Pop. Brains everywhere. 'The balance of his mind was disturbed.' "

He smelled of peppermint. I followed him out of the room. He had an attaché case in his hand. He half opened it; it was full of papers.

"Shall I just empty the lot on the top of the head of the chaste Miss Croft? Wager me I won't. Go on—wager me."

I was alarmed, but luckily Uncle was not there. We could hear his voice in the workshop. It really was remarkable that my Uncle Belton had no idea of what was going on.

"All right," I said.

Gloomily Phillimore picked up the attaché case, held it upside down with a finger on the lid, and went back into Miss Croft's room.

"Good-bye, Mother," were the strange words Mr. Phillimore was muttering as he went in. Then he came out with the case still in his hands. "Vernon, the bird—if that is the word—has flown."

Poor Miss Croft had gone to cry in the lavatory.

Phillimore sat down for a little while, nodding his head, and slowly his vacant face settled into a terrifying scowl. He went out to the workroom and at last Miss Croft came out. Her little eyes seemed to be full of pins and were pink-lidded with crying.

"He's drinking. Mr. Belton knew he would start drinking if he went down to see his mother. He knew it. Where is he? Oh, I'm frightened. Don't let him come near me."

I left her biting her lips. I put my arm round her, but she pushed me away.

"Dadda will make me give my notice when I tell him," she was sobbing. "He won't have me insulted."

"I didn't insult you," I said.

"Don't be a fool," said Miss Croft.

In the workshop when I went there I heard the sound of snoring. The packer was nailing up a case, hitting the nails as loudly as he could and giving a huge wink and a nod to the other men. They were nodding at Mr. Phillimore fast asleep on the heap of kapok. It was clinging to his trousers like burs.

"He's been boozed up since four o'clock yes'day," said the foreman. He winked. "He's a case."

Mr. Phillimore left the office when he woke up, and went away with the foreman, who beckoned to two of his mates to come with them. Miss Croft and I stood on the step watching Mr. Phillimore's hat, tipped back, wagging in a slowly advancing group of caps. Sometimes he stopped to put a hand on the foreman's shoulder and make a speech to him. A roar of laughter ended the speech and a man on the outside of the group swivelled round with his hands in his pockets and made a flying kick at a stone. We saw no more of Mr. Phillimore for a week. The people at the boarding-house where he lived telephoned to say he had influenza.

In the early days of their marriage my Uncle Belton would have called a taxi and raced to Mr. Phillimore's bedside; but now, bemused by the advance of his infidelities with Mr. Naseley, he did nothing. But he did make a speech to me in the train, for the motion of a train and its isolation from the world encouraged moral reflection in my uncle.

"The important thing in life," Uncle Belton said to me, getting out a toothpick, "is to do the right thing. The Devil is always on the lookout for our weaknesses. Two and two make four, you can't argue with the law of progress. Philli-more can't argue with it any more than I can or you can, Vincent. I am disappointed in Mr. Phillimore. I said to him, multitudes, multitudes in the valley of decision, the servant who buried his talents was made to give to the others. Thou base and foolish servant. I don't want to influence nobody. I'm just putting the case as God sees it; and when Mr. Naseley said something the other day about the partners in his firm, two brothers who don't get on—pretty dreadful that, isn't it, two brothers—I said 'God is my partner.' Naseley said to me: 'By God, Belton, you're right.' I said: '*I'm* not right. God is right. He will guide us.' By the way, I shouldn't mention Mr. Naseley's name at the office. . . ."

After a week Mr. Phillimore came back. He was wearing a new suit. He had a flower in his buttonhole. He whistled quietly to himself. Phillimore had improved his appearance by clipping his moustache. I do not know what passed between himself and my uncle except that I heard my uncle say: "Pull yourself together, Phillimore."

Phillimore's manner to me was an indication: "How's the Queen of Clapham, Vernon?" he said. "Dusting and tidying the eternal mantelpiece of her virginity?" Then he put his fingers under my chin and tipped it up. "What a bitch she must be, my poor boy!" he said, and walked away.

Miss Croft kept the door of her room open, hoping to catch sight of him. He came in at last. She was wearing a new, pale-blue frock and when she walked she made sudden half turns so that we saw the silk swimming over the full line of her leg, and she frowned when she looked back. Phillimore stopped in the doorway and clicked his tongue loudly.

"Woman," he said, giving me a nudge. He looked very vulgar. She put on a puzzled expression that asked Mr. Phillimore to explain. He just rolled his eyes. It was more than vulgar. She sat down quickly and began to type.

"I'm busy," she said. "Haven't you anything better to look at?"

"N'no. N'no," said Phillimore, advancing a step and leering.

"You are being rude, Mr. Phillimore," she said. He was punctured. His boldness went. He tried to explain. She became angrier. He went.

"Sometimes," sighed Miss Croft, "I'm frightened of what that man will do." And added: "It's a new dress. Dadda says blue is my colour."

Phillimore said to me: "What have I done? What have you done, Vernon? Why is it that you and I are unspeakable in the eyes of that virgin? Because we must, a little while longer, presume she is one. We are innocent. We are children, Vernon. She plays with us. I beg of you, Vernon," he said, seizing me by the shoulders and looking into my eyes; his own eyes were wild as though a pack of wolves were racing out of them towards me. "I beg of you for the sake of the peace of this office, save us from that torture."

I laughed. I laughed and stepped away because I thought he was going to cry and to kiss me: no, chiefly because I thought by all this acting he was laughing at me.

The hours went slowly. I did the stock books, the invoice books; then in the late afternoon I had to go and help Uncle and Phillimore in the workroom. Phillimore left us. Uncle had taken it into his head to investigate a collection of chair-springs. He hated being helped, but if you were there he obliged you to stand there and watch. I had to wait a long time before I could get step by step away from him, but at last I managed it and got back to his office. The workmen had gone and I sat reading a trade paper. Phillimore was in Miss Croft's office, sitting in his hat and coat. He too was waiting for my uncle. Miss Croft was not there. She was washing her hands and I saw her, through the open door, pass across the room and go to get her hat and coat. It was very quiet now the lathes had stopped, and the evening cries of children in the street could be heard now the traffic had gone.

Suddenly I heard Mr. Phillimore's voice. It was bold and decisive, the voice he had been training for use on our telephone.

"Duckie," I heard him say. "Don't be cross." No answer.

"I say don't be cross."

"I'm not cross."

"You look it."

Miss Croft was picking up her things.

"I must fly," she said.

"Fly, fly," he said. "My wings are broken. The wings of youth are strong."

"Don't," said Miss Croft.

"Take me in your strong wings," said Mr. Phillimore.

"Oh, don't," said Miss Croft.

Phillimore had got up and they were now both out of my sight.

"On your strong wings . . ." he was saying.

"I must catch my train," she said.

"I am wrecked. My life is ruined. . . ."

"I'll miss it if I don't dash," she said.

"Dash," he muttered very loudly. "Yes, dash. Don't you understand, I love you!" The sounds suggested that Mr. Phillimore had jumped across the room, or was about to do so. A chair fell over. "You say, dash," I heard him say.

And then a screech came from Miss Croft. I ran into the room. There was Mr. Phillimore with one foot standing on his hat, holding Miss Croft in his arms and trying to kiss her, and she was pushing away from him not with anger, but with an unnecessarily helpless, sulky expression.

"I'll miss my train," she was saying breathlessly. And then her face settled, she looked him in the eyes, stiffened, opened her mouth in a manner that I thought was inviting, but instead of a kiss, a high, pure, perfectly calculated, and piercing scream came out of her. It was a marvel. By the fight in her little eyes I would have said it was a challenge. She waited to see what Mr. Phillimore would do. My uncle came running up the passage and arrived with a plonk like a bouncing ball in the room.

Phillimore loosened his grip and the girl wriggled away. At the sight of my uncle she broke into tears.

"I—" gasped Phillimore. "I—I—was—saying—good-bye —to Miss Croft."

"Phillimore," said my uncle.

"Good-bye," said Phillimore to me. He did not look at my uncle. "Dash," he said.

And before we knew more about it, he *had* dashed. He dashed from the room and Uncle's new horn-rimmed glasses fell off.

"Oh—he's gone," said Miss Croft, looking at the empty doorway. We all looked at it. But in a second he was back, a scornful face printed with derision, which did not look at Miss Croft or myself but stared at Uncle Belton.

"I forgot to tell you I'm joining Salter's," he said ironically. And then his self-control went: "That's what you've all done to me." This time he went for good. Uncle Belton and Miss Croft stepped towards each other instinctively.

"Oh, Mr. Belton, did you hear?" she said. "How awful!"

"Mr. Belton," she said, "the deceit." She put her hand on my uncle's coat-sleeve; but he was simply staring. He always stood square-shouldered and now his shoulders seemed to spread wider. He was very pale, as pale as a loaf of bread. He still did not speak, but slowly sat down in a chair.

"The double-crossing swine," he said.

It was quite simple, my Uncle Belton explained to me. When he had seen that Mr. Phillimore was not going to keep his promise and bring in more capital, he had had to look elsewhere. It was hard to credit, but Mr. Phillimore thought he had been badly treated—"said I wasn't open with him"— and all the time he was seeing Salter! "But there is a law of justice in the world," Uncle said with a smile. "Salter is on the point of bankruptcy."

There were no more flowers on the desk now until Miss Croft started bringing them. She devoted herself to my uncle and every day came out with little pieces of news about the wickedness of Mr. Phillimore. I saw him once, it must have been eighteen months later. He was standing on London Bridge looking up at a high building where a man was cleaning windows.

"I should die," I heard him say to someone in the crowd. Then he saw me. He bared his teeth as if he were going to spit, but changed his mind. His look suggested that I was the most ridiculous thing on earth, as he turned away.

The Landlord

It was due to the boldness of Mrs. Seugar, who always got what she wanted, that they came to live in the semi-detached house called East Wind. They were driving through that part of the town one Sunday. Mrs. Seugar was bouncing on the seat and sighing: "Snobby district. I like it snobby, refined, a bit of class." And her little eyes, like caterpillars' heads, began eating up everything they passed until she saw East Wind. The adjoining house was called West Wind. "Oh stop!" she called out. "Look—posh! That's the house I want. You could live in a house like that. I mean, be one of the toffs and look down your nose at everyone. I don't mean anything nasty. Get out and see if they'll sell it."

Wherever Mrs. Seugar moved, a spotlight played on her; but Mr. Seugar lived in a deep, damp-eyed shade of shame, the shame of always obliging someone. Unable to step out of it, he had shuffled a lot of money out of his shop into his pocket and piled it on to Mrs. Seugar, who stood out in the spotlight seeing that she was taken notice of. Mr. and Mrs. Seugar left the car, went to the house, and were asked in by the man who was to be their landlord. He was having tea in a shabby room, with pictures and books, a very tall man with nothing to remark about him except that as the Seugars advanced he retreated, slipped back like a fish with eyes like lamps and with a coarse little open mouth. Mrs.

The Landlord

Seugar sat herself down and let her legs fall open like a pair of doors.

"I have set my heart on your house. Oh, it's posh, cute," she said. "Isn't it? Haven't I?" Mr. Seugar with his knees together confirmed it.

"Would you sell it to us?" Mrs. Seugar said.

The landlord poured them out two cups of tea and slipped back into the corner watching them as if he were having a dream of being robbed. (In the end, it was he who robbed them. A scholar and gentleman, he asked a tremendous price: Mrs. Seugar was knobbed with jewelry.) But first of all he put them off. They could have, not this house, but the one next door, he said.

"I own both."

"Who lives next door?" said Mrs. Seugar. "Ask him who lives next door. Why should I talk—oh, it's so posh," she said, elbowing her husband. "You make me wear out my voice."

"Who . . ." began Mr. Seugar.

"No one," said the landlord.

"Then you can move in next door and we can move in here," cried Mrs. Seugar. "What did I say? Would you believe it—I said to my husband: 'That's the house I want, go and ask,' but he wouldn't. He makes objections to every-thing—well, I call it daft to make objections all the time. It makes people look down on me for marrying him. I don't mean anything nasty."

The shadow of shame came down like a dark shop blind over Mr. Seugar, and indeed that is where his mind was—in his shop. In half an hour the landlord was showing them round the house, Mr. Seugar following them like a sin, giving a glance into every room after the other two had gone on, being called forward for lagging behind. When the visit was done, Mr. Seugar bought the house, wiping his feet up and down on the carpet as he did so, crying inside himself at the tremendous price, and bewildered because, in buying something that could not be wrapped up in paper and slipped into his overcoat pocket, he felt exposed.

When they got home and shut their door, Mrs. Seugar began to shout everything she said. He was snobby (the landlord); it was a pleasure to hear him talk the way the snobs talk, la-di-dai. It was lovely; but if you haven't the cash it doesn't help you being a snob. She felt at ease having someone to look down on straight away.

"He's a recluse," said Mr. Seugar.

"He isn't," shouted Mrs. Seugar, grabbing him back from her husband. "He never stopped staring at me. I could have died," shouted Mrs. Seugar. "Fancy him letting us have the house like that, no questions. It's barmy. Funny thing him living in that house all his life—he must have got pig-sick of it—and me killing myself to have it, it shows what I say, you never know. You say I'm mad."

At the end of the month Mrs. Seugar led her furniture into East Wind, and when it was all in, Mr. Seugar followed it like a mourner. They settled in and Mrs. Seugar sat there with her legs wide open and her shoes kicked off, going through the names of all the people she was going to look down her nose at. "Listen," said Mr. Seugar from the shade. No shop bell to call them, no one popping in from down street; they were hearing the only sound in their lives: the landlord poking his fire in the house next door.

"Talk!" said his wife to him. "But for me you wouldn't be here, say something. Not business. Talk. Talk snobby. Oh," sighed Mrs. Seugar, "I bet you talk in the shop. I've got everything on," she said, having a look at her gold watch, her diamond brooch, and so on, "and I feel a fool, you sitting with your trap closed. A snob would talk."

At that moment they both started. The front door was being opened, shoes were being wiped on the mat, there were steps in the hall.

"What's that?" said Mr. Seugar.

"Burglars, I'd welcome it," said Mrs. Seugar.

Mr. Seugar went out and met their landlord walking down the hall. He was just putting a key into his pocket. He was surprised by Mr. Seugar, murmured something, walked on, and then was stopped by the sight of their stair carpet. Murmuring again, he flicked like a fish sideways into the sitting-room, looked at Mrs. Seugar in a lost way, and then sat down.

"I've been for a walk," he said.

"A constitootional," said Mr. Seugar.

"Shut up, Henry," said Mrs. Seugar, "until remarks are addressed to you."

The landlord looked round the room where his pictures and his books had been and then glanced at the Seugars.

"Dreadfully late," he said suddenly, went to the window, which was a low one, opened it, and stepped over the sill. Once over, he walked down the garden into his own garden next door.

"Dreadfully, awfully, frightfully—late," Mrs. Seugar was repeating in ecstasy.

Mr. Seugar came out of his shame. "Blimey. See that? Forgot he's moved! He's still got the key."

A terrible quarrel broke out between the Seugars. That was a call, Mrs. Seugar said. No, it wasn't, said Mr. Seugar, it was a mistake. Mr. Seugar was so ill-bred he hadn't realized it was a call, but must pass remarks. If a visitor says "walk" you don't say "constitootional" afterwards, correcting him. Why repeat? It's daft. Not only that, he came to see her, not Mr. Seugar. A man, Mrs. Seugar said, was what she wanted, her ideal, who talked soft and gave you a good time, a lovely man, not the fairy prince and all that twaddle, but a recluse who could fascinate you and give you things.

"Out of mean spite you gave him the bird," she said to

Mr. Seugar. Mr. Seugar did not know what to do. At last he got a spade and went out to the garden to dig.

The next day just as lunch was put on the table, in came the landlord, walked straight into the dining-room, ahead of Mr. Seugar, sat down in Mr. Seugar's place before the joint, and started to carve.

"Henry!" Mrs. Seugar warned her husband.

Mr. Seugar said nothing. Their landlord handed them their plates and then rang the bell for an extra one. Mrs. Seugar talked about her summer holiday. People were stand-offish there, she said, and she couldn't get a corset.

"I apologize for the beef," said the landlord.

Mrs. Seugar kicked Mr. Seugar under the table.

"D'you believe millions now living will never die?" asked Mrs. Seugar to keep conversation going. "I mean they'll live, not pass out. It sounds daft. We had a circular. We put up a notice saying: No Hawkers. No Circulars; but that doesn't stop some people. Not never die, they must be fools to think that, what some people's minds get on, they must be empty. I want a bit of life. I'm not morbid."

"Millions now living?" said the landlord. "Will never die?"

"I'm surprised," said Mrs. Seugar, "they are allowed to give out circulars like that in a neighbourhood like this."

"I am sorry, I do apologize for the sweet," said the landlord. "It is my fault. I am awfully thoughtless. I will make a confession."

"A confession. Oh!" cried Mrs. Seugar clapping her hands.

"It is terrible," said the landlord. It was one of his longest speeches. "I forgot I asked you to lunch."

"Henry," said Mrs. Seugar. "Close your mouth, we don't want to see what you've eaten."

Presently the landlord looked at the pattern on the plates, then at the table, then at the walls. He got up and, murmuring, went suddenly out.

"You can see what has happened," said Mrs. Seugar.

"What I said yes'day, day before," said Mr. Seugar.

They sat there dwindling at the table, terrified.

"He's barmy," said Mr. Seugar humbly—the customer is always right. "He's forgot he's moved. Like people who order the same groceries twice."

"Father," said Mrs. Seugar—she always called him father when she was accusing him: he had failed in this respect. "Ever since we've been up here you've shown you're not used to it. Why didn't you tell me you asked him in for a bite?"

"Who carved the joint? Am I barmy or is he?" said Mr. Seugar.

"I was glad for him to carve. It used to be his house. I have manners if some people haven't," said Mrs. Seugar.

Mr. Seugar began one of his long, low, ashamed laughs, a laugh so common that Mrs. Seugar said he could keep that for the next time. Mr. Seugar stopped suddenly and kept it for that. He had kept so many things for the next time in his life that they got stale.

"If any person calls to be laughed at, it's you, father," said Mrs. Seugar. Mr. Seugar waited till she went out of the room and then did a small dance, which he stopped in alarm when he caught sight of himself in the mirror. A blush darkened his face and he went out to dig in the garden. Later his wife brought out a cap for him to wear; she didn't, she said, like to see a man digging without his cap.

If they had had a cat or a dog, Mrs. Seugar said, it would have been just the same; why make a difference when it was a human being who came in at the front door, said a word or two in the sitting-room, and went out by the window? For all the time she was left alone, Mrs. Seugar said, it was company.

"It's a man," said Mrs. Seugar.

"What's he say?" said Mr. Seugar.

"It isn't what he says," Mrs. Seugar said. "With those snobby ones it is the way they say it, it's what d'you call it, that pansy drawl. I love it. He likes to hear me talk."

"Oh," said Mr. Seugar.

"Yes," said Mrs. Seugar. "Why?"

"I just said 'Oh,' " said Mr. Seugar. "I'll try the window myself." And copying the landlord, Mr. Seugar himself stepped over the sill into the garden to his digging.

"That isn't funny, it's vulgar," called Mrs. Seugar after him.

Mr. Seugar said: "Oh, sorry. No harm," and came back over the sill into the room and went out the proper way to put things right.

One evening the following week he met their landlord coming downstairs fast in his slippers.

Mr. Seugar went into his storeroom at the shop on early closing day and sat on a sack of lentils. He was trying to get a few things clear in his mind. "He sold me the house. I bought it. But I hadn't the right to buy it, there was no notice up." Suddenly the truth was clear to him. "I bought *him* as well. He was thrown in. It's like sand in the sugar."

And then the cure occurred to him. Mr. Seugar went home to his wife and said:

"We must arst him in. We've never arst him in. If we arst him he'd see his mistake."

"He never wanted us to have this house," said Mrs. Seugar. Once a month she suffered from remorse. "We oughtn't to have done it. It's a judgment."

"Arst him."

They laid out a table of ham and cake and tea and put a bottle of port wine on the sideboard. Mr. Seugar lit a whiff to make the hall smell and went all over the house to be sure the landlord wasn't there already and then walked up and down there until he arrived. He came at last and gave a long hand to Mr. Seugar.

"I hope you are comfortably settled. I ought to have come before but I have been very busy. I must go and present my apologies to Mrs. S.," said the landlord.

"We have been meaning to ask you a long time," said Mrs. Seugar.

"I go away so often," said the landlord.

"You live next door to people all your life and never see them," said Mrs. Seugar, "yet someone from the other end of the earth you keep running into. How long is it since you've spoken a word to the people in the fish shop next door, Henry?"

"This morning," said Mr. Seugar.

"Don't tell lies," Mrs. Seugar said. "Ten years more like it."

Mrs. Seugar drank a glass of port and went red. An evening of pleasure succeeded. They were celebrating the normality of their landlord.

"Is a woman's life what you call over at forty-five?" asked Mrs. Seugar. "You work and what is there? You can't settle, you wish you could, but no, you must be up looking out of the window. *You* have settled. You've got your books, you can read. I can't, it's daft, I can't lose myself in something. If I could *lose* myself!"

Their landlord looked at Mr. and Mrs. Seugar and they could see he was appreciating them. Mrs. Seugar's voice went like a lawn-mower running over the same strip of grass, up and down, up and down, catching Mr. Seugar like a stone in the cutters every now and then, and then running on again. They had a long conversation about boiler coke. It turned out that their landlord used anthracite, which did not affect the lungs, and Mr. Seugar said they had paraffin at the shop in his father's time.

There was a pause in the conversation. The landlord looked at the clock and yawned. Presently he knelt down and they thought he was tying his bootlaces; he was untying them. He took his shoes off, then his collar and tie, unbuttoned his waistcoat.

"If you will forgive me," he said, "I'll go to bed now. Don't let me break up the party. I'll just slip off. You know your rooms."

"Sssh," said Mrs. Seugar when he had gone. "Say nothing. Listen."

Mr. and Mrs. Seugar sat like the condemned in their chairs. They heard their landlord go upstairs. They heard him walking in their rooms above. Then evidently he discovered his mistake, for they heard him rush downstairs and out of the house, banging the door after him. The following night Mr. Seugar went up to their bedroom at nine o'clock to get some matches and found their landlord fast asleep, in their bed.

Service was always Mr. Seugar's motto. He bent slightly over the bed, rubbing his hands. "And the next pleasure?" he appeared to say.

Mrs. Seugar came in. When she saw their landlord lying in his shirt, half out of the bedclothes, she made one of her sudden strides forward, squared her chins and her cheeks, and made a grab at her husband's pyjamas, which had been thrown on the bed. At the same time she gave him a punch that sent him through the doorway and threw the pyjamas after him. "Take those things away," she said.

Mr. Seugar was an inhuman man; he was not sorry for himself, but he was sorry for his pyjamas. He picked them up. As he did this, he saw Mrs. Seugar settling into an attitude of repose and heaving her breath into position. From Mr. Seugar's point of view, on the fourth stair outside and on an eye level with his wife's ankles, never had Mrs. Seugar seemed more beautiful; it was as if she were eating something that agreed with her and that other people could not get.

"Where are yours?" whispered Mr. Seugar emotionally.

The Landlord

Mrs. Seugar never answered questions. Now she came out of the room and quietly closed the door. "So refined!" she said. "His mouth was shut."

Mr. Seugar opened his mouth at once. He and Mrs. Seugar had not slept apart for twenty-eight years and, in a voice irrigated by what with him passed for feeling, Mr. Seugar mentioned this fact.

A new contralto voice came from Mrs. Seugar's bosom. "There are times," she said, "when a woman wants to be alone. I'll take the spare room."

And what Mrs. Seugar said she would take, she always took. In the spare room she lay awake half the night going over the past twenty-eight years of her life with a tooth comb. You make your circumstances or they make you, she thought. Which is it?

By "circumstances," she meant, of course, Mr. Seugar, who lay on the living-room sofa frivolously listening to the varying notes of the springs. An extraordinary dream came to him that night. He dreamed that thieves had removed the ham-and-bacon counter from his shop. At six o'clock he woke up, put on an overcoat, and went up to what was, after all, his bedroom. The landlord had gone. Mr. Seugar put his hand under one of the pillows and pulled out his wife's nightdress and threw it into the corner with his pyjamas when he had taken them off. Unfairness was what he hated.

"If I had had a different life," said Mrs. Seugar to her friends, "things would have been different for me. I sacrificed myself, but when you're young you don't know what you're doing. I don't mean anything nasty against father, he's done what he could, it's wonderful, considering. . . ."

Mr. Seugar went out and played bowls when the shop was closed. He pitched the ball down the green, watching it as it rolled, and when it stopped he called out: "How does that smell?"

The fishmonger at the other end called back: "Strong."

But what Mr. Seugar was really thinking as he pitched the ball was: "I lay he's in the kitchen making tea." Or "I lay a pound he's having a bath." Or "What you bet he's gone to bed?" Mr. Seugar was a betting man by nature. He would bet anyone anything, only they did not know he was doing so. "It's a mug's game," Mr. Seugar said, knowing that he was a mug. He did not bet only on the bowling green; he betted while he was digging in the garden, turning round suddenly and looking at the windows of both houses to see if anything had happened while his back was turned. A starling on the chimney would give him a start and he would stick the spade in the ground and go inside to see what had happened. One day when he thought he had betted on everything his landlord could possibly do, he met him upstairs on the landing of the house.

"Are you looking for someone?" said Mr. Seugar leaning forward over an imaginary counter as he spoke.

"Yes," said the landlord and walked on, disregarding Mr. Seugar as he always did, like a customer moving on to the next counter.

"My wife," said Mr. Seugar, always one to oblige, "is in the sitting-room."

The landlord stopped and considered Mr. Seugar with astonishment.

"*Your* wife!" he said.

"Oh," screamed Mr. Seugar—the scream was inside him, in his soul, and was not audible. "Oh," he screamed. "The deception. I never thought of that."

He saw how he had been diddled. He went out into the garden and dug, dug, dug. Worm after worm turned in the damp soil. "I am mad," said Mr. Seugar. Mr. Seugar dropped his spade and, pulling out his key, he opened his mouth, put on a fish-like expression, and went round to his landlord's house. He let himself in. Out of the study came the landlord.

The Landlord

"Good morning," said the landlord.

Mr. Seugar did not answer, but marched up the stairs and had a bath. After that he came down to the study. His landlord had gone, but Mr. Seugar sat there in front of the fire. Then, in order to annoy them next door, poked the fire.

Main Road

At the close of a December evening when the roads are like slugs, oozy and gleaming in the cold, two workless and sodden men were shambling along, lost in the side lanes of silent country. The darkness had come down to the roots of the trees and the fields. The houses with their yellow dabs of oil light had scattered and thinned away. Blistered and squelching and gone past the cravings of hunger into a hunched, mechanical misery, the two men went on. It was their third day on the road, and, no longer exchanging any words, cursing the lanes which had snared them into homeless, foodless darkness, they seemed to be groping round and round in a pit. Now they would almost sooner have found a main road than a plate of beef.

Suddenly the old one, who was ahead, stopped dead and then broke into a weak, gasping hobble.

" 'Ere y'are," he called.

Without warning, after a sudden rise, the lane had finished. They were out of it. They stood—oh miracle of miracles!—upon a main road. They gazed upon it with awe. Straight as a dull sword it carved the country in two, light-less, soundless, without signposts; and with it the double rows of telegraph poles and the low chopped hedges went. And now the two men were appalled. Which way? After the winding roads this great one seemed to strike them like a plank flat in the face. It jerked the knees in their sockets. It was as hard as iron to the weak bones.

On this third day the object of their journey had been driven from their minds altogether. They did not care if they never got to the town where the factory and the jobs were said to be, nor where they slept. They had eaten poorly on the first two days when the adventure was young, but on this day the singing had stopped and the whistling. The only sounds all day had been the dazed singing in their heads, the gritting of their teeth.

During the daytime, not work nor towns, but food had been their only thought. They ached and craved for it. Every step was for food, every glance sharpened the search for it, every sound was passed in judgment, every sight was questioned. The anarchy of hunger was in their bubbling bellies, which blew weakly out or cavernously sank.

Most of the time the younger one walked behind. Sometimes he had been only a few yards behind, sometimes the distance was twenty or thirty yards, once or twice it had been a quarter of a mile. He walked with belt tight and his hands in the sodden pockets of his overcoat, his straight shoulders rounded over his chest. He was a man of thirty with spikes of grey about the ears, his eyes were steely, the skin of his face stretched over the set bones. In his hunger he had begun to hate the man who was always in front.

He was a man near fifty, the older one, a man whose one-time florid corpulence had declined, like a leaking balloon, in two years of famine, to a bluish wobbling windiness. Dazed, vague, dreamy, his big arms lolling about loose, and with a lost look in his eyes, he stumbled ahead. Even when their hunger had started to put out claws he had continued to make jokes. They were always the same kind of joke.

"Cows doin' nicely," was one of them.

"Show me a stew now an' I'd throw it back at you," was another.

First of all, the younger man had begun hating him because he always got ahead. Then he hated his back and his figure and his ridiculous top-heavy way of walking on his toes. He hated him because, in the intolerable space and emptiness of the country and of the sky, it was necessary to hate someone. He hated him for being so bloody cocksure and humorous. He hated him for hearing of the job, thinking of the journey, for drinking their money on the second day, for leading this dance over the lanes when hunger had made them wander off the main road, so they were going round in circles, no doubt, like men lost in a forest—the forest of the cravings of hunger where everything reminds you of only one thing—looking for houses where there was food. But most of all he grew to hate the older man for begging. The young one had never begged, refused to beg, hung back if begging was on the cards. "The bloody old tramp!" he chewed away. "I'd sooner sock a man in the jaw than beg.

"And," he would add when the old man came away from a back door, where he had been refused, "he doesn't get anything when he does beg." Throughout the day the young one had looked at the baldish head of the older one, as he bared it with an absurd touch of ceremony at kitchen doors, with intensified disgust. He hated him when he tried, he hated him when he failed, and, finally, even more he got to hate him when, discouraged and dazed, he passed houses without begging at all.

The older man was innocently unaware of all this. In the afternoon they had come among people who lived in scattered shacks and bungalows. There were small holdings and gardens of vegetables, with patches of glass frame, and everyone had a few chickens. They were small careful people, with a little nervous independence—small builders, small shopkeepers, small coal merchants, small pensioners. They bent digging in their holdings and spoke arrogantly with fright when the big fellow went to a back door and asked for food. They had small, raging dogs. The two men walked closer together in these places. Lights were now lit, the yellow country lights, dabbed among the smeared blackness of the trees. The older man set the course. Instinctively he walked from light to light, stopping when he got to a lamp, wonderstruck because there was no food under it. Then on he went, lifting his feet high because of his blisters, the damp under his arms propping up his shoulders with spears of cold. Loosely his top teeth slid about on the lower ones; dazed and dreamy he walked. Tinned salmon, cabbage, suet pudding, and cheese, he dreamed. Fish and chips, ham and eggs, spaghetti. Grass and rubbish heaps, dogs and cats. Thrushes, sparrows, chickens, and canaries. In imagination he was grazing off everything he saw.

"We had a goat when I was a boy," he said. "And when it got a bit past it my ol' dad killed and skinned it." He jogged on, ruminating. "Show me a bit of goat and I'd throw it back in your face."

The other one didn't answer. Their breath was short. In a weak voice the big one continued:

"Seagull. I knew a man who ate a seagull. The French eat horse."

"Goose is another tough thing. Wild goose. When we was boys . . ."

"It's a bleedin' pity you're not a boy now," called the younger man.

"What?" called back the old one over his shoulder, still walking.

And now the old fool was deaf. The young one strained himself to catch up. He gasped along with his mouth open. At last he got within a couple of yards of the old man.

"A bleedin' pity you're not a boy now," the young one shouted out in a rage. Having got it home, he dropped back yard by yard.

After this they had been silent. The old one wobbled

along, deeply injured by the reproach; no more he laughed, no more he begged.

Then, suddenly, they had come upon the main road.

It was empty now. But when life came to this road it was not mean and made of little sounds, spade strokes, and footsteps as it had been in the lanes. Here, when life came, it was brilliant and roaring. Every few minutes fans of light would open slowly in the elms a mile ahead and then abruptly narrow and close; a few seconds would pass and then the long beams of a car's headlights would leap out and paint the poles and hedges gaudily with light. Long shadows rushed back from the two men, and then new shorter shadows jumped out of them, until in a cascade of rushing brilliance the car roared by and they were left like men slapped in the face, awakened. Gliding more slowly towards them and sloping to the camber of the road came soft two-decker buses. Like meat in a shop window the passengers seemed, women with full baskets, men with food inside them and pipes in their mouths. The two men stood upon the grass verge exalted by the light.

Now they were on the main road, the younger one took the lead. He lifted his head and stepped out. This was what he wanted. After the rasp of the wheels on this road, its silences were icy and momentous. The cars whined and expired like shells across an empty planet wilderness. There was no sound of people. There were no animals moving in the fields. An appalling inhuman vacancy opened in the road. The younger one understood this. But before they had gone a mile the old man was craving for the sight of a lane in which, broken at last but sheltered, he could crawl and hide from these blinding lights that seemed to go clean through his mind, from these silences of iron. He was paralysed. At the sight of the first signpost he hurried after his companion and got there with him.

"Lane," he said breathlessly, lifting an arm. The hedges

were high, a friendly warmth seemed to come from them. The young one was startled into stopping. The last mile had been vehement. Lane must lead somewhere. House? Light?

The old one's eyes swung about helplessly, pleading. "Bloke," he said. He hadn't strength to say more.

The young one was compelled to listen. The sound of footsteps was distinctly heard. He, too, heard the footsteps distantly in the lane coming nearer. The two men listened; the only sounds were from their breathing and the steps. Suddenly the old man stumbled off down the lane towards the steps. The young one gaped but did not move. A figure dimly appeared in the darkness. It was a man. It was a youth. It was a youth with a small playful ball of light from a torch dancing round his feet.

"God!" exclaimed the young man, all the hatred of the day returning to his body, so that he clenched his fists. "The old fool's going to beg! God, I'll—" he raised his fists.

But in spite of this he found himself making a few steps after the old man. He saw the youth coming out of the black silence with a small raffia bag in his hand. He saw the old man move nearer the youth. He saw the youth stop. The younger one sidled up slowly, but still hanging aloof, as he always did when the old one begged. He stood scowling, with tears of craving in his eyes, and a cold shiver of rage and shame sprang through him when he heard the old man's voice.

"No. I haven't." Distinctly he heard the youth's answer. The young man's held breath went out and he unclenched his fists at the reply. He was beaten. He could have broken into tears; but when he saw the youth step aside making a half circle round the big fellow, afraid to lift the torch to his face, but half raising it instead to shine on his stomach and neck, a wild contempt, a rage before prey, flung itself into his blood. Impelled by his day-long hatred of the old man, he stepped forward, taking a cold breath. "I'll show you,"

138

he muttered. There was the smell of cows, the smell of chickens, the smell of a farm, where animals and birds had been feeding all day. "Leave the bastard alone," he rapped out loudly to the old man. He strode forward into the circle of light and stopped the youth.

"What's that?" he said sharply, knocking the bag.

"Hyur—" blustered the young man, but his opened mouth would not make any more words. He flashed the light helplessly about him.

"Been pinching?" said the younger man.

The older man gaped but said nothing.

"Chicken," stammered the youth. "Mrs. Ross gave me a chicken."

"That's not a chicken," said the younger man.

The youth looked helplessly up and down the lane. He tried to skip away, but the older one woke up and stopped him.

"That's not a chicken." A sudden change had come over the older man. He copied the younger man's words. A feeling of intense new wakefulness was in both of them.

"Ah—" The youth tried to shout.

"Bleedin' thief," shouted the younger man. He trembled for a second and then suddenly let out a hard punch to the youth's wind and tripped him up. He went down flat in the mud.

Now there was no doubt about it. It was as if silently under all their talk and in all their silence they had been rehearsing this all day, working out every detail to perfection. They said nothing but sprang to it. The big fellow went down gay and hard on the gasping youth and sat on him. The younger one snatched up the bag and rummaged in the youth's coat pocket for a handkerchief. Money chinked. The youth feebly kicked. Without a word, the older man stuffed a bit of the handkerchief between the youth's teeth and tied it round his neck. A look of extraordinary pale,

breathless gaiety rose in the older man's exhausted face; a
look of keenness and shrewd skill sprang up in the eyes of
the other. Their breath came in helpless gasps.

" 'Ere y'are," they gasped together.

They lifted the youth up, giving a glance apiece up the
lane.

"There's a bus coming," said the older one. They pitched
the youth at the top of their strength through the hedge and
into the ditch and ran for the bus.

Out of the lane and across the road they went. They
were babbling, choking, half-laughing. They waved their
arms to signal to the large green bus softly swerving towards
them.

They grabbed frantically at the rail.

"Just in time," grinned the older man to the conductor.

The conductor, noting the numbers of tickets, hardly
smiled.

The big one flopped into a seat on one side of the gangway. He had the bag on his knee. The younger one sat on
the opposite side. They sat panting quietly. The passengers
stared at them stupidly. The dry warmth of the bus entered
into the bodies of the two men, and the pounding of their
hearts slackened. Their heads lolled weakly, luxuriously on
their necks.

"Two to the finish," said the older man in a hoarse voice.

The younger one paid up. What was more, there was a
shilling change. The older man glanced at the empty road
behind and then settled comfortably down. With its warm
soft roar the bus broke the dull air of the open country.
What a change! He winked at the younger one.

"Got a fag?" he teased.

The shadow of the grin he had had when he was a much
fatter and less crafty man came on his face. It made the
passengers smile. Reassured, the older man felt the bag with
his fingers. Cautiously he drew out the skewer and looked

down. He signalled across the gangway like a schoolboy. "Nt. Chkn. Fsnt," he was signalling with his lips. Not chicken, pheasant.

This made the passengers laugh. The grin on the older man's face became broader and deeper, feeding on his face. He loved the world. The light vans of tradesmen began to spin by, passing the speeding bus. There was light, speed, hilarity everywhere. A feeling of wild irresponsibility overcame the older man. Amid the laughter of the passengers, he pulled the pheasant's tail out of the bag.

But the younger one ignored all this. Crouching in his seat, he sat alert in the bitter vividness of his vengeance and his pride. There goes the bloody butcher, the bloody baker, money streaming down the world in petrol. Food! He looked at the old man with contempt. What he wanted, his tortured hating soul cried out within him, was not food.

Handsome Is as Handsome Does

In the morning the Corams used to leave the pension, which was like a white box with a terracotta lid among its vines on the hill above the town, and walk through the dust and lavish shade to the beach. They were a couple in their forties.

He had never been out of England before, but she had spent half her youth in foreign countries. She used to wear shabby saffron beach pyjamas with a navy-blue top that the sun had faded. She was a short, thin woman, ugly yet attractive. Her hair was going grey, her face was clay-coloured, her nose was big and long, and she had long, yellowish eyes. In this beach suit she looked rat-like, with that peculiar busyness, inquisitiveness, intelligence, and even charm of rats. People always came and spoke to her and were amused by her conversation. They were startled by her ugly face and her shabbiness, but they liked her lazy voice, her quick mind, her graceful good manners, the look of experience and good sense in her eyes.

He was a year older. On the hottest days, when she lay bare-backed and drunk with sunlight, dozing or reading a book, he sat awkwardly beside her in a thick tweed jacket and a white hat pulled down over his eyes. He was a thick-set, ugly man; they were an ugly pair. Surly, blunt-speaking, big-boned, with stiff short fair hair that seemed to be

142

struggling and alight in the sun, he sat frowning and glaring almost wistfully and tediously from his round blue eyes. He had big hands like a labourer's. When people came to speak to her, he first of all edged away. His instinct was to avoid all people. He wanted to sit there silently with her, alone. But if the people persisted, then he was rude to them, rude, uncouth, and quarrelsome. Then she had to smooth away his rudeness and distract attention from it. But he would ignore the person to whom she was talking and, looking down at her, would say: "What are you getting at me for, Julia?" There was a note of angry self-pity in his voice. She liked a man of spirit.

This started quarrels. They were always quarrelling. They quarrelled about their car, their food, where they would sit, whether on the beach or at cafés, whether they would read upstairs or downstairs. He did not really know he was quarrelling. The trouble was that everything seemed difficult to him. He had thoughts but he could not get them out. They were tied up in knots like snakes, squeezing and suffocating him. Whenever he made a suggestion or offered an opinion, his short brow became contorted with thick frowns, like a bull's forehead, and he coloured. He lowered his forehead, not as if he were going to charge with fury, but as if he were faced with the job of pushing some impossible rock uphill. He was helpless.

She would see this and, cunningly, tactfully, she would make things easy for him. They had no children and, because of the guilt she felt about this and because of the difficulties he saw everywhere, they had become completely dependent on each other.

First of all, they were alone at the pension. There were themselves and M. Pierre. He was the proprietor. At mealtimes they all sat together. M. Pierre was a plump grey man of sixty, with a pathetic, mean little mouth, a monocle in his eye. He was a short and vain little dandy and was given to boastfulness. The town was a gay place in the summer like a pink flower opening by the peacock sea, and M. Pierre was the butterfly that flutters about it. He had the hips of a woman. He was full of learned little proverbs and precise little habits. Certain hours he would devote to lying on a couch and reading detective stories in a darkened room. At another time he would sit in his dining-room with a patent cigarette-making machine, winding the handle, meddling with the mechanism, turning out the cigarettes. He gave a lick to each one as it came out. "So he won't have to offer you one," Coram said.

In the afternoon M. Pierre made a great fuss. Appearing in yellow vest and red trousers, he took out a new bicycle done in grey enamel and glittering with plated bars, gears, brakes, acetylene lamps, and elaborate looped wires. He mounted by a tree and, talking excitedly as if he were about to depart on some dangerous journey to the Alps or the Himalaya, he would whizz giddily down to the beach with his towel and striped gown on the carrier.

"You are going to bathe this afternoon?" M. Pierre asked. "I am going." It was a question he put to the Englishman regularly at lunch-time. M. Pierre would boast of his love of the sea.

Coram frowned and coloured and a veil of wetness, as if tears were being generated by the struggle within, came to his eyes.

"What's he say?" he asked his wife at last, for he understood French poorly.

"He wants to know whether we are going to bathe with him."

"Him!" said Coram in a surly voice. "Him bathe! He can't swim. He can't swim a yard. He just goes down to look at the women."

"Please, Tom!" she said in a sharp lowered voice. "You

144

mustn't say that in front of him. He understands more than you think."

M. Pierre sat at the head of the table, grey hair parted in the middle, monocle on expressionless face.

"He's a fraud," Coram said in his blunt grumbling voice. "If he understands English why does he pretend he don't?"

"Parlez français, Monsieur Coram," came the neat, spinsterly correcting voice of the Frenchman.

"Oui," said the wife very quickly, smiling the long, enchanting smile that transformed her ugly face. "Il *faut*."

M. Pierre smiled at her and she smiled at him. He liked her bad accent. And she liked him very much, but for her husband's sake she had to pretend to dislike him. Her life was full of pretences, small lies, and exaggerations which she contrived for her husband's sake.

But Coram disliked the Frenchman from the beginning. When M. Pierre saw the Corams had a car, he persuaded them to take him about the country; he would show them its beauties. Sitting like a little duke in the car he pointed out the torrid towns raked together like heaps of earthenware in the mountain valleys, the pale stairways of olives going up hills where no grass grew and the valleys filled with vines. Driving in the fixed, unchanging sunlight, M. Pierre directed them to sudden sights of the sea in new bays more extravagant in colour. Coram frowned. It was all right for his wife. She had been to such places before. Her family had always been to such places. This was the thing that always awed him when he thought about her; pleasure had been natural to her family for generations. But for him it was unnatural. All this was too beautiful. He had never seen anything like it. He could not speak. At noon when the mountains of the coast seemed to lie head down to the sea like savage, panting, and silver animals, or in the evening when the flanks and summits were cut by sharp purple shadows and the sea became like some murmuring lake of milky opal, he felt the place had made a wound in him. He felt in his heart the suspended anger of a man torn between happiness and pain. After his life in the villas and chemical factories of the Midlands, where the air was like an escape of gas and the country brick-bruised and infected, he could not believe in this beautiful country. Incredulous, he mistrusted.

"Garsong!" (There was a café near the harbour where the Corams used to sit for an hour before dinner.) "Garsong— encore—drinks!" That was the only way he could melt his mistrust.

Coram could not explain why. He was thwarted like his country. All he could do was frown and take it out of M. Pierre.

"He's a mean squirt," Coram said.

"He's a liar," he said.

"Look at him making those cigarettes."

"We've known him a week and what's he do but cadge drinks and rides in the car. He's a fraud."

His wife listened. Her husband was a man without subtlety or wit, quite defenceless before unusual experience. He was a child. Every day she was soothing this smouldering aching struggle that was going on inside him.

After they had been there a week a newcomer arrived at the pension. He arrived one morning by the early train, walking down from the station with his new light suitcase. He was a young man in his twenties, tall, dark, aquiline, a Jew.

"We will call you Monsieur Alex," said M. Pierre with his French love of arranging things.

"That is charming," said the Jew.

He spoke excellent English, a little too perfect, a little too round in the vowels, and excellent French, almost too pure. He talked easily. He had heard, he said, that there were some excellent pictures in the churches of the mountain towns.

146

"Rather sweet, isn't he?" said Mrs. Coram. The Jew was grave and handsome. Coram was admiring too, but he was more cautious.

"Yeah. He looks all right," he said.

His mother was French, the young Jew told them on the first evening, his father German. But they had both come from Austria originally. He had cousins in every country in Europe. He had been educated in England. Slender, with long hands, a little coarse in complexion in the Jewish way, he had grey and acute sepia eyes. He was so boyish, so free in his talk about himself, so shy and eager in his laugh—and yet—how could Mrs. Coram describe it?—he seemed ancient, like some fine statue centuries old that has worn and ripened in the sun. He was thick-lipped and had a slight lisping hesitance of speech and this sense of the ancient and profound came perhaps from his habit of pausing before he spoke as if judiciously cogitating. Mrs. Coram would sit there expectant and curious. She was used to the hesitations, the struggles with thought of her husband; but there was this difference: when the Jew spoke at last, what he said was serious, considered, a charming decoration of commentary upon their discussions.

M. Pierre always longed for fresh worlds to patronize; he was delighted with Alex. Too delighted for Coram and even for his wife. She could not help being on the point of jealousy when Alex sat and talked to the Frenchman. Coram bluntly wanted to rescue the young man from "the fraud."

"You know what's wrong . . . with this place," Coram said to Alex. "There's no industry."

"Oh, but surely agriculture, the wine," said Alex.

"Yeah, I know," said Coram. "I mean real industry. . . ."

"My husband's a chemist, industrial chemist," she explained.

"I mean," said Coram grinding on and frowning quizzically, "they just sit around and grow wine and batten on the visitors, like this fellow. What a town like this wants is a couple of good whore shops and a factory. . . ."

"Tom!" said Mrs. Coram. "How exotic you've become!"

"I expect ample provision has been made," said the Jew.

"No," said Coram, in his halting, muddling, bullying tone, "but you see what I mean."

He screwed up his eyes. He wished to convey that he had not quite found the words for what he had meant really to say.

The odd thing about the young Jew was that although he seemed to be rich and was cultivated, he had no friends in the town. The young always arrived in troops and carloads at this place. The elderly were often in ones and twos, but the young—never. Mrs. Coram detected a curious loneliness in him. Polite and formal, he sometimes seemed not to be there. Why had he come? Why to this pension? It was a cheap place and he obviously had money. Why alone? There were no relations, no women. When he went out he saw no one, spoke to no one. Why not? Alone he visited the mountain churches. He was equable, smiling, interested, happy—yet alone. He liked to be alone, it seemed, and yet when they spoke to him, when Coram—urged by her—asked him to come down to the beach or drive in the car, he came without hesitation, with the continuous effortless good manners and curious lack of intimacy that he always had. It baffled her. She wanted to protect and mother him.

"The Jewboy," Coram called him. His wife hated this. They quarrelled.

"Stop using that stupid expression," she said.

"He is," said her husband. "I've nothing against him. He's clever. But he's a Jewboy. That's all." He was not against the Jewboy. He even liked him. They talked together. Coram almost felt protective to him too.

"Aren't you being rather vulgar?" she said to her husband.

One effect the Jew had on them was to make them stop having this kind of quarrel in public. Coram did not change. He was as uncouth as ever. But his wife restrained herself. In mortification she heard his crude stumbling words and quickly interrupted them, smoothed them away hastily so that Alex should not notice them. Either she was brushing her husband away out of hearing, first of all, or she was working with every nerve to transform her husband in the young man's eyes. At the end of the day she was exhausted.

One evening when they went up to bed in the hot room at the top of the house, she said to her husband: "How old is he, Tom? Twenty-two?"

Coram stared at her. He did not know.

"Do you realize," she said, "we're nearly old enough to be his parents?" She had no children. She thought about him as her son.

She took off her clothes. The room was hot. She lay on the bed. Coram, slow and methodical, was taking off his shoes. He went to the window and emptied out the sand. He did not answer. He was working out how old he would have been if the young man had been his son. Before he found an answer, she spoke again.

"One forgets he must think we're old," she said. "Do you think he does? Do you think he realizes how much older we are? When I look at him it seems a century, and then other times we might all be the same age. . . ."

"Jews look older than they are," said Coram.

Her questioning voice stopped. Tom was hanging up his jacket. Every time he took off a garment he walked heavily across the room. Her questions went on silently in her mind. Twenty-two? And she was forty. What did he think of her? What did he think of her husband? Did her husband seem crude and vulgar? Did he seem slow-minded? What did the young man think of both of them? Did he notice things? Did he notice their quarrels? And why did he like to spend time with them, talk to them, go about with them? What was he thinking, what was he feeling? Why was he so friendly and yet, ultimately, so unapproachable?

She lay on her side with her slight knees bent. Out of her shabby clothes her body was thin but graceful. Her shoulders were slender, but there were lines on her neck, a reddish stain spreading over her breastbone, a stain hard with exposure to years. Her small breasts were loose and slack over the ribs. The skin creasing under them was sallow. She ran her hands over her hips. She moved her hands round and round on her small flat belly, caressing herself where she knew her body was beautiful. It seemed only a few days ago that this had been the body of a young girl. She was filled with sadness for her husband and herself. She could hear the beating of her heart. She found herself listening for the steps of the young man on the stairs. Her heart beat louder. To silence it she said in an anxious voice to her husband, lowering her knees:

"Tom—you haven't stopped wanting me." She knew her voice was false.

He was taking off his shirt.

"What do you want?" he said.

His face looked grotesque as it looked out of the shirt top.

"Nothing," she said.

Tom took off his shirt and looked out of the window. You could see the white farms of the valley with their heavy walls from the window. The peasants kept their dogs chained, and when there was a moon they barked, a dozen or more of them, one after the other, all down the valley.

"If those dogs—start tonight—we won't sleep," he said. He came to the bed and waited for her to get under the sheet. She felt his big-boned body beside her and smelled his sharp, curious smell.

"God," he said. He felt stupefied in this place. In five minutes he was asleep. But she lay awake. Forty she was thinking. A woman of forty with a son. No son. She heard, as she lay awake, the deep breathing of her husband, the curious whistlings of his breath. She lay thinking about her life, puzzling, wondering. Why had she no son? She dozed. She awakened. She threw back the sheet and sleeplessly sighed. If she slept, it was only in snatches and she woke up with her heart beating violently and to find herself listening for the sound of a step on the stairs. There was a sensation of inordinate hunger and breathlessness in her body.

Sometimes the young Jew waited for them in the morning and went down with them to the beach. He carried her basket for her or her book. He went back for things.

"Tom," she said in front of her husband, "has no manners."

She walked between them and talked excitedly to the young man about characters in books, or foreign towns, or pictures. She laughed and Coram smiled. He listened with wonder to them.

They sat on the beach. Under his clothes the Jew wore a black bathing suit. He undressed at once and went into the water. His body was alien and slender, the skin burned to the colour of dark corn. He dived in and swam far out into the blue water, beyond the other bathers. He did not laugh or wave or call back, but in his distant, impersonal way he swam far out with long, easy strokes. After a mile he lay floating in the sun. He seemed to pass the whole morning out there. She could see his black head. To be young like that and lie in the sea in the sun! And yet how boring to lie there for so long! She would have sudden pangs of anxiety. She would talk of the cold current that came out in the deeper water, from the harbour. She was always glad and relieved when she saw his head moving towards the shore. When he came out of the water he seemed to be dry at once, as if some oil were in his skin. She would see only beads of water at the back of his neck on the short black hair.

151

"You can swim!" she said.

He smiled.

"Not much," he said. "Why don't you?"

The question pleased her. She was astonished by the pleasure it gave her.

"I'm not allowed," she said with animation. "Tell me what were you doing out there. You were such a long time."

His dark eyes were large and candid as he turned to her and she caught her breath. There were three or four black freckles on his skin. Her older yellow eyes returned his innocent gaze. "Good heavens," she thought. "With eyes like that he ought to be a girl." But she did not know and did not feel that her eyes were older than his.

"I was nearly asleep," he said. "The sea is like a mattress."

He and Coram had a scientific discussion about the possibility of sleeping on the sea.

It was absurd of her, she knew, but she was disappointed. Had he not thought of them, of her? She had been thinking of him all the time.

Coram sat beside them. He talked about the business scandals and frauds in the chemical trade. The quick-minded Jew understood all these stories long before Coram got to their elaborate end. Coram had an obsession with fraud. His slow mind was angry about that kind of quickness of mind which made fraud possible. Coram sat inert, uncomprehending, quite outside the gaiety on the beach. He was not gloomy or morose. He was not sulking. His blue eyes glistened and he had the wistful face of a dog trying to understand. He sat struggling to find words which would convey all that he had felt in this fortnight. He considered the sea and the young man for a long time. Then he undressed. Out of his dark-red bathing suit his legs were white and were covered with thick golden hairs. His neck was pink where the sun had caught it. He walked down awkwardly over the pebbles, scowling because of the force of the sun, and straddled knee-deep into the water. Then he flung himself on it helplessly, almost angrily, and began clawing at it. He seemed to swim with clenched fists. They could see him clawing and crawling as the slow blue swell lifted him up. For a hundred yards he would swim not in a straight line but make a half circle from the beach, as if he were incapable of swimming straight or of knowing where he was going. When he waded out with the water dripping from him there was a look of grievance on his face.

"That water's dirty," he said when he got back. The Mediterranean was a fraud: it was too warm, thick as syrup. He sat dripping on his wife's books.

One morning when he came back and was drying himself, rubbing his head with the towel, he caught sight of M. Pierre. The Frenchman was sitting not many yards away. Short-sighted, no doubt M. Pierre had not seen them. Beside him were his towels, his red slippers, his red swimming helmet, his cigarette case, his striped bathing gown, and his jar of coconut oil. He was in his bathing suit. More than ever, but for his short grey hair, he looked like a pot-bellied middle-aged woman as he rubbed coconut oil on his short brown arms. His monocle was in his eye. He looked like a Lesbian in his monocle.

Coram scowled.

"You see," he blurted in a loud voice. "He hasn't been in. He won't go in either. He just comes—down here—all dolled up—to look at the women."

"Not so loud," his wife said. "Please." She looked with anxiety at the Jew. "Poor Monsieur Pierre," said Mrs. Coram. "Remember his age. He's sixty. Perhaps he doesn't want to go in. I bet you won't be swimming when you're sixty."

"He can swim very well," said the young Jew politely. "I went out with him a couple of days ago from the other

153

beach." He pointed over the small headland. "He swam out to the ship in the bay. That is three miles."

"There, Tom!" cried his wife.

She was getting bored with these attacks on M. Pierre.

"He's a fraud, a rotten fraud," said Tom in his smouldering, struggling voice.

"But Alex was with him!" she said.

"I don't care who was with him," said Tom. "He's a fraud. You wait till you know him better," said Tom bluntly to the Jew. "Believe me, he's a rotten little blackmailer."

"Ssh. You don't know that. You mustn't repeat things," she said.

"Well, you know it as well as I do," Tom said.

"Quiet, Tom, please," his wife said. "He's sitting there."

"He blackmails his brother-in-law," Tom persisted. He was addressing himself to the Jew.

"Well, what of it?"

She was angry. M. Pierre could easily hear. And she was angry, trembling with anger, because she did not want the young man to see the uncouthness of her husband and her mortification at it.

"Pierre's sister married a motor millionaire. That's where Pierre gets his money. He waits till his brother-in-law has a new woman and then goes to his sister and pitches the tale to her. She goes to her husband, makes a jealous scene, and, to keep her quiet, he gives her what she wants for Pierre."

"You don't know that," she said.

"I know it as well as you do," he said. "Everyone in the town knows it. He's a fraud."

"Well, don't *shout*. And use some other word. It's a bore," she said.

"I've no respect for a man who doesn't earn his living," Coram said. ("Oh God, she thought, now he's going to quarrel with this boy.")

The Jew raised an eyebrow.

"Doesn't he keep the pension?" the Jew inquired calmly.

"You mean his servants keep it," blustered Coram. "Have you ever seen him do a stroke?"

"Well," his wife said, "we can't all be like you, Tom. My family never earned a penny in their lives. They would have been horrified at the idea."

She was speaking not with irony but with indignation. At once she knew she had gone too far. She had failed for once to soothe, to smooth away.

"Ay! Didn't want the dirty work," Coram said, dropping into his Midland accent. He was not angry. He was, from his own stolid point of view, reasonable and even genial. He wondered why she was "getting at" him.

"Why, dearest," she said, knowing how irony hurt his vanity. "You've hit it. You've hit it in one. Bravo. They had no illusions about the nobility of work." She was ridiculing him.

"You don't believe in the nobility of work, do you?" she said to the Jew. "My husband's got a slave's mind," she said.

"Working is a habit, like sleeping and eating," said the Jew seriously in his lazy and too perfect enunciation. It had the well-oiled precision of a complexity of small pistons in an impersonal machine. She had heard him speak French and German with an equal excellence. It was predestined.

Living with her husband, always dealing with the inarticulate, she had injured her own full capacity to speak. The Jew stirred her tongue and her lips. She felt an impulse to put her lips to his, not in love, but to draw some of the magic of exposition from him. She wanted her head to be joined to his head in a kiss, her brow to be against his. And then his young face and his dark hair would take the lines from her face and would darken her greyness with the dark, fresh, gleaming stain of youth. She could never really believe that her hair was grey. Her lips were tingling and parted as, lost in this imagination, she gazed at him; innocent and cool-eyed, he returned her look. She did not lower her eyes. How young she had been! A shudder of weakness took her shoulders and pain spread like a burn from her throat and over her breasts into the pit of her stomach. She moistened her lips. She saw herself driving in the August sun on an English road twenty years ago, a blue tarred road that ran dazzling like steel into dense trees and then turned and vanished. That day with its climate and the resinous smells of the country always came back when she thought of being young. She was overwhelmed.

The sun had gone in and the sea was grey and sultry and, in this light, the water looked heavier and momentous, higher and deeper at the shore, like a swollen wall. The sight of the small lips of foam was like the sight of thirst, like the sudden inexplicable thirst she had for his lips.

Then she heard Tom's voice. It was explanatory. Sitting with people who were talking, he would sometimes slowly come to conclusions about a remark that had struck him earlier in the conversation. He would cling to this, work upon it, struggle with it. She often laughed affectionately at this lagging of his tortoise mind.

The frowns were deep in the thick pink skin of his forehead, the almost tearful glare was in his eyes.

"They didn't want the dirty work," he said. He was addressing the young man. "They have butlers. They have a grown man to answer doorbells and bring letters. Her family had. They corrupt people by making them slaves. . . ."

The Jew listened politely. Coram felt he hadn't said what he meant. The frown deepened as the clear eyes of the Jew looked at his troubled face.

"I was on a jury," Coram said. "We had to try a man. . . ."

"Oh Tom, not that story about the butler who stole elevenpence. Yes, Tom was on a jury and a man got six

months for obtaining a meal, value elevenpence, from an
A.B.C. or a Lyons or some place. . . ."

"Yes," said Coram eagerly, his glaring eyes begging the
Jew to see his point.

He wanted to explain that a man corrupts by employing
servants. No, not that. What Coram really meant in his
heart was that he would not forgive his wife for coming from
a rich family. And yet something more than that too, something not so ridiculous, but more painful. He was thinking of
some fatal difference between his wife and himself and their
fatal difference from society. He was thinking of the wound
which this place by the beautiful sea had made in him. He
struggled, gave it up.

But she looked scornfully at him. She wiped him out of her
sight. She was angry with him for exposing his stupidity
before the young Jew. She had fought against it in the last
few days; she had been most clever in concealing it. But now
she had failed. The thing was public.

She got up angrily from the beach.

"Pick up my book," she said to her husband. The Jew did
not quite hide his astonishment. She saw him gaze and was
angrier still with herself. Tactfully he let her husband pick
up the book.

They walked back to the pension. All the way along the
road she scarcely spoke to her husband. Once in their room,
she pulled off her hat and went to the mirror. She saw him
reflected in the glass, standing with a look of heavy resentment on his face, bewildered by her.

She saw her own face. The skin was swollen with anger
and lined too. Her grey hair was untidy. She was shocked by
her physical deterioration. She was ugly. When she heard
the young man's step on the stairs she could have wept. She
waited: he did not close his door. This was more than she
could bear. She turned upon her husband. She raised her
voice. She wanted the young man to hear her rage.

157

Handsome Is as Handsome Does

Why had she married such an oaf, such a boor! Her family had begged her not to marry him. She mocked him. He failed at everything. There he was stuck at forty, stuck in his career, stuck for life.

Sometimes he blurted out things in the quarrel, but most of the time he was speechless. He stood at the foot of the bed with his tweed coat in his hand, looking at her with heavy blue eyes, his face reddening under the insults, his tongue struggling to answer, his throat moving. He was not cold, but hot with goading. Yet he did nothing. The forces inside him were locked like wrestlers at each other's throats, muddled, powerless. As the quarrel exhausted itself she sank on to the bed. She was fascinated by his hulking incapacity. She had always been fascinated. From the very beginning.

He had not moved during all this, but when she lay down on the bed with her head in the pillow he went quietly to the clothes peg and hung up his coat. He stood there rolling up his sleeves. He was going to wash. But she heard him move. She suddenly could not bear that he move away, even those two steps, from her. She could not bear that he should say to himself: "One of Julia's scenes. Leave her alone. She'll get over it," and, taking his opportunity, slip away and go on as if nothing had happened.

She sat up on the edge of the bed. Tears were stinging her cheeks.

"Tom!" she called out. "What are we going to do? What are we going to do?"

He turned guiltily. She had made him turn.

"I want a child, Tom. What are we going to do? I must have a child."

Her tone made his blood run cold. There was something wild and horror-struck in her voice. It sounded like a piercing voice crying out in a cavern far away from any other living creature, outraged, animal, and incomprehensible.

'God,' he thought. 'Are we going over all that again? I thought we'd resigned ourselves to that.'

He wanted to say: 'You're forty. You can't have a child.' But he could not say that to her. He suspected that she was acting. He said instead what she so often said to him; it seemed to be the burden of their isolated lives.

"Quiet," he said. "People will hear."

"All you ever think of!" she cried out. "People. Drift. Do nothing."

They went down the tiled stairs to the dining-room. The sun had come out again, but it was weak. A thin film of cloud was rising in the east. The shutters of the dining-room were always closed early in the morning, and by noon the house was cool and dark. Before his guests came down, M. Pierre used to go round the room with a fly-swatter. Then the wine was brought in a bucket of water and he put it down beside his chair and waited. A clock clucked like some drowsy hen on the wall, and the coloured plates, like crude carnival wheels, glowed in the darkened room on the black carved shelves of the cupboard. Mrs. Coram came into the room and she heard the dust blowing outside in the breeze and the leaves moving in the vines. A bolt tapped on the shutters.

Their faces were dark in the room, all the faces except Mrs. Coram's. Her face was white and heavily powdered. She had been afraid that when she saw Alex she would be unable to speak, but would choke and have to run from the table. To her surprise, when she saw him standing by his chair in the room, with his brown bare arm on the chair top, she was able to speak. So easily that she talked a great deal.

"Red wine or white? The wishes of women are the wishes of God," said M. Pierre to her, paying himself a compliment at the same time.

159

She began to mock the young man. He laughed. He enjoyed the mockery. "The wishes of women are the sorrows of Satan," he said satanically. She went on to mockery of M. Pierre. He was delighted. She repeated in her own way the things that her husband said about him.

"Monsieur Pierre is a fraud," she said. "He goes to the beach. He pretends he goes there to swim. Don't you believe it! He goes there to look at the girls. And Alex—he has got a motor inside him. He goes straight out and anchors. You think he's swimming. But he's only floating."

"I can swim ten miles," said M. Pierre. He took a small mouthful of wine and boasted in a neat, deprecating way. "I once swam half across the Channel."

"Did you?" said the young man with genuine interest.

And once M. Pierre had started to boast, he could not be stopped. She egged him on.

"Challenge him," said Coram morosely to the young man, chewing a piece of meat.

"I challenge him," said M. Pierre.

But not at the town beach, he said, at the one beyond. It was true he rarely swam at the town beach. He liked to be alone when he swam . . . solitude . . . freedom. . . .

"You bet he does," grunted Coram.

"And Monsieur Coram too," said M. Pierre.

"I have been in once," Coram said.

"So have they!" she exclaimed.

When they got up from the table, Coram took his wife aside. He saw through it all, he said to her; it was a device of M. Pierre's to get a drive in his car. She was astonished at this remark. Before today she would not have been astonished, she would have tried to smooth away the difficulties he saw and the suspicions. But now everything was changed. He was like a stranger to her. She saw it clearly; he was mean. Men of his class who had worked their way up from nothing were often mean. Such a rise in the world was admired. She had once admired it. Now it amused her and made her contemptuous. Mean! Why had she never thought of that before? She had been blind.

When lunch was over, it was their habit in the house to go to their rooms and sleep. She waited. First M. Pierre went into his room, with his yellow novel. The Jew and her husband lingered. "The best thing about this place is the drinks," he was saying. "They're cheap. You can have as much as you like. Down at those hotels in the town they don't leave the bottle on the table." He was flushed and torpid. After a while he said: "I'm going up."

"I'm staying here. I shall take a deck chair outside. That room's too hot," she said.

He hesitated. "Go, go," she almost cried. She looked at the black shining hair of the young man, his full lips, the brown bare arms that came out of the blue vest, the large darker hands, redder with the flush of blood. They were spread on the table, stroking the cloth. She could feel, in imagination, those palms on her body. Her heart raced and shook her. She and he would be alone. She would talk to him, she would not listen to him, he should not have his own words, perfect, predestined, and impersonal. It was she who would talk. She would make him halt and stammer. She would break through this perfection of impersonal speech. She would talk and make him know her. She would bring herself close to him with words, and then with touch. She would touch him. He was young, he was without will: he would touch her. She saw in her mind the open door of his room. She thought all this as her husband hesitated, stupefied, by the table.

But when he went and she was alone with Alex, her heart stopped and there were no words in her throat. Her whole body was trembling, the bones of her knees were hard to her hands.

"I think," Alex suddenly said as he had often said before,

"I think I shall go for a walk. I'll be back for the swim," he said.

She gasped. She looked with intent irony at him. She saw him get up from the table and, in his oddly studied way, as if there were meat in his solitude no one else could know, he went.

"You fool," she said to herself. But as she stared out of the open door and heard his cool footsteps on the gravel outside until the sound of the breeze in the vines licked them away, she felt lost with relief.

In a deck chair under the mulberry tree she thought about herself and her husband. It was the time of year when the fruit of the mulberry falls. The berries dropped on the gravel, into the tank where the frogs croaked at night and on the table. They broke there. Sometimes they dropped like small hard hearts into her lap, and when she picked them off they crushed in her fingers and the red juice ran out. She breathed deeply, almost panting in her chair.

She had married an outcast. Her relations had said that and they had been right. Some of those who had been right—her mother and father, for example—were dead. Tom's father had had a small boot-repairing business in Leicester. He worked in the front room of their house, with its bay window. "Coram. Repairs While You Wait." That man and his wife had had seven children. Imagine such a life! Tom had studied, won scholarships, passed examinations. All his life he had been different from his brothers and sisters. Now his job was chemistry. Once he was going to be a famous chemist. Instead he got commercial jobs in the laboratories of big firms. He did not belong to the working class any more. He did not belong to her class. He did not belong to the class of the comfortable professional people he now met. He did not belong anywhere. He was lost, rough, unfinished, ugly, unshaped by the wise and harmonious hand of a good environment.

And she had really been the same. That was what had brought them together. He was ugly in life, she was ugly in body; two ugly people cut off from all others, living in their desert island.

Her family were country gentry, not very rich, with small private incomes and testy, tiresome genteel habits. The males went into the Army. The females married into the Army. You saw one and you had seen them all. She had always been small and thin; her long nose, her long mouth, her almost yellowish eyes and dead clay skin made her ugly. She had to be clever and lively, had to have a will or no one would have noticed her. At one time she supposed she would marry one of those tedious young men with dead eyes and little fair moustaches who were "keen" on gunnery and motor cars. She had thrown herself at them—thrown herself at them, indeed, like a bomb. That didn't suit the modern militarists. They had the tastes of clerks. They fingered their moustaches, looked dead and embarrassed at her, said they couldn't bear "highbrow" girls, and got away as quickly as they could. They were shocked because she didn't wear gloves. The naked finger seemed an indecency to them. "I could be a general's wife by now if I'd worn gloves," she used to say. Before they could throw her out and treat her as the bright, noisy, impossible woman who appears in every family, she threw them out.

So she married Tom. She got away from her home, went to live with a friend, met Tom, and married him. There was a row. "The toothpaste man," her relations called him. Thought she was going to live in a chemist's shop. He became a stick to beat her family with; he was going to be a great man, a great scientist—she flogged them. He was going to be a much greater man than those "keen" subalterns with their flannel bags, dance records, and little moustaches or those furtive majors, guilty with self-love.

She looked back on these days. She had always expected something dramatic and sudden to happen. But—what was it? —Tom had not become a great man. The emergence from his class had become really an obsession, and a habit. He was struggling to emerge long after he had emerged. He was always spending his energy on reacting from something that no longer existed. He lived—she could never quite understand it—in the grip of some thwarting inward conflict, his energy went into this invisible struggle. The veins and the muscles swelled as if they would burst. Torn between dealing with her—that is, with the simple business of giving her simple natural happiness—and himself, he was paralysed. And they had had no children. Whose fault was that? At first it was a mercy, because they were poor, but later? She slept with him. Her body had grown old trying to tear a child from him. Afterwards she attacked him. He listened stupefied.

Why had this happened to her? And why had she this guilt towards him so that now she pitied him and spent all her day coming between him and difficulty? She had sown her disappointment in him, he had sown his frustration in her. Why? And why did they live in a circle they could not break? Why did they live so long in it until suddenly she was forty, a grey-haired woman?

She went over these things, but she was not thinking and feeling them only. There was the soft stroke of a pulse between her breasts, making her breathless with every throb. Movement came to her blood from the sight of the blowing vines and the red soil of the olive fields and out of the wind-whitened sky. Her lips parted in thirst for the articulate lips of the young Jew. She could not sleep or read.

At last she went into the cool house. The flies, driven indoors by the wind, were swimming in the darkness. She went up the stairs to her room.

"Get up," she said to her husband. "We must go."

He couldn't go in these clothes, she said. He must get the car. She bullied him. She changed into a green dress. Grumbling, he changed.

She looked out of the window. Alex was not coming. She could see the valley and the trees flowing and silvered by the wind. Dust was blowing along the roads between the earth and sun giving it a weird and brilliant light like the glitter of silica in granite.

Tom went downstairs. His clothes were thrown all over the room.

"We're waiting," he said when she came down. The black car was there and M. Pierre. He stood by it as if he owned it.

"Women," said M. Pierre, "are like the bon Dieu. They live not in time but in eternity."

Coram glared at him. Alex was there, tall and impersonal. He had come back, he said, some other way. He gravely considered M. Pierre's remark. He made a quotation from a poet. This was obscure to her and everyone.

"Where the hell's this picnic going to be?" said Coram.

They disputed about where they should sit. That is, she said one thing and her husband another. At last M. Pierre was in front and she and the young man were at the back. Coram got in and sulked. No one had answered his question. "If anyone knows where they're going they'd better drive," he said.

"The far beach," she called out.

"Well, in God's name!" he muttered. Still, he drove off.

"Are you crowded at the back?" he said later in a worried voice. A sudden schoolgirl hilarity took her.

"We like it," she cried loudly, giggling. And pressed her legs against Alex.

She was immediately ashamed of her voice. Before she could stop herself she cried out: "I've got my young man."

She swaggered her arm through his and laughed loudly

close to his face. She was horrified at herself. He laughed discreetly, in a tolerant elderly way at her. So they bumped and brushed over the bad roads to the beach. Coram swore it would break the springs of his car, this damfool idea. She could see the sweat on her husband's thick pink neck. She goaded him. She called to him not to crawl, not to bump them about, not to take the town road but the other. Coram turned angrily to her.

She wanted to show the young man: "You see, I don't care. I don't care how revolting I am. I don't care for anything, I hate everything except a desire that is in me. There is nothing but that."

The car topped the hill and she turned her head to look back upon the town. She was surprised. Two belfries stood above the roofs. She had never seen them before. The clay-coloured houses were closely packed together by the hills, and those that were in the sun stood out white and tall. The roofs went up in tiers, and over each roof a pair of windows stared like foreign eyes. The houses were a phalanx of white and alien witnesses. She was startled to think that she had brought her life to a place so strange to her. She and her husband had lived in the deeply worn groove of their lives even in this holiday and had not noticed the place. Her mood quietened.

The outlying villas of this side of the town were newer, and the air burned with the new resinous odour of the pines and the two flames of sea and sky.

"I often come this way," said the Jew, "because there is more air. Do you know the waiter in the café by the harbour? On one hot day last year he chased his wife's lover down the street, loosing off a revolver. He breaks out once a year. The rest of the time he is the perfectly contented complaisant husband. If the café were up here, it would not happen. Or perhaps he might only be complaisant once a year. Probably our whole emotional life is ruled by temperature and air currents."

She looked at him. "You have read your Huxley," she said dryly, "haven't you?" But afterwards she felt repentant because she thought if he was showing off, it was because he was young. "*I* could cure him of that."

Presently the car stopped. They had got to the beach. They sat for a minute in the car studying it. It was a long beach of clean sand, looped between two promontories of rock, a wilder beach than the one by the town where people came to picnic. Now there was no one on it. And here the sea was not the pan of enamelled water they had known, but was open and stood up high from the beach like a loose tottering wall, green, wind-torn, sun-shot, and riotous. The sky was whitened on the horizon. The lighthouse on the red spit eight miles across the bay seemed to be racing through the water like a periscope. The whole coast was like groups of reddened riders driving the waves into a corral.

"The east wind," said M. Pierre, from his window, considering it.

They got out of the car. They walked on the sand, and the waves unrolled in timed relay along the shore. The three men and Mrs. Coram stood singly, separated by the wind, gazing at the tumult. They spoke and then turned to see where their words had gone. The wind had swept them from their lips and no one could hear.

Alex stayed behind, but soon he ran forward in his bathing suit.

"You're not going!" Tom said. The sea was too wild. The Jew did not hear him and ran down to the shore.

"Oh!" Mrs. Coram said anxiously, and moved to Pierre.

Without a word the Jew had dived in. Now he was swimming out. She held Pierre's arm tightly, and then slowly the grip of her fingers relaxed. She smiled and then she laughed.

Handsome Is as Handsome Does

It was like watching a miracle to see Alex rise and sink with those tall waves, strike farther out, and play like some remote god with their dazzling falls. Sometimes he seemed to drop like a stone to the sea's floor and then up he shot again as if he had danced to the surface. She watched him, entranced.

"He's fine," she called. She looked for Tom. He was standing back from them, looking resentfully, confusedly, at the sea. Suddenly all her heart was with the swimmer and her mind felt clean by the cleansing sea. Her fear for him went. She adored his danger in the water and the way he sought it, the way he paused and went for the greatest waves and sailed through.

"Tom!" she called.

Before he knew what she wanted, Coram said: "I'm not going out in that."

"Pierre is," she called. "Aren't you?"

The old man sat down on the shingle. Yes, he was going in, he said.

Alex came back. He came out and stood by the water, unable to leave it. He was fifty yards from them. Suddenly he had dived in again. Then he came out once more and stood throwing stones into the sea. She saw him crouch and his long arm fling out as he threw the stone. He was smiling when he came back to them.

They sat down and talked about the rough water. They were waiting for Pierre to go. He did nothing. He sat down there and talked. The Jew eyed him. Eagerly he wanted Pierre to come. The time passed and Pierre said this sea was nothing. He began to boast of a time when he had been in a yacht that had been dismasted in a gale. "I looked death in the face," he said. Coram glowered, and winked at the Jew.

The Jew grew tired of waiting and said he was going to try the other end of the beach. She watched him walk away over the sand. Like a boy he picked up stones to throw as he went.

168

She was hurt that he went away from her and yet she admired him more for this. She leaned back on her elbow; the soft stroke of pleasure and pain was beating between her breasts, a stroke for every step of his brown legs across the sand, a stroke for every fall of the sea on the shore. She saw him at last run down to the water and go in. He went far out of sight until there was a crest of fear to every breath of longing in her. He has gone far enough, she thought, far enough away from me.

She stood up. If she could fly in this wind over the sea and, like a gull, call to him from overhead and, pretending to be pursued, make him follow her to the shore! Then, to her surprise, he was suddenly on the shore again, standing as he had done before, studying the waves he had just been through. He stood there a long time and afterwards sat down and watched them. She called to him. It was too far. Timelessly he lived in his far-away youth. What was he doing, what was he thinking as he sat there remote in the other world of his youth?

Now M. Pierre had the beach to himself and there were no near competitors, he walked away and undressed. Presently he came back, short and corpulent in his bathing suit and his red slippers. He asked particularly that Mrs. Coram should be careful with his eyeglass. He fastened his helmet. Dandified, deprecating, like the leading dancer in a beauty chorus he stood before them.

"I float naturally in the sea," he observed as if he were a scientific exhibit, "because the balance of displacement in my case is exact."

He went to the sea's edge like royalty, pausing every few yards to nod.

"Look," she said.

It was odd, for the moment, to be alone with her husband, to feel that just he and she saw this as they alone had seen many other things in the world.

"He won't go in," said Coram.

M. Pierre had reached the sea's edge. Impertinently a large wave broke and he stood, surprised, like an ornament in a spread lace doily of surf. It swilled his ankles. He waited for it to seethe back a little and then he bent and wetted his forehead. He paused again. A green wave stood up on end, eight feet high, arched and luminous like a carved window in a cathedral. It hung waiting to crash. But before it crashed an astonishing thing happened. The fat little man had kicked up his heels and dived clean through it. They saw the soles of his red rubber shoes as he went through and disappeared. There he was on the other side of the wave in the trough and then, once again, he dived through the next wave and the next, clambering over the surf-torn ridges like a little beetle. The foam spat round him, suds of it dabbed his face. Now his head in its red bathing helmet bobbed up in dignified surprise at the top of a wave, now he was trudging out farther and farther into the riotous water.

"He's floating," said Tom.

"He's swimming," she said.

They talked and watched. She looked down the beach for Alex. He was lying full length in the sun.

Pierre was far out. How far they could not tell. Sometimes they saw the head bobbing in the water, sometimes they could not see him. They lost him. It was difficult to see against the flash of the sun. Nearer to them the emerald water fell in its many concussions on the shore and the shingle sang as the undertow drew back. She saw with surprise the lighthouse still racing, periscope-like, through the waves, dashing through the water and yet going nowhere. Why does he stay there, why doesn't he come back? She looked avidly to the young man stretched on the shore.

"Let's go up to the car and have a drink," said Tom.

"No," she said. "Wait."

She looked up for Pierre. He was not straight ahead of them.

"Where is Pierre?"

Ah, there he was; he was far out, swimming as far as they could see parallel to the beach.

She got up and walked along the beach. The mounting chaos of the sea was like the confusion of her heart. The sea had broken loose from the still sky and the stable earth; her life was breaking loose too from everything she had known. Her life was becoming free and alarmed. The prostration of each wave upon the sand mocked her with the imagination of desire forever fulfilling and satiate; satiate and fulfilling. She walked dazed and giddily towards Alex as if she were being blown towards him. Her dress blew and the wind wetted her eyes. She lifted her arms above her head and the wind blew into her legs, drove back her skirts. She paused. Did he see her? Did he see her miming her passion, with the wind?

She marched back to her husband. The wind caught and blew her almost unwillingly fast towards him.

"Tom!" she said. "I shall have a child by someone else."

He looked at her, in his habitual startled stupor. He hated this sea, this beach, this extraordinary country. He simply did not believe in it. Those words seemed like the country, wild and incredible. He just did not believe them, any more than he believed that the wind could speak. God, he thought she'd had her scene for the day and had got over it.

He was struggling.

"I have decided," she said. It was an ultimatum.

He smiled because he could not speak.

"You don't believe me."

"If you say so, I believe you."

She had terrified him. He was like a man blundering about a darkened room. Say? What could he say? She'd be crying

171

before the night was out that she could never leave him. Or would she? He was relieved to see her walk away and to sink back into his habitual stupor. When she had gone he wanted to seize her and shake her. He saw another man lying naked on her; the picture enraged him and yet it gave him the happiness of an inexpressible jealousy. Then tears came to his eyes and he felt like a child.

She was walking away looking for Pierre and thinking: "He doesn't believe me. He's a lout."

She watched Pierre as she walked. An old man, a nice old man, a funny old man. And very brave. Two unconcerned men, making no fuss, one old and one young: Pierre and the Jew.

The grace of the Jew, the comic strength of Pierre—they belonged to a free, articulate world. She was opposite to Pierre now. The sea was heavy in his course, the waves weightier there, and once or twice a roller cracked at the crest as he was swimming up it. But he was coming in, she saw, very slowly coming in. He was coming in much farther down. She came back to Tom.

"Look," she jeered. She seemed to have forgotten her earlier words. "You said he couldn't swim!" Coram screwed up his eyes. She walked down once more to the place where Pierre would land. The roar of the waves was denser and more chaotic. Tom followed her down. Pierre hardly seemed nearer. It was long waiting for him to come in.

At this end of the beach there was rock. It ran out from the promontory into the water. She climbed up to get a better view.

Suddenly she called out in a controlled voice: "Tom. Come here. Look."

He climbed up and followed her. She was looking down. When he got there he looked down too. "Hell," he said.

Below them was a wide cavern worn by the sea, with two spurs of rock running out into the water from either side of

it. The enormous waves broke on the outer spurs and then
came colliding with each other and breaking against the
tables of rock submerged in the water, jostled, punched, and
scattered in green lumps into the cave. With a hollow boom
they struck and then swept back on the green tongue of the
undertow. The place was like a wide gulping mouth with
jagged teeth. Mr. and Mrs. Coram could not hear themselves
speak, though they stood near together looking down at the
hole with wonder and fear.

"Tom," she said, clutching his arm. He pulled his arm
away. He was frightened too.

"Tom!" she said. "Is he all right?"

"What?"

"Pierre—he's not coming in here?" she said.

He looked at the hole and drew back.

"Tom, he is. He is!" she cried out suddenly in a voice
that stopped his heart. "He's drifting. He's drifting in here.
These rocks will kill him."

Tom glared at the sea. He could see it as plainly as she.
He backed away.

"The damn fool," Tom said. "He's all right."

"He's not. Look."

He was drifting. He had been drifting all the time they
had talked. They had thought he was swimming parallel to
the beach but all the time he had been drifting.

They could see M. Pierre plainly. In five minutes he would
be borne beyond the first spur and would be carried into the
hole.

As he came nearer they saw him at battle. They saw him
fighting and striking out with his arms and legs. His cap
had come loose and his grey hair was plastered over his head.
His face had its little air of deprecation, but he was gasping
and spitting water, his eyes were stern and bewildered as if
he had not time to decide which of the waves that slapped
him on the face was his opponent. He was like a man with

173

dogs jumping up at his waving arms. The Corams were above him on the rock and she called out and signalled to him, but he did not look up.

"Are you all right?" she called.

"Course he's all right," said Coram.

It seemed to her that Pierre refused to look up but kept his eyes lowered. Increasingly, as he got into the outer breakers he had the careless, dead look of a body that cannot struggle any more and helplessly allows itself to be thrown to its pursuers. The two watchers stood hypnotized on the rock. Then Mrs. Coram screamed. A wave, larger than the rest, seemed to dive under Pierre and throw him half out of the water. His arms absurdly declaimed in space, and a look of dazed consternation was on his face as he dropped into the trough. The sun in the sky flashed like his own monocle upon him and the rich foam.

"Quick. He is going," she cried to her husband, clambering down the rock to the beach.

"Come on," she said. He followed her down. She ran towards the surf. "We'll make a chain. Quick. Take my hand. He's finished. We'll get him before he goes."

She stretched out her hand.

"Get Alex," she said. "Run and get him. We'll make a chain. Quickly run and get him."

But Tom drew back. He drew back a yard, two yards, he retreated up the beach, backing away.

"No," he said angrily, waving his arm as though thrusting her away. Yet she was not near him or touching him.

"Tom!" she called. "Quick. You can swim. I'll come."

"No," he said.

She did not see for a moment that the look of angry stupor on his face was fear, that he was prepared to let Pierre drown; and then, as he half ran up the beach she saw it. He would not go in himself. He would not fetch Alex. He was going to stand there and let Pierre drown. "Tom," she called. She saw his thick red glistening face, his immovable glowering struggling stare. He stood like a chained man. He would stand there like that doing nothing and let Pierre drown. She was appalled.

So she ran. She ran down the beach, calling, waving to the Jew.

It happened that he had got up and was wandering idly along the surf towards them. He heard her cry and thought she was calling out with the excitement of the wind. Then he saw.

"Quick," she called. "Pierre is drowning."

She clutched his arm as the Jew came up to her. He gave a glance, jerked away her arm, and ran swiftly along the beach. She followed him. She saw him smile as he ran, the slight gleam of his teeth. When he got near the rock he broke into a short laugh of joy and rushed into the water. In two strokes he was there.

She feared for both of them. She saw a wave rise slowly like an animal just behind Pierre and a second greater one, green as ice and snowy with fluttering spume, following it closely. The two swimmers stared with brief, almost polite surprise at each other. Then the Jew flung himself bodily upon Pierre. An arm shot up. Their legs were in the air. They were thrown like two wrestlers in the water. There was a shout. The Jew came up, his arm went out, and his hand—the big hand she had seen upon the table that morning in the pension—caught the old man under the armpit. They were clear of the rock. They swayed like waltzing partners and then the enormous wave picked them both up, tossed them to its crest, and threw them headlong over and over on the shore. The falling wave soaked Mrs. Coram as they fell.

M. Pierre crawled dripping up the shingle and sank down

175

panting. His face was greenish in colour, his skin purple with cold. He looked astonished to be out of the sea. The Jew had a lump the size of an egg on his shin.

"I thought I was finished," Pierre said.

"I'll get some brandy," Mrs. Coram said.

"No," he said. "It is not necessary."

"You saved his life," she said excitedly to the Jew.

"It was nothing," he said. "I found myself the current out there is strong."

"I could do nothing against the current," Pierre said. "I was finished. That," he said in his absurd negligent way, "is the second time I have looked death in the face."

"Rub yourself with the towel," she said.

He did not like being treated as an old man.

"I'm all right," he said. After all, once he had attempted to swim the Channel. Perhaps they would believe now he was a swimmer.

"It is always you good swimmers who nearly drown," she said tactfully.

"Yes," Pierre boasted, becoming proud as he warmed up. "I nearly drowned! I nearly drowned! Ah yes, I nearly drowned."

The emotion of the rescue had driven everything else from her mind. The scene was still in front of her. She looked with fear still at the careless water by the rock where only a few minutes ago she had seen him nearly go. Never would she forget his expressionless head in the water. With the eyelids lowered it had looked grave, detached, like a guillotined head. She was shivering; her fingers were still tightly clenched. Supposing now they had M. Pierre dead beside them. How near they had been to death! She shuddered. The sea, green and dark as a blown shrub, with its slop of foam, sickened her.

"He is not very grateful," she thought. And she said aloud:

"Monsieur Pierre, but for Alex you would be dead."

"Ah yes," said M. Pierre turning to the Jew not very warmly. "I must express my warmest thanks to you. That is the second time I have looked . . ."

"You get no credit," she said to Alex in English just in her husband's way. It was odd how she had his habit in a time of stress. "He thinks he's immortal."

"Parlez français," said M. Pierre.

"She says," said Alex quickly, "that you are immortal."

All this time she was standing up. One side of her dress had been soaked by the wave that had borne them in. As she talked she could see Tom standing forty yards off. He was standing by the car as if for protection and half turned from the sight of the sea. She was still too much in the excitement of the rescue, going over it again and again, to realize that she was looking at him or to know what she thought of him.

"We must get you home," she said to M. Pierre, "quickly."

"There is no hurry," he said with dignity. "Sit down, madame. Calm yourself. When one has looked death in the face . . ."

She obeyed. She was surprised they thought her not calm. She sat next to Alex as all the afternoon, when he had gone off, she had wished to do. She looked at his arms, his chest, and his legs as if to find the courage shining on his body.

"It was nothing." She could see that this was true. It had been nothing to him. One must not exaggerate. He was young. His black hair was thick and shining and young. His eyes were young too. He had, as she had always thought, that peculiarly ancient and everlasting youth of the Greek statues that are sometimes unearthed in this Mediterranean soil. He was equable and in command of himself, he was at the beginning of everything, at the beginning of the mind and the body. There was no difficulty anywhere, it was all as easy as that smile of his when he ran into the water. Had she been like that when she was young? How had she been? Had everything been easy? No, it had been difficult. She could not remember truly, but she could not believe she had ever been as young as he was young. Without knowing it she touched his bare leg with two of her fingers and ran them down to his knee. The skin was firm.

"You're cold," she said. The coldness startled her. He had probably never slept with a woman. She found herself, as she touched that hard body which did not move under her touch, pitying the woman who might have slept with this perfect, impersonal, impenetrable man.

There was resentment against his perfection, his laugh in the water, his effortless achievement. He showed no weakness. There was no confusion in him. There was no discernible vice. She could not speak.

And now, as she calmed down and saw Tom, her heart started. She saw, really saw him for the first time since the rescue and went up the tiring shingle to him. He was still standing against the car.

"The damn fool," Coram said before his wife could speak. "Trying to drown others beside himself. They're all alike."

"It is no thanks to you that we saved him," she said. "Leave it to me! You ran away!" she said angrily.

"I didn't," he said. "Drown myself for a fool like that. What do you take me for? He wasn't drowning anyway."

"He was," she said. "And you ran away. You wouldn't even go for Alex. I had to go."

"No need to shout," he said. She stood below him on the shingle and he winced as if she were throwing stones at him. "These people get me down in this place," he said, "going into a sea like that."

"You ran away when I called," she insisted.

"Are you saying I'm a coward?" he said.

He looked at her small, shrilling figure. She was ugly when she was in a temper, like a youth, gawky, bony, unsensual. Now she had joined all the things that were against him. The beauty of this country was a fraud, a treachery against the things he had known. He saw the red street of his childhood, heard the tap of his father's hammer, the workers getting off the trams with their packages and little bags in their hands, the oil on their dungarees. He heard the swing door of his laboratory, the drum of machines, and smoke drooping like wool through the Midland rain, saw the cold morning placards. That was his life. The emeralds and ultramarine of this sea and the reddened, pine-plumed coast made him think of those gaudy cocottes he had seen in Paris. The beauty was corruption and betrayal.

He did not know how to say this. It was confused in his mind. He blustered. He glared. She saw through the glowering eyes the piteous struggle, the helpless fear. He was ugly. He stood there blustering and alone with his dust-covered car, an outcast.

"I'm saying you could have helped," she said.

She looked in anger at him. Her heart was beating loudly, her blood was up. It was not the rescue—she half realized now—which had stirred her—but the failure to rescue. From the very moment when he had run away, something in her had run after him, clamouring for him, trying to drag him back. Now, his muddle seemed to drag her in too.

"Help that swine!" he said.

M. Pierre and Alex came to the car carrying their towels.

"You think of no one but yourself," she said to her husband in front of them. "For God's sake let's get home."

Everyone looked at her apprehensively. Coram got into the car and she, determined not to let him escape one moment of her contempt, sat beside him. Pierre and Alex were at the back. In silence they drove from the beach and over the hill from which the white town could be seen stacked closely in the sun, like a pack of tall cards. As the car crawled through the narrow streets, which were crowded in the evenings with holiday-makers and workers who came up from the harbour or down from the fields, Pierre put his head out of the window. He waved to friends sitting in cafés.

"I nearly drowned!" he called out. "I nearly drowned."

"Drowned?" People laughed, getting up from their tables.

"For the second time in my life," he called, "I have looked death in the face."

"Tiens!"

"Yes, I nearly . . ."

Coram trod on the accelerator. M. Pierre fell back into his seat, his little scene cut short, as they swerved up the dusty road to the pension.

Coram was silent. They got out and he went to put the car away. Pierre went to his room and she and Alex went up the stairs of the shuttered house to their rooms. She was ahead of him. When she got to his landing she saw his door was open. She turned and said:

"May I see what you are like?"

"Of course," he said.

She went into his room and he followed her. The shutters were closed and the room was dark and cool. There was the white shape of the bed, the pile of books by its side, the white enamel basin on its iron stand, and his suitcase on a chair. He went to push open the shutters.

"Oh, don't do that," she said. But one shutter slipped open. Her face was white and hard, tragically emptied of all expression as she looked at his polite face.

There was nothing.

She went over and lay on the bed. He raised his eyebrows slightly. She saw him raise them.

"They are hard in this house," she said. "The beds."

"A bit," he said.

She leaned up on one elbow.

"You were plucky," she said, "this afternoon. But my husband ran away."

"Oh no," he said. "He had not changed. He had not been in."

"He ran away," she said. "He wouldn't even go and fetch you."

"One could not expect . . ." Alex began.

"You mean you are young?" she said.

"Yes," said Alex.

"My husband is my age," she said in a hard voice. "Turned forty.

"I admired what you did," she said.

He murmured something politely. She got up and sat on the edge of the bed.

"My skirt," she said, "was soaked. Look."

She pulled it above her knees. "Feel it," she said.

He came close to her and felt the frock. She stared into his eyes as he touched the cloth. She was shivering.

"Close the door," she said suddenly. "I must take it off. I don't want Monsieur Pierre to see me." He closed the door. While his back was turned she picked up the hem of her frock and pulled it over her head. She stood bare-legged in her white underclothes. The shoulder strap slipped over her arm. She knew that he saw her white breast.

"In England this might be misunderstood," she said, with a loud nervous laugh. "But not in France." She laughed and stared, frightened at him.

"I'm old enough to be your mother, aren't I?"

"Well, not quite," he said.

She was nearly choking. She could nearly scream. She was ugly and hideous. She had wanted to show him what she was. "Feel how cold I am," she said putting out her leg. He put his hand on her white thigh. It was soft and warm. He was puzzled.

"Do you mind?" she said. She lay back on the bed. Tears came into her eyes when she spoke.

"You are young," she said. "Come and sit here."

Handsome Is as Handsome Does

He came and sat on the edge of the bed beside her. He was very puzzled. She took his hand. But there was no desire in her. It had gone. Where had it gone? She dropped his hand and stared helplessly at him. She saw that he did not want her and that it had not occurred to him to want her. If she had drawn his head down to her breast she would have been cold to his touch. There was no desire, but only shame and anger in her heart.

"I suppose," she said suddenly, with a false yawn, "that this is a little unconventional."

To her astonishment, he got up.

"Have you ever been in love?" she asked in a mocking voice to call him back. "Hardly, I expect, not yet. You are only a child."

Before he could answer she said: "Too young to sleep with a woman."

Now he looked embarrassed and angry. She laughed. She got up. She was delighted she had made him angry.

She took her frock and waited. Perhaps he would attempt to kiss her. She stood waiting for him. But he did not move. Slowly a horror of what she was doing came over her. There was no desire. She saw too a remote fear of her in his brown eyes.

"Thank you," she said. She put the frock against her breast and went to the door. She hoped for one more humiliation when she opened it: that she should be seen, half naked, leaving his room. But there was no one on the stairs.

From the landing window as she went up she saw the familiar picture. The military rows of the vines in the red soil. The shadow-pocked mountains, the pines. It was like a postcard view taken in the sun, the sun not of today but of other days, a sun that was not warm but the indifferent, hard, dead brilliance of the past itself, surrounding her life.

She lay down on her bed and sobbed with misery and

shame as a broken creature will abase itself before a bloodless, unapproachable idol. She sobbed because of her ugliness
and of the ugliness of having no desire. She had abased and
humiliated herself. When had the desire gone? Before Alex
had rushed to the rescue into the sea it had been there. When?

It had gone when she had heard her husband's refusal and
had seen the fear and helplessness in his eyes, the muddle
in his heart. Her desire had not gone winged after the rescuer,
but angry, hurt, astounded, and shocked towards her husband. She knew this.

She stopped weeping and listened for him. And in this
clarity of the listening mind she knew she had not gone to
Alex's room to will her desire to life or even to will it out
of him, but to abase herself to the depths of her husband's
abasement. He dominated her entirely, all her life; she wished
to be no better than he. They were both of them like that;
helpless, halted, tangled people, outcasts in everything they
did.

She heard him coming up the stairs.

"Tom," she called. "Tom."

She went avidly to the door.

That evening in the quietness after dinner some friends of
M. Pierre's came in to hear about his escape. He wore his
yachting cap that night. Death, he said, had no terrors for
him, nor had the sea. In his case the balance of displacement
was exact; once already he had looked death in the face. . . .
He was the hero. He did not once refer to his rescuer. Two
of the guests were English, a colonel and his wife, and to
them Coram, also, told the story. He stumbled over his
words. He lumbered on. They sat under the massed black
leaves of the mulberry tree.

Mrs. Coram sat there calm, clever, and experienced, as
she always was. Here and there, as she always did, she

helped her husband over the story. "Let me tell you what happened," she said smiling. They turned to her with relief and Coram himself was grateful.

Wonderful story she always tells, they said. Ought to write. Why didn't she take it up? "Go on, Mrs. Coram, give us the lowdown."

They all laughed, except Pierre, under the trees. He was out of his depth in so much quick English.

It was ridiculous, she said, in her quickest voice, glancing at Alex, to go out in a sea like that. She described the scene.

"Tom tried to persuade him not to go, but he would. You know how vain they are," she said. "And then," she said as they laughed with approval and caught the excitement of her story, "poor Tom had to go in and rescue him."

She looked at them. Her eyes were brilliant, her whole body alive with challenge as she glanced from her visitors to Alex and Tom.

"B——" Tom began.

"Alex was at the other end of the beach and Tom had to go in and rescue him," she repeated.

She looked at all of them with defiance and a pause of pity for Alex; at Tom, like a cracking whip before a too docile lion. The Corams against the world.

Pocock Passes

The cities fall, but what survives? It is the common, patient, indigenous grass. After Mr. Pocock's death this thought lay in a muddle in Rogers's mind; if Rogers had a mind. He was enormously fat; a jellyfish which is washed and rocked by sensations and not by thought. The Wilcoxes, the Stockses and Rogerses, the three ordinary, far-back tribes who made the village, alone had history; and this plain corporate history, like the eternal grass, choked out the singular blooms. The death of a Rogers is something. A card is shuffled into another pack and he joins the great phalanx of village Rogerses beyond the grave, formidable in their anonymity. But the death of a stranger like Pocock, who had been in the place only a few months, was like a motor smash. Vivid but trivial, it sank out of village memory to the bottom of time.

Rogers admitted to himself that he had had a fright. Mr. Pocock had been a man of fifty like himself, as fat as Rogers was, too—they had compared waist measurements once—and he drank heavily: that came home rather close. So close that although Rogers was Mr. Pocock's only friend in the last months of his life, Rogers could not bring himself to go to the funeral. He put on his black to show willingness, but at the hour of the funeral slipped on the doorstep and twisted his knee and had to be kept in his house. With a sort of

185

penitence or hoping for a last order, Askew, the village publican, went—he followed all his customers to the end—and came back saying:

"Mr. Pocock, he drank too much. I often tried to stop him."

Then it was that Rogers, who had gone down to the pub once the funeral was over and Pocock was set in his grave—then it was that Rogers saw a profound truth:

"You're wrong there," he said.

"He didn't drink too much," he said. "The trouble with Mr. Pocock was that he didn't drink enough."

One thing the death of Mr. Pocock did for Rogers was to make him stay at home. There was nothing to go out for. Outside was the road, the village, the four-eyed faces of the villas called Heart's Desire Estate, which Rogers had built on the flat fields and had sold before anyone had discovered that the site was a water meadow. There was his wooden hut too, where he slept over the typewriter sometimes, with its estate-agent's plate on the door. His wife ran his business now—such as it was. Above all this was the sky. He was inclined to see a hole in things like the street or sky after Pocock's death, a hole with simply nothing beyond it. Staying at home with his family kept Rogers from seeing the hole. Hearing his wife use the typewriter or telephone in the office, drinking a cup of tea, listening to his two girls, torpidly watching them, his slow mind lay down like a dog in the domestic basket. "Wife and family—you're lucky, ol' boy," Mr. Pocock had said many times in his husky, half-rapacious voice. Rogers brooded. Perhaps he, surviving, was the better man.

Yet with all his heart and with some plain builder's shrewdness and village vanity, Rogers had wanted to believe in the singularity of Mr. Pocock. People came down from London and took a house in old age, and when they died, these strangers always turned out to be less than they had at

first seemed to be. He was used to that. A handful of dust—
often scandalous dust—was all they were against the great
tribal burial mound of the village Wilcoxes, Stockses, and
Rogerses. Pocock not only had looked different but had
sounded different and behaved accordingly. Yet the death of
Pocock had left in Rogers's mind some suspicion of fraud—
indeterminate yet disturbing, like waking in the night and
thinking you smell a carpet smouldering, and yet no coal on
it when you get out to look.

Pocock was a painter. Not only that, he was a well-known
painter from London; he knew other painters. Not only
other painters, but studios and actresses. He knew the stage.
Yet after the ambulance went like a soft clap of low white
wings between the hedges of the main road, taking Pocock
to the hospital and his end, Rogers said to people who had
come to look at property: "We had Pocock here." They
merely said blankly: "What's that? Never heard of him."
No one at all had heard of Mr. Pocock, the famous painter.

Rogers and Mr. Pocock had come together not because of
their minds or tastes, but because of their bodies. They were
drawn will-lessly together by the magnetic force of their
phenomenal obesities. There is a loneliness in fat. Atlas met
Atlas, astonished to find each saddened by the burden of a
world. Rogers was short and had that douce, pleading melancholy of the enormous. His little blue eyes, above the
bumps of fat on his cheek-bones, looked like sinking lights
at sea; and he had the gentle and bewildered air of a man who
watches himself daily getting uncontrollably and hopelessly
fatter. His outsize navy-blue jacket hung on him like another
man's overcoat. The coarseness and grossness of his appearance, the spread of his nostrils, the crease of his neck,
gave him a pathos: there is an inherent delicacy, a dignity
and spirituality in pork. He lived in a quiet sedentary fever
in which, as his own bounds daily grew, the world seemed
farther away to him. His gentleness was like that of the

blind, indicating how far he was from other people. There was no one like him in the village. Rogers was a show-piece. His visits to the public-house were a hopeless try for gregariousness, but there were no seats broad enough in the tap, it didn't "do" for him to go to the bar where his workmen were, and, anyway, there were no seats in it. He went instead to the small parlour and was usually there alone, like a human exhibit, with an aspidistra and a picture of Edward VII.

Rogers's first impression, as he came into the parlour one night, was that an enormous bull terrier in a black-and-white chessboard jacket had got up on a chair in the darker corner. Rogers's perceptions were slow; but at last he saw the figure was a man and not a dog. Between the check suit and check cloth hat was a face, a raw-meat face which had grown a grey moustache, and under that was a small, furiously proud and querulous mouth. An old dog who would fly out at you if spoken to. The check coat went on to check knickerbockers. There was a rose in Pocock's buttonhole—the smell of the rose and of Turkish cigarettes in the room—and he had a spotted bow to his collar. But what surprised Rogers, after he had said "Good evening" and was leaning forward with the usual difficulty to tap the bell on the table, was the stranger's voice. Husky, swaggering, full-tempered, it said, daring you to contradict and yet somehow weary: "What are you having, old boy?"

Deep called unto deep: Rogers saw to his astonishment, not a stranger, but a brother. Not his blood brother, of course, but something closer—a brother in obesity.

Mr. Pocock's was a different kind of fatness, tight where Rogers's was loose, dynamic where Rogers's was passive and poetic, aggressive where Rogers's was silkily receptive. Mr. Pocock's pathos was fiery and bitter. A pair of stiffly inflated balloons seemed to have been placed, one under and one above Mr. Pocock's waist-line, and the load forced his short legs apart on either side of the chair, like the splayed speckled legs of a frog. And there was another bond. Mr. Pocock, it was evident, was a drinker. A gentleman, too (Rogers observed), as the evening went on, arrogantly free with money. A sportsman also. There were a couple of illustrated papers on the table and one had a photograph of tropical game. A peeress had taken these photographs. One showed a hippopotamus rising like a sofa out of a lake.

"Damn cruel, old boy," said Mr. Pocock in a grating gasp, having an imaginary row with the aristocracy and Rogers about it. "All these bloody white women following poor defenceless animals around with cameras, old boy. Bloody hippopotamus can't even drink in peace. Animals much sooner be shot, old boy—what?"

Yes, Mr. Pocock was a sportsman, a blaspheming sportsman of some elegance, for now Rogers noticed a couple of rings on one hand.

Yet not a sportsman, after all, for he looked bored when Rogers spoke of the duck and snipe and the teal which float like commas on the meres at the back of the village.

"Can't eat it, old boy," replied Pocock. "Game's poison to me. Bloody waste of time following birds, if you ask me. Need every ounce of daylight for my work."

The bell on the table was tapped again and again. In and out went Askew, the publican. Even he straightened up under the snapping orders of Mr. Pocock.

And there was no reserve in Mr. Pocock. His talk was free and self-explanatory. "I've come down here to see if there is anything," said Pocock. "If there is, well and good. If not, all right. There may be something."

("What?" wondered Rogers.)

"I've got to, old boy," said Mr. Pocock. "I've got to cut down the overheads. Have another, old boy? With this bloody crisis," he said with an angry and frightened look in his eyes. "I had my own studio in London and a housekeeper, but with this crisis, and the critics in league against you, the bottom's gone out of things. There may be something here—I don't know. Two rooms, a bed, a table, do my own cleaning up and cooking—that's all I want and no women about. No," said Mr. Pocock, "no more women.

"You married, old boy?" asked Mr. Pocock.

"Yes," said Rogers.

"You're lucky, old boy," said Mr. Pocock. "Bloody lucky. Excuse my language, old boy, but woman's a b—"

"Oh, fifty-fifty," said Rogers, not clear whether he meant only half lucky or wholly lucky to have a wife he could share everything with, she doing the office work and looking after his house while he built up his figure and did the drinking. For Rogers had reached the point of saturation in his own life when drinking was work. It never stopped.

Rogers's slow mind wanted to explain, but Pocock interrupted.

"I know, old boy. You can't tell me anything about women. They're a bloody question-mark, old boy. There's two answers to it, one's right and one's wrong. When I want what I want, I don't ask anyone's opinion, I go and get it.

"What?" added Mr. Pocock.

"You're right," said Rogers in his slow, groping voice. "You know the story of the couple who . . ."

They didn't laugh out loud at the story. Rogers shook and shook and his eyes sank out of sight. Mr. Pocock strained in his chair and seemed to fizz with austere pleasure like a bottle of soda-water.

"It's nature," said Mr. Pocock when his head stopped fizzing.

Rogers was out of his depth here. His head was lolling forward. He had reached the stage when Mr. Pocock had a tendency to rise to the ceiling and then to drift away sideways towards the door in great numbers.

"Take salmon," said Rogers heavily, this coming into his mind at the moment.

"Salmon, old boy? Why bloody salmon?" said Mr. Pocock.

"They go—" said Rogers. "They go—up fresh water."

"Salmon?" said Mr. Pocock. "Salmon? They come from the sea."

"They don't breed in it," said Rogers uncertainly. He was beginning to forget why he had mentioned them.

"I know," said Mr. Pocock peremptorily. "They live in the sea and go up the river when they feel like it."

"Feel like it," repeated Rogers. Somewhere near here was the reason for raising the matter.

". . . I've seen 'em, old boy," continued Mr. Pocock, putting down his glass with a bang.

"Out of the sea," insisted Rogers.

"Don't be bloody funny, old boy," said Mr. Pocock, banging his glass again. "We know they do."

The landlord called: "Time."

Rogers and Mr. Pocock got up with common difficulty, exchanging a look of sympathy. Foot by foot, after they had unbent, stopping between paragraphs, they talked and stopped their way out of the public-house and outside its door. Facing the night, surprised by it, they halted again. The moon arrested them. It was a white full moon, the most obese of planets, with its little mouth open in the sad face.

"Just made for an artist, I should say," said Rogers, slapped across the face by the cold wind, but warm within in his linings. Yet as a villager he had an obscure feeling that for a London stranger to paint the place insulted it. His feeling was primitive; he did not want the magic of an alien eye upon his home.

"It *used* to be pretty, old boy," said Mr. Pocock. "Till some bastard ran up those bloody villas."

"I put them up ten years ago," said Rogers dispassionately; and he meant that time justified and forgave all things.

"Good God, old boy. Bloody ugly," fizzed Mr. Pocock.

They stared at the villas and grinned, almost sniggered, like boys peeping through a fence at something shocking. It gave Rogers and Mr. Pocock pleasure, they being human, to know the worst about each other. And as they gazed with tenderness upon the raped virgin, the sight started Pocock's mind on his own affairs and prompted him to the words which were the final thing to bind Rogers to him.

"I don't mind telling you, old boy, I've been hurt," Mr. Pocock said. "I've had a jerk. I haven't told a bloody soul so far, but I'll tell you. *Last year I started living on my capital.*"

Rogers turned his back on Mr. Pocock and affected to look up the road for traffic. It was empty. All lights in the village houses were out. He felt a stirring of the bowels. His wife did not know, he hardly let himself know—but he, too, had passed the crest of his life, he, too, was beginning the first harassed footsteps downhill, crumbling away to pieces like a town in a fog, and no one, hitherto, to watch or share the process. Rogers also had started living on his capital.

After this, day by day, they sought each other out like two dogs. First of all they were halting and suspicious. Rogers said: "Have you been painting, Mr. Pocock?" but this was not, he discovered, a welcome question. Mr. Pocock replied that he was sizing up the situation. Midday, Mr. Pocock could always be found sizing things up at The Grapes or The Waggoner. He was sizing up and settling in. And, anyway, he hadn't been feeling too well lately.

"Been having trouble with my foot," said Mr. Pocock defiantly at Rogers.

"It's the weight you carry," said Rogers. "I get it myself."

Mr. Pocock, as one heavy drinker to another, appreciated the tact of that lie.

"I keep clear of doctors, old boy," said Mr. Pocock. "Always have."

"They cut you down," said Rogers, emptying his glass.

"All wrong, old boy," said Mr. Pocock. "Want to kill you."

At night they met like lovers. They were religious drinkers. Whisky was Mr. Pocock's religion, beer was the faith of Rogers. An active faith ranges widely. After the public-houses of the village there were two or three on the main road. The headlights of cars howling through the dark to the coast picked out two balloons in coats and trousers, bouncing and blowing down the road. Dramas halted them.

"What's that, old boy?"

"Rabbit."

"No, old boy, not a rabbit. It was a fox. I know a fox."

"I reckon it was a stoat."

The point became intricate under the stars.

"Bring Mr. Pocock in to supper one evening," Mrs. Rogers said. She was a plump, practical woman, with hair set like a teacake. She was a one-time nurse, abnormally good-tempered, pleasantly unimaginative. She ate well and enjoyed the anxiety of being the business management of an exhibit like her husband. Incapable herself of his deterioration, hers was the craving, so strong in the orderly and new, for its opposite, the romantic ruin. Rogers, like many men, and especially drinking men, who neglect their wives and are slowly ruining their families, had an ideal picture of his family in his mind, a picture to which his fancy was always putting more delicate touches of reminiscence. For, like all the world beyond his hazy corpulence, his family became remote, a little farther away each day, like a memory of an old master.

"Bloody funny thing, old boy," Mr. Pocock said. "When I paint a picture, I get the feeling I have for a woman."

It was Rogers's feeling about his own picture, of his family, that private masterpiece of his. Rogers wasn't interested in any other pictures; Mr. Pocock wasn't interested in domestic life. And The Crown was placed strategically between their homes.

About once every couple of months, Mr. Pocock hinted, he "broke out." He always had. He always would. There was a large manufacturing town with a river, pleasure-boats and a Hippodrome twenty miles away, where life, said Rogers, abounded. He and Mr. Pocock put roses in their buttonholes, cigars in their mouths, and went. Rogers explained that he hadn't seen quite so much life since he was married, but when he was a youngster . . . Oh, dear. This stirred up memories in Mr. Pocock. They arrived and, to make a start, went to the station buffet. After this the past was vivid. They went to the Hippodrome for the second act of a play about divorce. The seats were narrow and Mr. Pocock said he couldn't breathe. They left. Mr. Pocock said all this modern stuff was dirty. Nothing but sex. (What's yours, old boy?) Dirt, like Epstein and Cézanne.

The last train back was the twelve seventeen. It brought the Hippodrome people. For a long time the station with its hoardings and iron and glass façade seemed unattainable, but at last, after a long time on the kerb opposite, they rushed it. The train was crowded. Rogers had been sorry to leave the Hippodrome. He smiled, wagging his head, thinking about it, then he began to laugh and nudge his neighbours. They were soon entertained by Rogers. It was like the old days.

"I've been divorced today," Rogers suddenly said; "and he's my co-respondent." Mr. Pocock at once offered him a cigarette. Rogers refused.

"Why do you refuse my cigarettes, old boy?" Mr. Pocock asked abruptly. He was out for a quarrel.

"Do you think I want your wife?" exclaimed Mr. Pocock angrily. Rogers laughed idiotically.

"Because you're a swine if you do," said Mr. Pocock.

But they didn't fight. They got out at their station, helped out by the passengers, and the guard, while the engine-driver watched from the cab. They passed Rogers's villas.

"Damned awful, old boy," said Mr. Pocock.

"Come in," said Rogers when they got to his house.

A look of sobered terror came into Mr. Pocock's face. "Your wife in?" he said.

"She's in bed," Rogers said.

"Thank God," said Mr. Pocock. "I'm drunk."

"Come in," said Rogers.

"She'd hear my language," said Mr. Pocock. Rogers opened the door and led the way into the sitting-room.

Mr. Pocock sat down while Rogers went to the whisky bottle.

"It's empty, old man," Rogers said, looking blankly at Mr. Pocock.

"Thank God, old boy." Mr. Pocock stood appalled, like a man who had never been in an inhabited house before. He looked shocked. He saw with horror the cretonne-covered sofa, the photographs, the slim silver vases with maidenhair fern in them.

"She's taken the other one away and put this one here."

"Women," said Mr. Pocock.

They stared at each other.

"Come round to my place," said Mr. Pocock.

Still talking, they went out, leaving the door open. A woman's head appeared at the window.

"Alfred!" the voice called.

Rogers stopped and stared at Mr. Pocock. Mr. Pocock stared back like a fierce dog at Rogers.

"Better answer, old boy," said Mr. Pocock, banging his stick on the ground.

"Yes," called Rogers.

"Had a good time?" said the woman's voice. They could not see her in the darkness, but Mr. Pocock raised his hat.

"Better go," he whispered.

He went off alone. Rogers followed him at last. Mr. Pocock's house was the last of a row of labourers' cottages, one room and the scullery downstairs and two little rooms up. Now Rogers was shocked by what he saw. In the downstairs room was an old bit of carpet laid to the edge of a cooking range, and the carpet was stained with grease. Tins and the remains of a meal were on the table. Mr. Pocock used only one of the rooms upstairs. They went up. Its boards were bare. There was a suitcase on the floor and there was an iron bed and a chair. The place smelled of mice and also of the smoking candle stuck on the mantelpiece. They sat down.

"That's what I ought to have done—got married," said Mr. Pocock. His face looked greenish in the candlelight. "Bloody lonely without a woman, old boy.

"There's a woman," Mr. Pocock exclaimed violently. There were canvases stacked against the dirty wall. He turned one round. He filled his glass. What Rogers saw shocked him. It was the picture of a thin, dark-haired woman sitting on a bed, naked. Not lascivious, not beautiful, not enticing, just naked and seeming to say: "It don't feel natural, I mean having nothing on."

"Oh dear, oh dear," was all Rogers could say. He went hot. It was the painting of the bed that shocked him. Mr. Pocock seemed to him a monster.

Mr. Pocock began to boast and Rogers hardly listened. There was a bottle of whisky. Rogers's eye kept going with astonishment to the picture. A dancer, Mr. Pocock said. He knew all the stage crowd, he said. Could have had her, he said. Words and words came out of Mr. Pocock, gobbling and strutting like a blown-out turkey in the room, words making an ever-softening roar in the set, cold silence of the cottage where no clock ticked.

Suddenly Rogers had a shock. It was daylight. He had been asleep on the floor and the sun was shining on him.

He gaped. There was Mr. Pocock on the bed. Still holding his cane, the rings shining on his podgy fingers, which had grey hair at the knuckles, Mr. Pocock lay. He was snoring. His body heaved up and down in the loud suit, like a marquee with the wind loose in it. Remote in sleep with his picture above him, Mr. Pocock looked sacred and innocent, in the bare room.

The spring came with its glassy winds, its air going warm and cold and the lengthening light becoming frail in the evenings. Rogers and Mr. Pocock were both ill. Rogers received illness as part of his burden; he was more aware of his wife and of his children when he was ill. But Mr. Pocock was an aggressive invalid. He saw conspiracy. He was terrified and he blustered to conceal this and made war on the doctor. He would not stay in bed.

"Kimble thinks he's got me, old boy. Knocked off my beer and cut me down to two whiskies a day. It isn't right! It isn't human! He's got to be fair."

When Rogers got up they met in the pub.

"I've had seven, old boy," Mr. Pocock said. "But if Kimble says anything to you about what I drink—it's two. I've treated him fairly. I've been reasonable. That man wants to kill me. But not a word to him! You've got to deal with these doctors."

First of all when he had come to the village Mr. Pocock had a charwoman to clean and wash up for him, but he was hardly ever in his cottage and he ate at any time. He had got rid of the charwoman and looked after himself. He had brought his bed downstairs when he was first ill because he had been frightened in the upstairs room. One night he felt tired and low. A bus-ride had upset him. He went to bed early. In the middle of the night he woke up in black terror. He felt sick and he was fainting, and he was sure he was in London. He reached for his stick and knocked on the floor to make the woman come up to him, the woman whose portrait Rogers had seen and who lived downstairs. All the night sleeping and waking he dreamed he was knocking to make himself heard on the floor. For the model, then for Mrs. Rogers, then for his mother.

In the morning he could hardly move. Then he remembered he was on the ground floor and had been knocking on the carpet which covered the flags, which covered the earth. He had been knocking on the hard crust of the earth. All he could do was to crawl from his bed to the cupboard where the whisky bottle was and then crawl back. But he called no one; he stiffened with anger if there were any signs of anyone coming to the door. He was not going to be caught like this. He was not going to admit anything. He cursed the doctor.

It was two days before Mr. Pocock's illness was discovered.

"Mr. Pocock's ill," Rogers's wife brought the news. She knew all the illnesses of the village.

Rogers sat up, alert. He was at once frightened for himself. He did not want to see Mr. Pocock before the doctor had been. Rogers sat in his chair, unable to move. He wanted to do something for Mr. Pocock, but he was paralysed. He sat in a stupor of inertia and incompetence. He looked appealingly at his wife. She got a car and had Mr. Pocock brought to the house.

"It's the bloody sugar, old boy," murmured Mr. Pocock with a regal weariness as three men carried him upstairs.

Mrs. Rogers was glad when the ambulance came that, for once in his life, Mr. Pocock had had a real home with a woman to look after him.

That was the last of him.

A dealer came down to look at the pictures after the funeral, but he would not take them. One or two others came hoping for frames. But the twenty-odd canvases there had no frames on them. A brother came down to clear up Mr. Pocock's affairs.

"We never corresponded," said the brother. Of all things he was a clergyman.

Two fair and tall young men in suède shoes and pull-overs, so alike they looked like a pair of tap-dancers, turned up at the same time. They *were* tap-dancers.

"Terrible," they said. They were looking at the pictures; but Rogers supposed they referred to the death, the poverty of the house—or perhaps the clergyman. Rogers had been told by Mr. Pocock that in reward for his kindness he might have one of the pictures, but he did not know which to choose. The only picture he felt anything about was the picture on the bedroom wall, the nude. He detested it.

"Women," he thought, "that must have been Mr. Pocock's trouble. Not drink. Oh dear, not drink, women." So when everyone had gone, he took the small picture, wrapped it in newspaper, and put it in a shed in his garden. That picture, and a corkscrew, which he stuffed in his pocket, because a corkscrew was useful. He took the picture because, without knowing it, he felt it symbolized the incomprehensibility of the existence of other people. The corkscrew was the man he knew, the picture the man he did not know at all. He thought that one day he had better destroy the picture—in case a bad impression of his friend was formed.

And so, slipping out of the funeral, keeping in the background afterwards, staying in his own house, Rogers eluded the memory of Mr. Pocock. Rogers was forgetting everything as he grew larger. He forgot yesterday, last week, last year—he dreamed through time like an idle whale, with its mouth open, letting what would come into it. He contemplated through a haze his own work of art—his family. He watched his wife's second chin when she gave her practical laugh. His two girls swam up to him like fish. They were an extra pair of eyes and ears for him. They saw things quickly. They laughed at things long before he heard them. On Saturdays he took them to the cinema. Every Saturday. A year passed, and then two years. He never said now: "We had Mr. Pocock, the painter, here." He had learned his lesson.

And then came the most extraordinary fortnight of Rogers's life. He was with his daughters in the cinema. They were watching a gangster film. A film four years old: they only got the old films in these country towns. Two men were going quietly up the stairs of a hotel and then along a corridor. It was at night. They were making for the room where a Mexican, behind closed doors, was covering a girl with a gun. But they were not sure of the room. They hesitated at doors. It was trying for Rogers, because his mind was still in the pillared lounge below, reminded by it that he was living on his capital. How had the Mexican got the girl in the room? Then the two men stopped. One said: "O.K.," and they pushed open a door marked 13 and switched on the light. Rogers's daughters jumped in their seats and a shout of laughter came from the audience. A large, round-faced man with a huge stomach was lying on a bed in check suit and knickerbockers, asleep and snoring, with a bottle, rolled on its side, near by.

"Mr. Pocock!" the girls shouted.

It was. Rogers's heart went small in his chest and seemed to shoot like a stone in his throat. The gangsters rolled their eyes ironically. The audience laughed. One of the gangsters picked up the bottle and made to prod Mr. Pocock with it. The audience sent up blast after blast of laughter; especially shrill laughter went up first from the children in front. The other gangster touched his friend's arm, raised his eyes to the ceiling, and said: "R.I.P." Wave after wave of laughter passed by as the snores stopped and then began again like a car toiling and missing uphill.

"It's Mr. Pocock, Mr. Pocock, Dad," Rogers's daughters cried, jumping on their seats. And the laughter went on. For the achievement of Mr. Pocock was that he did nothing, nothing at all. He just lay and snored, the human balloon.

Rogers couldn't believe it.

It became urgent for him after this to decide the matter. Films in the town moved down the road, ten or twenty miles to the next place in the week. Four times he followed that film in a fortnight. Four times he saw that scene. It was unmistakably Pocock. And each place the audience roared until one night at the Hippodrome, where it was the big picture, he heard a packed house shout out with enthusiasm at Pocock's sublime unconsciousness. He had three minutes of the film, but those three minutes brought the house down.

It terrified Rogers. Pocock was lying exactly as Rogers had seen him that morning after the binge when he had waked up in Pocock's cottage. He dreaded that the eyes would open, the voice speak. And then, after the sixth time of seeing the film, as he walked home down the village street, he longed to meet that preposterous figure, to slap him on the back and tell him. He longed for him to wake up on the screen and hear that helpless applause, to see those wide-open laughing mouths. "He kept it quiet," thought Rogers. And the drowning soul saw no irony in it all; but rather felt that life was incomprehensible no more. Something had been settled.

When he took the picture from his garden shed and burned it on the rubbish heap soon after, Rogers heard in the husky roar of the flame the sound of a soul set free, all stain removed.

The Sniff

It is hard to say what the present situation is, whether it is improving or whether it is becoming one of those everlasting situations that mark the characters and memories of children. These have all noticed their mother's habit of looking up from her sewing, raising her straight nose, and giving a sniff as if she were going to say: "Pop outside and see what's burning"—that sniff has become established since their father came back from the war. Her candid children glance at one another and then, without self-betrayal, they copy the sniff. The last one copies it loudly. It is not a snuffling nor a weeping sound; it is alert, questing and suspicious: "I think I smell burning *again*." After a few of these sniffs there is a look of wooden melancholy on her face and she sighs, she looks sullenly up at the window and the continuing daylight. She listens for footsteps upstairs and one would say that (for her) the ceiling is like dirty thawing snow, trodden all over, by the hundreds of footmarks of someone who will not come down. She is a woman of thirty-seven who has dull, fair hair, a long face, warm-tempered grey eyes; and her arms and elbows are going all day long. She has what she calls "a woman's life."

Mrs. N.'s husband (who is the man upstairs) is her age and works in the boys' outfitting department of a big shop. He is one of those men who like to see other people promoted over their heads. The manager, Mr. Frederick, for example, began in the shop, at the same counter with him. Between these two, Mr. Frederick and her husband, Mrs. N. feels—how can she put it?—she feels that her heart has become a cage and that she cannot get out of it. Perhaps "cage" is the wrong word; for what she really feels is that she is enclosed not in bars but in a smell. She really means that: a literal smell. It is not a strong smell, for sometimes it is hardly noticeable; but it is always there, and on Saturdays and Sundays it is openly there, strong, animal, and violent; so that she gets up restlessly and goes round the house unconsciously following it, searching for it, until at last she finds it. And when she finds it, she stands, as still as stone, unable to speak. Her husband looks up and tells her that what she needs is a holiday.

Mr. N. is not as tall as she is; indeed, he is not as tall as most people. His large astounded dark-blue eyes are raised under caterpillar eyebrows as if he were standing on tiptoe. He has a wide swarthy face—though he lost colour when he came back from the war—a low, monkeyish forehead, and a cap of black curls over his head. The widely opened eyes appear to be talking with astonishment, though in fact his lips hardly talk at all. He is astonished by the goods he sells, the customers he sees, by every woman he sees; by his wife, his children. Astonished at being married now fifteen years, astonished by what happened to him during the war. There is only one thing that does not astonish him.

When he came back from the war she saw with relief he had aged as much as she had. Those gazing doll's eyes of his, so childish and so surprised, were beginning to look out of the stupor of middle age. He looked like a man who is going to live on his kindness to himself. "One good thing" (she thought with pleasure, with pity and the spite that comes of dealing with children all day for years), "one good thing" (she thought), "the girls won't be after you." In the old days at the shop the girls were mad about him and he was mad about them. But only mad. Before she was married to him, she would have done anything to get him away from them; but once she was married she did not mind. That was the one certain control of him: the shop. The hateful thing about the war was that neither she nor the shop ruled him, and what he would be like then she could not imagine. What had happened to him during the war? He told her everything, but surely there was something else? He came back. She watched the crust of Italy and Africa pass from his skin and saw the paler man underneath appear.

"I used to think," he would begin.

Think! Imagine it, he had time to think! For five years she had been trailing after children, cooking, cleaning, mending, queueing, and he came home and told her he used to "think." Well, what was the marvellous "thought"? "Five years out of our lives," he said. Good heavens, do you call that a "thought"? There was no time to waste, you must get what you can out of life, he said. The children might be calling and she would be glad to leave the room. No wonder he never got on at the shop, if that was what he called "thinking."

When she went out shopping she listened to some of the other women. To the woman next door:

"They're lazy. The Army made them forget what life is like. They go round looking for one another like dogs. Don't worry. They'll settle down."

What the other women were saying with their eyes and sometimes with their tongues was "I bet there's been another woman. They are doped with memory. Have *you* got a clear conscience?"

She almost wished there had been another woman, almost wished she had not got a clear conscience.

He was a good husband. On Saturday afternoons she went out and he stayed at home and looked after the children. She used to go out giving orders in all directions and came back to see which had been disobeyed. One of the satisfying things about him was that he was always reproachable. One Saturday when she came back from shopping and got to the gate of the house, she saw the lights were not lit. The curtains were not drawn.

In the hall, no light, and in the house no sound. The air was still. The coats on their hooks, the closed doors of the rooms, the silence, indicated a place absorbed in itself. And then—her heart jumped. She was in the wrong house. This place did not *smell* like hers. She was treading on some other woman's floor polish. She took a breath, and the skin of her nostrils moved to the prick of some new smell that might have been the smell of an unsweet flower, like the garlic flower. She opened the sitting-room door and, for the first time, sniffed. The smell was not in the sitting-room. She went to the foot of the stairs and again she sniffed, but there too the scent weakened. For a moment she thought another woman was in the house and, trying the dining-room, she expected to find her sitting there, an odorous creature with bare, vaccinated arms and hot flowered lap, painting her nails, but the dining-room was empty. The scent strengthened as she approached the kitchen. Perhaps he had washed the dog, polished the brass. She opened the kitchen door and the wild smell raced to her.

"Where's the light?" she called out.

In the kitchen the daylight had decayed. He was sitting at the kitchen table with a box of oil paints before him, his thumb in a gaudy palette. He was painting a small picture of the kitchen with its plate rack and sink, and beside him the children stood watching silently. Even he did not look up, but went on painting.

"Ssh," said the eldest girl as her mother went to put her bag on the table. "Don't jog him."

The children moved nearer to protect the sacred figure of

their father, who had suddenly, gloriously, without warning, taken up painting.

"Look," the children said. They opened a roll of sketches he had done in the war: crayon drawings, water colours of soldiers, the pyramids, sand dunes, Italian towns. She could not speak.

"You never told me," she said.

She gazed at his secret life with consternation. The look of astonishment had gone from him. He looked determined, ashamed, and unnaturally boastful.

"I thought I'd have a go at the old oils," he said in a dishonest voice. She looked at the sink. The washing up was done. The room was clean. Newspaper had been spread on the table. He was wearing an old jacket. Nothing (she had to agree) was "wrong."

She laughed.

"What a blessed kid you are!" she said. "Where's these poor children's teas?"

"We don't want any tea," the children said together.

"I bought myself some paints," he said in an ashamed voice. "Secondhand."

He put his brushes down.

"No," cried the children. "You haven't finished."

"The light's gone," he said. And he spoke so sadly that the children turned indignantly towards the window at the fading sky. His wife switched on the light and she could have died laughing when she saw his face change.

"It's wrong," he said. "It's the perspective. I'll have to start again."

"Is this what they taught you in the Army?" she said.

"Yes," he said. "The only thing. Time drags, you've got to do something."

Their neighbour was a dirty, gleeful woman bobbing up and down with curiosity about everything. She wore horn-rimmed spectacles and she used to stand on a box and look over the fence by the kitchen door. Her shoulders were out of sight and the head appeared to rest on top of the fence by itself, like a hairy bird's egg.

"We don't know what they've been through," the neighbour said.

"A man wants a hobby," his wife explained.

"Some men spend it on drink and some on women or the dogs," said the neighbour.

"He" (his wife nodded to her husband, who was crouching over his oil paints on a kitchen chair at the end of the garden), "he doesn't even smoke. Every night he comes home, it's the same. I wish he'd paint the kitchen."

"It keeps him in, mine's always out," said the neighbour greedily. "Has he done your picture?"

"Years ago," said his wife, "when I was in the shop all the girls were after him saying: 'Draw me, draw me,' posing for him, anyone would think they were I don't know what they thought themselves."

"Film stars," said the neighbour, tidying her hair.

"Cheapening their faces, I used to tell them," his wife said remembering.

"He asked me, but I wouldn't let him. It's funny how things begin. I said to him: 'Can't you find something better to do? Or are you soft?' " She laughed.

"What did he say?" said the neighbour.

"That's how we got married. I made him stop it," she said. He stopped drawing altogether when he was in love with her.

Now he came up from the bottom of the garden, astonished of course. Astonished by the sight of the neighbour's bodiless head balanced on the wooden fence; even more astonished when a hand came up from nowhere and removed the spectacles.

"When are you going to do my portrait?" said the neighbour with a rich and sickly smile.

The Sniff

He had no sense. A few weeks passed and he showed his pictures to Mr. Frederick, the manager.

"Mr. Frederick says I have genius," he said. That was the thing that did not astonish him.

"How that man's got on!" she said. "Climbing on other people's shoulders," she said.

"You're unfair to him," he said.

"Only because he flatters you you like him," she said.

The smell was the worst thing. Sometimes he painted flowers, sometimes a corner of the garden, sometimes he tried to turn his Italian sketches into a large oil painting; and they all smelled. He took to standing his best ones on the mantelpiece and she knew at once. They were awkward, living, chopped-off little pictures, unbearably new—not like pictures you see in a shop or a magazine—like small joints of meat. When she knew Mr. Frederick had praised them she saw that Mr. Frederick had "got on" by sheer unscrupulousness. Her husband came home, changed his jacket, and went up to the box room, and if she went there he was so absorbed he did not answer. The smell made her sniff, but he took no notice of that; he simply grunted. She sniffed. He grunted. He would sit there holding his breath for as much as a minute, and then puff it out with the labour of a man lifting a heavy piece of furniture upstairs. Sniff. Grunt. That animal grunt: that was their only conversation.

All these years trailing after children, all these years waiting for your husband to come home, all these years getting older—and then, when he did come, he didn't speak! Not much of a life for a woman.

"As long as it keeps him happy," the neighbour said. "I like a contented man."

"By the pound, in a shop," her husband said.

What began to alarm her was that this painting did not make him happy. Hear him! How he carried on, moaning and groaning! It was: "I can't paint" or "It's all wrong."

Or he got stuck and painted it all out (that was waste for you) and started again. "Well," she told him, "if I couldn't do a thing, I'd give it up, not make myself miserable. I mean, what's the use of giving yourself the pip?"

He grunted.

"You say all your life you wanted to paint; if only you could paint you'd be happy," she said. "You said I stopped you when we were married." She sniffed.

"I didn't say that," he said with astonishment. She had got a reply from him at last!

"It's what you meant," she said.

He put his brush sideways in his mouth; the brush looked like a moustache there; he gazed at her.

"Well, look at you," she said. "It makes you miserable and me miserable and the children." (That was untrue: the children loved him to paint. She could not forgive them that.) "You don't think of us. It's turned you selfish. Always breathing that stuff into your system. It's poisoning you."

He put the brush down and started explaining to her about the picture. She was not listening; she was riding her wrongs, galloping away on them; but all the same, the words that caught her ear "persp"—what was it?—"chiara"—how d'you do? His eyes got larger and larger, astonished by the difficulty he had in trying to say what was in his mind.

"You're too trustful of people, showing that picture to Mr. Frederick. He'll genius you out of the shop," she said.

"I'd be free then," he said. "An artist can't work without time and freedom. I was sort of free in the Army," he said.

"Free of me," she said.

"No, free," he said, "for the first time in my life. That's what made me start."

"Give up the shop!" she cried out.

"That's what I want to do," he said. "I give up the shop or give up my work."

"Your work!" she said. "Are you crazy or what? Here,"

she said in a panic. "You're kidding yourself. You're not an artist. Not a real artist."

She waited for his answer, anxiously fixing her look upon him. He waited a long time before answering. He seemed to be clambering over obstacles, puffing and struggling to get to something that eluded him; he failed. For he replied: "No."

"What?" she said to be sure of it.

"No," he said. "I'm not."

"Oh!" she said. And then her argument died on her tongue. If he had said "Yes" she could have had it out with him then and there. He had always been a boaster—"Look what I've done"—like a child. But his "No" shocked her. It was spoken in such a cold voice out of a frozen, obdurate, empty desolation. He might have been a marooned man, someone who has been put off alone on an ugly island. She felt an emotion that was half pity and half rage at this denial of himself. It was frightening to her, now, that he should agree with her and she said to soothe him after she had wounded him:

"Are you going to draw the woman next door? She asked you. You never offer to draw me."

"That old owl," he said. "You said you hated being drawn."

"You never asked me," she said. "Draw me—not my face.

"Like artists do," she said. "With nothing on.

"I'll let you," she said eagerly.

"Now," she said when she had taken off her clothes and sat on a chair. "This is not to be an excuse. The children will be back soon."

He was shy and uncertain.

"A painter doesn't think like that," he said. "Move your arm back. He's thinking of the composition. He's thinking of beauty."

"You don't love me," she said. "Not like you used to in

the shop. You wanted to draw me then. Now any woman would do.

"I can't keep my arm like that all the time," she said.

"Just a moment, only a moment," he said.

It was terrible. The way his astonished eyes looked at her, how composed his astonishment was. The way he measured her, as though she was in some way wrong. Imagine what the neighbours would say. Suppose one of the children came in. He grunted as he drew.

"You have a hard life," he said, suddenly talking, talking for the first time, as he drew. "Shut up with three children, always at the stove or at the sink. You don't have a chance. I often think," he said, "you never have a life, not to call it life."

Her lips straightened.

"Go on telling me," she said.

"You need a rest, a change," he said, measuring her shoulders with the pencil.

"You don't say," she said, "and who's going to give it to me?"

And then she slowly came to see what it was that she hated about this painting of his. *He* had a life, a life she couldn't share, a secret life she could not enter. Wonderfully kind he sounded—wonderfully kind, just like a man who is being unfaithful to you. Telling her. Telling her to go and have a life of her own. She sat there, naked, ironical, muttering her thoughts. "You thank your stars," she said (but not to him), "I don't go after a life of my own. A woman's life is a man, a child, another person. If I had had a life of my own, it wouldn't be you."

"Oh, don't move," he said.

"If I had had a life of my own, as you have, it would be a man." She saw now clearly how it was with him: this painting was an infidelity. It was like another woman. She took a long breath. She smelled the sharp smell of the paint and she remembered what she had thought at once when she smelled it in the house: another woman was there. He was unfaithful to her.

She got up without warning and covered herself with a vest. It humiliated her to sit before him.

That is still the situation. Mr. Frederick, the manager, has been to the house. He is a shy, hard-mouthed man with a narrow face and grey hair. Unmarried. He is the kind of man who has to have some power and usually you see his kind standing for hours outside chicken runs at the end of a garden, fancying he is the cock. You can see he's gone farther with this husband of hers; leads him round like a tame bear. The fool! The enemy! "Didn't I say he wished him no good?" He has bought one of her husband's pictures for ten pounds.

"Your husband is a born artist," he says to her. "He needs time. He needs peace. He needs . . . He needs . . ."

She can see he is dropping hints to her. What have they been saying about her? She says nothing. She just hates Mr. Frederick. And yet—she can't understand why she does this, why she should enslave herself to this new mistress of his—she tiptoes to his room at dinner-time with a tray; if he is working she puts the tray down without a word, so as not to disturb him, and goes out. She asks no questions. She makes no difficulties. She keeps the children away. And then one of the children begins to sniff, the next one sniffs, and the third one sniffs louder; she herself goes into the sitting-room and sniffs again, sniffing round the walls. Where is it? What has he done with it? Has he brought it down yet—the new picture?

The Scapegoat

There were long times when we were at peace and when the world left us alone. We could go down Earl Street and, although we did not like the place and it felt strange to us and the' women stared down from the windows and a child here and there might call out a name after us, we just walked on thinking of something else. But we were always more at ease and more ourselves, even in the quietest times of truce, when we had turned the corner by the hop ware-house and had got back into Terence Street, which was our own. The truth is that you can't live without enemies, and the best enemies are the ones nearest home; and though we sometimes went out to the Green to boo the speakers, and some of our lads went after the Yids or joined a procession up west, that was idleness and distraction. The people we hated were not a mile away on the main road where the trams and the buses are and you don't know one man from the next; no, the people we hated were round the corner, next door, in Earl Street. They were, we used to say, a different class of people from ourselves altogether.

I don't know why, but if there was any trouble in the world, we turned out and attacked them. I don't know either how these things began. You would know there was trouble coming when you heard the voices of the children getting shriller and more excited, until their cries became rhythmic like the pulse of native war cries in the forest. We were, indeed, lost in a *jungle* of streets. Somehow the children would have sticks, old pieces of board, and stones in their hands and they would be rushing in groups to the hop warehouse and jeering and then scattering back. A similar thing would be happening in Earl Street. Usually this happened in the warm long evenings of the summer. Then, after the children, the thing got hold of the women and they came down from their windows where they had been watching and scratching their arms, very hot and restless, and would stand at their doorsteps and start shouting at their children. A stone would fly up and then the women would be down in the middle of the street.

It might take a day to work up or it might take longer. You would get the Earl Street girls going down our street talking in loud voices daring us, and our young lads would stand by saying nothing until the girls got to the corner. And then those girls would have to bolt. Towards closing time the Gurneys, the fighting family in Earl Street, would be out and we had our Blackers and then it was a question of who came out of the Freemasons and how he came out. But perhaps nothing would happen and we would just go down Earl Street after dark and merely kick their milk bottles down the basements.

This has been going on ever since the old people can remember. When the war came we knew everyone in Earl Street was a spy or a Hun or a Conchie. The Great War, for us, was between Earl Street and Terence Street. They had a V.C. and we hadn't, though we had a bunch of other stuff and one man who escaped from the Turks and was in the papers; and though we did our best, the tea we gave was nothing to the tea they did in Earl Street for their V.C. Where they got the money from was the puzzle. Thirty-two pounds. Some of our women said the Earl Street girls must have been on the streets; and at the Freemasons, the men said half of Earl Street were nothing but bloody pensioners. The police came in before we had the question settled. But when the war ended, things changed. Half of our lot was out of work and when we went down Earl Street we would see half of their lot out of work too, and Earl Street did not seem quite so strange to us. One street seemed to blend into the other. This made some of our lot think and they gave their steps an extra clean to show there was a difference between Earl Street and Terence Street after all.

In the years that followed, sometimes we were up on Earl Street, sometimes we were down. We were waiting for some big event. It did not come for a long time and a stranger might have thought that the old frontiers had gone and the reign of universal peace was upon us. It was not. The Jubilee came and we saw our chance. Earl Street had collected thirty-two pounds for its V.C.'s tea party. We reckoned we would top that for the Jubilee. We would collect forty.

There was a red-haired Jew in our street called Lupinsky. He was a tailor. He was round-shouldered from bending over the table, and his eyes were weak from working by gas at night. In the rush season he and his family would be up past midnight working. He was a keen man. He came out in pimples, he was so keen. Lupinsky saw everything before any of us. He saw the Jubilee before the King himself. He had got his house full of bunting and streamers and Union Jacks. "Get in at the early doors," he said. "What'll you have?" he used to say to us when we went to his shop. "*Rule, Britannia*, or *God Save the King*?" "Who's that?" we said. "The King of the Jews?" "Getcha," said Lupinsky. "He's dead. Didn't you hear?" He raked in the money. They had another Jew in Earl Street doing the same. "I say!" called Lupinsky. "I say!"—we used to call him "I-say-what'll-you-have"—"Cohen's sold one hundred and twenty yards to Terence Street and you've only done seventy." So we doubled. "I say," says Lupinsky. "I say. When you going

215

to start collecting? They got ten quid in Earl Street and you haven't started."

And this was true. The trouble was we couldn't agree upon who should collect. We had had a nasty experience with the club a few years back. And then Lupinsky was hot for doing it himself. He'd got the bunting. He'd seen it coming. He'd even got boxes. He'd thought of everything. We had nothing against Lupinsky, but when we saw him raking in the money on his God Saves and Kiss-me-quicks and his flags of all the nations, we thought he was collecting enough as it was. He might mix up the two collections. "No," we said to Lupinsky. "You're doing your bit, we'll do the rest." "That's O.K.," Lupinsky said. He never bore resentment, he was too keen. "But I hear Earl Street's up to twelve ten." He wasn't upset with us, but he couldn't bear to see us shilly-shallying around while Earl Street walked away with it. "If you don't trust me," he said, "can't you trust yourselves? I don't know what's happened to this street." And he spat from the top of his doorstep into the gutter.

Lupinsky was wrong about us. We trust each other. There is not a man in Terence Street you cannot trust. In that nasty business we had with the club, the man was not a Terence Street man. We could trust one another. But we were frightened. Forty pounds! We thought. That's a big sum. We didn't like the handling of it. There wasn't one of us who had seen forty pounds in his life. The Blackers, a good fighting lot, were terrified. Albert Smith and his uncle were the most likely, but they said they were single and didn't like the idea. And we, for some reason, thought a single man wasn't right for the job. And the wives, the married ones, though eagerly wanting their husbands to do it, were so afraid the honour would go to someone else that they said to give it to a married man was tempting Provi-

216

dence. Lupinsky went down the street almost in tears saying
Earl Street had touched seventeen ten.

Then suddenly we saw the right man had been staring us
in the face all the time. He was not single and he was not
married. He was a widower, made serious by death: Art
Edwards. We chose Art Edwards and he agreed.

Art Edwards was a man of forty-seven and the moment
he agreed, we were proud of him. He was a grey-haired
man, not very talkative and of middle height, very patient
and looked you straight in the face. He lived with his sister,
who looked after his two children, he had a fruit stall in
the main road—he had been there for twenty years—and
every Sunday he used to go alone with a bunch of flowers
for his wife's grave at the cemetery. The women admired
him very much for doing this. He never changed. His house
was the neatest house in our street and he never seemed to
get richer or poorer. He just went on the same.

He had been a widower a good long time, too, and some
thought he ought to marry again. The women were curious
about him and said you couldn't but respect a man who
didn't take a second, and Art was held up as a model. This
didn't prevent many of them running after him and spreading
the rumour afterwards that his sister was a woman who
wouldn't let a man call his soul his own. But the way Art
mourned for the dead and kept faithful to The First, the
ONE AND ONLY, as the women said, was striking. Some of
the men said that being a model wasn't healthy and that if
they had been in Art's shoes they would muck around on
the quiet. They wondered why the hell he didn't, yet admired
him for his restraint. Some of us couldn't have lived with
temptation all those years without slipping up.

Art had put a black band on his sleeve when his wife
died and had worn it ever since. But when he started collecting for the tea we had the feeling he had put off his

217

mourning and had come alive again. We were pleased about this because, with his modest, retiring ways, we hardly knew him. "It will bring him out," we said. He came round with his little red book and his tin and we said: "What's it now, Art? How we doin'?" Art was slow at adding up, but accurate. He told us. We made a big effort and we touched the ten-pound mark pretty soon.

This woke us up and made us feel good, but Lupinsky came round and said it wasn't any bloody good at all. They'd touched nineteen pounds in Earl Street. So one of the women said they'd help Art. He didn't want this, or his sister didn't. So she joined in, too, to keep the other women off him. They knocked at his door at all hours and stopped him in the street. And when she saw this, his sister put on her best hat and coat and went round and stopped their men. The result was everyone was collecting and came round to Art and said:

"Here y'are, Art. One and eight," or "Here y'are, Art, eight and six."

And two of the Blacker girls had a fight because one said the other wasn't collecting fair but was cheapening herself to get the money. For we touched seventeen and went on to twenty-one.

The night we passed Earl Street some of our girls went out and just walked down Earl Street telling them. They didn't like it. A crowd from Earl Street came round and called "Down with the Yids," outside Lupinsky's. Then Earl Street picked up and passed us again. We went round to Art and planked down more money. Art got out his book and he couldn't write it down fast enough.

"Where do you keep it, Art?" we said.

He showed us a box in the cupboard. It was a fine sight, all that money.

His sister said: "Art's picked up a bit in the High Street."

We looked at him as if he were a hero. " 'Slike business,"
he said. "You've got to go out for it."

We looked with wonder at him. We had chosen the right
man. It was bringing him out. And he had ideas too. He got
some of the kids to go out at night with tins.

We passed Earl Street and they passed us. Then we passed
them again. It was ding-dong all the time. Lupinsky flew in
and out with the latest like a wasp and stung us to more.
Art Edwards, he said, had no life in him. After this it became
madness. People got out their savings.

There was a funny case at Harry Law's. He was a boozer,
a big, heavy man, very particular in the house and very religious. Some nights when he was bad he used to beat his
wife and we used to look down into their basement window
wondering what would be happening inside, for something
usually was happening. There were often shouts and curses
and screams coming from that room and then times, which
made you uncomfortable, when everything was quiet. Harry
Law was often out of a job. Mrs. Law was a timid woman
and everyone was sorry for her. She used to go up to the
Freemasons and look through the door at him. She was a
thin, round-shouldered woman, always anxious about her
husband and sorry that he made a fool of himself, for he got
pompous when he was drunk and she hated the way people
laughed at him. He used to say she had no ambition and he
had dragged her out of the gutter. She said: "*Down* into
the gutter, you mean." They used to have guilty arguments
like this for hours, each boasting they were better than the
other and wondering all the time why they had got into
their present situation. Then Harry Law would go to church
so as to feel good and find out why, and his wife used to
stop at home and think about it, too. She would put her
arms round him and love him when he came back. And he
would be all right for a few days until he got some scheme

into his head for making money. When he had the scheme he would go out and get drunk again.

Harry Law wanted to show everyone that he was a man of ideas and ambitions, and better than the rest of us in Terence Street. He used to dress up on Sundays. He used to say he had been better off once and had had a shop. The truth was, as his wife bitterly told everyone, he'd always been the same; up and down all his life. She couldn't bear other people laughing at him, but she used to tear his reputation to bits herself and get great pleasure out of doing it.

It was just at the height of our madness that he came into the Freemasons and instead of cadging for drinks, he began to order freely. A funny thing had happened, he said. And he said, in his lordly voice: "I want Art Edwards." It turned out that he had been going across the room while his wife was out and had tripped up on something on the floor. There was a bump in the lino. Being a very inquisitive man who never had anything to do, he knelt down and felt the lump. "I thought it was dirt," he said. One of the things he always said about his wife was that she was dirty. He was a very clean man himself. He decided to take up the lino, and underneath he found a lump of money wrapped up in notes. It was his wife's savings.

That was why Harry Law was lording it at the Freemasons. He had hardly given a penny to the collection, but now, when everyone was present, he was going to make a great gesture and show his greatness. When Art came in, he said: "Here Art. Have a fiver."

We all stared. Harry Law was leaning against the bar with the notes in the tips of his fingers as if they were dirt, like a duke giving a tip.

At that moment his wife came in.

"That's mine," she screamed. "It's mine."

There was a row and Art wouldn't take the money. Everyone said that a man hadn't the right to take his wife's money.

But Harry said: "What!" Wasn't his money as good as anybody's and we said: "Yes, Harry, but that belongs to your missus." She was crying and he kept saying: "Go home. I'll teach you to come round here. It is my money. I earned it."

This was awkward. Between her tears, with her hands covering her face, Mrs. Law was saying she had saved it. He was always ruining them, so she had to save. Still, if he'd earned it, it was his.

"Take that money," says Harry, dropping it like a lord on the floor. The notes fell down, we all looked at them, and no one moved. Mr. Bell of the Freemasons got a laugh by saying we were littering up his bar with paper. Then Harry turned his back and we picked it up and were going to give it to Mrs. Law, but Harry says in a threatening voice: "That's Art's. For the collection. I reckon I got Earl Street knocked silly." •

That part of the statement was irresistible. While we hesitated, Art said: "Give it here, then. I'll look after it."

Lupinsky, who had been sitting there all the time clutching his hands and his eyes starting out of his head with misery at the sight of money lying in the sand, gave a shout.

"That's the boy," he said. "We've got 'em."

We all felt uncomfortable with Harry and we went away in ones and twos, and Mrs. Law went out still crying. After she went out, Art went too and when we got down the street, Art stopped and told Mrs. Law he wasn't going to take the money and he made her take it back. She clutched it with both hands and looked at him like a dog with gratitude.

That night half the men in Terence Street wanted to take up their lino and sat up late arguing with their wives; but the madness was still in the air, especially when Earl Street, hearing our news, sent all their kids up west and passed us. There was a fight in the High Street between our kids and the Earl Street kids, and one of ours lost her box. But there was nothing in it except stones. They put stones in to make a rattle so that people would think they were doing well. If there had been any money in that box there wouldn't have been a pane of glass in Earl Street left.

"They've passed us," the cry went down our street. In the middle of this Mrs. Law came over to Art and gave him back the money. She made him take it.

"Your husband made you," says Art.

"Him," she said scornfully. "He don't know anything about it. I told him you gave it me back and he said, 'A good thing too,' he's feeling sorry for himself. I'll teach him to touch my money, I said. If there's going to be any giving in this house, it's me that's got the money. I'm going to teach my husband a lesson," she said.

This surprised Art, for he had been very sorry for poor Mrs. Law and had shown it. But I've no doubt she was tired of being pitied. That money was all she had. She was going to show us that the Laws had their pride and she wasn't going to let them down. Only *she* was going to give it.

Her eyes shone and were sharp. They were greenish miserly grey eyes, yet she was not miserly. Now she was proud and not bedraggled with tears and misery, she looked jubilant and cunning. She had been a gay, quick-tongued woman in her time.

"I kept it under the floor. That was wrong of me," she said. "I oughter have put it in the Post Office."

She said she knew her husband was right. It was not right to hide money.

Everyone in Terence Street had supposed Mrs. Law to be a poor, timid, beaten soul and Art had always thought the same, he said; but now he said that she had some spirit. She had opened her heart to him because he had been kind to her and now she said, very proudly, that he should come and have a chat with her husband. She took Art triumphantly to her basement just to show her husband there were other men in the world. Old Harry Law saw this at once—he was always on his dignity—so he just talked largely to Art about the shops he had had, the ups and downs, his financial adventures. Investments, he called them. We had all heard of investments but none of us had ever had any. If he had his life over again, Harry Law said, he'd invest every penny.

"There's a man," Art said when he went, "who doesn't practice what he preaches." But he respected Harry's preaching though he despised him a bit. And Harry said: "There's a man who stays the same all his life. Never made a penny, never lost a penny. The only money he's got," said Harry, "isn't his—this collection."

And Harry asked him how much it was. There were some thirty-odd pounds, Art said.

Harry respected him when he heard that and said with a sigh: "Money makes money."

When Art got back, his sister was short with him. "Going after other men's wives," she said. And she lectured him about Mrs. Law. It had been such a warm, pleasant, friendly evening over at Harry Law's that Art was hurt about this.

"Him and her," he said, "has got more brains than you think. They've lived, all right. They've had their ups and downs."

"He's a boozer."

"We've all got our faults. He's had his ups and downs."

And that was the phrase he kept repeating. It fascinated him. He felt generous. It came to him that he had never felt anything for years. He had just gone on standing in the High Street by the stall. He had never taken a holiday. He had never bought himself anything he wanted. He had never done anything. It startled him—but he suddenly did not want his wife, who was in the grave. The street had chosen him, singled him out above all others, and there he stood naked, nothing. He was shy about his nonentity. He felt a curious longing for ups and downs.

223

The Scapegoat

You will say: how did we know what Art Edwards thought? That was the strange thing: we did know. We knew as if he had told us, as if we were inside him. You see, because we had singled him out he was, in a sense, ourselves. We could see him thinking and feeling and doing what we would. He had taken the burden off us. By doing that he had become nearer and more precious to us than any other person.

And there was Terence Street two pounds ahead of Earl Street, drunk with the excitement of it. Art used to get out the money and count it—it was the biggest sum of money he had ever seen—and a sober pride filled him. He had done this. People like Mrs. Law had just thrown in all they had. He had put in his bit cautiously, but everyone had scraped and strained and just wildly thrown in the cash. It made him marvel. He marvelled at us, he marvelled—as his hands trembled over the money—that he had been picked out by us to hold it.

We went round once or twice to look at the money too. What a nest egg, what an investment! Over thirty pounds! We said we wished it was ours. We said we wished we could give more, or double it. We all wanted to double it. We looked at it sadly. "If that thirty pounds had been on the winner today," someone said. "Or on the dogs."

We laughed uneasily. And we dreamed. The more we looked at that money, the more we thought of things you could do with it—mad things like backing a horse or sensible things like starting a business or having a holiday.

When we got up in Art's kitchen and saw him put the money in the cupboard and lock the door, we nodded our heads sadly. It was like burying the dead.

"It's sad it's got to go," we thought.

And it seemed to us fitting that Art, who had buried the dead and who was a dour man with iron-grey hair and level-looking eyes, should have the grim task of keeping that money, like some sexton. And we were glad to have him doing it, to have him be responsible instead of us. For some of us had to admit we'd go mad at times with temptation tingling in our fingers and hissing like gas in coal in our hearts.

When we left him we felt a kind of sorrow for Art for bearing our burden, for being the custodian of our victory over Earl Street.

It made us all very friendly to Art. The time went by. We used to stop and have a word with him in the street. And Art became friendly too. But he wasn't at the Freemasons much. He went over to Mrs. Law's. And Harry Law didn't go on the booze. He stayed at home talking largely to Art. Once or twice Art went out in the evenings with Mr. and Mrs. Law. Lupinsky used to see them up at the pictures.

Lupinsky was our reporter of everything and gradually, expressing no doubt the instinct of the street, he had become our reporter on Art Edwards. We wanted a friendly eye kept on him, not because he was valuable, but because he was—well, as you would keep an eye on a sick man, say, a man who might have a heart attack or go dizzy in the street. When Lupinsky came back and said: "I see Art Edwards getting on a tram," we used to look up sharply and then, annoyed with ourselves, say: "What of it? What was he doing, having a ride?"

That Jew used to make us tired. And he'd started worrying already about the catering. They'd started arranging about the catering already in Earl Street. "It's a funny thing," we said, "about the Yids. He's only been here fifteen years and you'd think he'd been here forever. Anyone'd think he'd been born in the street. You'd bloody well think it was Jerusalem."

We had been born there, most of us, and we said: "It *will* be Jerusalem soon."

But we would have been nowhere without Lupinsky.

And then one morning he came along and said:

"Seen Art?"

"No," we said.

"He's not up in the High Street," said Lupinsky. "And he's not at his house."

"What of it?" we said.

Lupinsky was breathless. All the pimples on his face seemed about to burst. He had the kind of red hair that is coarse and stands up on end and thick arched eyebrows, which were raised very high but were now higher, for his eyes were starting out of his head. There were always bits of cotton from tailoring on his clothes and he was as I have said rather humpbacked from leaning all day over his machine.

"I saw him last night at the station. Nine o'clock. He took a ticket on the North London and hasn't been back."

"Smart baby," we said. But we were thinking of Lupinsky. We didn't believe him and yet we did believe him. "What were you doing up at the station—brother had another fire?" we said. Lupinsky's brother was always having fires.

But it was true. Art hadn't been home that night and his sister was very shifty when we went to see her. We never liked Art's sister and we grinned to think he'd got away from her for a night.

"Art had to go away on business," she said.

Theirs was a tidy house and Art's sister worked hard in it. The window-sills were hearthstoned. That woman never stopped. She always came to the door with an iron in her hand or a scrubbing-brush or with something she was cleaning or cooking. She was a tall, straight-nosed woman and she had the best teeth I've ever seen, but there was no thickness in her, no give.

She used to say: "I've never had justice done me."

And Art used to sigh and say: "I can never do justice to her."

"What about it now?" said Lupinsky, who was waiting for us.

"Art can go away if he likes," we said. "Why not?"

"Sure, yes, why not?" said Lupinsky. "What you worrying about?"

Later on, Lupinsky came and told us Art was still away. His stall was still in the shed and he hadn't been down to the market. Lupinsky had a friend who had told him. Then Lupinsky had another friend who said he'd seen Art at Wembley.

"Too many Yids here," said Albert Blacker. "You can't move but you catch one in your clothes. What's up with Wembley?"

We went over to Mrs. Law's and called down to her. She was ironing in the light of the window.

"Seen Art Edwards?" we said.

"No," she said. "He hasn't been here for two or three days."

"Oh," we said.

Then Harry Law got up from his chair by the stove and said: "Art gone?"

"We're just looking for him. Thought he might be with you."

Mrs. Law gazed at us and then she looked at her husband. She was one of those women who when anything serious or unexpected happens, when they don't know what to think, when they are bewildered, always turn to their husbands; as if by studying him she would always know the worst about any event in the world and would be prepared. It was like looking up something in a book or gazing into a crystal. And when she had gazed at her husband and thought about him, she said: "Oh dear."

And she put down her iron, and her shoulders hunched up. She looked accusingly at her husband and he lowered his eyes. He knew she could read him like that.

The Scapegoat

We did not think so at the time, but afterwards we said we had the feeling that when Mrs. Law looked at her husband in that accusing way, she knew something about Art Edwards that we did not know. It turned out that she did not know. I looked out of the window that night when I went to bed. It was a warm night. I work in a fur warehouse and the air had the close, dead, laid-out smell of ladies' furs. There was a cold hollow lilac light over the roofs from the arc lamps in the High Street. At night our street is quiet and often you can hear the moan of a ship's siren from the river like the hoarse voice of someone going away. But the commonest sound is the clinking of shunting trucks on the railway—a sound that is meaningless, as if someone who couldn't play the piano had struck the keys anyhow, trying to make a tune. It is a sound that makes you think the city has had an attack of nerves. As I stood there on one leg, undoing my boots, I heard quick footsteps coming along. They were Lupinsky's. Lupinsky was always up late.

"I say. I say," he called up to me. "Art's come back. I just seen him. He came back and let himself in."

That night Art Edwards went into the shed in his yard and, attaching his braces to a hook in the roof, he hanged himself. The box in the cupboard was empty. He had gone off to Wembley and lost all the money on the dogs.

We went out into the street in the morning and stood outside the house and stared at the windows. The people from Earl Street came too. All the children came and stared and no one said anything in the street. Albert Blacker went into the yard at the back and Lupinsky was there with the police. Mrs. Law would not leave her house, but stood on her doorstep holding the railing tightly, watching from a distance. Harry Law would not come out. He walked up and down the room and called up to his wife to come down. He could not bear being left alone. She was afraid to leave her house and yet, I thought, wanted to be with Art.

228

"The bloody twister," we said between our teeth.

"That bloody widower," we said.

"Takes our money and has a night out. Our savings! Our money!"

"The rotten thief."

We muttered like this standing in front of the house. We were sorry for the police who had to touch the body of a man like that.

"You wouldn't trust me," Lupinsky said.

We looked at him. We turned away. We couldn't bear the sight of that man's pimples.

"I'm used to money," Lupinsky said.

I could not repeat all the things we said. I remember clearly the red, white, and blue streamers drooping over the street and looking dirty, with "God Save the King" on them. "God Save Art Edwards," said Harry Law coming up. He was tight.

We thought of the spirit of Art Edwards's sister being humbled. All down the street, at all the windows, the women leaned on their bare arms thinking about this. They cuffed their children and the children cried. There was the low murmur of our voices in the street and then the whining voices of children. Presently a couple of women came down, pushed their way through the crowd, and went in to help Art's sister. We gaped at them.

And then Lupinsky, who gave the lead to everything and always knew what we were thinking underneath, said: "They're jeering at us in Earl Street."

They were. We set our teeth. Kids came round shouting: "Who swiped the money box! Who swiped the money box!" Our kids did nothing for a long time. Then they couldn't stand it. Our kids went for the Earl Street kids. Some of our women came down to pull their kids off and this drew out the Earl Street women. In half an hour Albert Blacker came out of the Freemasons with his sleeves rolled up, just when the Earl Street men were getting together and then Harry Law came out roaring. Mrs. Law ran towards him. But it was too late. A stone went and a window crashed and that brought out the rest of the Blacker family. We got it off our chests that night and we crowded into Earl Street. Half their milk bottles had gone before the police whistles went.

And then it was clear to us. We knew what to do. Lupinsky headed it. Art Edwards was suddenly our hero. We'd kill the man who said anything against Art Edwards. In our hearts, we said, it might have been ourselves. Thirty pounds, we remembered the sight of it! We even listened to Harry Law.

"He was trying to double it at the dogs," he said. "Investing it. Every man has . . ."

His wife pulled his coat and tried to stop him.

"Every man," continued Harry Law, "has his ups and downs."

And to show Earl Street what we were and to show the world what we thought of Art Edwards, we got up the biggest funeral that has ever been seen in our street. He was ourselves, our hero, our god. He had borne our sins. You couldn't see the hearse for flowers. The street was black with people. The sun shone. We'd been round and got every stall-holder, every barrow man in the neighbourhood. That procession was a mile long when it got going. There was a Jubilee for you, covered in red, white, and blue wreaths. Art Edwards our king. It looked like a wedding. The great white trumpets of the lilies rocked thick on the coffin. Earl Street couldn't touch that. And Lupinsky collected the money.

The Lion's Den

Oh, there you are, that's it, dear," said the mother,
timidly clawing her son out of the darkness of the
doorway and kissing him. "You got here all right. I couldn't
look out for you; they've boarded up the window. We've
had a land-mine. All the glass went last week. Have you
had your tea? Have a cup of tea?"

"Well, let's see the boy," said the father. "Come in here
to the light."

"I've had tea, thanks," Teddy said.

"Have another cup. It won't take a tick. I'll pop the kettle
on. . . ."

"Leave the boy alone, old dear," the father said. "He's
had his tea. Your mother's just the same, Teddy."

"I only thought he'd like a cup of tea. He must be tired,"
said the mother.

"Sit down, do, there's a good girl," said the father.

"Now—can Father speak? Thank you. Would you like
to wash your hands, old chap?" the father said. "We've
got the hot water back, you know."

"Yes, go on," said the mother, "wash your hands. They
did the water yesterday."

"There she goes again," the father said. "Wonderful,
isn't it?"

"No, I don't want to wash," said Teddy.

231

The Lion's Den

"He doesn't want to wash his hands," said the father, "so leave him alone."

"It's hot if he wants to."

"We know it's hot," said the father. "Well, my boy, sit down and make yourself comfortable."

"Take this chair. Don't have that one. It's a horrible old thing. Here, take this one," the mother said.

"He's all right. He's got a chair," the father said.

"Let him sit where he likes," the mother said. "You do like that chair, Teddy, don't you?"

"Well," said Teddy, "you're looking well, Mother." This was not true; the mother looked ill. Her shoulders were hunched, her knees were bent, and her legs bowed stiffly as she walked. When she smiled, tears ran to the corners of her eyes as if age were splitting them; and dirty shadows like fingermarks gave them the misplaced stare of anxiety. Her fingers, too, were twisting and untwisting the corners of her cardigan.

"Of course she's looking well. Nothing wrong with her, is there? What I keep saying," the father said.

He was a bit of a joker. He resembled a doll-like colonel from a magazine cover, but too easy in manner for that.

"I'm well now," said the mother. "It's just these old raids. They upset me, but I get over it."

"We worry about you," Teddy said.

"You shouldn't worry," said the father. "There's nothing to worry about, really. We're here, that's the chief point. We just don't worry at all."

"It doesn't do any good, Teddy dear," said the mother. She was sitting by the fire and she leaned over to him and gripped his knee hard. "We've had our life. I'm seventy, don't forget."

"Seventy," laughed his father. "She can't forget she's seventy. She doesn't look it."

232

"But I am," said his mother fiercely.

"Age is what you make it," the father said. "That's how I feel."

"There's a lot in that," said the son.

"I go to bed . . . and I lie there listening," the mother said. "I just wait for it to go. Your father, of course, he goes to sleep at once. He's tired. He has a heavy day. But I listen and listen," the mother said, "and when it goes I give him a shake and say 'It's gone.' "

"I don't want to sound immodest," the father laughed, "but she nearly has my—my confounded pyjamas off me, sometimes."

"He just lies there. He'd sleep through it, guns and all," the mother went on. "But I couldn't do that. I sit on the edge of the bed. If it's bad I sit on the top of the stairs."

"We both do if it's bad," the father said. "I get up if it's bad."

"You ought to sit under the staircase, not on top," said Teddy.

"Just in case," said the mother. "I like to feel I can get out."

"You see, you want to get out," the father said. "It isn't that one's afraid, but—well—you feel more comfortable."

"I sit there and I know it's wrong of me, I think of you all, if I'll ever see any of you again. I wish you were with me. I never see you all, not together like we used to be. . . ."

"It is natural for a mother to feel like that," said the father.

"I mean if we could be not so far apart."

"We wish you'd come down to us," Teddy said.

"I wish I could, dear," said the mother.

"Why don't you? You could, easily."

"I'd like to, but I can't."

233

"I don't see why not. Why don't you send her, Dad? Just for the rest."

"I've got to stay with Dad," she said.

"Your mother feels she's got to stay with me."

"But," Teddy said, "you could look after yourself for a while."

"I could look after myself all right," said the father. "Don't you worry about that."

"Well," said Teddy, "what's against it?"

"Nothing's against it," said his father. "Just herself. She feels her place is here. She just feels this is her place."

His father raised his chin and lowered his eyes bashfully. He had a small white moustache as slight as a monkey's, and it seemed to give a twist to the meaning of his words, putting them between sets of inverted commas.

The mother read his eyes slowly and fidgeted on her stool by the fire. She nodded from habit when she had got through her husband's words, but she glanced furtively at her son. She put on an air of light-heartedness, to close the subject.

"Some day I'll come," she said. "The Miss Andersons are very kind. They had us down last Sunday when the windows went. . . . It's safer downstairs."

"You know what I feel?" said his father, in a sprightly way. "I feel it's safe everywhere."

The son and the mother both looked at the father with very startled concern and sympathy, recognizing that in danger everyone lives by his own foible. Then guiltily they glanced at each other.

"I feel it," said the father apologetically, when he saw their expression.

"I know it," he asserted, feebly scowling. Seeing he had embarrassed them, he escaped into a businesslike mood. "Now I'm going down to see about the coal for the morning. I always do it at this time."

"He's wonderful," said the mother. "He always does the coal."

When the father left the room, a great change came over the mother and son.

"Come nearer the fire, dear," said the mother. They were together. They came closer together like lovers.

"Just a minute, dear," she said. And she went to the curtains and peeped into the night. Then she came back to the stool.

"You see how it is, dear," she said. "He has faith." The son scowled.

"It's wonderful, his faith," she said. "He trusts in God."

A look of anger set on the son's jaw for a moment, then he wagged his head resignedly.

"He always did. You remember, when you were a boy?" said the mother, humouring her son. "I never could. He did from the beginning when I met him. Mind you, Teddy, I don't say it's a bad thing. It's got him on. When one of those old things starts he goes to his room and he prays. I know he's praying. Really he's praying all the time, for me, for you children—"

"For us!" exclaimed the son.

"Yes, for everyone," said the mother. "The world—oh, I don't understand. If there's a God, why did He let it happen in the first place?—but your father, he always did do things on a big scale."

She was speaking in a whisper and glancing now and then at the door.

"Too big," she murmured.

"If there is a God," said the son, "he is pitiable, weak, small. Hardly born—"

He checked himself when he saw that his mother looked at him without comprehension. "I am old." She shivered and he saw the tears cracking in her eyes. "I used to live in hope

—you know, for the future. You know, hope things would go right, hoping things for you children, but now I haven't even got hope." She looked wildly. "It's gone."

She stared over his shoulder to the walls of the room and the heavy curtains.

"It isn't this old war and these old raids," she said. "Life's gone, it's gone too quickly. There's nothing, Ted, that's how it seems to me, except if we could just be together as we were."

"Don't cry, Mother."

"No, mustn't cry, mustn't let him see I cried. Women do cry. It's silly. What shall we talk about? Let's think of something else."

She became sly and detached like a young girl running away, daring him to catch her. He knew these changes of mood in his mother very well. She began to talk in a bold, taunting way.

"It's the house," she said scornfully. "He doesn't like the house to be left. Someone must be in the house. It won't run away I tell him. Good thing if it was bombed. But his mother was just the same, cling on, cling on, scrubbing, polishing. 'You can't take it with you,' I used to say to her. She used to give me a look. 'Eh,' she said, 'you want me to die.' I can see her now. 'You wicked woman,' I said. And when they carried her out, the men bumped the coffin, dear, on the chest of drawers and I thought: 'If you could see that scratch!' Some call it faith. I call it property. Property."

His mother's eyes became sly and malicious. She laughed.

"Oh, there are things I could tell you," she cried recklessly, looking at the door. "When it starts and I hear the guns, I think of you. Things you don't know about, you were just a baby at the time. No one knows them. It's my life. All those years. Can you hear him? Is he coming upstairs?"

"No, I don't hear him."

"No, he'll be another minute or two. Quick, I'll show you something. Come along."

She got up and, seizing her son's sleeve, she nearly ran with him from the room.

"You're not to say anything," she said.

"His bedroom," she said. "Look at it."

It was simply a bedroom with too much furniture in it.

"Three chests of drawers," the son said. "What does he want with three?"

A look of wicked delight came into his mother's face, a look so merry that he knew he was saying what she wanted him to say.

"Two wardrobes," he exclaimed.

"Three with this!" exclaimed his mother, touching a cupboard in the corner, as if she were selling it.

"And then—just in case you want to read," his mother said satirically. She pointed one by one to several reading lamps by the bed, on the chests, on the dressing-table.

"What's he want five for?" said the son.

"Shave?" said his mother excitedly, opening a heavy drawer. Inside were a number of razors and shaving things of all kinds. She bent to the drawer below.

"Locked," she said. Undismayed, she led him to the far wall. "Count," she said. The son began to count. At seventeen he stopped. There were many more than seventeen pairs of boots lined up, and at the end the son stopped with astonishment.

"Riding-boots. When does he ride?"

"He's never ridden in his life, my dear."

"Waders, climbing-boots . . ." The son began to laugh. "He never fished, did he? When did he buy all this gear?"

"Oh, we haven't begun, dear. Look at this."

One by one she opened the wardrobes swiftly, allowed

her son to glance, even to touch for a moment, and then swiftly closed the door. She showed him some thirty suits of clothes and more hats than he could count.

"I'll try one on," said the son, laughing.

"No," said the mother, "he'd know you'd touched them."

"What's the idea of this hoard? It's madness," he said.

The word "madness" came to his head because, at this triumph of her secret-telling, she looked mad herself. Her eyes stared with all the malice of the mad, intent on their message. Then quickly as a mouse she scurried to the door and listened.

The son stood by the fireplace when she went to the door, and looked at a picture over the mantelpiece. It was the only picture in the room. It was a picture of a tall, bareheaded, austere man in ancient robes, standing in the shadows of a crowded place, alone. And in those shadows crouched a prowling group of lions, their surly faces barred with scowls of anger and fear.

"Daniel in the Lion's Den. He loves old Daniel," said his mother, coming up behind him. "He's always talking of Daniel."

The son gaped at the picture. The room was filled with his father's life, but this picture seemed to be more profoundly his father's life than anything else in the room. He suddenly felt ashamed of being in his father's room.

"Let's go back to the fire," the son said.

"Look, dear." The mother was pulling at his sleeve. "Something else, quick."

She took him to a chest of drawers and opened the drawers one by one.

"Pants," she said in her deceptive voice, and as she spoke she carefully lifted one or two of the garments. Underneath them was a silver cruet.

"Solid silver," she said. "Wait. Two dozen teaspoons. A set of fish-knives. All silver."

238

"Come along, Mother. I know, I know."

"Silver tea-tray. Kettle." She was at another drawer, ignoring him.

"Fish-knives, spoons, ink-stands . . ."

"Mother, stop. . . ."

"You move this. It's heavy. Look at this one. Shirts." She was lifting the shirts and revealing under them a cache of silver cream-jugs, hot-water jugs . . .

"Oh dear," said his mother. "We never use them. We never see them. He thinks I don't know. He just comes home and goes straight to his bedroom and slips them in."

"Where does he pick up all this?" said the son.

"Ask no questions, hear no lies," said his mother.

"No, seriously, what's the idea?"

The old lady's face was marked suddenly by all the bewilderment of a lifetime. She was helpless.

"Don't ask me, dear," she said. "It's him. It's how he's always been."

She looked at her son, exhausted and inquiring. She had suddenly lost interest. She was also frightened.

"Come out, in case he comes. You see, dear, how it is. We couldn't leave all that."

She turned out the lights and they walked back into the sitting-room.

"You're looking tired, dear," she said, in an unnatural voice, making conversation. "Do you sleep well?"

She went over to the curtain again and peeped out as she said this.

"Pretty well."

She came back to the fire.

"I know. You dream. Do you dream? I dream something chronic. Every night. Your father doesn't dream, of course. He just sleeps. He's always been like that. Sometimes I have a terrible dream. I dream, dear, that I'm in a palace, a king's palace, something like Windsor Castle, and I go into a great hall and it's filled with—treasure: well, things, beautiful—you know, armour, pictures, china, and I stand there and I can't get my breath and I say 'Oh, I must get out.' And I go out of a door just to get air to breathe. . . ."

"Indigestion," said her son.

"Is it? Well, through this door there's another room, just the same, but it's filled with commoner things—crockery, ironmongery, furniture—just like a secondhand shop, but thousands, dear, and I think: 'Oh, let me breathe,' and I hurry out of it by the door, and beyond that door," said the mother, holding his hand, "is another room. Ted, it's full of everything decaying, filthy. Oh, it's horrible, dear. I wake up feeling sick."

"What is that?" asked the son, nodding to the ceiling. "Up there."

"On the ceiling?" she said. "Oh, that's our crack. It's getting bigger," she said. "It's a bad one. That was the land-mine, dear, the one that broke the windows. The one that killed old Mrs. Croft . . ."

"I know, Mother, don't . . ."

"I thought we had gone and I said: 'Oh, Dad. We've gone.' Ted, dear, the dust!"

They looked at the ceiling. Beginning at the wall by the window, the crack was like a cut that has not closed.

"And perhaps it would have been a good thing if we had gone," she said, narrowing her eyes and searching her son's face with a look that terrified him. "We've had our life. What is your life? I watch that old crack and I say: 'Let's see. Are you getting larger?' But he sits there, quiet at his table, and says: 'Remember Daniel. There's nothing to be afraid of.' It's wonderful, really. He believes it. It does him good. There's just ourselves, dear, you see. You've all grown up, you've gone your own ways, you can't be here with me and it wouldn't be right if you could be. I always feel I've got you. I think to myself: 'I've got something, I've got you children.' But he's got nothing. You mustn't take any notice of the things I say. I expect you know women just say things and don't know why they say them. . . . When I see him sitting there under the lamp, praying for me and you and all of us, I think: 'Poor old Daddy, that's all he's got—his faith. But I've got him.' "

"Ssh, Mother, don't cry. He's coming now," the son said. Quickly she sat on the stool by the fire and put her head forward so that the disorder of her face should be hidden in the glow of the flame.

The father tapped his fingers comically on the panel of the door.

"May I come in? Sure I'm not interrupting? Thank you. Mother and son," he smiled, nodding his head. "The old, old story, mother and son."

A flush of annoyance and guilt passed over the son's body and came to his lips in a jaunty, uneasy laugh.

The father frowned.

"I say, old girl," he said, "I've just been outside. There was a chink of light showing in my room. We must be careful. . . ."

"I was just showing Ted round," said the mother.

"Showing me round the estate," Ted said.

"I've switched it off," the mother said.

"Switch it on, old girl. Let's have that tea." He settled himself innocently on the edge of his chair with his legs tucked under it, and his pleased fingers joined over his waistcoat.

"It's a good thing I know your mother. How old are you, my boy—forty? In forty-five years I've got to know her," the father smiled.

The old lady nodded her head as she went over his words, and then she got up from her stool to make the tea.

"I don't think they'll come tonight, dear," she said with spirit.

"I'm here," the son laughed.

"Run along, old girl. Of course they won't," the father said, ordering and defending his own. "I just *know* they won't."

Eleven O'Clock

From years of habit the mare stopped a minute or two at the right houses in all the streets waiting for the milk-man's voice to call: "Good day, ma'am, thank you, ma'am," in the alleys. Then she gave a slouching heave, the cans and bottles would start jingling, and, with the man following, she was off to the next stop. But when eleven o'clock came she stopped dead. She knew the house they were at now. She knew it well. An ungainly, warty, and piebald creature, she loosened her shoulders, her head and neck hung to the ground, her forelegs splayed out, and she looked old, rakish, and cynical.

For here was no stop of a minute or two. Down the passage strode the milkman, his lips whistling. Five minutes passed into ten, ten into twenty. Some mornings it was half an hour, three quarters, or the full hour. And when the milkman came back he was not whistling.

He was a short, ruddy man in a brown dustcoat with the firm's name on it and a hat like a police inspector's. But there is nothing like a uniform for concealing the soul. He was bald and battered under his hat, and his eyebrows were thick and inky. If he took his hat off in the middle of a sentence, that sentence would become suddenly very easy and rather free; if he wiped his bald head with his handkerchief, *that* was a sign he might get freer.

Eleven O'Clock

The first time the milkman went to the house a woman came across the kitchen towards him. The fire was murmuring in the range and a pot of coffee was standing on it. A tray of cakes had just been taken out of the oven and was standing on the table. The milkman's nostrils had small sensitive black hairs in them, and they quivered.

"Oh, I do like a nice mince pie," said the milkman.

She was a kind woman. "The early bird catches the worm," she said. "Have one."

She was a big creature, lazy and soft in the arms and shoulders. She had several chins. The small chin shook like a cup in its saucer on the second chin that was under it, and she had freckles on her neck. She was warm and untidy with cooking, and her yellow hair was coming undone at the back. Her mouth was short and surly, but now it softened in harmony with the rest of her into an easy placid smile; the rest of her body seemed to be laughing at her fatness, and the smile broadened from her lips to her neck and so on downwards, until the milkman put his foot on the doorstep, took off his hat, and wiped his bald head with pleasure.

"I'm a rollin' stone, ma'am," said the milkman. "I don't mind if I do."

She turned round and walked slowly to the table and the cakes. They were small cherry cakes. When she turned, the crease in the back of her neck seemed to be a smile and even her shoes seemed to be making smiles of pleasure on the floor.

"Come in," she said. "I'm Yorkshire. I'm not like the people round here. I'm neighbourly."

"I'm Yorkshire. I'm neighbourly too," said the milkman, rubbing his hands, and he stepped in. It was warm and cosy in the kitchen, warm with the smell of the cakes and the coffee, and warm with the good-natured woman.

"Take a seat," said the woman. "I'm sitting down myself.

I've been on my feet all morning. I come from Leeds and this is my bake."

"I come from Hull," said the milkman. "We never say no and we never say die. I've been on my feet too. What I mean to say—in my job, you can't ride because you're always stopping, and you can't stop because you've got to keep moving, if you get me." The milkman sat down opposite to her.

"I could tell you were from the north," said the hospitable woman. She pushed the cakes towards him. "Go on," she said. "Take one. Take two. They're a mean lot of people down here. There's nothing mean about me."

"After you, ma'am," he said.

"No," she said. "I dassn't."

She laughed.

"Slimming?" said the milkman.

"Oh, ha ha," laughed the woman. "That's a good one. Look at me. I've got the spread. I don't get any exercise." She went into a new peal of laughter. "And I don't want it."

"We're as God made us," said the milkman. "All sizes."

"And all shapes," said the woman, recovering. "It wouldn't do for all of us to be thin."

"You want some heavyweights," said the man.

"They're all thin round here, and mean," said the woman.

The woman laughed until tears came into the small grey eyes which were sunk like oyster pearls between her plump fire-reddened cheeks and her almost hairless brows. She laughed and laughed, and her laughter was like her smile. She laughed not only with her mouth, but her cheeks gave a jump and her chins jumped together and her big breasts shook, and she spread her legs with laughter, too, under the table.

"Oh dear! Oh dear!" she said. "When I was a girl I was in the catering business and they starved me. One house I was in the boss used to follow me into the kitchen when I was

245

putting away the snacks to see I didn't pinch anything. And I can tell you it was a work of art slipping a bit of cheese down the neck of me blouse to eat when I got up to bed, it was."

The milkman looked at her blouse.

The milkman widened one eye and winked with the other.

"Oh, don't!" cried the woman, going off again. "Don't! Stop it! Don't start me off.

"Don't mind me," said the woman wiping her eyes. "I've been here seven weeks and this is the first laugh I've had. My husband's a cripple. He's a watch-maker. Tick-tock, tick-tock, tick-tock, all day long. He hangs up the watches on the wall and that's all I've heard for seven weeks! Tick-tock, tick-tock, tick-tock."

She wiped the tears from her eyes with her apron and waved an arm to the wall.

There were four clocks on the kitchen wall and three on the mantelpiece, and there were watches hanging on nails. The tall brown clock with the pendulum gave a slow grating "Tock"; the blue alarm on the mantelpiece went at a run; the big wooden clock next to it made a sweet sound like a man sucking a pipe, and the rest croaked, scratched, ticked and chattered. Carved in fretwork was a small cuckoo clock beside the door.

"Who winds them?" asked the milkman with his mouth full of cake.

"Who winds them?" said the woman. "He winds them. He comes home and spends all night winding them. Have some coffee. You ought to see what I've got inside and up-stairs."

"I bet," said the milkman, gazing at her from his still wide eyes. "If there's a drop of coffee I'll have it."

"Laugh," said the woman. "You can't tell night from day in this house. They all say something different. I've been seven weeks here, but it might be seven years. It's a good thing I can laugh."

"It's slimming," he said.

"It's spreading," she said.

"Well, I like a bit of spread myself," said the milkman.

The milkman watched her go to the range. He watched her bring the coffee-pot over and bring a couple of white cups from the dresser. He got up and went to the door.

"My Jenny," he said. "My mare. Whoa! Listen to her. She's kicking up the pavement."

The mare was kicking the kerb. She was standing with her forelegs on it, gazing down the alley and striking a hoof on the pavement.

"She knows I'm in here," he said, coming back. "I bet she knows I'm having a cup of coffee. I bet she's wondering what's happening. I bet she's thinking it out. Wonderful things horses are. Jealous, you know, too," he said. "If she knew you was in here, I'd never hear the last of it.

"Eating's her trouble. She's old," said the milkman. "She's terrible. I've never seen an animal eat what she does. I bet she knows there's something going on."

The milkman sipped his coffee. His lips made bubbling sounds as he drank. Soon there were no sounds in the room but the ticking of the clocks and the bubbling noise of the woman's lips and the man's lips at their cups, and a click of the cups and a murmur of laughter from the woman.

Then the little fretwork clock which hung by the door gave a small sneezing buzz, a door clipped open, a tiny hammer rang, and out bobbed the bird. "Cuckoo! Cuckoo!" it called, and "Clap" went the door. The milkman put down his cup with a start and gaped.

"They're all wrong," said the woman. "Sit down. Have another cake, just a little one. Have a tart? That cuckoo's never right. 'Oh, shut up,' I tell it. 'Keep quiet.' "

"I used to do fretwork myself," said the milkman.

"Sit down," she pressed him. "Another cup will warm you up."

"You're warm in here," said the milkman.

"I'm warm anywhere," the woman said.

"Don't want winding up, I bet," said the milkman with a wink. He was short beside her and he took a long easy look at her. He wiped his bald head and put on his hat.

"Well," he said. "Talking of time, one thing leads to another."

She looked at him sadly, and with a lazy yawn raised her big arms above her head.

"Come and see those clocks."

The milkman had his pencil in his ear, a small red stump of pencil. He took it out and, quickly, he gave her a soft poke in the waist with it and went off.

"Good day, ma'am, thank you, ma'am," he called, and went off whistling.

The next day the milk-cart stopped again at the house. Behind the cart the milkman walked, humming to himself. He looked up at the house. There was the short brick wall and the iron rail on top of it. There was the green hedge coming into leaf. He took his basket, he swung open the gate and he went down the alley. There was a smell of pastry just out of the oven. For a long time while he was gone the mare stood, then she stepped on to the kerb and began knocking her hoof upon it. The sound could be heard down the deserted road. "Whoa!" shouted the milkman down the alley. The mare stretched her neck and sniffed the ground and then began pawing again. She got both forefeet on the pavement and kept stretching and shaking her smooth white neck. "Whoa!" shouted the milkman's voice. She pricked her ears. He was shouting from the front-room window.

Half an hour passed. The mare had now stepped farther on to the pavement. Her neck was stretched out to its full length. She was sniffing the wall, the iron rail, and behind it the juicy green shoots of the hedge. She strained, her nostrils trembling, her soft mouth opening to seize a shoot in her old

248

yellow teeth. She paused and made a greater effort, pulling
the cart, and now her nose was over the top of the railing.
Grunting, chewing, slopping, crunching sounds came from
her mouth. She had bitten off her first piece. And, once on it,
appetite leapt. She gave a wilder tug and now she could get
at the hedge. Her teeth dragged at the hedge and crunched.
She raised her neck, looked with discrimination at the shoots,
then went on quietly browsing.

No sounds came from the house, no sound from the road
but the chewing of the horse, the bit chinking like marbles in
her slobber. Hearing him come at last, she backed on to the
the road. He came out very thoughtful and not whistling.

And some mornings there was the smell of cake in the
alley, sometimes it was pie, and sometimes it was coffee.
Again a quarter of an hour passed, or maybe twenty minutes
or half an hour, and often enough a full hour, and a shout of
"Whoa!" came from an upstairs window. He had his coat
off. "That clock's wrong," said the woman. "They're all
wrong." The mare's neck was right over the railings and this
was necessary because, as she chewed, the hedge got lower
and lower.

"Eh, whoa there!" the milkman shouted down from the
top floor of the house one morning and, looking in amaze-
ment at the torn and bitten green hedge and the mare still
tearing it, he came down to the street.

"What's the idea? Come off it," he said, taking the mare
by the bridle and jerking her head off the hedge.

He drew her off the pavement and went back and looked
over the railings at the hedge, ruined by weeks of eating.

"Been getting your greens, haven't you?" he said. He
stared at the mare and, bright under their blinkers, he saw
the eyes of that cynical animal, secretive and glistening,
gazing back at him.

You Make Your Own Life

Upstairs from the street a sign in electric light said "Gent's Saloon." I went up. There was a small hot back room full of sunlight, with hair clippings on the floor, towels hanging from a peg, and newspapers on the chairs. "Take a seat. Just finishing," said the barber. It was a lie. He wasn't anywhere near finishing. He had in fact just begun a shave. The customer was having everything.

In a dead place like this town you always had to wait. I was waiting for a train, now I had to wait for a haircut. It was a small town in a valley with one long street, and a slow mud-coloured river moving between willows and the backs of houses.

I picked up a newspaper. A man had murdered an old woman, a clergyman's sister was caught stealing gloves in a shop, a man who had identified the body of his wife at an inquest on a drowning fatality met her three days later on a pier. Ten miles from this town the skeletons of men killed in a battle eight centuries ago had been dug up on the Downs. That was nearer. Still, I put the paper down. I looked at the two men in the room.

The shave had finished now, the barber was cutting the man's hair. It was glossy black hair and small curls of it fell on the floor. I could see the man in the mirror. He was in his thirties. He had a swarthy skin and brilliant long black eyes.

250

The lashes were long too and the lids when he blinked were pale. There was just that suggestion of weakness. Now he was shaved, there was a sallow glister to his skin like a Hindu's, and as the barber clipped away and grunted his breaths, the dark man sat engrossed in his reflection, half smiling at himself and very deeply pleased.

The barber was careful and responsible in his movements, but nonchalant and detached. He was in his thirties too, a young man with fair receding hair, brushed back from his forehead. He did not speak to his customer. His customer did not speak to him. He went on from one job to the next silently. Now he was rattling his brush in the jar, wiping the razor, pushing the chair forward to the basin. Now he gently pushed the man's head down, now he ran the taps and was soaping the head and rubbing it. A peculiar look of amused affection was on his face as he looked down at the soaped head.

"How long are you going to be?" I said. "I've got a train."

He looked at the clock. He knew the trains.

"Couple of minutes," he said.

He wheeled a machine on a tripod to the back of the man. A curved black thing like a helmet enclosed the head. The machine was plugged to the wall. There were phials with coloured liquids in them and soon steam was rushing out under the helmet. It looked like a machine you see in a Fun Fair. I don't know what happened to the man or what the barber did. Shave, hot towels, haircut, shampoo, this machine, and then yellow liquid like treacle out of a bottle—that customer had everything.

I wondered how much he would have to pay.

Then the job was over. The dark man got up. The clippers had been over the back of his neck and he looked like a guardsman. He was dressed in a square-shouldered grey suit, very dandyish for this town, and he had a silk handkerchief sticking out of his breast pocket. He wore a violet and silver tie. He patted it as the barber brushed his coat. He was delighted with himself.

"So long, Fred." He smiled faintly.

"Cheero, Albert," said the upright barber, and his lips closed to a small, hardly perceptible smile too. Thoughtfully, ironically, the barber watched his handiwork go. The man hadn't paid.

I sat in the chair. It was warm, too warm, where the man had sat. The barber put the sheet round me. The barber was smiling to himself like a man remembering a tune. He was not thinking about me.

The barber said that machine made steam open the pores. He glanced at the door where the man had gone. "Some people want everything," he said, "some want nothing." You had to have a machine like that.

He tucked in the cotton wool. He got out the comb and scissors. His fingers gently depressed my head. I could see him in the mirror bending to the back of my head. He was clipping away. He was a dull young man with pale-blue eyes and a look of ironical stubbornness in him. The small dry smile was still like claw marks at the corners of his lips.

"Three bob a time," he said. He spoke into the back of my neck and nodded to the door. "He has it every week."

He clipped away.

"His hair's coming out. That's why he has it. Going bald. You can't stop that. You can delay it but you can't stop it. Can't always be young. He thinks you can." He smiled dryly but with affection.

"But he wasn't so old."

The barber stood up.

"That man!" he said. He mused to himself with growing satisfaction. He worked away in long silence as if to savour every possible flavour of my remark. The result of his meditation was to make him change his scissors for a finer pair.

"He ought to be dead," he said.

"T.B.," he said with quiet scorn.

He looked at me in the mirror.

"It's wonderful," he said, as if to say it was nothing of the sort.

"It's wonderful what the doctors can do," I said.

"I don't mean doctors," he said. "Consumptives! Tuh! They're wonderful." As much as to say a sick man can get away with anything—but you try if you're healthy and see what happens!

He went on cutting. There was a glint in his pale-blue eyes. He snipped away amusedly as if he were attending to every individual hair at the back of my head.

"You see his throat?" he said suddenly.

"What about his throat?" I asked.

"Didn't you notice anything? Didn't you see a mark a bit at the side?" He stood up and looked at me in the mirror.

"No," I said.

He bent down to the back of my neck again. "He cut his throat once," he said quietly. "Not satisfied with T.B.," he said with a grin. It was a small, firm, friendly grin. So long, Fred. Cheero, Albert. "Tried to commit suicide."

"Wanted everything," I said.

"That's it," he said.

"A girl," the barber said. "He fell in love with a girl."

He clipped away.

"That's an item," said the barber absently.

He fell in love with a local girl who took pity on him when he was in bed, ill. Nursed him. Usual story. Took pity on him but wasn't interested in him in that way.

"A very attractive girl," said the barber.

"And he got it badly?"

"They get it badly, consumptives."

"Matter of fact," said the barber, stepping over for the clippers and shooting a hard sideways stare at me. "It was my wife.

"Before she was my wife," he said. There was a touch of quiet, amused resolution in him.

He'd known that chap since he was a kid. Went to school with him. Used to be his best friend. Still was. Always a lad. Regular nut. Had a milk business, was his own guv'nor till he got ill. Doing well.

"He knew I was courting her." He smiled. "That didn't stop him." There was a glint in his eye.

"What did you do?" I asked.

"I lay low," he said.

She had a job in the shop opposite. If you passed that shop you couldn't help noticing her at the cash desk near the door. "It's not for me to say—but she was the prettiest girl in this town," he said. "Still is," he mused.

"You've seen the river? You came over it by the station," he said. "Well, he used to take her on the river when I was busy. I didn't mind. I knew my mind. She knew hers. I knew it was all right.

"I knew him." He grinned. "But I knew her. 'Let him take you on the river,' I said."

I saw the barber's forehead and his dull blue eyes looking up for a moment over my head in the mirror.

"Damp river," he said reflectively. "Damp mists, I mean, on the river. Very flat, low-lying, unhealthy," he said. "That's where he made his mistake. It started with him taking her on the river."

"Double pneumonia once," he said. "Sixty cigarettes a day, burning the candle at both ends."

He grunted.

"He couldn't get away with it," he said.

When he got ill, the girl used to go and look after him.

254

She used to go and read to him in the afternoons. "I used to turn up in the evenings too when we'd closed."

The barber came round to the front and took the brushes lazily. He glanced sardonically at the door as if expecting to see the man standing there. That cocksure irony in the barber seemed to warm up.

"Know what he used to say to her?" he said sharply and smiled when I was startled. " 'Here, Jenny,' he used to say, 'tell Fred to go home and you pop into bed with me. I'm lonely.' " The young barber gave a short laugh.

"In front of me," he said.

"What did you say?"

"I told him to keep quiet or there'd be a funeral. Consumptives want it, they want it worse than others, but it kills them," he said.

"I thought you meant *you'd* kill him," I said.

"Kill him?" he said. "Me kill him?" He smiled scornfully at me: I was an outsider in this. "He tried to kill *me*," he said.

"Yeah," he said, wiping his hands on a towel. "Tried to poison me. Whisky. It didn't work. Back O.K.?" he said, holding up a mirror. "I don't drink.

"I went to his room," he said. "I was his best friend. He was lying on the bed. Thin! All bones and blue veins and red patches as if he'd been scalded and eyes as bright as that bottle of bath salts. Not like he is now. There was a bottle of whisky and a glass by the side of the bed. He wanted me to have a drop. He knew I didn't drink.

" 'I don't want one,' I said. 'Yes, you do,' he said. 'You know I never touch it,' I said. 'Well, touch it now,' he said. 'I tell you what,' he said; 'you're afraid.' 'Afraid of what?' I said. 'Afraid of catching what I've got.' 'Touch your lips to it if you're not afraid. Just have a sip to show.'

"I told him not to be a fool. I took the bottle from him. He had no right to have whisky in his state. He was wild when I took it. 'It'll do some people a bit of good,' I said, 'but it's poison to you.'

" 'It *is* poison,' he said.

"I took the bottle away. I gave it to a chap in the town. It nearly finished him. We found out it *was* poison. He'd put something in it."

I said I'd have a singe. The barber lit the taper. I felt the flame warm against my head. "Seals up the ends," the barber said. He lifted up the hair with the comb and ran the flame along. "See the idea?" he said.

"What did you do?"

"Nothing," he said. "Just married my girl that week," the barber said. "When she told him we were going to get married he said: 'I'll give you something Fred won't give you.' We wondered what it would be. 'Something big,' he said. 'Best man's present,' he said. He winked at her. 'All I've got. I'm the best man.' That night he cut his throat." The barber made a grimace in the mirror, passed the scissors over his throat, and gave a grin.

"Then he opened the window and called out to a kid in the street to fetch *her*. The kid came to me instead. Funny present," he said. He combed, he patted, he brushed. He pulled the wool out of the back of my neck. He went round it with the soft brush. Coming round to the front he adroitly drew off the sheet. I stood up.

"He got over it," he said. "Comes round and plays with my kids on Sundays. Comes in every Friday, gets himself up. See him with a different one every week at the pictures. It's a dead place this; all right in the summer on the river. You make your own life. The only thing is he don't like shaving himself now, I have to go over every morning and do it for him."

He stood with his small grin, his steady eyes amused and resolute. "I never charge him," he said. He brushed my coat, he brought my hat.

256

Miss Baker

When Easter came she knew that her time of fasting was drawing to a close; for three weeks she had not spoken. God had given her nothing to say to the world. She had prayed—for prayer always transposed her great sorrow—but He had become very small and far away like a very high and soundless bird. Yet in these days of the triumph of Spring and of His Son she had heard Him moving. On Easter Monday she got up from her chair and looked into the mirror and spoke for the first time.

"There you are, Miss Baker!" she said to her image. "Your hair is beautiful and yellow."

She watched the image, expectantly crinkling her pale eyes—there might be a miracle—but her lips in the mirror did not move.

"Poor darling," said Miss Baker to the image at last. "You are caught." And she smiled sadly though there was a fine curl of slyness at the corner of her lips. It was at this point when she might have broken down in a passion of sadness, when she had already the silver hairbrush in her hand raised to smash the mirror into a great gasping star, that the Voice of God stopped her with a whisper. So quietly the Voice spoke that for the moment she might have been deceived. It said: "Go ye into all the world." That was all.

She wanted to hear more, but when nothing came she understood.

She washed her face and brushed back her yellow hair over her ears to hear and understand the Voice again. She put on her white dress for her purity. "You are good to me, too good to me, Miss Baker," she said to the image in the mirror, thanking it with her repentance.

Then with a devout languor, very slowly before the glass she raised her arms in their long white sleeves, leaned back and closed her eyes; she was crucified upon herself.

When she came down from the cross the devils had gone. She put on a white straw hat with a broad brim and daisies round the crown. She took her umbrella, saw that the gas was turned off and that her key was in her bag and every window closed, and went out. To her surprise night had already fallen and the stairs were dark. Down six flights of stairs she went lower and lower into all the world. Sounds of traffic and of people walking came nearer and nearer from the street, starting like birds from her descending feet and rising in flocks until as she stepped down on to the pavement she was surrounded by them.

But like a ghost in her white dress she moved untouched by the things and creatures she touched. It was a cold night and people were wearing coats and hurrying. Their breath puffed out in clouds. The world smelled. It smelled of beer and frying meat, of vegetables in the market, of motor cars and oil, and the steam of a laundry. The world made noises. The scrawling noise of boots on the pavement, the sizzle of motor-car wheels, the deep mayoral bark of horns, the vicissitudes of voices. She walked through the music of a barrel organ, through halls and fountains of music, but her mind listened to none of the sounds that her ears heard. When she stopped dead still and listened, it was to hear again the guiding Voice.

She prayed in these moments humbly, not with the ar-

rogance of expecting to be heard, though when she opened
her eyes again it seemed the world was more contented and
long and happily married. The eyes of the houses were alight,
and in the early darkness, she thought, they looked so nice
and comfortable like old gentlemen with spectacles on,
smoking their pipes. She walked on and on, from street to
street, going into as many streets as she could and saying
nothing, her lips very full and still and slightly smiling and
the colour of her eyes fading as the inner light shone brighter.
Wherever she took her whiteness she could feel the pain of
the world going away.

Yet she was not white and pure enough, for the Voice did
not come again though she listened for it. Why did the
Voice not speak again? Perhaps an hour had passed or two
or three hours. People looked at her. Then when she opened
her eyes from prayer she saw on the opposite side of the
street a shining pool. "I do not hear His Voice," she said,
"but He leadeth me beside still waters, even though it is
only a puddle." And she had a very clever pouting and joking
look on her face as she waited for the traffic to pass and
crossed the street. On the pavement she found a dry, clean
spot, dusted it with her handkerchief, and sat down. "It is
not very comfortable," she said aloud in case people should
think her foolish, "but it will do." Very decently she pulled
her dress down to her ankles and sighed, closing her eyes
but too tired for prayer, and in those unguarded minutes an
errand boy went by and staggered into a long, walking-back-
wards stare. An old woman passed with a chain of three
children walking backwards, too. A young man in a mackintosh took his pipe out of his mouth, swivelled round, and
then turned back to her.

"Excuse me—er—miss," he said. "Allow me," he said
touching her shoulder. "Are you ill?"

She was charming and frigid to him. His face was stupid
with health.

"No, I am merely resting, thank you," she said.

A fat carpenter with a sandy moustache, and a bag of tools in his hand, came up and nudged the young man.

"What's up?" he asked. "Bin knocked down?"

"Dunno," said the young man. "Says she's resting."

The carpenter stared and then bent down himself.

"Anything the matter, miss?" he said.

"Nothing, thank you. It's not very comfortable, but I am resting," she said.

Oh, for five minutes' rest! Would God not give her just five minutes? Great weariness was streaming up out of the pavement into her and the street was heaving as if in it some tide had turned. Three young girls from a factory stopped chattering to look at her. Two of them giggled with embarrassment, but the third, who was dark and compassionate, knelt at Miss Baker's feet and looked clearly into her eyes.

"There is nothing the matter," said Miss Baker before the girl could speak. "I am only waiting for Someone. Please go!" she said, turning to the small crowd. They were very startled because she had a ladylike voice. They shifted their feet, glanced up and down the empty street looking out for danger, saw people in the distance, and, re-encouraged by the sight, closed round her again.

"Where do you live?" asked the kneeling girl. "Let me take you home."

"Where do she live?" asked the carpenter.

"She says she's waiting for someone," said the girl.

"For Someone," Miss Baker subtly corrected. They were puzzled and abashed. Malign, she studied their feet to embarrass the people, and when she put on the look of adding up their faces they turned away. But they did not go. The crowd had greatly increased. There was the inner ring composed of the young man, the carpenter, the kneeling girl, and two or three others at the heart of the mystery. There was the second ring. There was a third ring which, between trying to reply to the outer ring and ask the second ring for information at the same time, got no satisfaction and could not get away either. The crowd stood there like oxen with all their weight. Their pipes smoked. Their breath steamed. Their eyes, like bright creeping things, she felt, wandered over her. "It's a girl," said the carpenter, swelling out in the chest. At last the outer ring forced a victory. "Here's a copper," cried a boy at the back, and the circles opened to admit the weight of the policeman. They made way for him and closed in after him. He was a young policeman with very clean cheeks and all his weight went from one foot to the other. He was very heavy and calm, but he was blushing.

"Stand back," he said raising his voice, to give himself more space to be calm in. He put his hands on his knees and bent down to Miss Baker.

"Please, officer," she said. "Tell all these people to go away."

"Stand back," said the policeman again to cover his bewilderment.

"If you are all right you must move on, ma'am," he said uncertainly. "You are obstructing, miss."

"I am not obstructing," said Miss Baker very sharply and tightening her long white gloves on her fingers.

"Causing a crowd to collect . . ." said the policeman in his quoting voice. "Causing an obstruction. . . ."

"I am not obstructing. It is all these people who are obstructing. Please, officer," said Miss Baker with imperious lucidity, "please tell them to go away."

The policeman swallowed and stood up because his back was uncomfortable and so was his reason. He advanced upon the crowd waving his arms. "Move along there," he said. "Move along now. Hear what I say?"

The ranks thinned out before him and as they did so Miss Baker very quickly, quietly, and cleverly got up and walked away in the opposite direction, at first lightly shaking the looks of the gaping crowd off her back. She walked on twenty or thirty yards and one or two ran on to get ahead of her and some nervously followed to be within reach but without responsibility if something happened again. The rest had wavered backwards and forwards and the policeman stood in the middle of the pavement, his head held together by his helmet strap. She walked on blindly straight. The heads of the crowd still seemed to her to be stretching after her like the shooting heads of serpents. She waved her umbrella to beat them off, but the miserable heads came on. She hurried to get out of reach. If she could only get a few yards ahead of them into solitude and into the charmed circle of prayer. If she could stop and hear the Voice. If only she could hear the Voice!

But now the invisible serpents had caught her and were in her head, filling it with their thoughts. She struggled bravely against them. And it was this struggle which filled her with towering rage. They were slaves. She was free. What right had the slaves of the serpent over the free? She trembled with rage. Defiantly sure of her right, she sat down on the pavement again.

She sat down and her spirit darkened with passionate affirmations of her freedom. It was her pavement as much as anyone else's. She had a right in law. Her cheeks flushed and she felt giddiness and darkness of blood in her head and the answering heat of defiance in her hands, her bosom and throat. She gathered all her forces into this narrow compass of personal assertion and defiance and magnified herself until there was no room for the Voice of God; and only the roar of the world was in her ears. She pushed back her white hat, and her yellow hair began to fall over her face. She dug her nails into her umbrella. She was weeping passionately, and with shudders of hatred, abandoning herself to sin; beside her now was no healing pool. In the bars of the drain of the gutter beside her was the entrance into hell and the fingers of .

Anti-Christ were clawing at the bars. Down and down she was being dragged. It was with unspeakable gratitude she rose to go away with the policeman when he came again.

The following crowd stared at the empty door of the police station long after she had gone in. Generations of minutes bred and passed like ants. She seemed to be sitting on a bench in the police station and sometimes she was interested when a face with moving lips came nearer to her, but she could not think about the questions the lips asked her. She saw a man with a number on his collar, scratching his head, staring at his writing, and two or three times he spoke into the telephone. It did seem that they wanted something that she could give, but when she gave them her handbag they returned it to her. The policeman with the clean face who had brought her took her umbrella. When she got her handbag back, she opened it and looked into the mirror.

"Oh, Miss Baker, you are a dear to come with me," she murmured, glancing slyly to see if anyone was watching her. "Where would I be without you! You and I in a police station, Miss Baker!"

She tidied her hair and before she had done this—which was very embarrassing—the man with the number on his collar put down his glasses and got down from his high desk. He walked across to her quietly and again began to ask her things. And at last it came to her very clearly that he wanted to know her name. Clearly as she heard the Voice speaking she heard another voice speak distinctly in her throat: "Legion," it answered.

"L-E-G-I-O-N?" spelled the surprised officer. "And what address?"

But the other voice saw the trap and would not answer. Inside her it laughed like a flame.

They led her into an inner room and gave her some tea. She heard them telephoning again, far away the voices alighting in the places where the bells had rung, clapping down upon them quickly. Her mind drifted through parks and gardens and fountains, which slowly quenched her inward flame. The room was peaceful and she could feel peace returning. And then, far away among the telephoning voices, she heard a stirring in the air like the movement that came when the Voice was going to speak. She looked up quickly in this direction. And she saw a man in the room. There was peace in him she saw at once. He was huddled on a bench near her, his legs sprawling wide. His body lay in big, smiling curves of fatness. His sandy hair was sprinkled neatly and thinly over his head and in the gas light gleamed like a halo. But his features were ugly, brutal, and sodden, his thick mouth had dropped open, many of his front teeth were chipped, and he grunted half-asleep with the snort of a pig. His little blue eyes were half-blindly peeping. Once or twice he muttered and wagged his head and the policeman who was at the door of the room grinned.

She smiled and gazed at the man, not pushing herself out to him, but casting aside all aggression of the bodily will so that it was Sight that saw him and not herself. There poured out love and compassion for the man who was drowned in sleep. Out of him the Voice could speak. And in this knowledge she forgot about herself and her right, about drunkenness; and where the drunk man was, was a shape that would become the figure of God. The Voice was coming. Distantly like a high bird descending she could see the Voice; nearer and near it circled down, till as pure as a far-away bugle the sound came into her, saying to all her blood:

"Speak to me."

Speak to Him. She who had always listened *for* Him, now to speak *to* Him! She rose up with no hesitation and touched the drunk man on the shoulder and shook him. His eyes opened and quivered and closed again. She took him by his hand, and his eyes opened very wide and stared. Then slowly he gave a long, creeping, dirty grin.

264

"This is Peniel," she said, "the place of names. What is your name?" she asked him earnestly.

He stared and his face sank deeper and deeper, more satiate into his folds of smile, and a sparkle of wetness came on the corner of his lower lip.

"Tell me your name," she begged.

He looked at her doubtfully and at last muttered thickly: "Shepherd."

Her face became radiant. Her neck was pale and her throat beseeching as she took his hand in both of hers and said rapturously:

"Then I am one of Your Sheep!"

"Here," muttered the drunk man, pulling his hand away and recoiling at the meaning in her eyes and lips. "You know shlot 'bout this shex stuff, donchyer."

And pushed her violently away. But she stood up and said aloud, laughing mildly in the duplicity of the revelation her great sorrow had given her and holding out her arms in trembling white sleeves and raising her head:

"I have found my Lord! Miss Baker, darling, we have found our Lord."

The Ape

The fruit robbery was over. It was the greatest fruit robbery, and from our point of view the most successful, ever known in our part of the jungle. Not that we can take all the credit for that, for it was not ourselves who started the fight, but our enemies, a colony of apes who live in another tree. They were the first to attack, and by the time the great slaughter was over, hundreds of their dead, of both sexes, lay on the ground, and we had taken all their fruit. It was a fortunate triumph for us.

But apes are not a complacent or ungrateful race. Once we were back in our tree binding up our wounds, we thought at once of commemorating our victory and thanking our god for it. For we are aware that if we do not thank our god for his benefactions, he might well think twice before he sent us another fruit robbery of this triumphant kind. We thought therefore of how we might best please him. We tried to put ourselves in his place. What would most impress him? There were many discussions about this: we screamed and screeched in passionate argument and the din grew so loud—far louder than the noise we make in the ordinary business of eating or defending our places in the tree or making love and dying— that at last our oldest and wisest ape, who lived at the very top, slyly observed: "If I were god and had been looking down at this tree of screeching monkeys for thousands of years, the thing that would really impress me would be silence." We were dumbfounded. Then one or two of us shouted: "That's got it. Let silence be the commemoration of our victory."

So at last it was arranged. On the anniversary of the day when the great fruit robbery began, we arranged that all of us would stop whatever we were doing and would be silent.

But nothing is perfect in the jungle. You would think that all apes would be proud to be alike and would have the wisdom to abide by the traditions of their race and the edicts of their leader. You would think all would destroy the individual doubt with the reflection that however different an ape may fancy he is, the glory of the ape is that as he is now so he always has been, unchangeable and unchanged. There were, however, some, and one in particular as you will see, who did not think so.

We heard of them from a pterodactyl, a rather ridiculous neighbour of ours.

The pterodactyl lived on a cliff just above our tree and often, scaly and long-necked, he would flop clumsily down to talk to us. He was a sensationalist and newsmonger, a creature with more curiosity than brains. He was always worried. What (he would ask us) is the meaning of life? We scratched our heads. Where was it all leading? We spat out fruit pips. Did we apes think that we would always go on as we were? That question was easy. Of course, we said. How fortunate we were, he said, for he had doubts about himself. "It seems to me that I am becoming—extinct," he said.

It was all very well of us to make light of it, he said, but "if I had not lived near you such an idea would never have entered my head." We replied that we did not see what we had done to upset him. "Oh, not you in particular," he said. "It is your young apes that are worrying me. They keep talking about their tails."—"No livelier or more flourishing subject," we said. "We apes delight in our tails."—"As far as I can see," the pterodactyl said, "among your younger apes, they are being worn shorter and will soon be discarded altogether."—"What!" we exclaimed—he could have touched us on no more sensitive spot—"How dare you make such a suggestion!"—"The suggestion," the pterodactyl said, "does not come from me but from your young apes. There's a group of them. They caught me by the neck the other day—I am very vulnerable in the neck—and ridiculed me publicly before a large audience. 'A flying reptile,' they said. 'Study him while you can, for the species won't exist much longer—any more than *we apes shall go about on four legs and have tails.* We shall, at some unknown time in the future, but a time that comes rapidly nearer, cease to be apes. We shall become man. The pterodactyl, poor creature, came to the end of his evolutionary possibilities long ago.' "

"Man!" we exclaimed. "Man! What is that?" And what on earth, we asked the pterodactyl, did he mean by "evolution." We had never heard of it. We pressed the pterodactyl to tell us more, but he would only repeat what he had already said. When he had flopped back to his cliff again, we sat scratching ourselves, deep in thought. Presently our old and wisest ape, a horny and scarred old warrior who sits dribbling away quietly to himself all day and rubbing his scars on the highest branch of all, gave a snigger and said: "Cutting off their tails to spite the ape." We did not laugh. We couldn't take the matter as lightly as he took it. We, on the contrary, raged. It was blasphemy. The joy, the pride, the whole apehood of us apes is in our tails. They are the flag under which we fight, the sheet-anchor of our patriotism, the vital insignia of our race. This young, decadent post-fruit-robbery generation was proposing to mutilate the symbol that is at the base of all our being. We did not hesitate. Spies were at once sent down to the lower branches to

see if what the pterodactyl had told us was true and to bring
the leader into our presence.

But before I tell what happened I must describe what life
in our tree is like. The tree is a vast and leafy one, dense in
the ramification of its twigs and branches. In the upper
branches where the air is freer and purer and the sunlight
is plentiful, live those of us who are called the higher apes;
in the branches below, and even to the bottom of the trunk,
swarm the thousands of lower apes, clawing and scrambling
over one another's backs, massing on the boughs until they
nearly break, clutching at twigs and leaves, hanging on to
one another's legs and tails, and all bellowing and screeching
in the struggle to get up a little higher and to find a place to
sit, so that when we say, as we do, that the nature of life is
struggle and war we are giving a faithful report from what
is going on below us.

We in the upper branches eat our fruit in peace and spit
out the pips and drop the rind upon the crowd below. It is
they who, without of course intending to do so, bring us our
food. Each of them carries fruit for himself, but the struggle
is so violent that it is hard for them to hold the fruit or to
find a quiet place where they can eat it. Accordingly we send
down some of our cleverer apes—those who are not quite
at the top of the tree yet and perhaps will never get there
because they have more brain than claw—and these hang
down by their tails and adroitly flick the fruit out of the
hands of the climbers. Very amusing it is to watch the
astonishment of the climbers when they see their fruit go,
because a minute before, they were full of confidence; then
astonishment changes to anger and you see them grab the
fruit from their nearest neighbours, who in turn grab from
the next. Failing in this, they have to go down once more to
the bottom to get more fruit and begin again; and as no part
of the struggle is more difficult than the one which takes
place at the bottom, an ape will go to any lengths, even to the

risk of his life, to avoid that catastrophe. So for thousands of years have we lived and only when fruit on our own tree is short or when we can bear no longer the sight of an abundance of fruit on another tree, occupied by just such a tribe of apes as ourselves, do our masses cease their engaging civil struggle and, at an order from us higher apes above, go forth upon our great fruit robberies. It is plain that if in any respect an ape ceased to be an ape, our greatness would decline, and anarchy would follow—that is, how would we at the top get our food?—and we should lose our tree and be destroyed by some stronger tribe. Our thoughts can therefore be imagined when the spies brought before us the leader of that group of apes who were preparing to monkey with our dearest emblem. He stood before us—and that is astonishing, for we apes do not habitually stand for long. Then he was paler than our race usually is, less hairy, fearless—very un-apelike that—and upright on his hind legs, not seeking support for his forelegs on some branch. These hung at his side or fidgeted with an aimless embarrassment behind his back. We growled at him and averted our eyes from his stupidly steadfast stare—for as a fighting race we are made subtle by fear and look restlessly, suspiciously around us, continually preparing for the sudden feint, the secret calculation, the necessary retreat, the unexpected attack. Nothing delivers an ape more readily to his enemy than a transparently straightforward look; but this upright ape had already lost so much of his apehood that he had forgotten the evasions of a warrior race. He was not even furtive. And in another way, too, he had lost our tradition. He spoke what was in his mind. This, I need hardly say, is ridiculous in a warrior whose business is to conceal his real purpose from his enemy. I note these facts merely as a matter of curiosity and to show how this new ape, from the very beginning, gave himself helplessly into our hands. We had supposed him to be guilty of race treachery only, a bodily perversion which is, perhaps, a sin and not a crime—but the moment he spoke he went much farther. He accused himself of sedition from his own mouth. He spoke as follows:

'Since my arrest has given me an opportunity of speaking to higher apes for the first time in my life, I will speak what (perhaps unknown to you) has been in the minds of us who are lower in the tree for hundreds of years. We think that there is no greater evil than the vast fruit slaughters. Now there could be no slaughter if our teeth and claws were not sharp, and they would not be sharp if we were not perpetually engaged in struggle. We believe that a crucial time has arrived in the evolution" (we pricked up our ears at that word) "of the ape. Our tails, which used to swirl us (as they waved above our heads) into blood-thirsty states of mind, are shortening; we have not shortened them ourselves by any act of will. If we apes will work to order our lives in a new way, the struggle will cease, no more great fruit slaughters will be necessary, and everyone will have all the fruit he needs and can eat in peace in his appropriate place in the tree. For we do not think that even you in the higher branches, for whom unconsciously we labour, really benefit by the great slaughters. Some of you are killed as thousands of us are, many of you are maimed and carry unbeautiful scars. From what we below hear of your private lives and talk in the upper branches, your privileges do not make you either sensible or happy."

We were ready to fall upon him after this blasphemous speech, but our oldest ape, steeped in the wisdom and slyness of his great age, silenced us. "And when there is a shortage of fruit for everyone in the tree, high and low alike?" he asked. "If our teeth and claws are not sharpened," replied the new ape, "we shall not want to attack other trees but, when we need fruit, we shall go to the others and instead of tearing them apart we shall talk to them, stroke them, and persuade them. They, seeing how gentle our hands are, will

The Ape

like being stroked and will smile and coo in their pleasure; for, as all of us apes know from intimate experience, there is nothing more delightful than a gentle tickling and scratching —and then they will share their fruit with us."—"What a hope!" We laughed. And some cried with disgust: "That ape's a pansy!" But a shout went up from the lower branches where a mass of his supporters were gathered. "You'd better do as he says," the cry came, "or soon there will be none of us left to bring you your fruit." "Yes," said the leader, "another fruit robbery and there will be no more workers for you to steal from."

"Now," we whispered to our oldest ape on the highest branch, "now let us kill him."

"Remember," said the old one, "that he has followers. They are too many for us and we are unprepared."

This was true, so, reluctantly, we let the leader go and swing back down the branches to his own people.

After he had gone we gathered in conference in the upper branches. When we were seated, our oldest ape said: "No doubt to you there seems to be something new, startling, and dangerous in the speech you have just heard. I expect you think it the speech of a revolutionary. So it is—but there's nothing new in that. From the beginning of time there have been revolutions, and what difference do they make? None whatever. Everything goes on afterwards exactly as it went on before. Do not worry therefore about revolutionaries. I have seen dozens of such people, and with a little art they can be made to die very comfortably of their own enthusiasm. And, in one way, I agree with what that strange ape said. He said that violence is wasteful. It is—for to exterminate our own workers would mean that we would be without food or would have to go down out of our comfortable places in the tree and get it for ourselves. That would indeed be a calamity. No, I think if we wish to remove the danger from this particular movement we should support it."

"Support blasphemy and treachery!" we cried with indignation.

"Ah!" exclaimed the old ape wistfully. "There speaks the honest warrior. But I am old and political and it would seem to me a mistake to let all that enthusiasm get out of our hands. After our last great fruit robbery we are rather tired, you know, and enthusiasm is not easily come by again."

"But our tails!" we shouted.

"Your honour and your tails!" said our weary and ancient one. "I guarantee to show you such a display of tails wagging, curling, prehensile, and triumphant as you have never seen before."

"Well, if your plan will safeguard our sacred tails and preserve us from evolution," we said, "there may be something in it. Tell us what it is."

"It is very simple," he said. "First of all we shall announce the end of all fruit robbery—"

"Impossible," we interrupted.

"It is never impossible to *announce* anything," he said. "I repeat we shall announce the end of all fruit robbery. But the lower ape is an emotional creature. It is useless to argue with him—indeed, we know that the free interchange of ideas in open argument is extremely dangerous, for the lower apes are hungry, and hunger sharpens the mind, just as it sharpens the claws. No, we must appeal to his emotions, for it is here that he is untrained and inexperienced. So when we announce the end of all fruit robbery, we must perform an act that shall symbolize our intention. That is easy. Almost anything would do. The best, I think, would be merely to alter the date of the commemoration of our last robbery from the anniversary of its call to battle, to the day on which it ended and when peace was declared. I'll lay you a hundred to one in pomegranates that you will see the tails wag on that day."

We who listened were doubtful of the success of a trick so simple and, moreover, we were disappointed not to have the opportunity of killing the rebel ape. But when we heard the enthusiasm in the lower branches, we realized that our oldest ape had judged rightly. Those short-tailed evolutionists were so diddled that they shouted for joy. "Peace!" "The end of all fruit robberies," "To each according to his needs"—we above heard their delirious cries and winked. And when the inquisitive pterodactyl came down to see what it was all about, we slapped him on the back and pulled his wings about merrily and nearly choked him with pomegranate seeds, which do not agree with him. "Cheer up, you're not extinct yet," we said. And even that cheerless reptile, though he said his nerves couldn't stand monkey tricks any more, had to smile.

And the ceremony took place. We appointed the day, and just before noon the yelling ceased and all the struggling and climbing. Just where they were, on whatever twig or branch, our apes coiled their tails and squatted in silence. The only movement was the blinking of our eyes, thousands of eyes in the hot rays of the sun. I do not know if you have ever seen a tree full of apes squatting in silence on their haunches. It is an impressive sight. There was our oldest ape on the topmost branch; a little beneath him was our circle of privileged ones, and below, thick in the descending hierarchy, were the others.

And then, before a minute had gone by, an event occurred which filled us with horror. The lengths to which blasphemy will go were revealed to us. Taking advantage of the stillness of the multitude, an ape leapt up the tree, from back to back, from branch to branch, and burst through our unprepared ranks at the top. It was the leader to whom we had spoken.

"This is a fraud," he shouted. "You are pretending to commemorate peace when all the time you are planning greater robberies. You are not even silent. Listen to the grinding and sharpening of your claws and teeth."

It was, of course, our habit. We do it unconsciously.

The Ape

Too startled for a moment to act, we hesitated. Then: "Lynch him. Kill him," cried the crowd with a sudden roar. We hesitated no more and at least a score of us leapt upon him. You would think we had an easy task. But there was extraordinary strength in that creature. He fought like a god, skillfully, and he had laid out half of our number with a science and ferocity such as we had never seen before our numbers overwhelmed him. Some spirit must have been in him and we still wonder, not without apprehension, if that spirit is lying asleep in his followers. However that may be, we threw him down at last upon the branch. Our oldest ape came down to look upon the panting creature and then what we saw made us gasp. He was lying on his face. There was a backside bare and hairless—he had no tail. No tail at all. "It is man!" we cried. And our stomachs turned.

The Chestnut Tree

The first firm I worked for was a leather merchants' in
the south of London. To look at, their place was like a
pair of muddy Methodist chapels with a jail attached; there
were bars to the windows and, inside, the office smelled of
feet, ink and boots. The name of the firm was Greenhythe &
Co. They had been established for one hundred and fifty
years.

I was fifteen when my father took me there. I had never
been to London before and in the train, after the ticket col-
lector had passed, we walked down the corridor to an empty
first-class carriage, pulled down the blinds, and then knelt in
prayer. Afterwards we read the Ninety-first Psalm. I had
diarrhœa that morning because I was afraid.

When we came to the office we were shown at once to Mr.
Greenhythe's room.

"I want this boy to begin at the bottom of the ladder," my
father said, speaking as a self-made man.

"Do you speak French, boy? *Parlez-vous français?*" said
Mr. Greenhythe. I could not answer. He was a very old
man with long white hair that was the colour of Vaseline at
the roots. He had a hump on one shoulder and the head of a
lion.

He then said there was a French proverb which went:
"*C'est le premier pas qui coûte.*"

After that my father and Mr. Greenhythe exchanged memories about the Wesleyan movement and the two men walked to the door. There was something noble, savage, and prophet-like about Mr. Greenhythe. But as he walked nimbly and cautiously to the door, with his bearded head sunk forward, his long arms hanging loosely, his old, cracked blue eyes raised, and his boots hissing on the ground like a boxer's in the sawdust, I noticed he had the punched-in face of a fighter and wicked little teeth. Only people, he said, who had been recommended by the chapel and were known for their seriousness ever worked for the firm of Greenhythe & Co. And so it seemed. Ten clerks were bending over their ledgers as if over the Scriptures when I was led to the cashier's desk.

My work began at eight in the morning. First of all I went down into the basement where the lavatory was to collect the pads used for copying the letters. The pads had been soaking all night. A smell of cigar smoke and scent came from the water closet and the sound of a newspaper being unfolded. Then of singing. Out came Mr. Cook, a fat bald man of sixty with a pair of nostrils like pink bubbles, and as fresh and perfumed as a flower; he had indeed a carnation in his buttonhole, for he grew these plants in his garden. "La da, di da, hijorico," he sang, and stood biting his fingernails sulkily and scratching his womanish backside. Mr. Cook opened the office every morning at half past seven. Later, when we went upstairs and while I was filling the ink-wells, this old man would lift up his desk lid, peep over the top, and shout: "Ya! Ya! Ya!" and duck again. Then, once more, he sat biting the nails of his short, dirty fingers.

At ten to nine the clerks began to arrive. When they had hung up their coats and hats they came to the fireplace and stood warming themselves. If there was no fire, they stood there all the same. Williams, the sandy, flat-footed one, with a sneering voice and misery in his skinny legs; Hodgkin, like a young actor, raising dark eyebrows as if he were looking

at himself sideways in a mirror, and very stage-struck;
Porter, the shipping clerk, with food stains on his waistcoat,
the puffing father of a large family who was often making
mistakes in an authoritative way, sending bills of lading to
the wrong ports, delivery orders to the wrong wharves, and
who sat among the muddle of his papers like a hen having a
dust bath; Turpin, the limp dandy in patent shoes, lined and
sick-looking, always with a smile stamped dead on his face,
and smelling of cachous; then Sawston. Cook did not join
them. Popping his head above his desk lid he shouted out:
"Ha ya! Ha ya!" And when they turned in condescension,
some word like "Flambustigation." Sawston used to turn to
him and tell him, in dry, morose voice, to shut up. Cook put
down his lid and laughed till the tears ran down his face.

Then the outer door swung and in came Drake, the cashier
and head of the office. All the clerks moved guiltily to their
desks. Except Sawston. He glanced up at the clock. If it
wanted two minutes or one minute of nine, he stayed where
he was and watched Drake, a tall man with a gloomy voice
like a chapel organ and grizzled hair and gold-rimmed
glasses, come glowering towards him, clearing his throat.
"Good morning, Mr. Drake," said Mr. Sawston with loud
effrontery. Drake looked at the clock; Sawston's small black
eyes in his baldish, bullet head dared Mr. Drake to have the
courage to tell him to go to his desk. Mr. Drake blew his
nose and did not dare. "Um. Um. Umph." Mr. Drake made
a characteristic sigh on three notes, a noise famous in the
office, and at once perfectly imitated by Mr. Cook, who
again lifted his desk lid, ducked his head, and spluttered with
laughter. Nine o'clock struck and slowly Mr. Sawston
walked to his desk, carefully cleaned his pens, wiped his
ruler, sharpened his pencils, put a pile of invoices tidily on
his blotter, and began writing in his small girlish hand.
Moodily Mr. Drake gazed at the back of Mr. Sawston's
cheap grey suit and shook his head.

In Greenhythe's office the hours were long. At seven in the evening when I left, Williams and Sawston were still at their books under the green shades of the lights, Porter the shipping clerk was sunk in his muddle; the partners, Mr. Greenhythe's sons, had gone, but a bell that snapped outside his office and a weak bad light shining through the glass door showed that Mr. Greenhythe was still working. On Saturdays we left early—four o'clock. Only Mr. Cook enjoyed this régime. Leaving the office at eleven o'clock in the morning to take documents or large cheques to the City, he would waggle his rump as he went out, saying: "Ya! Ya! dears!" and would spend the next few hours in the West End, sometimes at theatres for an act or two, sometimes in pubs, and occasionally with girls. He came back short-tempered, rosy, and smelling of cigars.

One Monday when I had been four or five months in the firm, a woman came to the office counter. She was a tall, soft woman who wore a big floating hat with flowers on it and a blue serge coat and skirt. She had the bust of a draper's model. "I have an appointment with Mr. Greenhythe," she said in a delicate, aloof, and dreamy voice, looking down at me as if I were a fly on the counter. She was touching her nose affectingly with a handkerchief and I thought she was a royalty with a cold.

"What name, please?"

"Miss Browne," she said. "Browne with an 'e.' "

After an hour she came out of Mr. Greenhythe's room with Mr. Drake as well and they led her to the street door. They were talking about Mr. Greenhythe's Bible class. A week later she came again and then two days running. In his harmonium voice, Mr. Drake murmured to Mr. Porter that the firm were thinking of employing "a lady book-keeper."

The word "lady" fell like a boulder upon us. There were typists upstairs who arrived late and who never spoke to us; in the General Office there were no women at all.

The Chestnut Tree

"A leedy book-keepah!" called Mr. Cook from his desk. "Ya ha!"

"Who's getting the sack?" said Williams.

"Who's getting the bird?" said Hodgkin, and hummed an air from *La Bohème*.

"There are two," said Turpin, the tired sick young man who always knew everything. "She said she could not work in an office unless she were chaperoned by her sister."

"One for you, one for Mr. Turpin," sneered Williams.

"Let us pray," called Mr. Cook, hiding behind his desk lid.

Mr. Drake was coming in. The clerks moved to their desks. The lines on Mr. Turpin's face became deep seams. He was a martyr to the seduction of women. Women set him off, like a machine, against his will. They confided in him at once; just as Mr. Drake confided to him the worries of a cashier, Mr. Porter the muddles of his shipping, Mr. Williams his troubles with his stomach, Mr. Greenhythe the number of well-known preachers he had heard. The bold sick eyes of Mr. Turpin, the sympathy of his manners, even his large ears, which stuck out like comical microphones from his long head, the smile, which was the tired smile of a man with a headache, brought men and women to him helplessly. He was a clever man from the flat, singsong Midlands, but he had the long, stupid face of an animal that is mindless and sad.

The two lady book-keepers arrived. Miss Browne the elder, whom we had seen, was like a swan and thought so herself. Her fair hair, she conveyed to you, was her glory. She was curving and sedate. With the sleepy smile of one lying on a feather bed in Paradise, with tiny grey eyes behind the pince-nez which sat on her nose, with the swell of long low breasts balanced by the swell of her dawdling rump, she moved swanlike to her desk. But not like a swan in the water; like a swan on land. She waddled. Her feet were planted obliquely. One would have said that they were webbed.

Behind her came the cygnet and chaperon, her sister and protector. When I saw her I felt I had been struck in the heart by a stone. Mr. Drake frowned and drummed his fingers, Mr. Cook began biting his thumbnail and leered in fury, Mr. Porter became homely and paternal, Williams gave a scheming look at her legs, the stage-struck Hodgkin took a comb out of his pocket and ran it through his waved hair. Turpin and Sawston, who were on opposite sides of the same high, tilted desk, looked at each other fixedly. They looked as though they were trying to hypnotize each other. Taking small hard steps, her red lips pettishly drooping, her head in a cap of short black curls, her small breasts, her hips, her waist, set off by her silk dress, the sister of Miss Browne walked as if at any moment, if she shrugged her shoulders again, she could make her clothes fall off her. Her dress had some small design of red and white daisies. She looked at us tenderly and without innocence. She was as hard as a bird. When she spoke, her voice was like a high cross voice in a garden.

Turpin put one leg down from his stool at once. He was about to introduce himself to the women; to walk between them with his hand just touching their waists. In such times his limpness went; he was decided. The dull buzz of his voice was the sound of the machine that had started inside him. But this time he sat back on his stool. Sawston was looking at him. Sawston's face was bloodless, as set and chalky as a clown's. The thick black brows were rigid and seemed to have been painted on, his eyes had a light so peremptory in them that one might have been looking into a pair of pistol barrels. Turpin was arrested by Sawston's eyes.

"O.K., laddie," Turpin said. A slight smile came to Sawston's face and he went on staring with indulgence at Turpin, whom he had silently conquered. Sawston's eyes appeared to be printing off thousands of words, which Turpin read as rapidly as they were printed. Sawston folded his arms, and his fists were clenched. His coat-sleeves were short and his wrists were spidery, with black hair. The smile became fainter, more ironically acid and delighted.

At the end of the morning Sawston, who had worked very little—and ordinarily he worked hard—but had sat staring defiantly at his own life, got down from his stool and walked back to the desk by the fireplace where Mr. Drake ruled. Drake was tall. Sawston was a short man, wide for his size, and he wore collars so low that they did not show above his jacket. This gave the impression that he was a collarless workman or was perhaps wearing a boxer's sweater. He was one of those men who have to shave twice a day and whose beard leaves a dark indigo stain like ink on a blotter. He was a curt man, blunt and independent.

"I think, Mr. Drake," he said, "I think the younger Miss Browne had better work with me."

It was a demand, an order. Drake's jaws chewed, he blew into his moustache and was flustered. He tried to glower. He looked sideways up at the bars of the window, he made his harmonium noises. In the office he had the kind of authority which is despised but obeyed. But with Sawston Mr. Drake could do nothing. He looked down resentfully at Sawston as if Sawston were a bear who had put him up a tree.

"Obviously," continued Sawston, "the girl hasn't got a brain in her head. I'll teach her."

Sawston had a cocky habit of clicking his tongue in his mouth when he was amused by his own self-possession. Having said this, he walked back to his desk.

After lunch Sawston called across two rows of desks in a clear voice which was much louder than the tone that was thought suitable in this office:

"Miss Browne. Will you come over here, please."

She pouted and, affecting lack of interest, walked over to him. The black curls shook on her head, the small breasts pushed like nuts against her blouse. Her eyes were hot-blue with freckles on the pale skin under them and her clockwork voice said: "Yes, what do you want?"

"Call over these invoices," he said. She shrugged her rounded shoulders and held a pencil in her teeth. Sawston put his hand out and took the pencil out of her mouth. She was astonished. Sitting behind them, the elder Miss Browne saw this incident and awoke from her dream. She gazed at Sawston's shiny back with dislike.

We were afraid of Sawston, all of us. Without authority he suggested independent power. He was small, but our fear was physical. His walk, for example—he walked, not as some swaggerers did, who thought the place belonged to them, but as if he owned the precise yard of floor he happened to stand on. That was a vaster claim. His desk was his, not the firm's. His pens were his. He sharpened *his* pencils. He made no mistakes in his books—well, once a year he might make a mistake and no one cared to mention it to him. He would admit it. This was inhuman and alarming; there was no one else in the building who did not make a scene about their mistakes and try to argue them on to someone else. A peculiar physical thing about him was the smallness of his wrists and his hands. Then of what were we afraid? His indifference. He was a man, Mr. Turpin said admiringly, who would ruin himself. And Mr. Turpin understood ruin.

Sometimes the two sisters sat together, sometimes the elder Miss Browne sat beside Mr. Drake, calling over the big ledgers. High on their stools these two looked like a King and Queen. Mr. Drake was respectful to her. She had a romantic queenly air, sighed majestically or made little regal yawns behind her hands, sometimes stretching her arms to the back of her head and looking at us from a great, pale

pillow of voluptuousness through her rimless glasses. No
one, not even Mr. Turpin, responded to the voluptuousness
of the elder Miss Browne. She dropped her pens, but only
Mr. Drake grovelled on the floor for them. She watched him
grovelling, thanked him with languor, spoke in the exhausted
voice of a great hostess. Her favourite subject was Woman.

When the sisters sat together was the time to attempt a
flirtation with the younger one. The swan prevented it. She
had a weary musical sarcasm:

"Have you nothing else to occupy yourself with, Mr.
Williams?"

One day she said: "Heestings is a beautiful spot. One can
have any kind of holiday there—quiet, noisy, or musical."

"Quiet with her about," said Williams, digging his pen in
the younger one's ribs. The younger one astonished us, as
pretty women do, by making a horrible face, squaring her
mouth as if she were going to be sick, and nodding at her
sister. Delight! The two sisters detested each other. The
great actress was jealous; the chaperon was venomous. Left
alone together, they bickered in refined voices.

"But you did, Hester, you said so yourself."

"I didn't."

"You did. You said he said . . ."

"I said nothing of the sort."

We rolled our eyes. Lovely! Lady book-keepers! The
young one saw me listening and turned and smiled intimately
at me. I went scarlet, and when she spoke to me I could not
answer. The elder sister looked over the young one's black
curls at me and said remotely: "He's only a child." She
pronounced it "charld."

Turpin and I sat opposite Sawston, and when the young
one was with him we heard him reading the invoices and she
copying or checking; but between the dates and the figures
a low conversation was interpolated. Sitting side by side,
they did not look at each other but looked across at Turpin

and me, or at their books. But all the time, like the dry
mutter of a telegraph, their talk went on.

Lady book-keepers! What happiness it was to see them
arrive in the morning! The elder one, holding her hair at the
back and tilting her flowery hat forward, came in with her
coat flying and swayed as if drunk to the cloakroom, murmuring loudly to the young one, who came pattering trimly,
crossly, shrugging her shoulders and snapping out words,
behind.

"Ha ya," called Mr. Cook. "Late again."

"And hot," said Mr. Williams. Covering his mouth with
his hand, he added to the remark.

"Sisters, sisters," called Mr. Cook when they came to
their desk. "Do not quarrel." The young one ignored him
and went to Sawston and started intense whispering.

"The big cow," said Sawston aloud one morning.

"What do you want?" he snapped at me, seeing I was
listening. She smiled at me. She reached across to the library
book I had on the desk and said:

"What are you reading?"

It was poetry, the poetical works of Sir Walter Scott. I
was reading *The Lay of the Last Minstrel*.

"Pooh," she said. "Dry."

Sawston looked quizzically at me.

"The boy's brain will bust," he said.

They both smiled, united by the same irony. I felt sad; I
might have been their son.

But the cashier was watching our little group. "Press on,
Mr. Sawston," he moaned. "Press on! Boy. Come here."
Colouring, I went to the side of his desk. He had his pen
longways in his teeth and he went on turning the pages of his
ledger.

"I do not want you to waste Miss Hester's time," he said.
"We are very busy. How old are you?"

"Sixteen," I lied. I was fifteen years and two months old.

The Chestnut Tree

I stood there waiting for his next remark. He went on turning the pages of his ledger. "Um. Um. Um," he sighed on his three notes. I had never been so near to this legendary noise before. It was like the rumination of humanity. A cage had been opened and out had come the humdrum rumour of the human race, the neutral, aimless, mindless rumble of the ape, digesting its inexplicable years on earth.

"Yes?" said Mr. Drake, observing me again, surprised to see me still there. Then: "That's all." I went back in a sulk. My cheeks were hot. I scowled at Miss Hester Browne. She had been my undoing.

In the garden of the house where I lodged was a chestnut tree. In the morning when I left to catch my train the sky was clear and blue and against it the leaves of the tree hung down like the tongues of dark green dogs and the pink candles of blossom stood up from among them. I listened to the sound of my feet on the pavement. It was without will of mine that they touched the ground. There was a throbbing in my ears, so that I could hear only my own body, the clapping of my heart. I seemed to be flying, not walking. Would people in the train be uneasy because I was mad? The spirit and the flesh—two animals that were always in my head—were pulling me apart. The spirit was desire, the spirit was Hester Browne; the flesh had no desire, it clothed the torpor and the innumerable dreads of the mind and body.

My train went on to London, past the factories. Why were there no lakes, no mountains? For: "He, neglected and oppressed, wished to be with them and at rest." And why was great literature so boring? Into the pages of *The Lay of the Last Minstrel* I had put a folded sheet of the *Windsor Magazine* with a poem printed on it.

> *Stars of the heavens I love her*
> *Spread the glad news afar,*

it began. I was ashamed to think that terrible poem described my feelings better than anything in Scott.

"I should say you were an idealist," Mr. Turpin said gravely to me while he opened the firm's letters. In the morning, when he was tired, he used to talk about life.

But now Mr. Drake had broken me. I was watched. Shame, vanity, spite thickened my head and bit my throat. The spirit and the flesh turned a somersault inside me, I tore up my cutting from the magazine; the flesh triumphed. I hated Hester Browne. My desire had become a poison. I saw the deadly nightshade shadows under her eyes and I was pleased by what Mr. Turpin had said.

Turpin wore a small, mauve silk handkerchief in his breast pocket, and it was very long. An idealist! I bought myself a handkerchief and wore it like his. Williams shuffled over to me and, putting his hand over his mouth in his secretive way, bent towards me slyly so that I could smell the tobacco on his breath.

"Imitation," he sneered, "is the sincerest form of flattery."

Giving a sharp look back at me, he went off.

Now I hated Hester Browne I had the courage to observe her. She began to arrive after her sister and went breathless and damp-skinned to her desk. The pretty eyes were sticky with sleep as if she hadn't washed. To a connoisseur like Turpin this was very attractive. Her dress, the one with the small daisies, had scores of small creases in it. There was a week like this, her lips sulked, and an exciting hay-like smell followed her in a warm current as she walked.

"Do you notice, Mr. Turpin, anything about the atmosphere?" said Williams.

"Yes, I do," said Mr. Turpin shortly. "Pleasanter than leather, isn't it?"

"A matter of opinion," leered Mr. Williams. Up went the inevitable hand to his lips. "Perhaps a matter of experience."

The Chestnut Tree

There was a lift up to the top floor of the warehouse and sometimes I had to take messages there. I was waiting on the third floor when the lift went groaning past me. Inside were two people, a man and a woman. The man was limp and tall and his head was close to her, looking down at her neck. She was the elder Miss Browne. She was talking violently and the man was Mr. Turpin, who paid no attention to what she said but kept murmuring:

"You great big doll."

"He's a married man," she was saying. "Look at his face. It's a cruel face. The way he speaks to her even."

Two coats, a skirt, and a pair of trousers were carried upstairs out of my sight.

"I can be cruel too, duckie," Mr. Turpin was saying as his patent shoes went up beyond me.

It was August. Mr. Cook put his carnation in a glass of water and smelled it from time to time. He was sixty-two on the bank holiday and went up in an aeroplane. Mr. Greenhythe's secreaty, an elderly woman who looked like Queen Victoria, put a pamphlet with the heading *Repent Ye* on our desks. Turpin read it through carefully. Then he lit his cigarette with it and said respectfully:

"I must go upstairs and thank her." Hodgkin took a clean sheet of paper and wrote with flourishes the words *The Marriage of Figaro*. Underneath he wrote in smaller letters: The Duke: Rupert Hodgkin. He looked in a pocket mirror and watched the movements of his mouth. "Press on, Mr. Hodgkin," said Mr. Drake. Mr. Sawston and Hester Browne went out to lunch together, waiting for Mr. Drake to go first.

On an afternoon in the middle of that week children in the street began shouting at a balloon in the sky. "Listen to those children," said Mr. Porter tenderly, making a mistake in a weighing slip as he spoke. Between two and three was a slow hour; we all went to look at the balloon.

"Before the war," said Mr. Drake, unbending, "there used to be a number of balloons." We did not notice the elder Miss Browne get down from her desk and go into Mr. Greenhythe's room and so we were astonished to see her coming out of it. The top part of her was gliding in a drowsy and smiling dream. She had the smile of one who has opened a bazaar, of a boa constrictor that has fed.

Mr. Drake pulled himself together.

"March 1," came Mr. Drake's voice. "By goods, cash. £26 17s. 1d." And her voice repeated: "£26 17s. 1d."

"March 3," Mr. Drake went on. "By goods, cash. £462 16s. 3d. March 14," the voice was chanting the office litany. "Have you got March 14, Miss Browne? Goods, thirteen and a penny? Put a query against that."

He peered over Miss Browne to the page to see she had done this. As she wrote in the great ledger she was looking at the childish pink and white frock of her sister like a woman who is thinking of lengthening the sleeves. She also looked ironically at the slack, shiny coat of Mr. Sawston.

There was a bell over Mr. Greenhythe's door and it snapped two or three times. It was my business to answer the bell and sometimes the old man used to ring it by mistake or forget what he wanted. I went into his office, which had a green light, for the sun-blind was down. His elderly secretary was just leaving the room. The old lion put down the telephone.

"Boy," he said breathlessly, "the *Alexandra Castle* has docked."

I stared at him. He looked at me suspiciously.

"Is your father well?" he asked.

I said he was.

He looked absently at his secretary.

"What was I thinking about?" he asked pathetically.

"Mr. Sawston," she said.

"Ah, boy!" he barked at me, showing his little teeth. "Send Mr. Sawston to me."

Mr. Sawston went into Mr. Greenhythe's room.

"Sawston's on the carpet," Williams said.

"Hi yi," said Cook, smelling his carnation. "What do I ca-ah? What do I ca-ah? I've got tickets for the Palladium."

Turpin leaned across to Hester Browne, who was looking resentfully towards Mr. Greenhythe's door and straightening her shoulder straps.

"Keep on doing that," said Mr. Turpin in a dead voice. "And I will bite your shoulders."

"I was thinking, Mr. Drake," said the elder Miss Browne with a yawn, "what thousands of people there must be at the sea."

A pencil rolled down the desk and dropped on to the floor. "Boy," called a curt voice. "Pick up my pencil." It was Sawston. He was back again. Suddenly sitting at the desk. His eyebrows appeared to be stamped an inch higher on his forehead. His eyes seemed to be filled with points of flint. I picked up the pencil.

"The damned, impudent old man," he said so loudly that everyone looked up. He did not look at Hester Browne. She spoke to him.

"Shut up," he said very loudly.

He collected his invoice forms together, folded his blotter, and put those into his desk. Then he put away his pens and his round ruler.

The girl put her hand on his sleeve, but he lifted it off. Then he got down, looked round the office, taking in every detail of it, and after that walked to the cloakroom. He came out in his bowler hat with his mackintosh over his shoulder. He stopped, lit a cigarette, and threw the match-stick over counter. We all stared. At three o'clock in the afternoon, smoking without permission, Mr. Sawston walked out of the office.

A moan, indignant, and forlorn, like the sound of a ship's siren as it goes out with foreboding into the ruin of the sea, went up from Mr. Drake.

"Mr. Sawston!" called the appalled voice. Mr. Sawston glanced back, showed the whites of his eyes, and raised his bowler hat. He was gone. Hester Browne jumped down, knocked her stool over, and ran to the counter.

"Hetty," shouted her sister, and came heavily after her. "Leave that man alone!"

She was in time to catch Hester by the sleeve.

"Stop it," shouted Hester and, turning like a rat, struck at the elder one's face.

"Ooh you, you . . . you," cried Miss Browne and hit out. The young one's sleeve tore, down went the elder's glasses.

"Just look at that," said Williams.

They were at each other's hair, screeching and shouting.

"You little tart! You little tart! You—you—you—little tart!" screamed Miss Browne.

The swing door on the counter flew open and Miss Browne fell through on to the floor.

We rushed to them. Their blouses were ripped, their hair was down, their faces were bleeding. The little one underneath was biting her sister's wrist, the big one was striking out and hitting the counter. They rolled.

"Miss Browne. Miss Hester," sobbed Mr. Drake shaking his pen at them and spattering them with ink. He bent to pull down Miss Browne's skirt, which was round her waist and exposing thighs whose might astonished us.

At once the pair of them got free and flew at Mr. Drake. This was beyond us. Mr. Hodgkin stepped back, Mr. Cook lowered his head and blushed, Mr. Williams cried out.

The Chestnut Tree

"Remove them, remove them," pleaded Mr. Drake. Mr. Porter, eternally wrong, began to pull at Mr. Drake. A loud slap startled us. Miss Hester had caught Mr. Drake on the cheek. There was silence. And then we saw Mr. Turpin. Sitting sideways on his stool, detached, interested, and thoughtful, he was watching us.

"Mr. Turpin!" Drake and Porter called out together. It was a cry to the expert. Sadly he got down from his stool and came to the two panting girls.

"Darlings . . ." he began, and put his arms round their waists, but at this word the big one swooned and hung on him so that he was hardly able to support her. "I told Mr. Greenhythe," she was gasping quietly. "Save her, save her. He's a married man."

But the little one had jumped away. Screeching, she escaped us and ran into the street to follow Mr. Sawston. And that was the last we saw of either of them. The thing that struck us all dumb was that Mr. Sawston had not fallen to the fear that hung over all of us: he had not been sacked. He had sacked himself.

The Evils of Spain

We took our seats at the table. There were seven of us. It was at one of those taverns in Madrid. The moment we sat down Juliano, the little, hen-headed, red-lipped consumptive who was paying for the dinner and who laughed not with his mouth but by crinkling the skin round his eyes into scores of scratchy lines and showing his bony teeth—Juliano got up and said: "We are all badly placed." Fernando and Felix said: "No, we are not badly placed." And this started another argument shouting between the lot of us. We had been arguing all the way to the restaurant. The proprietor then offered a new table in a different way. Unanimously we said: "No," to settle the row; and when he brought the table and put it into place and laid a red and white check tablecloth on it, we sat down, stretched our legs, and said: "Yes. This table is much better."

Before this we had called for Angel at his hotel. We shook his hand or slapped him on the back or embraced him and two hung on his arm as we walked down the street. "Ah, Angel, the rogue!" we said, giving him a squeeze. Our smooth Mediterranean Angel! "The uncle!" we said. "The old scoundrel." Angel smiled, lowering his black lashes in appreciation. Juliano gave him a prod in the ribs and asked him if he remembered, after all these years, that summer at Biarritz. When we had all been together? The only time

293

we had all been together before? Juliano laughed by making
his eyes wicked and expectant, like one Andalusian remind-
ing another of the great joke they had had the day poor
So-and-So fell down the stairs and broke his neck.

"The day you were nearly drowned," Juliano said.

Angel's complexion was the colour of white coffee; his
hair, crinkled like a black fern, was parted in the middle, he
was rich, soft-palmed, and patient. He was the only well-
dressed man among us, the suavest shouter. Now he sat
next door but one to Juliano. Fernando was between them,
Juan next to me, and at the end Felix. They had put Cæsar
at the head of the table, because he was the oldest and the
largest. Indeed, at his age he found his weight tiring to the
feet.

Cæsar did not speak much. He gave his silent weight to
the dinner, letting his head drop like someone falling asleep,
and listening. To the noise we made, his silence was a balance
and he nodded all the time slowly, making everything true.
Sometimes someone told some story about him and he listened to that, nodding and not disputing it.

But we were talking chiefly of that summer, the one when
Angel (the old uncle!) had nearly been drowned. Then Juan,
the stout, swarthy one, banged the table with his hairy hands
and put on his horn-rimmed glasses. He was the smallest and
most vehement of us, the one with the thickest neck and the
deepest voice, his words like barrels rumbling in a cellar.

"Come on! Come on! Let's make up our minds! What
are we going to eat? Eat! Eat!" he roared.

"Yes," we cried. "Drink! What are we going to drink?"

The proprietor, who was in his shirt-sleeves and braces,
said it was for us to decide. We could have anything we
wanted. This started another argument. He stepped back a
pace and put himself in an attitude of self-defence.

"Soup! Soup? Make up your minds about soup! Who
wants soup?" bawled Juan.

"Red wine," some of us answered. And others: "Not red, white."

"Soup I said," shouted Juan. "Yes," we all shouted. "Soup."

"Ah," said Juan, shaking his head, in his slow miserable disappointed voice. "Nobody have any soup. I want some soup. Nobody soup," he said sadly to the proprietor.

Juliano was bouncing in his chair and saying, God, he would never forget that summer when Angel was nearly drowned! When we had all been together. But Juan said Felix had not been there and we had to straighten that matter out.

Juliano said: "They carried him on to the beach, our little Angel on to the beach. And the beach superintendent came through the crowd and said: 'What's happening?' 'Nothing,' we said. 'A man knocked out.' 'Knocked out?' said the beach superintendent. 'Nothing,' we said. 'Drowned!' A lot of people left the crowd and ran about over the beach saying: 'A man has been drowned.' 'Drowned,' said the beach superintendent. Angel was lying in the middle of them all, unconscious, with water pouring out of his mouth."

"No! No!" shouted Fernando. "No. It wasn't like that."

"How do you mean, it wasn't like that?" cried Juliano. "I was there." He appealed to us: "I was there."

"Yes, you were there," we said.

"I *was* there. I was there bringing him in. You say it wasn't like that, but it was like that. We were all there." Juliano jumped protesting to his feet, flung back his coat from his defying chest. His waistcoat was very loose over his stomach, draughty.

"What happened was better than that," Fernando said.

"Ah," said Juliano, suddenly sitting down and grinning with his eyes at everyone, very pleased at his show.

"It was better," he said. "How better?"

Fernando was a man who waited for silence and his hour.

The Evils of Spain

Once getting possession of the conversation he never let it go, but held it in the long, soothing ecstasy of a pliable embrace. All day long he lay in bed in his room in Fuencarral with the shutters closed, recovering from the bout of the day before. He was preparing himself to appear in the evening, spruce, grey-haired, and meaty under the deep black crescents of his eyebrows, his cheeks ripening like plums as the evening advanced, his blue eyes, which got bloodshot early, becoming mistier. He was a man who ripened and moistened. He talked his way through dinner into the night, his voice loosening, his eyes misting, his walk becoming slower and stealthier, acting every sentence, as if he were swaying through the exalted phase of inebriation. But it was an inebriation purely verbal; an exaltation of dramatic moments, refinements upon situations; and hour after hour passed until the dawn found him sodden in his own anecdotes, like a fruit in rum.

"What happened was," Fernando said, "that I was in the sea. And after a while I discovered Angel was in the sea. As you know, there is nothing more perilous than the sea, but with Angel in it the peril is tripled; and when I saw him I was preparing to get as far away as possible. But he was making faces in the water and soon he made such a face, so inhuman, so unnatural, I saw he was drowning. This did not surprise me, for Angel is one of those men who, when he is in the sea, he drowns. There is some psychological antipathy. Now, when I see a man drowning my instinct is to get away quickly. A man drowning is not a man. He is a lunatic. But a lunatic like Angel! But unfortunately he got me before I could get away. There he was," Fernando stood up and raised his arm, confronting the proprietor of the restaurant, but staring right through that defensive man, "beating the water, diving, spluttering, choking, spitting, and, seeing he was drowning, for the man *was* drowning, caught hold of me, and we both went under. Angel was like a beast. He

clung to me like seaweed. I, seeing this, awarded him a
knock-out—zum—but as the tenacity of man increases with
unconsciousness, Angel stuck to me like a limpet, and in
saving myself there was no escape from saving him."

"That's true," said Angel, admiring his fingernails. And
Cæsar nodded his head up and down twice, which made it
true.

Juan then swung round and called out: "Eat! Food! Let
us order. Let us eat. We haven't ordered. We do nothing
but talk, not eat. I want to eat."

"Yes, come on," said Felix. "Eat. What's the fish?"

"The fish," said the proprietor, "is bacalao."

"Yes," everyone cried. "Bacalao, a good bacalao, a very
good one. No, it must be good. No. I can't eat it unless it's
good, very good *and* very good."

"No," we said. "Not fish. We don't want it."

"Seven bacalaos, then?" said the proprietor.

But Fernando was still on his feet.

"And the beach inspector said: 'What's his name and
address and has he any identity papers?' 'Man,' I said, 'he's
in his bathing dress. Where could he keep his papers?' And
Juan said: 'Get a doctor. Don't stand there asking questions.
Get a doctor.'"

"That's true," said Juan gloomily. "He wasn't dead."

"Get a doctor, that was it," Angel said.

"And they got a doctor and brought him round and got
half the Bay of Biscay out of him, gallons of it. It astonished
me that so much water could come out of a man."

"And then in the evening"—Juliano leaped up and clipped
the story out of Fernando's mouth. "Angel says to the
proprietor of the hotel—"

Juan's head had sunk to his chest. His hands were over his
ears.

"Eat," he bawled in a voice of despair so final that we all
stopped talking and gazed at him with astonishment for a

few moments. Then in sadness he turned to me, appealing. "Can't we eat? I am empty."

". . . said to the proprietor of the hotel," Fernando grabbed the tale back from Juliano, "who was rushing down the corridor with a face like a fish. 'I am the man who was drowned this morning.' And the proprietor who looked at Angel like a prawn, the proprietor said: 'M'sieu, whether you were drowned or not drowned this morning, you are about to be roast. The hotel is on fire.'"

"That's right," we said. "The hotel was on fire."

"I remember," said Felix. "It began in the kitchen."

"How in the kitchen?"

This then became the argument.

"The first time ever I heard it was in the kitchen."

"But no," said Angel, softly rising to claim his life story for himself. Juliano clapped his hands and bounced with joy. "It was not like that."

"But we were all there, Angel," Fernando said; but Angel, who spoke very rapidly, said:

"No and no! And the proof of it is. What was I wearing?" He challenged all of us. We paused.

"Tripe," said Juan to me, hopelessly wagging his head. "You like tripe? They do it well. Here! Phist!" he called the proprietor through the din. "Have you tripe, a good Basque tripe? No? What a pity! Can you get me some? Here! Listen," he shouted to the rest of the table. "Tripe," he shouted, but they were engrossed in Angel.

"Pyjamas," Fernando said. "When you are in bed you wear your pyjamas."

"Exactly, and they were not my pyjamas."

"You say the fire was not in the kitchen," shouted Fernando, "because the pyjamas you were wearing were not yours!" And we shouted back at Angel.

"They belonged to the Italian Ambassador," said Angel, "the one who was with that beautiful Mexican girl."

The Evils of Spain

Then Cæsar, who, as I have said, was the oldest of us and sat at the head of the table, Cæsar leaned his old big pale face forward and said in a hushed voice, putting out his hands like a blind man remembering:

"My God—but what a very beautiful woman she was," he said. "I remember her. I have never in my life," he said speaking all his words slowly and with grave concern, "seen such a beautiful woman."

Fernando and Angel, who had been standing, sat down. We all looked in awe at the huge, old-shouldered Cæsar with his big pale face and the pockets under his little grey eyes, who was speaking of the most beautiful woman he had ever seen.

"She was there all that summer," Cæsar said. "She was no longer young." He leaned forward with his hands on the table. "What must she have been when she was young?"

A beach, the green sea dancing down white upon it, that Mexican woman walking over the floor of a restaurant, the warm white houses, the night glossy black like the toe of a patent shoe, her hair black. We tried to think how many years ago this was. Brought by his voice to silence us, she was already fading.

The proprietor took his opportunity in our silence. "The bacalao is done in the Basque fashions with peppers and potatoes. Bring a bacalao," he snapped to a youth in the kitchen.

Suddenly Juan brought his fists on the table, pushed back his chair, and beat his chest with one fist and then the other. He swore in his enormous voice by his private parts.

"It's eleven o'clock. Eat! For God's sake. Fernando stands there talking and talking and no one listens to anybody. It is one of the evils of Spain. Someone stop him. Eat."

We all woke up and glared with the defiance of the bewildered, rejecting everything he said. Then what he said to us penetrated. A wave roared over us and we were with him. We agreed with what he said. We all stood up and, by our private parts, swore that he was right. It was one of the evils of Spain.

The soup arrived. White wine arrived.

"I didn't order soup," some shouted.

"I said 'Red wine,' " others said.

"It is a mistake," the proprietor said. "I'll take it away." An argument started about this.

"No," we said. "Leave it. We want it." And then we said the soup was bad, and the wine was bad and everything he brought was bad, but the proprietor said the soup was good and the wine was good and we said in the end it was good. We told the proprietor the restaurant was good, but he said not very good—indeed, bad. And then we asked Angel to explain about the pyjamas.

The Voice

A message came from the rescue party, who straightened up and leaned on their spades in the rubble. The policeman said to the crowd: "Everyone keep quiet for five minutes. No talking, please. They're trying to hear where he is."

The silent crowd raised their faces and looked across the ropes to the church which, now it was destroyed, broke the line of the street like a decayed tooth. The bomb had brought down the front wall and the roof, the balcony had capsized. Freakishly untouched, the hymnboard still announced the previous Sunday's hymns.

A small wind blew a smell of smouldering cloth across people's noses from another street where there was another scene like this. A bus roared by and heads turned in passive anger until the sound of the engine had gone. People blinked as a pigeon flew from a roof and crossed the building like an omen of release. There was dead quietness again. Presently a murmuring sound was heard by the rescue party. The man buried under the debris was singing again.

At first difficult to hear, soon a tune became definite. Two of the rescuers took up their shovels and shouted down to encourage the buried man, and the voice became stronger and louder. Words became clear. The leader of the rescue

The Voice

party held back the others, and those who were near strained to hear. Then the words were unmistakable:

> *"Oh Thou whose Voice the waters heard,*
> *And hushed their raging at Thy Word."*

The buried man was singing a hymn.

A clergyman was standing with the warden in the middle of the ruined church.

"That's Mr. Morgan all right," the warden said. "He could sing. He got silver medals for it."

The Reverend Frank Lewis frowned.

"Gold, I shouldn't wonder," said Mr. Lewis, dryly. Now he knew Morgan was alive he said: "What the devil's he doing in there? How did he get in? I locked up at eight o'clock last night myself."

Lewis was a wiry, middle-aged man, but the white dust on his hair and his eye-lashes, and the way he kept licking the dust off his dry lips, moving his jaws all the time, gave him the monkeyish, testy, and suspicious air of an old man. He had been up all night on rescue work in the raid and he was tired out. The last straw was to find the church had gone and that Morgan, the so-called Rev. Morgan, was buried under it.

The rescue workers were digging again. There was a wide hole now and a man was down in it filling a basket with his hands. The dust rose like smoke from the hole as he worked.

The voice had not stopped singing. It went on, rich, virile, masculine, from verse to verse of the hymn. Shooting up like a stem through the rubbish, the voice seemed to rise and branch out powerfully, luxuriantly, and even theatrically, like a tree, until everything was in its shade. It was a shade that came towards one like dark arms.

"All the Welsh can sing," the warden said. Then he remembered that Lewis was Welsh also. "Not that I've got anything against the Welsh," the warden said.

"The scandal of it," Lewis was thinking. "Must he sing so loud, must he advertise himself? I locked up myself last night. How the devil did he get in?" And he really meant: "How did the devil get in?"

To Lewis, Morgan was the nearest human thing to the devil. He could never pass that purple-gowned figure, sauntering like a cardinal in his skull cap on the sunny side of the street, without a shudder of distaste and derision. An unfrocked priest, his predecessor in the church, Morgan ought in strict justice to have been in prison, and would have been but for the indulgence of the bishop. But this did not prevent the old man with the saintly white head and the eyes half-closed by the worldly juices of food and wine from walking about dressed in his vestments, like an actor walking in the sun of his own vanity, a hook-nosed satyr, a he-goat significant to servant girls, the crony of the public-house, the chaser of bookmakers, the smoker of cigars. It was terrible, but it was just that the bomb had buried him; only the malice of the Evil One would have thought of bringing the punishment of the sinner upon the church as well. And now, from the ruins, the voice of the wicked man rose up in all the elaborate pride of art and evil.

Suddenly there was a moan from the sloping timber, slates began to skate down.

"Get out. It's going," shouted the warden.

The man who was digging struggled out of the hole as it bulged under the landslide. There was a dull crumble, the crashing and splitting of wood, and then the sound of brick and dust tearing down below the water. Thick dust clouded over and choked them all. The rubble rocked like a cake-walk. Everyone rushed back and looked behind at the wreckage as if it were still alive. It remained still. They all stood there, frightened and suspicious. Presently one of the men with the shovel said: "The bloke's shut up."

Everyone stared stupidly. It was true. The man had

stopped singing. The clergyman was the first to move. Gingerly he went to what was left of the hole and got down on his knees.

"Morgan!" he said in a low voice.

Then he called out more loudly: "Morgan!"

Getting no reply, Lewis began to scramble the rubble away with his hands.

"Morgan!" he shouted. "Can you hear?" He snatched a shovel from one of the men and began digging and shovelling the stuff away. He had stopped chewing and muttering. His expression had entirely changed. "Morgan!" he called. He dug for two feet and no one stopped him. They looked with bewilderment at the sudden frenzy of the small man grubbing like a monkey, spitting out the dust, filing down his nails. They saw the spade at last shoot through the old hole. He was down the hole widening it at once, letting himself down as he worked. He disappeared under a ledge made by the fallen timber.

The party above could do nothing. "Morgan," they heard him call. "It's Lewis. We're coming. Can you hear?" He shouted for an axe and presently they heard him smashing with it. He was scratching like a dog or a rabbit.

A voice like that to have stopped, to have gone! Lewis was thinking. How unbearable this silence was. A beautiful proud voice, the voice of a man, a voice like a tree, the soul of a man spreading in the air like the cedars of Lebanon. "Only one man I have heard with a bass like that. Owen the Bank, at Newtown before the war. Morgan!" he shouted. "Sing! God will forgive you everything, only sing!"

One of the rescue party following behind the clergyman in the tunnel shouted back to his mates.

"I can't do nothing. This bleeder's blocking the gangway."

Half an hour Lewis worked in the tunnel. Then an extraordinary thing happened to him. The tunnel grew damp and its floor went as soft as clay to the touch. Suddenly his knees went through. There was a gap with a yard of cloth, the vestry curtain or the carpet at the communion rail was unwound and hanging through it. Lewis found himself looking down into the blackness of the crypt. He lay down and put his head and shoulders through the hole and felt about him until he found something solid again. The beams of the floor were tilted down into the crypt.

"Morgan. Are you there, man?" he called.

He listened to the echo of his voice. He was reminded of the time he had talked into a cistern when he was a boy. Then his heart jumped. A voice answered him out of the darkness from under the fallen floor. It was like the voice of a man lying comfortably and waking up from a snooze, a voice thick and sleepy.

"Who's that?" asked the voice.

"Morgan, man. It's Lewis. Are you hurt?" Tears pricked the dust in Lewis's eyes, and his throat ached with anxiety as he spoke. Forgiveness and love were flowing out of him. From below, the deep thick voice of Morgan came back.

"You've been a hell of a long time," it said. "I've damn near finished my whisky."

"Hell" was the word which changed Mr. Lewis's mind. Hell was a real thing, a real place for him. He believed in it. When he read out the word "Hell" in the Scriptures he could see the flames rising as they rise out of the furnaces at Swansea. "Hell" was a professional and poetic word for Mr. Lewis. A man who had been turned out of the church had no right to use it. Strong language and strong drink, Mr. Lewis hated both of them. The idea of whisky being in his church made his soul rise like an angered stomach. There was Morgan, insolent and comfortable, lying (so he said) under the old altar-table, which was propping up the fallen floor, drinking a bottle of whisky.

"How did you get in?" Lewis said, sharply, from the hole.

The Voice

"Were you in the church last night when I locked up?"

The old man sounded not as bold as he had been. He even sounded shifty when he replied: "I've got my key."

"*Your* key. I have the only key of the church. Where did you get a key?"

"My old key. I always had a key."

The man in the tunnel behind the clergyman crawled back up the tunnel to the daylight.

"O.K.," the man said. "He's got him. They're having a ruddy row."

"Reminds me of ferreting. I used to go ferreting with my old dad," said the policeman.

"You should have given that key up," said Mr. Lewis. "Have you been in here before?"

"Yes, but I shan't come here again," said the old man.

There was the dribble of powdered rubble, pouring down like sand in an hour-glass, the ticking of the strained timber like the loud ticking of a clock.

Mr. Lewis felt that at last after years he was face to face with the devil, and the devil was trapped and caught. The tick-tock of the wood went on.

"Men have been risking their lives, working and digging for hours because of this," said Lewis. "I've ruined a suit of . . ."

The tick-tock had grown louder in the middle of the words. There was a sudden lurching and groaning of the floor, followed by a big heaving and splitting sound.

"It's going," said Morgan with detachment from below. "The table leg." The floor crashed down. The hole in the tunnel was torn wide and Lewis grabbed at the darkness until he caught a board. It swung him out and in a second he found himself hanging by both hands over the pit.

"I'm falling. Help me," shouted Lewis in terror. "Help me." There was no answer.

306

"Oh, God," shouted Lewis, kicking for a foothold. "Morgan, are you there? Catch me. I'm going."

Then a groan like a snore came out of Lewis. He could hold no longer. He fell. He fell exactly two feet.

The sweat ran down his legs and caked on his face. He was as wet as a rat. He was on his hands and knees gasping. When he got his breath again, he was afraid to raise his voice.

"Morgan," he said quietly, panting.

"Only one leg went," the old man said in a quiet grating voice. "The other three are all right."

Lewis lay panting on the floor. There was a long silence. "Haven't you ever been afraid before, Lewis?" Morgan said. Lewis had no breath to reply. "Haven't you ever felt rotten with fear," said the old man, calmly, "like an old tree, infested and worm-eaten with it, soft as a rotten orange? You were a fool to come down here after me. I wouldn't have done the same for you," Morgan said.

"You would," Lewis managed to say.

"I wouldn't," said the old man. "I'm afraid. I'm an old man, Lewis, and I can't stand it. I've been down here every night since the raids got bad."

Lewis listened to the voice. It was low with shame, it had the roughness of the earth, the kicked and trodden choking dust of Adam. The earth of Mr. Lewis listened for the first time to the earth of Morgan. Coarsened and sordid and unlike the singing voice, the voice of Morgan was also gentle and fragmentary.

"When you stop feeling shaky," Morgan said, "you'd better sing. I'll do a bar, but I can't do much. The whisky's gone. Sing, Lewis. Even if they don't hear, it does you good. Take the tenor, Lewis."

Above in the daylight the look of pain went from the mouths of the rescue party, a grin came on the dusty lips of the warden.

"Hear it?" he said. "A ruddy Welsh choir!"

The Fly in the Ointment

It was the dead hour of a November afternoon. Under the
ceiling of level mud-coloured cloud, the latest office buildings of the city stood out alarmingly like new tombstones,
among the mass of older buildings. And along the streets, the
few cars and the few people appeared and disappeared slowly
as if they were not following the roadway or the pavement,
but some inner, personal route. Along the road to the main
station, at intervals of two hundred yards or so, unemployed
men and one or two beggars were dribbling slowly past the
desert of public buildings to the next patch of shop fronts.

Presently a taxi stopped outside one of the underground
stations and a man of thirty-five paid his fare and made off
down one of the small streets.

"Better not arrive in a taxi," he was thinking. "The old
man will wonder where I got the money."

He was going to see his father. It was his father's last
day at his factory, the last day of thirty years' work and life
among these streets, building a business out of nothing, and
then, after a few years of prosperity, letting it go to pieces
in a chaffer of rumour, idleness, quarrels, accusations, and,
at last, bankruptcy.

Suddenly all the money quarrels of the family, which
nagged in the young man's mind, had been dissolved. His
dread of being involved in them vanished. He was overcome

by the sadness of his father's situation. "Thirty years of your life come to an end. I must see him. I must help him." All the same, knowing his father, he had paid off the taxi and walked the last quarter of a mile.

It was a shock to see the name of the firm, newly painted too, on the sign outside the factory and on the brass of the office entrance, newly polished. He pressed the bell at the office window inside and it was a long time before he heard footsteps cross the empty room and saw a shadow cloud the frosted glass of the window.

"It's Harold, Father," the young man said. The door was opened.

"Hullo, old chap. This is very nice of you, Harold," said the old man shyly, stepping back from the door to let his son in, and lowering his pleased blue eyes for a second's modesty.

"Naturally I had to come," said the son, shyly also. And then the father filled out with assurance again and, taking his son's arm, walked him across the floor of the empty work-room.

"Hardly recognize it, do you? When were you here last?" said the father.

This had been the machine-room, before the machines had gone. Through another door was what had been the show-room where the son remembered seeing his father, then a dark-haired man, talking in a voice he had never heard before, a quick, bland voice, to his customers. Now there were only dust-lines left by the shelves on the white brick walls, and the marks of the showroom cupboards on the floor. The place looked large and light. There was no throb of machines, no hum of voices, no sound at all, now, but the echo of their steps on the empty floors. Already, though only a month bankrupt, the firm was becoming a ghost.

The two men walked towards the glass door of the office. They were both short. The father was well dressed in an

309

excellent navy-blue suit. He was a vigorous, broad man with a pleased impish smile. The sunburn shone through the clipped white hair of his head and he had the simple, trim, open-air look of a snow man. The son beside him was round-shouldered and shabby, a keen but anxious fellow in need of a haircut and going bald.

"Come in, professor," said the father. This was an old family joke. He despised his son, who was, in fact, not a professor but a poorly paid lecturer at a provincial university.

"Come in," said the father, repeating himself, not with the impatience he used to have, but with the habit of age. "Come inside, into my office. If you can call it an office now," he apologized. "This used to be my room, do you remember, it used to be my office? Take a chair. We've still got a chair. The desk's gone, yes, that's gone, it was sold, fetched a good price—what was I saying?" he turned a bewildered look to his son. "The chair. I was saying they have to leave you a table and a chair. I was just going to have a cup of tea, old boy, but—pardon me," he apologized again, "I've only one cup. Things have been sold for the liquidators and they've cleaned out nearly everything. I found this cup and teapot upstairs in the foreman's room. Of course he's gone, all the hands have gone, and when I looked around just now to lock up before taking the keys to the agent when I hand over today, I saw this cup. Well, there it is. I've made it. Have a cup?"

"No, thanks," said the son, listening patiently to his father. "I have had my tea."

"You've had your tea? Go on. Why not have another?"

"No, really, thanks," said the son. "You drink it."

"Well," said the father, pouring out the tea and lifting the cup to his soft rosy face and blinking his eyes as he drank, "I feel badly about this. This is terrible. I feel really awful drinking this tea and you standing there watching me, but you say you've had yours—well, how are things with you? How are you? And how is Alice? Is she better? And the children? You know I've been thinking about you—you look worried. Haven't lost sixpence and found a shilling have you, because I wouldn't mind doing that?"

"I'm all right," the son said, smiling to hide his irritation. "I'm not worried about anything, I'm just worried about you. This—" he nodded with embarrassment to the dismantled showroom, the office from which even the calendars and wastepaper basket had gone—"this—" what was the most tactful and sympathetic word to use?—"this is bad luck," he said.

"Bad luck?" said the old man sternly.

"I mean," stammered his son, "I heard about the creditors' meeting. I knew it was your last day—I thought I'd come along, I . . . to see how you were."

"Very sweet of you, old boy," said the old man with zest. "Very sweet. We've cleared everything up. They got most of the machines out today. I'm just locking up and handing over. Locking up is quite a business. There are so many keys. It's tiring, really. How many keys do you think there are to a place like this? You wouldn't believe it if I told you."

"It must have been worrying," the son said.

"Worrying? You keep on using that word. I'm not worrying. Things are fine," said the old man, smiling aggressively. "I feel they're fine. I *know* they're fine."

"Well, you always were an optimist," smiled his son.

"Listen to me a moment. I want you to get this idea," said his father, his warm voice going dead and rancorous and his nostrils fidgeting. His eyes went hard, too. A different man was speaking, and even a different face; the son noticed for the first time that like all big-faced men his father had two faces. There was the outer face like a soft warm and careless daub of innocent sealing wax and inside it, as if thumbed there by a seal, was a much smaller one, babyish, shrewd, scared and hard. Now this little inner face had gone greenish and pale and dozens of little veins were broken on the nose and cheeks. The small, drained, purplish lips of this little face were speaking. The son leaned back instinctively to get just another inch away from this little face.

"Listen to this," the father said, and leaned forward on the table as his son leaned back, holding his right fist up as if he had a hammer in his hand and was auctioning his life. "I am sixty-five. I don't know how long I shall live, but let me make this clear: if I were not an optimist I wouldn't be here. I wouldn't stay another minute." He paused, fixing his son's half-averted eyes to let the full meaning of his words bite home. "I've worked hard," the father went on. "For thirty years I built up this business from nothing. You wouldn't know it, you were a child, but many's the time, coming down from the north, I've slept in this office to be on the job early the next morning." He looked decided and experienced like a man of forty, but now he softened to sixty again. The ring in the hard voice began to soften into a faint whine and his thick nose sniffed. "I don't say I've always done right," he said. "You can't live your life from A to Z like that. And now I haven't a penny in the world. Not a cent. It's not easy at my time of life to begin again. What do you think I've got to live for? There's nothing holding me back. My boy, if I wasn't an optimist I'd go right out. I'd finish it." Suddenly the father smiled and the little face was drowned in a warm flood of triumphant smiles from the bigger face. He rested his hands on his waistcoat and that seemed to be smiling too, his easy coat smiling, his legs smiling, and even winks of light on his shining shoes. Then he frowned.

"Your hair's going thin," he said. "You oughtn't to be losing your hair at your age. I don't want you to think I'm criticizing you, you're old enough to live your own life, but your hair you know—you ought to do something about it. If you used oil every day and rubbed it in with both hands, the thumbs and forefingers is what you want to use, it would be better. I'm often thinking about you and I don't want you to think I'm lecturing you, because I'm not, so don't get the idea this is a lecture, but I was thinking, what you want, what we all want, I say this for myself as well as you, what we all want is ideas—big ideas. We go worrying along, but you just want bigger and better ideas. You ought to think big. Take your case. You're a lecturer. I wouldn't be satisfied with lecturing to a small batch of people in a university town. I'd lecture the world. You know, you're always doing yourself injustice. We all do. Think big."

"Well," said his son, still smiling, but sharply. He was very angry. "One's enough in the family. You've thought big till you bust."

He didn't mean to say this because he hadn't really the courage, but his pride was touched.

"I mean," said the son, hurriedly covering it up in a panic, "I'm not like you—I—"

"What did you say?" said the old man. "Don't say that." It was the smaller of the two faces speaking in a panic. "Don't say that. Don't use that expression. That's not a right idea. Don't you get a wrong idea about me. We paid sixpence in the pound," said the old man proudly.

The son began again, but his father stopped him.

"Do you know," said the bigger of his two faces, getting bigger as it spoke, "some of the oldest houses in the city are in Queer Street, some of the biggest firms in the country? I came up this morning with Mr. Higgins, you remember Higgins? They're in liquidation. They are. Oh yes. And Moore, he's lost everything. He's got his chauffeur but it's his wife's money. Did you see Beltman in the trade papers? Quarter of a million deficit. And how long are Prestons going to last?"

The big face smiled and overflowed on the smaller one. The whole train, the old man said, was practically packed with bankrupts every morning. Thousands had gone. Thousands? Tens of thousands. Some of the biggest men in the City were broke.

A small man himself, he was proud to be bankrupt with the big ones; it made him feel rich.

"You've got to realize, old boy," he said gravely, "the world's changing. You've got to move with the times."

The son was silent. The November sun put a few strains of light through the frosted window, and the shadow of its bars and panes was weakly placed on the wall behind his father's head. Some of the light caught the tanned scalp that showed between the white hair. So short the hair was that his father's ears protruded and, framed against that reflection of the window bars, the father suddenly took (to his son's fancy) the likeness of a convict in his cell, and the son, startled, found himself asking "Were they telling the truth when they said the old man was a crook and that his balance sheets were cooked? What about that man they had to shut up at the meeting, the little man from Birmingham, in a mackintosh . . ."

"There's a fly in this room," said the old man suddenly, looking up in the air and getting to his feet. "I'm sorry to interrupt what you were saying, but I can hear a fly. I must get it out."

"A fly?" said his son listening.

"Yes, can't you hear it? It's peculiar how you can hear everything now the machines have stopped. It took me quite a time to get used to the silence. Can you see it, old chap? I can't stand flies, you never know where they've been. Excuse me one moment."

The old man pulled a duster out of a drawer.

"Forgive this interruption. I can't sit in a room with a fly in it," he said apologetically. They both stood up and listened. Certainly in the office was the small dying fizz of a fly, deceived beyond its strength by the autumn sun.

314

"Open the door, will you, old boy," said the old man with embarrassment. "I hate them."

The son opened the door and the fly flew into the light. The old man struck at it but it sailed away higher.

"There it is," he said, getting up on the chair. He struck again and the son struck too as the fly came down. The old man got on top of his table. An expression of disgust and fear was curled on his smaller face; and an expression of apology and weakness.

"Excuse me," he said again, looking up at the ceiling.

"If we leave the door open or open the window it will go," said the son.

"It may seem a fad to you," said the old man shyly. "I don't like flies. Ah, here it comes."

They missed it. They stood helplessly gaping up at the ceiling where the fly was buzzing in small circles round the cord of the electric light.

"I don't like them," the old man said.

The table creaked under his weight. The fly went on to the ceiling and stayed there. Unavailingly the old man snapped the duster at it.

"Be careful," said the son. "Don't lose your balance."

The old man looked down. Suddenly he looked tired and old, his body began to sag and a look of weakness came on to his face.

"Give me a hand, old boy," the old man said in a shaky voice. He put a heavy hand on his son's shoulder and the son felt the great helpless weight of his father's body.

"Lean on me."

Very heavily and slowly the old man got cautiously down from the table to the chair. "Just a moment, old boy," said the old man. Then, after getting his breath, he got down from the chair to the floor.

"You all right?" his son asked.

315

"Yes, yes," said the old man out of breath. "It was only that fly. Do you know you're actually more bald at the back than I thought. There's a patch there as big as my hand. I saw it just then. It gave me quite a shock. You really must do something about it. How are your teeth? Do you have any trouble with your teeth? That may have something to do with it. Hasn't Alice told you how bald you are?"

"You've been doing too much. You're worried," said the son, soft with repentance and sympathy. "Sit down. You've had a bad time."

"No, nothing," said the old man shyly, breathing rather hard. "A bit. Everyone's been very nice. They came in and shook hands. The staff came in. They all came in just to shake hands. They said: 'We wish you good luck.' "

The old man turned his head away. He actually wiped a tear from his eye. A glow of sympathy transported the younger man. He felt as though a sun had risen.

"You know—" the father said uneasily, flitting a glance at the fly on the ceiling as if he wanted the fly as well as his son to listen to what he was going to say—"you know," he said. "The world's all wrong. I've made my mistakes. I was thinking about it before you came. You know where I went wrong? You know where I made my mistake?"

The son's heart started to a panic of embarrassment. "For heaven's sake," he wanted to shout, "don't! Don't stir up the whole business. Don't humiliate yourself before me. Don't start telling the truth. Don't oblige me to say we know all about it, that we have known for years the mess you've been in, that we've seen through the plausible stories you've spread, that we've known the people you've swindled."

"Money's been my trouble," said the old man. "I thought I needed money. That's one thing it's taught me. I've done with money. Absolutely done and finished with it. I never want to see another penny as long as I live. I don't want to see or hear of it. If you came in now and offered me a thousand pounds I should laugh at you. We deceive ourselves. We don't want the stuff. All I want now is just to go to a nice little cottage by the sea," the old man said. "I feel I need air, sun, life."

The son was appalled.

"You want money even for that," the son said irritably. "You want quite a lot of money to do that."

"Don't say I want money," the old man said vehemently. "Don't say it. When I walk out of this place tonight I'm going to walk into freedom. I am not going to think of money. You never know where it will come from. You may see something. You may meet a man. You never know. Did the children of Israel worry about money? No, they just went out and collected the manna. That's what I want to do."

The son was about to speak. The father stopped him.

"Money," the father said, "isn't necessary at all."

Now like the harvest moon on full glow the father's face shone up at his son.

"What I came round about was this," said the son awkwardly and dryly. "I'm not rich. None of us is. In fact, with things as they are we're all pretty shaky and we can't do anything. I wish I could but I can't. But"—after the assured beginning he began to stammer and to crinkle his eyes timidly—"but the idea of your being—you know, well, short of some immediate necessity, I mean—well, if it is ever a question of—well, to be frank, *cash*, I'd raise it somehow."

He coloured. He hated to admit his own poverty, he hated to offer charity to his father. He hated to sit there knowing the things he knew about him. He was ashamed to think how he, how they all dreaded having the gregarious, optimistic, extravagant, uncontrollable, disingenuous old man on their hands. The son hated to feel he was being in some peculiar way which he could not understand mean, cowardly, and dishonest.

The Fly in the Ointment

The father's sailing eyes came down and looked at his son's nervous, frowning face and slowly the dreaming look went from the father's face. Slowly the harvest moon came down from its rosy voyage. The little face suddenly became dominant within the outer folds of skin like a fox looking out of a hole of clay. He leaned forward brusquely on the table and somehow a silver-topped pencil was in his hand preparing to note something briskly on a writing-pad.

"Raise it?" said the old man sharply. "Why didn't you tell me before you could raise money? How can you raise it? Where? By when?"

The Night Worker

A marriage was in the air. In a week the boy's Cousin Gladys was going to be married. The boy sat in a corner of the room out of the way. Uncle Tom and Aunt Annie danced round the girl all day, pushing her this way, pulling her that; only a week to go and now—as the boy watched them in the little dark kitchen, out of the way of people's feet—the dance got fiercer, gayer, rougher. "Do what you like, you're free already," they seemed to say to her. And then: "You dare! You wait! You're still our daughter. Do as you're told." The boy watched them. He was seven. He did not know what a marriage was, and he gazed at them, expecting it to come into the room like a bird, or to be put on the table like a cake.

Aunt Annie stood at one end of the table with her back to the window, making a pie. He watched the mole move on her bony arm as she rolled the pastry.

"Hurry up with that sleeve, my girl. Haven't you taken out the tacking?"

"It's a fiddling job," said Gladys, holding up her needle.

"Here, give it us," said Aunt Annie, wiping the pastry off her fingers and snatching the needle. "Who's taking the Bible class on Sunday, then?"

"Not me," said Gladys.

The Night Worker

Aunt Annie flopped the pastry over the pie-dish and the boy saw it hang in curtains over the edge, while his Aunt stood straight looking down at the parting in Gladys's thick hair. Aunt Annie's grey hair was screwed back and in her bony face she had bold false teeth, so that she clucked when she talked and had the up-and-down smile of a skull. She had the good nature of a skeleton.

The boy was waiting for her to trim the pastry on the pie-dish. When she had done this she opened the oven door and a smell of hot cake came across the room. In came the boy's Uncle Tom, a sad, cake-eating man. How did a man so short come to marry a woman so tall? It must have been because Uncle Tom looked like a crouching animal who lived by making great jumps. He was a carpenter, whose skin was the colour of chapel harmonium keys; a yellow, Chinese-looking man with split thumbnails and a crinkled black beard and he frightened because he never quite came into the room, but stood in the doorway, neither in nor out, with a hammer or a chisel in his hand.

"I done them stair-rods, my girl," he said. It was like a threat.

"I'll take them round," Gladys said.

"She's going at twelve," said Aunt Annie.

"Jim be there?" asked her father.

"Yes," said Aunt Annie. She seemed to the boy to have the power to make her tall teeth shine on the scowl of Uncle Tom, and to put the idea of springing on us all out of his head. "Jim'll be there. She's taking the boy."

Then Gladys laughed and, leaning down the table, put her soft arm round the boy's waist and rubbed her cheek in his hair.

"I'm taking my young man round. You'll look after me, won't you?" she said. One of their inexplicable fits of laughter started. Aunt Annie's teeth clucked and clicked. Uncle Tom went "Ha, ha, ha," like a saw and lit a pipe.

"Only another week, Glad. It's just because of the neighbours," said Aunt Annie.

"Ay, my girl, neighbours talk," said Uncle Tom, and blew out violet smoke as if he were smoking the neighbours out.

The girl put on a prim, concealing expression. One minute she was a girl and the next a woman, then a girl again.

"Stars above, look at the time. Quick," she cried to the boy, getting up from the table.

They ran upstairs to her room at the back, where he slept too, a room which did not smell of camphor like his Aunt's room. He did not like to see Gladys take off her kitchen dress and stand, with bare shoulders and bare arms, in her petticoat, and bare-legged too, because then she became a person he did not know. She was shorter and more powerful. But when her Sunday blue dress was over her head and after she had said "Oh, these blooming things," when the hooks caught in her hair, he liked her again.

"How do I look?" she said, when she had her straw hat on, and, not waiting for an answer, she said: "Now, there's you! Brush your jersey! Quick."

Jim was waiting, she said. They went out of the room like the wind and the text "Honour Thy Father" swung sideways on the wall. Down those dark stairs they went, two at a time, and were half out of the door when Uncle Tom made his great jump after them.

"Don't forget them stair-rods."

"Goodness," she said, grabbing them, "I'm going dippy."

And then she was going down the street so fast that the boy had to trot.

"Oh!" She breathed more easily when they had got out of her street. "That's better. You ain't seen my new house." But she was talking to the street, not to him, smiling at it. She went along, smiling at the sky and the children playing hopscotch on the pavement, and the greengrocer's cart, as though she were eating the world like an orange and throwing away the skin as she went along. And her breasts and her plump chin jumped in time with her step.

"Which house is it?" the boy said.

"Not yet. Round the corner."

They turned the corner and there was another long street. "In this street?" he said.

"No. Round another corner."

He took her hand. She was walking so fast he was afraid of being lost. And then, down the next street, she calmed down.

Her face became stern. "Look at him, standing like a dummy! He hasn't seen us."

A man in a grey cap and a blue serge suit was standing on the pavement.

"Smoking," she said. "Bold as brass. There's men for you. He promised he'd give it up. Standing there daft and idle."

They were all workers in this family. Everything was work to them. Uncle Tom was always sawing and hammering. He had made the chests of drawers and the tables in his house. Aunt Annie scrubbed and cooked. Cousin Gladys was always sewing and even when she came in from her factory, she had, as they said, "something in her hands"—a brush, a broom, a cleaning cloth, or scissors. Jim was a worker, too. He worked at the post office in the middle of the town. One day Uncle Tom took the boy on top of a tram, and when they came near the post office, he said: "Eh, look out this side and you'll see Gladys's Jim working. He's got a good job. Sometimes he's on nights. He's a night worker. Now, look out for him when the tram slows down." The boy looked into the grey window of the post office as the tram passed by. Inside were dim rows of desks and people and presently he saw Jim in his shirt-sleeves. He was carrying a large wastepaper basket.

"What's he doing?" said the boy.

"Sorting," said Uncle Tom. "Sorting the mail. His father put him into that job when he was fourteen."

The boy saw Jim lift the wastepaper basket and then suddenly empty it over the head of another man who was sitting at a desk. He saw Jim laughing. He saw the man jump down and chase Jim across the office, laughing too.

"Larking about," said Uncle Tom indignantly. "That's government work."

The boy stopped laughing. He was scared of Jim after this. Jim was a tall man with a hungry face, but there was a small grin on his lips and after seeing him empty the wastepaper basket the boy did not know what to make of him. It made him feel there was something reckless and secretive in the lives of Cousin Gladys and Jim.

Jim stood outside the gate of the house.

"You come to see the house," he said to the boy. The boy murmured.

"Lost his tongue," said Jim.

"I've been in," he said to Gladys.

Gladys took his arm.

"Have you brought the things? I've got the stair-rods."

"I put them inside," he said.

"Oh, let me see," she said eagerly. The three went to the green front door of the house and Jim let them in. It was a small house of grey brick with a bay window.

"There," Jim said, pointing to the things. "I didn't take them upstairs. I waited for you."

On the floor was a washbasin and a jug.

"I must wash them before we go," she said. "Take them to the kitchen."

Jim stood and winked at the boy.

"Orders," said Jim.

"I can't stand dirt," she said, getting up.

"Well," said Jim, "I'm waiting, aren't I?" He put this question to the boy and winked again.

"Oh," Gladys said, "don't be soft."

"Don't look," said Jim to the boy.

And then Gladys and Jim put their arms round each other and kissed. He saw her heels come off the ground and her knees bend. Gladys blushed and stepped back.

"Oh no, you don't, does she?" Jim said to the boy. And he pulled Gladys and gave her another kiss.

"Jim!" she cried. "You'll have me over."

The boy laughed and pulled at her waist from behind and they were all laughing until her shoe kicked the china basin on the floor. That stopped them.

"What'll Ma say when she sees my dress," Gladys said.

"Oh," said Jim. "*He* won't tell." Winking again at the boy. "Here's a penny. Go into the garden and see if you can find some chocolate."

"No," said Gladys, kissing the boy and holding his hand. "He's my young man. He's looking after me."

They walked from room to room in the house. After Uncle Tom's house it was bare and smelled of size and new paint. The curtains were up but there was very little furniture. In the sitting-room there was only a blue carpet and a small settee. Jim and Gladys stood at the door and took deep breaths when they looked at this room. There was a vase on the mantelpiece and Gladys moved the vase from the middle to the end.

"Now I've made it lopsided," she said. "It wants two."

"It wants a picture," said Jim, looking at the bare, lilac-coloured walls. "It looks bare."

"Don't complain," said Gladys, pouting.

"I'm not. I was only thinking," he said, putting his arm round her waist, but she stepped away. Jim gave her a look. The boy had seen her sulk before. He loved her and when she sulked he was frightened.

Jim went out into the hall, and while he was out she stroked the boy's head and pressed him against her leg.

"You like it, don't you?" she said. "You don't think it's bare?"

"No," he said.

"I'll marry you. You don't grouse."

"Here—Glad—what's this here?" called Jim sharply from the hall. "When you've done spooning. . . ."

Her sulk went at once. She went out. Jim and she were looking at a small dark spot on the ceiling.

"A leak!" she cried.

"From the bathroom," he said.

"Who left the water on last time?" she said.

"Your mother—washing things," Jim said.

"She never," Gladys said.

They both rushed upstairs. The carpet was not yet down on the stairs, and their steps and voices echoed. It was a house of echoes. The boy did not follow. He went to see the painters' pails in the kitchen and to stir the oily remains of paint in them with a stick. He looked into the clean sink. He could not understand why Gladys and Jim were going to live in this house. He wanted to live there with them. He could not understand the laugh of his aunt and uncle, that peculiar laughter, so pleased and yet jealous, so free and yet so uneasy, when they talked about Gladys living in this house. It was a laughter marked by side glances. The boy couldn't understand why it was important for him to be there, and he felt lost. He went at last upstairs, and on the landing he heard them in the bathroom. They were talking. They had forgotten him. In the evasive way of grown-up people they had gone upstairs to look at the cause of the water coming through the ceiling and, now they were there, they were not talking about that at all. They were talking about people, about some person. The boy stood still and listened.

"They don't want him. *He's* away all the time travelling and she's having another, that'll be the fifth. Terrible, isn't it? Five, imagine it," Gladys was saying.

"Can't someone put her wise?" Jim said.

"I'd throw myself in the river."

The boy saw Gladys falling into the river. He thought: "I wonder why Gladys wants to get her clothes wet and what will Aunt Annie say."

"I dunno. Kids are nice. I'd like one like that," Jim said.

"Nobody's kid. That's what he is," Gladys said. When he heard the word "kid," the boy seemed to himself to swell and to lean and to topple with importance towards the bathroom door, but some fear of a woman's hand catching him by the leg or the arm made him seem to go thin again and lean away, till he crept quickly to the landing. There were two doors. Quietly he opened one door and went into a small room. There was nothing in it at all, no curtains to the windows, no linoleum on the floor, no firegrate either, but only a mousehole. He looked down the mousehole and watched it for a long time but nothing came out of it. There was a smell of mouse which reminded him of his home and he looked out of the window down into three back gardens, but no child was there. He wondered where nobody's kid was, but no child came. So he went to another room, for this was the house he wanted to live in with one room after another, if people would come and live in it and silence the echoes. Quietly he edged out of the room and guiltily looked into the next one. It was in the front of the house and looked on to the street. Each thing in the room seemed to look at him. There was a small carpet on the floor. There was a wardrobe, a dressing-table, and a large bedstead with a mattress on it, but no sheets or blankets. It was like his mother's and father's room, but this one was cold and smelled of the furniture shop. It had the mystery and watchful quietness of an empty bedroom.

"Where are you?" called Gladys. "Where's the boy gone?"

"He's round about," said Jim easily. They were walking

towards the room. The boy could not escape. He stood still.

"Ah, there he is," Gladys cried. And they were both in the room with him.

"Who sleeps in this bed?" said the boy. Gladys went red. Jim winked.

"Gladys, who sleeps here?" Jim said.

"I don't know," said Gladys.

"Getcha, she does. She knows," Jim said. "Ask her."

"You do," the boy said, pointing at Gladys. "She does."

"I don't," said Gladys sternly. "Jim does," she said sharply.

"He doesn't," the boy said. He had seen the lies rolling in their glances at each other.

"I do," said Jim.

"You don't," said the boy. "You're a night worker."

"That's a good one," said Jim, who never laughed but only smiled at the corner of his lips, and now suddenly shouted with laughter. "That's it. That's where I do my work. A night worker, that's where I do my work. Eh, Glad?"

"Jim, shut up," said Gladys primly. "Don't tease."

"I'm not teasing," laughed Jim. "I'm a hell of a night worker." And he made a grab at Gladys, who moved away.

"Jim," she said, "the neighbours. They can hear everything. These walls are like paper."

"You and the neighbours," laughed Jim, and he caught up the boy high in the air and sat on the side of the bed. "One, two, three," he said, and at three he brought the boy down on the bed.

"Come here, Glad," he said, "you have a go. He's ticklish."

The boy called out and kicked.

"Don't," said Gladys, coming to rescue him.

"Ticklish yourself," said Jim, catching her arm and pulling her on the bed. The boy was free.

"Kiss her. Kiss her," cried the excited boy.

"Don't," said Gladys.

"I'll neighbour you," said Jim.

The boy watched them struggling and then he saw Jim was not kissing her but whispering in her ear.

"You are too real, Jim," she said tenderly. And then they were all lying quiet, Jim in the middle of them, with one arm round Gladys's neck and one arm round the boy and the boy wishing he could get away.

"Family already," Jim said. "You must have been on night work, Glad."

"Oh, give it a rest," said Glad. "Remember everything is taken back home. Little pigs have big ears."

"Very nice work too," said Jim.

"Don't be so awful," she pleaded.

"What's awful about it?"

A sigh came from Gladys.

"Very nice, I was saying," said Jim. "Sunday morning. Who's getting up to light the fire?"

"You."

"Me?—No, you."

"Married life," said Jim. "Hear that?"

"Who does sleep here truthfully?" said the boy.

"Nobody does," said Gladys. "But Jim and me are going to when we are married. That satisfy you?"

The boy knew it was true. It was true because it was far beyond his understanding. Jim and Gladys watched him silently, but Jim's arm tightened on her. They nodded to each other watching the boy.

"And we'll have you for our little boy," said Gladys.

He knew this was not true. He did not want to be their little boy. They cuddled and kissed and danced about too much; and then people smiled and laughed at them.

"Leave him alone," said Jim. And they all lay there silently, but he was aching to move from Jim's arm and to go.

328

He was thinking of nobody's child and wishing he could find him, see him, watch him, talk to him.

"First question when I get back," Gladys said. "Did you put the stair-rods down? They think it's *their* house."

Yes, the boy wanted to get away from this house that wasn't a house yet, from this bed that was not a bed, and to see Aunt Annie and Uncle Tom, who sat still for hours after they had worked. He was going to ask her who nobody's child was and how big he was, where he lived, to see him, to watch for a long time what he did, to throw something to him to see if he moved, to see if he talked and how his mouth looked when he talked.

"When are we going home?" he said.

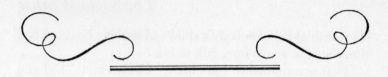

The Satisfactory

"When one says that what one is still inclined to call civilization is passing through a crisis," Mr. Plymbell used to say during the last war and after it when food was hard to get, and standing in his very expensive antique shop, raising a white and more than Roman nose and watching the words go off one by one on the air and circle the foreign customer, "one is tempted to ask oneself whether or not a few possibly idle phrases that one let fall to one's old friend Lady Hackthorpe at a moment of national distress in 1940 are not, in fact, still pertinent. One recalls observing, rightly or wrongly, at that time that one was probably witnessing not the surrender of an heroic Ally but the defeat of sauces. Béarnaise, hollandaise, madère—one saw them overrun. One can conceive of the future historian's inquiring whether the wars of the last ten years, and indeed what one calls 'the peace,' have not been essentially an attack on gastronomy, on the stomach and palate of the human race. One could offer the modest example of one's daily luncheon. . . ."

Mr. Plymbell can talk like *The Times* forever. Not all the campaigns of our time have been fought on the battlefield. His lunch in those bad days was a study.

At two minutes before half past twelve every day, Plymbell was first in the queue in the foyer outside the locked glass doors of Polli's Restaurant, a few yards from his shop. On one side of the glass Plymbell floated—handome, Roman, silver-haired, as white-skinned and consequent as a turbot of fifty; on the other side of the glass, in the next aquarium, stood Polli with the key in his hand waiting for the clock to strike the half hour—a man liverish and suspended in misanthropy like a tench in the weed of a canal. Plymbell stared clean through Polli to the sixty empty tables beyond; Polli stared clean through the middle of Plymbell into the miasma of the restaurant-keeper's life. Two fish gazed with the indifference of creatures who have accepted the fact that neither of them is edible. What they wanted, what the whole of England was crying for, was not fish but red meat, and to get meat at Polli's one had to be there at half past twelve, on the dot.

First customer in was Plymbell. He had his table, in the middle of this chipped Edwardian place, with his back to one of those white pillars that gave it the appearance of a shop-soiled wedding cake mounted on a red carpet, and he faced the serving hatch. Putting up a monocle to his more annoyed eye, he watched the chef standing over his pans, and while he watched he tapped the table with lightly frantic fingers. Polli's waiters were old men, and the one who served Plymbell had the dejected smirk of a convict.

Plymbell used hardly to glance at the farcical menu and never looked at the waiter when he coldly gave his order. "Two soups," said Plymbell. "Two roast beefs. . . . Cheese and biscuits," he added. "Bring me mine now and you can bring the second order in a quarter of an hour, when my secretary arrives."

It was a daily scene. Plymbell's waiter came forward with his dishes like one hurrying a funeral in a hot country, feebly averting his nose from the mess he was carrying on his dish. He scraped his serving spoons and, at the end, eyed his customer with criminal scorn. Plymbell's jaws moved over this stuff with a slow social agony. In fifteen minutes he had eaten his last biscuit and was wetting his finger to pick up the small heap of crumbs he had worked to one side of his plate. Plymbell looked at his watch.

Exactly at this moment Plymbell's assistant used to come in. Shabby, thin, with wrinkled cotton stockings and dressed in black, a woman of forty-five, Miss Tell scraped on poor shoes to the table. She carried newspapers in a bundle under an arm and a basket in her hand. He would look carefully away from her as she alighted like some dingy fly at the other side of the table. It was astonishing to see a man so well dressed lunching with a woman so bowed and faded. But presently she used to do a conjuring trick. Opening her bundle, Miss Tell put a newspaper down on the roll of bread on her side plate and then picked it up again. The roll of bread had gone. She had slipped it into her lap. A minute passed while she wriggled to and fro like a laying hen, and and then she would drop the roll into the basket by the leg of her chair.

Plymbell would be looking away from her while she did this and, his lips hardly moving, he would speak one word. "What?" was the word.

She replied also with one word—the word naturally varied—cringing toward him, looking with fear, trying to get him to look at her.

"Sausages," she might whisper.

"How many?" Plymbell would ask. He still did not look at her.

"Half pound," she said. On some fortunate days: "A pound."

Plymbell studied the domed skylight in the ceiling of the restaurant. The glass was still out in those days; the boards put there during the war when a bomb blew out the glass had not been replaced. Meanwhile the waiter brought a plate of soup to Miss Tell. She would stare at the soup without interest. When the waiter went, she lifted the plate across the table and put it in Plymbell's place and then lowered her head in case other customers had seen. Plymbell had not seen, because he had been gazing at the ceiling, but, as if absent-mindedly, he picked up a spoon and began to drink Miss Tell's soup, and when he had finished, put her plate back on her side of the table, and the waiter took it away.

Plymbell had been lunching at Polli's for years. He used to lunch there before the war with Lady Hackthorpe. She was a handsome woman—well-cut clothes, well-cut diamonds, brilliantly cut eyes, and sharply cut losses. Plymbell bought and sold for her, decorated her house.

Miss Tell used to go home to her parents in the evenings and say: "I don't understand it. I make out her bill every month and he says: 'Miss Tell, give me Lady Hackthorpe's bill,' and tears it up."

Miss Tell lived by what she did not understand. It was an appetite.

After 1940, no more Lady Hackthorpe. A bomb cut down half of her house and left a Hepplewhite bed full of broken glass and ceiling plaster on the first floor, and a servant's washstand on the floor above. Lady Hackthorpe went to Ireland.

Plymbell got the bed and a lot of other things out of the house into his shop. Here again there was something Miss Tell did not understand. She was supposed to "keep the books straight." Were Lady Hackthorpe's things being "stored" or were they being "returned to stock"?

"I mean," Miss Tell said, "if anyone was killed when a thing is left open it's unsatisfactory."

Plymbell listened and did not answer. He was thinking of other things. The war on the stomach and the palate had begun. Not only had Lady Hackthorpe gone. Plymbell's business was a function of Lady Hackthorpe's luncheons and dinners, and other people's, too. He was left with his mouth open in astonishment and hunger.

. . .

The Satisfactory

"Trade has stopped now," Miss Tell said one night when she ducked into the air-raid shelter with her parents. "Poor Mr. Plymbell never goes out."

"Why doesn't he close the business, Kitty?" Miss Tell's mother said.

"And leave all that valuable stock?" said Mr. Tell. "Where's your brain?"

"I never could fathom business," said Mrs. Tell.

"It's the time to pick up things," said Mr. Tell.

"That's a way to talk when we may all be dead in a minute," said Mrs. Tell.

Mr. Tell said something about prices being bound to go up, but a huge explosion occurred and he stopped.

"And this Lady Hackthorpe—is she *friendly* with this Plymbell?" said old Mrs. Tell when the explosion settled in as part of the furniture of their lives.

"*Mr.* Plymbell," Miss Tell corrected her mother. Miss Tell had a poor, fog-coloured London skin and blushed in a patch across her forehead. "I don't *query* his private life."

"He's a man," sighed Mrs. Tell. "To hear you talk he might be the Fairy Prince or Lord Muck himself. Listen to those guns. You've been there fifteen years."

"It takes two to be friendly," said Miss Tell, who sometimes spoke like a poem. "When one goes away, it may be left open one way or another, I mean, and that—" Miss Tell searched for a new word but returned to the old one, the only one that ever, for her, met the human case. "And that," she said, "is unsatisfactory."

"You're neurotic," her mother said. "You never have any news."

And then Miss Tell had a terrible thought. "Mum!" she cried, dropping the poetic accent she brought back from the West End every night; "where's Tiger? We've left him in the house."

Her mother became swollen with shame.

"You left him," accused Miss Tell. "You left him in the kitchen." She got up. "No one's got any heart. I'm going to get him."

"You stay here, my girl," said Mr. Tell.

"Come back, Kitty," said Mrs. Tell.

But Miss Tell (followed across the garden, as it seemed to her, by an aeroplane) went to the house. In her panic Mrs. Tell had left not only the cat; she had left her handbag and her ration books on the kitchen table. Miss Tell picked up the bag and then kneeled under the table looking for Tiger. "Tiger, dear! Tiger!" she called. He was not there. It was at this instant that the aeroplane outside seemed to have followed her into the house. When Miss Tell was dug out alive and unhurt, black with dust, six hours later, Mr. and Mrs. Tell were dead in the garden.

When Plymbell talks of that time now, he says there were moments when one was inclined to ask oneself whether the computed odds of something like eight hundred and ninety-seven thousand to one in favour of one's nightly survival were not, perhaps, an evasion of a private estimate one had arrived at without any special statistical apparatus—that it was fifty-fifty, and even providential. It was a point, he said, one recollected making to one's assistant at the time, when she came back.

Miss Tell came back to Plymbell's at lunch time one day a fortnight after she had been dug out. She was singular: she had been saved by looking for her cat. Mr. Plymbell was not at the shop or in his rooms above it. In the vainglory of her escape she went round to Polli's. Plymbell was more than half-way through his meal when he saw her come in. She was wearing no hat on her dusty black hair, and under her black coat, which so often had ends of cotton on it, she was wearing navy-blue trousers. Plymbell winced: it was the human aspect of war that was so lowering; he saw at once that Miss Tell had become a personality. Watching the wag

of her narrow shoulders as she walked, he saw she had caught
the general immodesty of the "bombed out."

Without being invited, she sat down at his table and put
herself sideways, at her ease, crossing her legs to show her
trousers. Her face had filled out into two little puffs of
vanity on either side of her mouth, as if she were eating or
were containing a yawn. The two rings of age on her neck
looked like a cheap necklace. Lipstick was for the first time
on her lips. It looked like blood.

"One inquired in vain," said Plymbell with condescension.
"I am glad to see you back."

"I thought I might as well pop round," said Miss Tell.

Mr. Plymbell was alarmed; her note was breezy. "Aren't
you coming back?"

"I haven't found Tiger," said Miss Tell.

"Tiger?"

Miss Tell told him her story.

Plymbell saw that he must try to put himself for a moment
in his employee's situation and think of her grief. "One recalls the thought that passed through one's mind when one's
own mother died," he said.

"They had had their life," said Miss Tell.

A connoisseur by trade, Plymbell was disappointed by the
banality of Miss Tell's remark. What was grief? It was a
hunger. Not merely personal, emotional, and spiritual; it was
physical. Plymbell had been forty-two when his mother died,
and he, her only child, had always lived with her. Her skill
with money, her jackdaw eye had made the business. The
morning she died in hospital he had felt that a cave had been
opened inside his body under the ribs, a cave getting larger
and colder and emptier. He went out and ate one of the
largest meals of his life.

While Miss Tell, a little fleshed already in her tragedy,
was still talking, the waiter came to the table with Plymbell's
allowance of cheese and biscuits.

Plymbell remembered his grief. "Bring me another portion for my secretary," he said.

"Oh no, not for me," said Miss Tell. She was too dazed by the importance of loss to eat. "I couldn't."

But Polli's waiter had a tired, deaf head. He came back with biscuits for Miss Tell.

Miss Tell looked about the restaurant until the waiter left and then coquettishly she passed her plate to Plymbell. "For you," she said. "I couldn't."

Plymbell thought Miss Tell ill-bred to suggest that he would eat what she did not want. He affected not to notice and gazed over her head, but his white hand had already taken the plate, and in a moment, still looking disparagingly beyond her, in order not to catch her eye, Mr. Plymbell bit into one of Miss Tell's biscuits. Miss Tell was smiling slyly.

After he had eaten her food, Mr. Plymbell looked at Miss Tell with a warmer interest. She had come to work for him in his mother's time, more than fifteen years before. Her hair was still black, her skin was now gray and yellow with a lilac streak on the jaw, there were sharp stains like poor coffee under her eyes. These were brown with a circle of gold in the pupils, and they seemed to burn as if there were a fever in their shadows. Her black coat, her trousers, her cotton blouse were cheap, and even her body seemed to be thin with cheapness. Her speech was awkward, for part of her throat was trying to speak in a refined accent and the effect was half arrogant, half disheartened. Now, as he swallowed the last piece of biscuit, she seemed to him to change. Her eyes were brilliant. She had become quietly a human being.

What is a human being? The chef, whom he could see through the hatch, was one; Polli, who was looking at the menu by the cash desk, was another; his mother, who had made remarkable ravioli; people like Lady Hackthorpe, who had given such wonderful dinner parties before the war— that circle which the war had scattered and where he had moved from one lunch to the next in a life that rippled to the sound of changing plates that tasted of sauces now never made. These people had been human beings. One knew a human being when the juices flowed over one's teeth. A human being was a creature who fed one. Plymbell moved his jaws. Miss Tell's sly smile went. He looked as though he was going to eat *her*.

"You had better take the top room at the shop," he said. "Take the top room if you have nowhere to live."

"But I haven't found Tiger," Miss Tell said. "He must be starving."

"You won't be alone," said Plymbell. "I sleep at the shop."

Miss Tell considered him. Plymbell could see she was weighing him against Tiger in her mind. He had offered her the room because she had fed him.

"You have had your lunch, I presume," said Plymbell as they walked back to the shop.

"No—I mean yes. Yes, no," said Miss Tell secretively, and again there was the blush like a birthmark on her forehead.

"Where do you go?" said Plymbell, making a shameful inquiry.

"Oh," said Miss Tell defensively, as if it were a question of chastity. "Anywhere. I manage. I vary." And when she said she varied, Miss Tell looked with a virginal importance first one way and then the other.

"That place starves one," said Plymbell indignantly. "One comes out of there some days and one is weak with hunger."

Miss Tell's flush went. She was taken by one of those rages that shake the voices and the bones of unmarried women, as if they were going to shake the nation by the scruff of its neck. "It's wrong, Mr. Plymbell. The government ought to give men more rations. A man needs food. Myself, it never worries me. I never eat. Poor mother used to say: 'Eat, girl, eat.' " A tear came to Miss Tell's right eye, enlarged it, and made it liquid, burning, beautiful. "It was funny, I didn't seem to fancy anything. I just picked things over and left them."

"I never heard of anyone who found the rations too much," said Mr. Plymbell with horror.

"I hardly touch mine since I was bombed out," said Miss Tell, and she straightened her thin, once humble body, raised her small bosom, which was ribbed like a wicker basket, gave her hair a touch or two, and looked with delicate resolution at Plymbell. "I sometimes think of giving my ration books away," she said in an offhand way.

Plymbell gaped at the human being in front of him. "Give them away!" he exclaimed. "Them? Have you got more than one?"

"I've got father's and mother's, too."

"But one had gathered that the law required one to surrender the official documents of the deceased," said Plymbell, narrowing his eyes suggestively. His heart had livened, his mouth was watering.

Miss Tell moved her erring shoulders, her eyes became larger, her lips drooped. "It's wicked of me," she said.

Plymbell took her thin elbow in his hand and contained his anxiety. "I should be very careful about those ration books. I shouldn't mention it. There was a case in the paper the other day."

They had reached the door of the shop. "How is Lady Hackthorpe?" Miss Tell asked. "Is she still away?"

Miss Tell had gone too far; she was being familiar. Plymbell put up his monocle and did not reply.

A time of torture began for Plymbell when Miss Tell moved in. He invited her to the cellar on the bad nights, but Miss Tell had become lightheaded with fatalism and would not move from her bed on the top floor. In decency Plymbell had to remain in his bed and take shelter no more. Above him slept the rarest of human beings, a creature who had three ration books, a woman who was technically three people. He feared for her at every explosion. His mouth watered when he saw her: the woman with three books who did not eat and who thought only of how hungry Tiger must be. If he could have turned himself into a cat!

At one point Plymbell decided that Miss Tell was like Lady Hackthorpe with her furniture; Miss Tell wanted money. He went to the dark corner behind a screen between his own office and the shop, where sometimes she sewed. When he stood by the screen he was nearly on top of her. "If," he said in a high, breaking voice that was strange even to himself, "if you are ever thinking of *selling* your books . . ."

He had made a mistake. Miss Tell was mending and the needle was pointing at him as she stood up. "I couldn't do that," she said. "It is forbidden by the law." And she looked at him strictly.

Plymbell gaped before her hypocrisy. Miss Tell's eyes became larger, deeper, and liquid in the dusk of the corner where she worked. Her chin moved up in a number of amused, resentful movements; her lips moved. "Good God," thought Plymbell, "is she eating?" Her thin arms were slack, her body was inert. She continued to move her dry lips. She leaned her head sideways and raised one eye. Plymbell could not believe what he saw. Miss Tell was plainly telling him: "Yes, I *have* got something in my mouth. It is the desire to be kissed."

Or was he wrong? Plymbell was not a kissing man. His white, demanding face was indeed white with passion, and his lips were shaped for sensuality, but the passion of the gourmet, the libidinousness of the palate, gave him his pallor. He had felt desire, in his way, for Lady Hackthorpe, but it had been consummated in bisques, in *crêpes*, in *flambées*, in *langouste* done in many manners, in *ailloli*, in bouillabaisse and vintage wines. That passion had been starved, and he

340

was perturbed by Miss Tell's signal. One asks oneself (he reflected, going to his office and considering reproachfully his mother's photograph, which stood on his desk)—one asks oneself whether or not a familiar adage about Nature's abhorrence of a vacuum had not a certain relevance, and indeed whether one would not be justified in coining a vulgar phrase to the effect that when one shuts the front door on Nature, she comes in at the back. Miss Tell was certainly the back; one might call her the scullery of the emotions.

Plymbell lowered his pale eyelids in a flutter of infidelity, unable honestly to face his mother's stare. Her elderly aquiline nose, her close-curled silver hair tipped with a touch of fashionable idiocy off the forehead, her too-jewelled, hawking, grabbing, slapdash face derided him for the languor of the male symptom, and at the same time, with the ratty double-facedness of her sex, spoke sharply about flirtations with employees. Plymbell's eyes lied to her image. All the same, he tried to calm himself by taking a piece of violet notepaper and dashing off a letter to Lady Hackthorpe. Avocado pear, he wrote, whitebait (did she think?), *bœuf bourguignon*, or what about *dindonneau* in those Italian pastes? It was a letter of lust. He addressed the envelope, and, telling Miss Tell to post it, Plymbell pulled down the points of his slack waistcoat and felt saved.

So saved that when Miss Tell came back and stood close to his desk, narrow and flat in her horrible trousers, and with her head turned to the window, showing him her profile, Plymbell felt she was satirically flirting with his hunger. Indignantly he got up and, before he knew what he was doing, he put his hand under her shoulder blade and kissed her on the lips.

A small frown came between Miss Tell's eyebrows. Her lips were tight and set. She did not move. "Was that a bill you sent to Lady Hackthorpe?" she asked.

"No," said Plymbell. "A personal letter."

Miss Tell left his office.

Mr. Plymbell wiped his mouth on his handkerchief. He was shocked by himself; even more by the set lips, the closed teeth, the hard chin of Miss Tell; most of all by her impertinence. He had committed a folly for nothing and he had been insulted.

The following morning Plymbell went out on his weekly search for food, but he was too presumptuous for the game. In the coarse world of provisions and the black market, the monocle was too fine. Plymbell lacked the touch; in a long day all he managed to get was four fancy cakes. Miss Tell came out of her dark corner and looked impersonally at him. He was worn out.

"No offal," he said in an appalled, hoarse voice. "No offal in the whole of London."

"Ooh," said Miss Tell, quick as a sparrow. "I got some. Look." And she showed him her disgusting, blood-stained triumph on its piece of newspaper.

Never had Miss Tell seemed so common, so flagrant, so lacking in sensibility, but also never had she seemed so desirable. And then, as before, she became limp and neutral and she raised her chin. There were the unmistakable crumb-licking movements of her lips. Plymbell saw her look sideways at him as she turned. Was she inviting him to wipe out the error of the previous day? With one eye on the meat, Plymbell made a step toward her, and in a moment Miss Tell was on him, kissing him, open-mouthed and with frenzy, her fingernails in his arms, and pressing herself to him to the bone.

"Sweetbreads," she said. "For you. I never eat them. Let me cook them for you."

An hour later she was knocking at the door of his room, and carrying a loaded tray. It was laid, he was glad to notice, for one person only. Plymbell said: "One had forgotten what sweetbreads were."

"It was nothing. I have enjoyed your confidence for fifteen years," said Miss Tell in her poetic style. And the enlarged eyes looked at him with an intimate hunger.

That night, as usual, Plymbell changed into a brilliant dressing-gown, and, standing before the mirror, he did his hair, massaging with the fingers, brushing first with the hard ivory brush and then with the soft one. As he looked into the glass, Miss Tell's inquiring face kept floating into it, displacing his own.

"Enjoyed my confidence!" said Plymbell.

In her bedroom Miss Tell turned out the light, drew back the curtains, and looked into the London black and at the inane triangles of the searchlights. She stood there listening. "Tiger, Tiger," she murmured. "Where are you? Why did you go away from me? I miss you in my bed. Are you hungry? I had a lovely dinner ready for you—sweetbreads. I had to give it to him because you didn't come."

In answer, the hungry siren went like the wail of some monstrous, disembodied Tiger, like all the dead cats of London restless beyond the grave.

Miss Tell drew the curtains and lay down on her bed. "Tiger," she said crossly, "if you don't come tomorrow, I shall give everything to him. He needs it. Not that he deserves it. Filling up the shop with that woman's furniture, storing it free of charge, writing her letters, ruining himself for her. I hate her. I always have. I don't understand him and her, how she gets away with it, owing money all round. She's got a hold—"

The guns broke out. They were declaring war upon Lady Hackthorpe.

Tiger did not come back, and rabbit was dished up for Plymbell. He kissed Miss Tell a third time. It gave him the

343

agreeable sensation that he was doing something for the war. After the fourth kiss Plymbell became worried. Miss Tell had mentioned stuffed veal. She had spoken of mushrooms. He had thoughtlessly exceeded in his embrace. He had felt for the first time in his life—voluptuousness; he had discovered how close to eating kissing is, and as he allowed his arm to rest on Miss Tell's lower-class waist, he had had the inadvertent impression of picking up a cutlet in his fingers. Plymbell felt he had done enough for the vanity of Miss Tell. He was in the middle of this alarmed condition when Miss Tell came into his office and turned his alarm to consternation.

"I've come to give my notice," she said.

Plymbell was appalled. "What is wrong, Miss Tell?" he said.

"Nothing's wrong," said Miss Tell. "I feel I am not needed."

"Have I offended you?" said Plymbell suspiciously. "Is it money?"

Miss Tell looked sharply. She was insulted. "No," she said. "Money is of no interest to me. I've got nothing to do. Trade's stopped."

Plymbell made a speech about trade.

"I think I must have got—" Miss Tell searched for a word and lost her poetic touch—"browned off," she said, and blushed. "I'll get a job in a canteen. I like cooking."

Plymbell in a panic saw not one woman but three women leaving him. "But you are cooking for me," he said.

Miss Tell shrugged.

"Oh, yes, you are. Miss Tell—be my housekeeper."

"Good God," thought Plymbell afterwards, "so that was all she wanted. I needn't have kissed her at all."

How slowly one learns about human nature, he thought. Here was a woman with one simple desire; to serve him—to slave for him, to stand in queues, to cook, to run his business, do everything. And who did not eat.

"I shall certainly not kiss her again," he said.

At this period of his life, with roofs leaving their buildings and servants leaving their places all round him, Plymbell often reflected guardedly upon his situation. There was, he had often hinted, an art in keeping servants. He appeared, he noted, to have this art. But would he keep it? What was it? Words of his mother's came back to him: "Miss Tell left a better job and higher wages to come to me. This job is more flattering to her self-importance." "Never consider them, never promise; they will despise you. The only way to keep servants is to treat them like hell. Look at Lady Hackthorpe's couple. They'd die for her. They probably will."

Two thousand years of civilization lay in those remarks.

"And never be familiar." Guiltily, he could imagine Lady Hackthorpe putting in her word. As the year passed, as his nourishment improved, the imaginary Lady Hackthorpe rather harped on the point.

There was no doubt about it, Plymbell admitted, he *had* been familiar. But only four times, he protested. And what is a kiss, in an office? At this he could almost hear Lady Hackthorpe laughing, in an insinuating way, that she hardly imagined there could be any question of his going any farther.

Plymbell, now full of food, blew up into a temper with the accusing voices. He pitched into Miss Tell. He worked out a plan of timely dissatisfaction. His first attack upon her was made in the shop in the presence of one of the rare customers of those days.

"Why no extra liver this week, Miss Tell? My friend here has got some," he said.

Miss Tell started, then blushed on the forehead. It was, he saw, a blush of pleasure. Public humiliation seemed to delight Miss Tell. He made it harder. "Why no eggs?" he

345

shouted down the stairs, and on another day, as if he had a whip in his hand: "Anyone can get olive oil." Miss Tell smiled and looked a little sideways at him.

Seeing he had not hurt her in public, Plymbell then made a false move. He called her to his room above the shop and decided to "blow her up" privately.

"I can't *live* on fish," he began. But whereas, delighted to be noticed, she listened to his public complaints in the shop, she did not listen in his room. By his second sentence, she had turned her back and wandered to the sofa. From there she went to his writing-table, trailing a finger on it. She was certainly not listening. In the middle of his speech and as his astounded, colourless eyes followed her, she stopped and pointed through the double doors where his bedroom was and she pointed to the Hepplewhite bed.

"Is that Lady Hackthorpe's, too?" she said.

"Yes," said Plymbell.

"Why do you have it up here?" she said rudely.

"Because I like it," said Plymbell, snubbing her.

"I think four-posters are unhealthy," said Miss Tell, and circled with meandering impertinence to the window and looked out on the street. "That old man," she said, admitting the vulgar world into the room, "is always going by."

Miss Tell shrugged at the window and considered the bed again across the space of two rooms. Then, impersonally, she made a speech. "I never married," she said. "I have been friendly but not married. One great friend went away. There was no agreement, nothing said, he didn't write and I didn't write. In those cases I sympathize with the wife, but I wondered when he didn't communicate. I didn't know whether it was over or not over, and when you don't know, it isn't satisfactory. I don't say it was anything, but I would have liked to know whether it was or not. I never mention it to anyone."

"Oh," said Plymbell.

"It upset Dad," said Miss Tell, and of that she was proud.

"I don't follow," said Plymbell. He wanted to open the window and let Miss Tell's private life out.

"It's hard to describe something unsatisfactory," said Miss Tell. And then: "Dad was conventional."

Mr. Plymbell shuddered.

"Are you interested?" asked Miss Tell.

"Please, please go on," said Plymbell.

"I have been 'the other woman' three times," said Miss Tell primly.

Plymbell put up his monocle, but as far as he could judge, all Miss Tell had done was make a public statement. He could think of no reply. His mind drifted. Suddenly he heard the voice of Miss Tell again, trembling, passionate, raging as it had been once before, at Polli's, attacking him.

"She uses you," Miss Tell was saying. "She puts all her rubbish into your shop, she fills up your flat. She won't let you sell it. She hasn't paid you. Storage is the dearest thing in London. You could make a profit, you would turn over your stock. Now is the time to buy, Dad said. . . ."

Plymbell picked up his paper.

"Lady Hackthorpe," explained Miss Tell, and he saw her face, small-mouthed and sick and shaking with jealousy.

"Lady Hackthorpe has gone to America," Plymbell said, in his snubbing voice.

Miss Tell's rage had spent itself. "If you were not so horrible to me, I would tell you an idea," she said.

"Horrible? My dear Miss Tell," said Mr. Plymbell, leaning back as far as he could in his chair.

"It doesn't matter," said Miss Tell, and she walked away. "When is Lady Hackthorpe coming back?" she said.

"After the war, I suppose," said Plymbell.

"Oh," said Miss Tell, without belief.

347

"What is your idea?"

"Oh no. It was about lunch. At Polli's. It is nothing," said Miss Tell.

"Lunch," said Plymbell with a start, dropping his eyeglass. "What about lunch?" And his mouth stayed open.

Miss Tell turned about and approached him. "No, it's unsatisfactory," said Miss Tell. She gave a small laugh and then made the crumb movements with her chin.

"Come here," commanded Plymbell. "What idea about lunch?"

Miss Tell did not move, and so he got up, in a panic now. A suspicion came to him that Polli's had been bombed, that someone—perhaps Miss Tell herself—was going to take his lunch away from him. Miss Tell did not move. Mr. Plymbell did not move. Feeling weak, Mr. Plymbell decided to sit down again. Miss Tell came and sat on the arm of his chair.

"Nothing," she said, looking into his eyes for a long time and then turning away. "You have been horrible to me for ten months and thirteen days. You know you have." Her back was to him.

Slices of pork, he saw, mutton, beef. He went through a nightmare that he arrived at Polli's late, all the customers were inside, and the glass doors were locked. The head waiter was standing there refusing to open. Miss Tell's unnourished back made him think of this. He did no more than put his hand on her shoulder, as slight as a chicken bone, and as he did so, he seemed to hear a sharp warning snap from Lady Hackthorpe. "Gus," Lady Hackthorpe seemed to say, "what are you doing? Are you mad? Don't you know why Miss Tell had to leave her last place?" But Lady Hackthorpe's words were smothered. A mere touch—without intention on Plymbell's part—had impelled Miss Tell to slide backward on to his lap.

"How have I been horrid to you?" said Plymbell, forgetting to put inverted commas round the word "horrid."

348

"You know," said Miss Tell.

"What was this idea of yours," he said quietly, and he kissed her neck. "No, no," she said, and moved her head to the other side of his neck. There was suddenly a sound that checked them both. Her shoe fell off. And then an extraordinary thing happened to Plymbell. The sight of Miss Tell's foot without its shoe did it. At fifty, he felt the first indubitable symptom. A scream went off inside his head—Lady Hackthorpe nagging him about some man she had known who had gone to bed with his housekeeper. "Ruin," Lady Hackthorpe was saying.

"About lunch—it was a good idea," Miss Tell said tenderly into his collar.

But it was not until three in the morning that Miss Tell told Plymbell what the idea was.

And so, every weekday, there was the modest example of Mr. Plymbell's daily luncheon. The waiter used to take the empty soup plate away from Miss Tell and presently came forward with the meat and vegetables. He scraped them off his serving dish on to her plate. She would keep her head lowered for a while, and then, with a glance to see if other customers were looking, she would lift the plate over to Mr. Plymbell's place. He, of course, did not notice. Then, absently, he settled down to eat her food. While he did this, he muttered, "What did you get?" She nodded at her stuffed basket and answered. Mr. Plymbell ate two lunches. While this went on, Miss Tell looked at him. She was in a strong position now. Hunger is the basis of life and, for her, a great change had taken place. The satisfactory had occurred.

But now, of course, French cookery has come back.

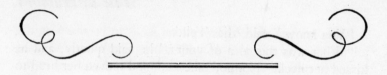

Sense of Humour

It started one Saturday. I was working new ground and I decided I'd stay at the hotel the weekend and put in an appearance at church.

"All alone?" asked the girl at the cash desk.

It had been raining since ten o'clock.

"Mr. Good has gone," she said. "And Mr. Straker. He usually stays with us. But he's gone."

"That's where they make their mistake," I said. "They think they know everything because they've been on the road all their lives."

"You're a stranger here, aren't you?" she said.

"I am," I said. "And so are you."

"How do you know that?"

"Obvious," I said. "Way you speak."

"Let's have a light," she said.

"So's I can see you," I said.

That was how it started. The rain was pouring down on the glass roof of the office.

She'd a cup of tea steaming on the register. I said I'd have one, too. What's it going to be and I'll tell them, she said, but I said just a cup of tea.

"I'm T.T.," I said. "Too many soakers on the road as it is."

I was staying there the weekend so as to be sharp on the job on Monday morning. What's more it pays in these small towns to turn up at church on Sundays, Presbyterians in the morning, Methodists in the evening. Say "Good morning" and "Good evening" to them. "Ah!" they say. "Church-goer! Pleased to see that! T.T., too." Makes them have a second look at your lines in the morning. "Did you like our service, Mr.—er—er?" "Humphrey's my name." "Mr. Humphrey." See? It pays.

"Come into the office, Mr. Humphrey," she said, bringing me a cup. "Listen to that rain."

I went inside.

"Sugar?" she said.

"Three," I said. We settled to a very pleasant chat. She told me all about herself, and we got on next to families.

"My father was on the railway," she said.

" 'The engine gave a squeal,' " I said. " 'The driver took out his pocket-knife and scraped him off the wheel.' "

"That's it," she said. "And what is your father's business? You said he had a business."

"Undertaker," I said.

"Undertaker?" she said.

"Why not?" I said. "Good business. Seasonable like everything else. High-class undertaker," I said.

She was looking at me all the time wondering what to say, and suddenly she went into fits of laughter.

"Undertaker," she said, covering her face with her hands and went on laughing.

"Here," I said, "what's up?"

"Undertaker!" She laughed and laughed. Struck me as being a pretty thin joke.

"Don't mind me," she said. "I'm Irish."

"Oh, I see," I said. "That's it, is it? Got a sense of humour."

Then the bell rang and a woman called out "Muriel!

Muriel!" and there was a motor bike making a row at the front door.

"All right," the girl called out. "Excuse me a moment, Mr. Humphrey," she said. "Don't think me rude. That's my boy friend. He wants the bird turning up like this."

She went out, but there was her boy friend looking over the window ledge into the office. He had come in. He had a cape on, soaked with rain, and the rain was in beads in his hair. It was fair hair. It stood up on end. He'd been economizing on the brilliantine. He didn't wear a hat. He gave me a look and I gave him a look. I didn't like the look of him. And he didn't like the look of me. A smell of oil and petrol and rain and mackintosh came off him. He had a big mouth with thick lips. They were very red. I recognized him at once as the son of the man who ran the Kounty Garage. I saw this chap when I put my car away. The firm's car. Locked up, because of the samples. Took me ten minutes to ram the idea into his head. He looked as though he'd never heard of samples. Slow—you know the way they are in the provinces. Slow on the job.

"Oh, Colin," says she. "What do you want?"

"Nothing," the chap said. "I came in to see you."

"To see me?"

"Just to see you."

"You came in this morning."

"That's right," he said. He went red. "You was busy," he said.

"Well, I'm busy now," she said.

He bit his tongue and licked his big lips over and took a look at me. Then he started grinning.

"I got the new bike, Muriel," he said. "I've got it outside. It's just come down from the works," he said.

"The laddie wants you to look at his bike," I said. So she went out and had a look at it.

When she came back she had got rid of him.

352

"Listen to that rain," she said. "Lord, I'm fed up with this line," she said.

"What line?" I said. "The hotel line?"

"Yes," she said. "I'm fed right up to the back teeth with it."

"And you've got good teeth," I said.

"There's not the class of person there used to be in it," she said. "All our family have got good teeth."

"Not the class?"

"I've been in it five years and there's not the same class at all. You never meet any fellows."

"Well," said I, "if they're like that half-wit at the garage, they're nothing to be stuck on. And you've met me."

I said it to her like that.

"Oh," says she. "It isn't as bad as that yet."

It was cold in the office. She used to sit all day in her overcoat. She was a smart girl with a big friendly chin and a second one coming, and her forehead and nose were covered with freckles. She had copper-coloured hair too. She got her shoes through the trade from Duke's traveller and her clothes, too, off the Hollenborough mantle man. I told her I could do her better stockings than the ones she'd got on. She got a good reduction on everything. Twenty-five or thirty-three and a third. She had her expenses cut right back. I took her to the pictures that night in the car. I made Colin get the car out for me.

"That boy wanted me to go on the back of his bike. On a a night like this," she said.

"Oh," she said, when we got to the pictures. "Two shillings's too much. Let's go into the one-and-sixes at the side and we can nip across into the two-shillings when the lights go down."

"Fancy your father being an undertaker," she said in the middle of the show. And she started laughing as she had laughed before.

353

She had her head screwed on all right. She said:

"Some girls have no pride once the lights go down."

Every time I went to that town I took a box of something. Samples, mostly, they didn't cost me anything.

"Don't thank me," I said. "Thank the firm."

Every time I took her out I pulled the blinds in the back seat of the car to hide the samples. That chap Colin used to give us oil and petrol. He used to give me a funny look. Fishy sort of small eyes he'd got. Always looking miserable. Then we would go off. Sunday was her free day. Not that driving's any holiday for me. And, of course, the firm paid. She used to take me down to see her family for the day. Start in the morning, and taking it you had dinner and tea there, a day's outing cost us nothing. Her father was something on the railway, retired. He had a long stocking, somewhere, but her sister, the one that was married, had had her share already.

He had a tumour after his wife died and they just played upon the old man's feelings. It wasn't right. She wouldn't go near her sister and I don't blame her, taking the money like that. Just played upon the old man's feelings.

Every time I was up there Colin used to come in looking for her.

"Oh, Colin," I used to say. "Done my car yet?" He knew where he got off with me.

"No, now, I can't, Colin. I tell you I'm going out with Mr. Humphrey," she used to say to him. I heard her.

"He keeps on badgering me," she said to me.

"You leave him to me," I said.

"No, he's all right," she said.

"You let me know if there's any trouble with Colin," I said. "Seems to be a harum-scarum sort of half-wit to me," I said.

"And he spends every penny he makes," she said.

Well, we know that sort of thing is all right while it lasts, I told her, but the trouble is that it doesn't last.

We were always meeting Colin on the road. I took no notice of it first of all and then I grew suspicious and awkward at always meeting him. He had a new motor bicycle. It was an Indian, a scarlet thing that he used to fly over the moor with, flat out. Muriel and I used to go out over the moor to Ingley Wood in the firm's Morris—I had a customer out that way.

"May as well do a bit of business while you're about it," I said.

"About what?" she said.

"Ah ha!" I said. "That's what Colin wants to know," I said.

Sure enough, coming back we'd hear him popping and backfiring close behind us, and I put out my hand to stop him and keep him following us, biting our dirt.

"I see his little game," I said. "Following us."

So I saw to it that he did follow. We could hear him banging away behind us, and the traffic is thick on the Ingley road in the afternoon.

"Oh, let him pass," Muriel said. "I can't stand those dirty things banging in my ears."

I waved him on and past he flew with his scarf flying out, blazing red into the traffic. "We're doing fifty-eight ourselves," she said, leaning across to look.

"Powerful buses those," I said. "Any fool can do it if he's got the power. Watch me step on it."

But we did not catch Colin. Half an hour later he passed us coming back. Cut right in between us and a lorry—I had to brake hard. I damn nearly killed him. His ears were red with the wind. He didn't wear a hat. I got after him as soon as I could, but I couldn't touch him.

Nearly every weekend I was in that town seeing my girl, that fellow was hanging around. He came into the bar on Saturday nights, he poked his head into the office on Sunday mornings. It was a sure bet that if we went out in the car he would pass us on the road. Every time we would hear that scarlet thing roar by like a horse-stinger. It didn't matter where we were. He passed us on the main road, he met us down the side roads. There was a little cliff under oak trees at May Ponds, she said, where the view was pretty. And there, soon after we got there, was Colin on the other side of the water, watching us. Once we found him sitting on his bike, just as though he were waiting for us.

"You been here in a car?" I said.

"No, motor bike," she said, and blushed. "Cars can't follow in these tracks."

She knew a lot of places in that country. Some of the roads weren't roads at all and were bad for tires and I didn't want the firm's car scratched by bushes, but you would have thought Colin could read what was in her mind. For nine times out of ten he was there. It got on my nerves. It was a red, roaring, powerful thing and he opened it full out.

"I'm going to speak to Colin," I said. "I won't have him annoying you."

"He's not annoying me," she said. "I've got a sense of humour."

"Here, Colin," I said one evening when I put the car away. "What's the idea?"

He was taking off his overalls. He pretended he did not know what I was talking about. He had a way of rolling his eyeballs, as if they had got wet and loose in his head, while he was speaking to me, and you never knew if it was sweat or oil on his face. It was always pale, with high colour on his cheeks and very red lips.

"Miss MacFarlane doesn't like being followed," I said.

He dropped his jaw and gaped at me. I could not tell whether he was being very surprised or very sly. I used to call him "Marbles" because when he spoke he seemed to have a lot of marbles in his mouth.

Then he said he never went to the places we went to,

except by accident. He wasn't following us, he said, but we were following him. We never let him alone, he said. Everywhere he went, he said, we were there. Take last Saturday, he said, we were following him for miles down the by-pass, he said. "But you passed us first and then sat down in front," I said. "I went to Ingley Wood," he said. "And you followed me there." No, we didn't, I said, Miss MacFarlane decided to go there.

He said he did not want to complain, but fair was fair. "I suppose you know," he said, "that you have taken my girl off me. Well, you can leave *me* alone, can't you?"

"Here," I said. "One minute! Not so fast! You said I've taken Miss MacFarlane from you. Well, she was never your girl. She only knew you in a friendly way."

"She was my girl," was all he said.

He was pouring oil into my engine. He had some cotton wool in one hand and the can in the other. He wiped up the green oil that had overflowed, screwed on the cap, pulled down the bonnet, and whistled to himself.

I went back to Muriel and told her what Colin had said.

"I don't like trouble," I said.

"Don't you worry," she said. "I had to have someone to go to all these places with before you came. Couldn't stick in here all day Sunday."

"Ah," I said. "That's it, is it? You've been to all these places with him?"

"Yes," she said. "And he keeps on going to them. He's sloppy about me."

"Good God," I said. "Sentimental memories."

I felt sorry for that fellow. He knew it was hopeless, but he loved her. I suppose he couldn't help himself. Well, it takes all sorts to make a world, as my old mother used to say. If we were all alike it wouldn't do. Some men can't save money. It just runs through their fingers. He couldn't save money, so he lost her. I suppose all he thought of was love.

357

I could have been friends with that fellow. As it was, I put a lot of business his way. I didn't want him to get the wrong idea about me. We're all human after all.

We didn't have any more trouble with Colin after this until bank holiday. I was going to take her down to see my family. The old man's getting a bit past it now and has given up living over the shop. He's living out on the Barnum Road, beyond the tram stop. We were going down in the firm's car, as per usual, but something went wrong with the mag and Colin had not got it right for the holiday. I was wild about this. What's the use of a garage who can't do a rush job for the holidays! What's the use of being an old customer if they're going to let you down! I went for Colin bald-headed.

"You knew I wanted it," I said. "It's no use trying to put me off with a tale about the stuff not coming down from the works. I've heard that one before."

I told him he'd got to let me have another car, because he'd let me down. I told him I wouldn't pay his account. I said I'd take my business away from him. But there wasn't a car to be had in the town because of the holiday. I could have knocked the fellow down. After the way I'd sent business to him.

Then I saw through his little game. He knew Muriel and I were going to my people and he had done this to stop it. The moment I saw this I let him know that it would take more than him to stop me doing what I wanted.

I said: "Right. I shall take the amount of Miss Mac-Farlane's train fare and my own from the account at the end of the month."

I said: "You may run a garage, but you don't run the railway service."

I was damned angry going by train. I felt quite lost on the railway after having a car. It was crowded with trippers too. It was slow—stopping at all the stations. The people come in, they tread all over your feet, they make you squeeze up till you're crammed against the window, and the women stick

out their elbows and fidget. And then the expense! a return
for two runs you into just over a couple of quid. I could have
murdered Colin.

We got there at last. We walked up from the tram stop.
Mother was at the window and let us in.

"This is Miss MacFarlane," I said.

And mother said: "Oh, pleased to meet you. We've heard
a lot about you."

"Oh," Mother said to me, giving me a kiss, "are you tired?
You haven't had your tea, have you? Sit down. Have this
chair, dear. It's more comfortable."

"Well, my boy," my father said.

"Want a wash," my father said. "We've got a washbasin
downstairs," he said. "I used not to mind about washing upstairs before. Now I couldn't do without it. Funny how your
ideas change as you get older."

"How's business?" he said.

"Mustn't grumble," I said. "How's yours?"

"You knew," he said, "we took off the horses: except for
one or two of the older families we have got motors now."

But he'd told me that the last time I was there. I'd been at
him for years about motor hearses.

"You've forgotten I used to drive them," I said.

"Bless me, so you did," he said.

He took me up to my room. He showed me everything he
had done to the house. "Your mother likes it," he said. "The
traffic's company for her. You know what your mother is for
company."

Then he gives me a funny look.

"Who's the girl?" he says.

My mother came in then and said: "She's pretty, Arthur."

"Of course she's pretty," I said. "She's Irish."

"Oh," said the old man. "Irish! Got a sense of humour,
eh?"

359

"She wouldn't be marrying me if she hadn't," I said. And then I gave *them* a look.

"Marrying her, did you say?" exclaimed my father.

"Any objection?" I said.

"Now, Ernest dear," said my mother. "Leave the boy alone. Come down while I pop the kettle on."

She was terribly excited.

"Miss MacFarlane," the old man said.

"No sugar, thank you, Mrs. Humphrey. I beg your pardon, Mr. Humphrey?"

"The Glen Hotel at Swansea, I don't suppose you know that?" my father said. "I wondered if you did, being in the catering line."

"It doesn't follow she knows every hotel," my mother said.

"Forty years ago," the old man said. "I was staying at the Glen in Swansea and the head waiter—"

"Oh no, not that one. I'm sure Miss MacFarlane doesn't want to hear that one," my mother said.

"How's business with you, Mr. Humphrey?" said Muriel. "We passed a large cemetery near the station."

"Dad's Ledger," I said.

"The whole business has changed so that you wouldn't know it, in my lifetime," said my father. "Silver fittings have gone clean out. Everyone wants simplicity nowadays. Restraint. Dignity," my father said.

"Prices did it," my father said.

"The war," he said.

"You couldn't get the wood," he said.

"Take ordinary mahogany, just an ordinary piece of mahogany. Or teak," he said. "Take teak. Or walnut."

"You can certainly see the world go by in this room," I said to my mother.

"It never stops," she said.

Now it was all bicycles over the new concrete road from the gun factory. Then traction engines and cars. They came up over the hill where the A.A. man stands and choked up round the tram stop. It was mostly holiday traffic. Everything with a wheel on it was out.

"On this stretch," my father told me, "they get three accidents a week." There was an ambulance station at the crossroads.

We had hardly finished talking about this—in fact, the old man was still saying that something ought to be done—when the telephone rang.

"Name of MacFarlane?" the voice said on the wire.

"No. Humphrey," my father said. "There is a Miss MacFarlane here."

"There's a man named Colin Mitchell lying seriously injured in an accident at the Cottage Hospital, gave me the name of MacFarlane as his nearest relative."

That was the Police. On to it at once. That fellow Colin had followed us down by road.

Cry, I never heard a girl cry as Muriel cried when we came back from the hospital. He had died in the ambulance. Cutting in, the old game he used to play on me. Clean off the saddle and under the Birmingham bus. The blood was everywhere, they said. People were still looking at it when we went by. Head on. What a mess! Don't let's talk about it.

She wanted to see him, but they said "No." There wasn't anything recognizable to see. She put her arms round my neck and cried: "Colin, Colin," as if I were Colin, and clung to me. I was feeling sick myself. I held her tight and I kissed her and I thought: "Holiday ruined.

"Damn fool man," I thought. "Poor devil," I thought.

"I knew he'd do something like this."

"There, there," I said to her. "Don't think about Colin."

Didn't she love me, I said, and not Colin? Hadn't she got

me? She said, yes, she had. And she loved me. But, "Oh, Colin! Oh, Colin!" she cried. "And Colin's mother," she cried. "Oh, it's terrible." She cried and cried.

We put her to bed and I sat with her, and my mother kept coming in.

"Leave her to me," I said. "I understand her."

Before they went to bed they both came in and looked at her. She lay sobbing with her head in the pillow.

I could quite understand her being upset. Colin was a decent fellow. He was always doing things for her. He mended her electric lamp and he riveted the stem of a wine-glass so that you couldn't see the break. He used to make things for her. He was very good with his hands.

She lay on her side with her face burning and feverish with misery and crying, scalded by the salt, and her lips shrivelled up. I put my arm under her neck and I stroked her forehead. She groaned. Sometimes she shivered and sometimes she clung to me, crying: "Oh, Colin! Colin!"

My arm ached with the cramp and I had a crick in my back, sitting in the awkward way I was on the bed. It was late. There was nothing to do but to ache and sit watching her and thinking. It is funny the way your mind drifts. When I was kissing her and watching her I was thinking out who I'd show our new Autumn range to first. Her hand held my wrist tight, and when I kissed her I got her tears on my lips. They burned and stung. Her neck and shoulders were soft and I could feel her breath hot out of her nostrils on the back of my hand. Ever noticed how hot a woman's breath gets when she's crying? I drew out my hand and lay down beside her and "Oh, Colin, Colin," she sobbed, turning over and clinging to me. And so I lay there, listening to the traffic, staring at the ceiling, and shivering whenever the picture of Colin shooting right off that damned red thing into the bus came into my mind—until I did not hear the traffic any more, or see the ceiling any more, or think any more, but a change

happened—I don't know when. This Colin thing seemed to
have knocked the bottom out of everything and I had a funny
feeling we were going down and down and down in a lift.
And the further we went, the hotter and softer she got.
Perhaps it was when I found with my hands that she had very
big breasts. But it was like being on the mail steamer and
feeling engines start under your feet, thumping louder and
louder. You can feel it in every vein of your body. Her
mouth opened and her tears dried. Her breath came through
her open mouth and her voice was blind and husky. Colin,
Colin, Colin, she said, and her fingers were hooked into me.
I got out and turned the key in the door.

In the morning I left her sleeping. It did not matter to me
what my father might have heard in the night, but still I
wondered. She would hardly let me touch her before that. I
told her I was sorry, but she shut me up. I was afraid of her. I
was afraid of mentioning Colin. I wanted to go out of the
house there and then and tell someone everything. Did she
love Colin all the time? Did she think I was Colin? And every
time I thought of that poor devil covered over with a white
sheet in the hospital mortuary, a kind of picture of her and
me under the sheets with love came into my mind. I couldn't
separate the two things. Just as though it had all come from
Colin.

I'd rather not talk any more about that. I never talked to
Muriel about it. I waited for her to say something, but she
didn't. She didn't say a word.

The next day was a bad day. It was grey and hot and the
air smelled of oil fumes from the road. There's always a
mess to clear up when things like this happen. I had to see
to it. I had the job of ringing up the boy's mother. But I got
round that, thank God, by ringing up the garage and getting
them to go round and see the old lady. My father is useless
when things are like this. I was the whole morning on the
phone: to the hospital, the police, the coroner—and he stood

fussing beside me, jerking up and down like a fat indiarubber ball.

I found my mother washing up at the sink and she said: "That poor boy's mother! I can't stop thinking of her."

Then my father comes in and says—just as though I was a customer: "Of course if Mrs. Mitchell desires it we can have the remains of the deceased conveyed to his house by one of our new specially sprung motor hearses and can, if necessary, make all the funeral arrangements."

I could have hit him because Muriel came into the room when he was saying this. But she stood there as if nothing had happened.

"It's the least we can do for poor Mrs. Mitchell," she said. There were small creases of shadow under her eyes, which shone with a soft strong light I had never seen before. She walked as if she were really still in that room with me, asleep. God, I loved that girl! God, I wanted to get all this over, this damned Colin business that had come right into the middle of everything like this, and I wanted to get married right away. I wanted to be alone with her. That's what Colin did for me.

"Yes," I said. "We must do the right thing by Colin."

"We are sometimes asked for long-distance estimates," my father said.

"It will be a little something," my mother said.

"Dad and I will talk it over," I said.

"Come into the office," my father said. "It occurred to me that it would be nice to do the right thing by this friend of yours."

We talked it over. We went into the cost of it. There was the return journey to reckon. We worked it out that it would come no dearer to old Mrs. Mitchell than if she took the train and buried the boy here. That is to say, my father said, if I drove it.

364

"It would look nice," my father said. "Saves money and it would look a bit friendly," my father said. "You've done it before."

"Well," I said. "I suppose I can get a refund on my return ticket from the railway."

But it was not as simple as it looked, because Muriel wanted to come. She wanted to drive back with me and the hearse. My mother was very worried about this. It might upset Muriel, she thought. Father thought it might not look nice to see a young girl sitting by the coffin of a grown man.

"It must be dignified," my father said. "You see, if she was there, it might look as though she were just doing it for the ride—like these young women on bakers' vans."

My father took me out into the hall to tell me this because he did not want her to hear. But she would not have it. She wanted to come back with Colin.

"Colin loved me. It is my duty to him," she said. "Besides," she said, suddenly, in her full open voice—it had seemed to be closed and carved and broken and small—"I've never been in a hearse before."

"And it will save her fare too," I said to my father.

That night I went again to her room. She was awake. I said I was sorry to disturb her, but I would go at once only I wanted to see if she was all right. She said, in the closed voice again, that she was all right.

"Are you sure?" I said.

She did not answer. I was worried. I went over to the bed. "What is the matter? Tell me what is the matter," I said.

For a long time she was silent. I held her hand, I stroked her head. She was lying stiff in the bed. She would not answer. I dropped my hand to her small white shoulder. She stirred and drew up her legs and half turned and said, "I was thinking of Colin. Where is he?" she asked.

"They've brought him round. He's lying downstairs."

"In the front room?"

"Yes, ready for the morning. Now be a sensible girl and go back by train."

"No, no," she said. "I want to go with Colin. Poor Colin. He loved me and I didn't love him." And she drew my hands down to her breasts.

"Colin loved me," she whispered.

"Not like this," I whispered.

It was a warm grey morning like all the others when we took Colin back. They had fixed the coffin in before Muriel came out. She came down wearing the bright blue hat she had got off Dormer's millinery man and she kissed my mother and father good-bye. They were very sorry for her. "Look after her, Arthur," my mother said. Muriel got in beside me without a glance behind her at the coffin. I started the engine. They smiled at us. My father raised his hat, but whether it was to Muriel and me or to Colin, or to the three of us, I do not know. He was not, you see, wearing his top hat. I'll say this for the old boy, thirty years in the trade have taught him tact.

After leaving my father's house you have to go down to the tram terminus before you get on the by-pass. There was always one or two drivers, conductors, or inspectors there, doing up their tickets, or changing over the trolley arms. When we passed I saw two of them drop their jaws, stick their pencils in their ears, and raise their hats. I was so surprised by this that I nearly raised mine in acknowledgment, forgetting that we had the coffin behind. I had not driven one of my father's hearses for years.

Hearses are funny things to drive. They are well-sprung, smooth-running cars, with quiet engines, and, if you are used to driving a smaller car, before you know where you are, you are speeding. You know you ought to go slow, say twenty-five to thirty maximum, and it's hard to keep it down. You can return empty at seventy if you like. It's like

driving a fire engine. Go fast out and come back slow—only
the other way round. Open out in the country, but slow down
past houses. That's what it means. My father was very
particular about this.

Muriel and I didn't speak very much at first. We sat
listening to the engine and the occasional jerk of the coffin
behind when we went over a pot-hole. We passed the place
where poor Colin—but I didn't say anything to Muriel, and
she, if she noticed—which I doubt—did not say anything to
me. We went through Cox Hill, Wammering, and Yodley
Mount, flat country, don't care for it myself. "There's a
wonderful lot of building going on," Muriel said at last.

"You won't know these places in five years," I said.

But my mind kept drifting away from the road and the
green fields and the dullness, and back to Colin—five days
before, he had come down this way. I expected to see that
Indian coming flying straight out of every corner. But it was
all bent and bust up properly now. I saw the damned thing.

He had been up to his old game, following us, and that
had put the end to following. But not quite; he was following
us now, behind us in the coffin. Then my mind drifted off
that and I thought of those nights at my parents' house, and
Muriel. You never know what a woman is going to be like.
I thought, too, that it had put my calculations out. I mean,
supposing she had a baby. You see I had reckoned on waiting
eighteen months or so. I would have eight hundred then. But
if we had to get married at once, we should have to cut
right down. Then I kept thinking it was funny her saying
"Colin!" like that in the night; it was funny it made her
feel that way with me, and how it made me feel when she
called me Colin. I'd never thought of her in that way, in
what you might call the "Colin" way.

I looked at her and she looked at me and she smiled but
still we did not say very much, but the smiles kept coming to
both of us. The light-railway bridge at Dootheby took me

by surprise and I thought the coffin gave a jump as we took it.

"Colin's still watching us," I nearly said.

There were tears in her eyes.

"What was the matter with Colin?" I said. "Nice chap, I thought. Why didn't you marry him?"

"Yes," she said. "He was a nice boy. But he'd no sense of humour.

"And I wanted to get out of that town," she said.

"I'm not going to stay there, at that hotel," she said.

"I want to get away," she said. "I've had enough."

She had a way of getting angry with the air, like that. "You've got to take me away," she said. We were passing slowly into Muster, there was a tram ahead and people thick on the narrow pavements, dodging out into the road. But when we got into the Market Square, where they were standing around, they saw the coffin. They began to raise their hats. Suddenly she laughed. "It's like being the King and Queen," she said.

"They're raising their hats," she said.

"Not all of them," I said.

She squeezed my hand and I had to keep her from jumping about like a child on the seat as we went through.

"There they go."

"Boys always do," I said.

"And another.

"Let's see what the policeman does."

She started to laugh, but I shut her up. "Keep your sense of humour to yourself," I said.

Through all those towns that run into one another as you might say, we caught it. We went through, as she said, like royalty. So many years since I drove a hearse, I'd forgotten what it was like.

I was proud of her, I was proud of Colin, and I was proud of myself. And after what had happened, I mean on the last two nights, it was like a wedding. And although we knew it was for Colin, it was for us too, because Colin was with both of us. It was like this all the way.

"Look at that man there. Why doesn't he raise his hat? People ought to show respect for the dead," she said.

A NOTE ON THE TYPE

This book was set on the Monotype in JANSON, *a recutting made direct from the type cast from matrices made by Anton Janson. Whether or not Janson was of Dutch ancestry is not known, but it is known that he purchased a foundry and was a practicing type-founder in Leipzig during the years 1660 to 1687. Janson's first specimen sheet was issued in 1675. His successor issued a specimen sheet showing all of the Janson types in 1689.*

His type is an excellent example of the influential and sturdy Dutch types that prevailed in England prior to the development by William Caslon of his own incomparable designs, which he evolved from these Dutch faces. The Dutch in their turn had been influenced by Garamond in France. The general tone of Janson, however, is darker than Garamond and has a sturdiness and substance quite different from its predecessors. It is a highly legible type, and its individual letters have a pleasing variety of design. Its heavy and light strokes make it sharp and clear, and the full-page effect is characterful and harmonious.

This book was composed, printed, and bound by Kingsport Press, Inc., Kingsport, Tennessee. The paper was made by P. H. Glatfelter Co., Spring Grove, Pa. The typography, decorations, and binding were designed by

WARREN  CHAPPELL